"I'VE BROUGHT YOU A PR[...]
SIR THORTON SAID SLYLY.

He held out a wrapped package. Fiona, not liking
the look on his face, was reluctant to take it.

His face darkened with anger. "You wanted a book
to read, and I've gone to considerable trouble to
buy you one. Open it!"

Trembling with emotion, Fiona pulled off the
wrapping. She opened the book and discovered,
to her horror, that it was a series of very detailed
plates depicting sex in all aspects.

Thorton's anger turned rapidly to lust as he
leafed quickly through the pages. "Look at this!
I've never done it that way." He flung the book
down and reached for Fiona. *And we're going to
work our way right through that book!"*

Other books by
RACHEL COSGROVE PAYES

BRIDE OF FURY
THE COACH TO HELL
MOMENT OF DESIRE

SATAN'S MISTRESS

RACHEL COSGROVE PAYES

PLAYBOY
PAPERBACKS

SATAN'S MISTRESS

Copyright © 1981 by Rachel Cosgrove Payes

Cover illustration copyright © 1981 by PEI Books, Inc.

Published simultaneously in the United States and Canada by Playboy Paperbacks, New York, New York. Printed in the United States
of America. Library of Congress Catalog Card Number: 80-81632.
First edition.

Books are available at quantity discounts for promotional and indus-
trial use. For further information, write to Premium Sales, Playboy
Paperbacks, 747 Third Avenue, New York, New York 10017.

ISBN: 0-872-16726-7

First printing March 1981.

This one is for Laura Haywood,
for many reasons

CHAPTER 1

Fiona McQuade had found, to her sorrow, that the streets of London were not paved with gold. In April of the year of our Lord 1753 they were awash with mud. Before she left the ribboner's shop, she pulled up the hood of her dark-red cloak to keep the drizzle from her glossy black curls. Fiona's aunt expected her to be well groomed in the exclusive millinery shop she owned on a quiet street just off Bond. Her customers were ladies of fashion, elegant creatures who lived in that never-never world of society that Fiona viewed with awe and envy from her position as lowly shop assistant.

Carefully tucking the ribbons in an embroidered satin pocket under the looped-up overskirt of her bright-blue gown, Fiona ventured out into the wet, holding up her skirt and petticoats to keep the hems from getting muddy. She'd worn stout shoes for this foray to the ribboner's, leaving her daintier black kid slippers in the back room of Aunt Eulalia's shop. It would never do to assist Lady Loverich or the Duchess of Danbury while wearing muddy slippers.

In the months that Fiona had been in London, she had learned the alleys and byways near her aunt's shop so that she could get back quickly. The Duchess of Lawton was coming at three to pick up two new bonnets, and Aunt Eulalia had discovered, to her dismay, that she needed a bit more rose ribbon to finish one of them.

"Hurry, Fiona. Don't stop to gaup at the sights," her aunt had cautioned. "And tell Mr. Beeson to put it on my account. It wouldn't do for you to carry money. Even in broad daylight, footpads might steal it."

Fiona was sure her aunt's constant fears of thieves were exaggerated, but she raced off on her errand, hoping that she might have a chance to see the famed Duchess of Lawton when she arrived. Usually Fiona had to stay in the back, stitching the bonnets. Only occasionally did her aunt allow her into the shop when the most important of her customers were there. And the duchess was probably the wealthiest of all of Aunt Eulalia's fine ladies. Whenever Fiona had a chance, she slipped the copy of *The Gazette* up to her tiny attic room over the shop to read the gossip about the fine lords and ladies of London. Aunt Eulalia didn't approve of such frivolity. She acknowledged that it was useful for her niece to be able to read and do sums as she could then help with the bookkeeping chores of the shop, but to read such things as the juicier bits in *The Gazette* was not to be tolerated. Aunt Eulalia was very religious, and the goings-on of the nobility scandalized her.

When Fiona first came from Edinburgh, newly orphaned by the smallpox epidemic that raged there, she'd made the mistake of saying, "But if they are so scandalous, why do you treat them with such great politeness when they come here?"

Drawing herself up to her full height, which was considerable, Aunt Eulalia had said coldly, "It's good business. Never forget that, Fiona. I must be polite so that they'll give me their patronage, which keeps clothes on your back, remember, and food in your mouth. But I don't have to approve of them."

It had put Fiona quite in her place. At sixteen, she was full of life and eager to meet the world; but she saw that Aunt Eulalia's shop might not be the best place for this meeting to happen. When a butcher's apprentice came to deliver a chicken her aunt had ordered and stood chatting with Fiona for a moment, her aunt had been enraged.

"Be off with you!" she yelled at the hapless youth in his blue linen smock. "I shall report you to your master if this happens again." Red-faced, he scurried away. Then Eulalia turned on her niece. "How dare you waste precious minutes chattering to the likes of him, a butcher's apprentice! Next thing I know, you'll be slipping out to meet him. Then you'll be expecting a child—from a lout who has no prospects."

"But he was only passing the time of day, Aunt Eulalia."

Her hatchet face dark with rage, the woman snapped, "Don't answer back, missie. Keep a civil tongue in your head. Be glad that I was willing to take you in when my poor sister and her husband died, and left you to fend for yourself. If I'd not sent you the fare for the stage, you'd be on the streets of Edinburgh this minute, selling yourself into sin to keep alive."

"Yes, Aunt Eulalia. I'm sorry."

Fiona knew real fear. She had been so demoralized when her parents died within hours of each other, leaving her alone, that she'd leaped at the chance to accept her aunt's offer of a home and employment in London. London! She'd thought it would have buildings of the whitest marble, set with jewels, and gold cobblestones. Instead it was very like Edinburgh, only sootier and grimier; larger, of course—so that all of its ills could be greater. She had dreams of meeting a wealthy lord who would fall instantly in love with her and carry her away to be his bride. That dream seemed less likely as the days went by. How would she meet a handsome lord in a millinery shop?

Fiona was passing the watchmaker's shop on the street next to her aunt's millinery establishment when she heard the cuckoo clock in his window call the hour of three. Oh, Aunt Eulalia would be furious. The duchess was to arrive at this time. Racing along, Fiona ducked into a noisome passage that led to the next street, slipping precariously on the slimy cobbles. She managed to keep her footing only by the most agile hopping. Through the dark, narrow way at last, she darted out into the street to cross to her aunt's shop. A carriage was drawn up before the door, a shiny varnished landau with a coat of arms emblazoned on the door. Aunt Eulalia would be livid with rage that she was late.

Throwing caution to the winds, Fiona ran across the muddied street, looking neither right nor left. It was her undoing. Another coach, a landaulet, came careening around the corner from Bond Street, its team of chestnuts clattering along at top speed. At the last moment, Fiona realized her danger. Instead of running on to escape this second carriage, she froze in her tracks, stopping stock-still in the middle of the narrow street. There wasn't room for the coach to pass her on either side. With horror she watched the enormous horses bearing down on her. In a moment she would be trampled beneath their iron-shod hooves.

The coachey yelled at her and hauled on the reins, but Fiona knew it wouldn't save her; she'd be knocked down by the chestnuts and run over by the wheels of the coach. Not able to bear to see her death approach, she closed her eyes and willed herself to faint. Not being a fainting type, though, it did no good. She could almost feel the breath of the horses on her face when she was caught about her waist very urgently, lifted right off her feet, and whirled about, so that the rain fell onto her uptilted face. There was an odor of scent in her nostrils, a very masculine odor, combined with the smells of brandy and tobacco.

Then Fiona's eyes flew open, and she found herself looking up at one of the handsomest men she had ever seen. His dark eyes flashed, and she knew that the hair hidden under his well-powdered bag wig was as black as her own, for his eyebrows were raven's wings over his eyes. As he set her onto her feet before Aunt Eulalia's door, he raised those brows and smiled at her, a crooked smile, tipped up at one corner, that set her heart to thudding.

"My, my, what have I here?" he asked, laughing in a way that made Fiona's bones feel like they were made of jelly. "What a pity it would have been to have such a delightful face stepped on by one of those horses."

Speechless from fright, and from the reaction to her last-minute rescue, Fiona could only look up at her tall savior with wide eyes, bosom heaving with emotion.

Two voices broke the spell. From nearby, Fiona heard a woman's peevish command: "Whatever do you think you are doing, Will? Put the little chit down and let her go on her way. Do you realize that you could have been killed, dashing out into the street to snatch her from in front of that coach?" And in the background, Aunt Eulalia's indignant, "Fiona McQuade, what are you doing? Get inside this instant!"

Pulling away from the handsome gentleman's hands, Fiona dropped him a sketchy curtsy, murmured "Thank you, milord," and fled into her aunt's shop.

She hurried into the back room, pulling off her cape as she went. Her aunt stalked in behind her just as she was shedding her muddy brogues for her black kid slippers.

"And what is the meaning of that performance I just witnessed? Allowing a man to embrace you in broad daylight right in front of my shop . . . For shame, Fiona! You'll turn into a trollop."

"I . . . he rescued me from being run down by a carriage that came racing around the corner. Truly, Aunt Eulalia, that is all. If he hadn't caught me up and put me out of harm's way, I'd now be lying dead in the street."

Her aunt sighed loudly. "Always with an answer. Your ready tongue will get you into trouble yet. Did you get the ribbon?"

Fiona got it out of her pocket and held it out to her aunt. Just then the little bell over the outer door tinkled. Her aunt peeked through the green stuff drapes that hung over the doorway into the shop.

"It's the Duchess of Lawton. Get those ribbons on her bonnet at once. I'll show her the other one while you work."

Picking up a bonnet of dark-green satin, Aunt Eulalia bustled into the shop, and Fiona heard her saying, "Good afternoon, Your Grace. I have your bonnets ready. If you'd care to try this one first . . ."

Catching up needle and thread, Fiona quickly stitched the rose ribbons to the other hat the duchess had ordered, a delectable concoction of shades of pink and rose, trimmed with a curled ostrich plume. She was just biting off the thread when she heard her aunt call, "Fiona, bring in the other bonnet for the duchess."

Having had a few moments to compose herself after her dreadful fright, Fiona moved through the curtains, carrying the just-finished bonnet with her. Her eyes went to the people in the shop. It was her Aunt Eulalia, in her good navy gown with a white lawn fichu, and the lord and lady who had been with her outside. Stunned, Fiona stopped short.

Her aunt turned and scowled at her. "Come, come, girl, whatever ails you? Bring me the bonnet for Her Grace."

As if in a dream, Fiona moved forward, her eyes on the man who had rescued her from certain death. Tall, devastatingly handsome, he was not looking toward her at all. Instead he was admiring the green bonnet the duchess was trying on. He had thrown back his black marten-trimmed cloak, and the gold lining gleamed dully in the subdued light of the small shop. His coat was of a pale-green velvet laced with gold, the buttons also of gold, and his waistcoat a darker green, embroidered all over in a leaf motif of gold thread, quite striking. Fawn knee breeches buckled with gold, pale oyster-white silk hose with clocks of gold, and black calf shoes with gold buckles completed his elegant attire. His neckcloth and sleeves were of the finest white lawn trimmed with a deep ruffle of handmade lace.

"Do you like it, Will?" the duchess asked. She preened in front of the mirror and held a hand mirror as well to see the back of the fetching hat.

Fiona disliked her on sight. Tall, buxom, wearing a silk gown with a shockingly low décolletage, from which her ample bosom seemed ready to tumble, she was the epitome of arrogance and high breeding. Her wig was dressed with one long white curl, which hung over her shoulder, calling attention to the cleavage of her bosom.

My bosom is just as lovely, Fiona thought rebelliously. *Lovelier, in fact. I'm firm and she's going flabby. I can see the beginnings of a crepy skin where her stays push her up.*

The young lord said, "The color becomes you, Sarah. I like it."

"Then I'll take it." She turned to Fiona's aunt and asked, "And the other bonnet? Is it ready?"

Aunt Eulalia motioned Fiona forward. Dropping a slight curtsy, she handed the pink bonnet to Lady Lawton, realizing as she did so that the color would be most unbecoming to the duchess. Although she was heavily painted, her hazel eyes betrayed her natural coloring. As the duchess perched the pink bonnet atop her well-powdered wig, with a burst of audacity Fiona said, "There's another hat in the back that would be more becoming to Your Grace."

Aunt Eulalia's mouth dropped open at her niece's forward manner.

The duchess turned slowly, looking at Fiona with eyes narrowed, frightening the girl with the intensity of her gaze. "Indeed? You don't think that Miss Goodbody's taste is the best?"

"It's not that, Your Grace," Fiona stammered, wishing now that she'd bitten her tongue instead of volunteering her implied criticism of both her aunt and this valued customer. "It's not that," she repeated, voice quaking, "but there's a lovely bonnet in back, the color of beech leaves in autumn, that would set off Your Grace's beautiful hazel eyes." Watching the slow smile come over Her Grace's countenance, Fiona relaxed a bit. The duchess wasn't angry now.

Aunt Eulalia, ever alert to the nuances of a customer's reaction, smiled her public smile and said, "I do believe that Fiona is right, Your Grace. The gold would be perfect for you." Turning to her niece, she said, "Well, go fetch the hat!" The glare she gave Fiona while her back was turned to the duchess boded no good for the girl later.

Fiona hurried into the workshop and came out carrying the bonnet she'd suggested, a very plain hat made of a very elegant imported French velvet. With loving care she placed the bonnet on the duchess's head, taking care not to crush the elaborate wig. Fiona couldn't help a little smile of satisfaction. She'd been right: the bonnet was perfect.

The duchess frowned at herself in the mirror, turned her head this way and that, then turned to her male companion. "What do you think, Will? It's awfully plain. Maybe an ostrich plume?"

Again Fiona said, without thinking, "Oh, no, Your Grace; that would ruin it."

She held her breath as the man, presumably the Duke of Lawton, looked carefully at the duchess. Would he agree with her? If he didn't, Fiona was lost, for she was no fool where women were concerned, and knew they dressed to please their men.

Then the handsome lord turned to Fiona with a little smile on his face. "You have an excellent eye, Miss Fiona. The bonnet suits Her Grace admirably."

Fiona felt herself flushing at the attention of this man who had saved her life. He was everything she had ever dreamed of, as she watched the wealthy clientele of her aunt's shop and read the forbidden society gossip in *The Gazette*. Today her fondest dream had been realized—to be rescued from imminent danger by a fabulous man—only this man was married to a lady, and Fiona was a lowly shopgirl.

"Well, if you like it, Will . . ."

Fiona could see her aunt let out the breath she'd been holding. Momentarily she was saved from Aunt Eulalia's wrath, since her idea had been a good one. She knew all too well, though, that she'd be scolded later for being so forward.

The young Scottish lassie boxed the two bonnets and brought them back into the shop. By now the duchess and her handsome escort were getting into their coach.

"Hurry—take out the boxes, Fiona. We must never keep our valued customers waiting."

Scurrying out in the drizzle without even her cloak on, Fiona passed the boxes up to the coachman.

As she turned to go back to the shop, the duchess rapped on the window of her coach to get Fiona's attention. The duke opened the coach door a trifle, and the haughty beauty asked, "Would you be interested in leaving Miss Goodbody so that you could come to work for me as my wardrobe girl?"

Fiona was so stunned by the offer that she just stood there, eyes rounded with surprise, unable to answer the duchess.

"Well, girl? I haven't all day."

"Oh, Your Grace, it would be wonderful; but I

don't know whether or not my Aunt Eulalia would permit it."

"Miss Goodbody is your aunt?"

Fiona nodded, feeling that person's eyes boring into her back as she stood by the coach. She'd catch it when she went back in.

"Perhaps something could be arranged with her," the man called Will—the duke?—murmured.

"Of course." The duchess smiled at him. "A bit of money solves all problems, eh, Will?" She turned back to Fiona. "Your aunt will be hearing from me." Then she nodded to Will who rapped on the carriage roof, signaling the coachey to drive off.

Hair curling up from the droplets of moisture that had collected on it, Fiona scurried back into the shop.

"What were you talking about?" her aunt asked sternly. "I do hope you weren't being forward and impertinent. It worked out this time for you to suggest a different bonnet to Her Grace, but don't ever let it happen again. You could have caused great embarrassment for me."

"I'm sorry, Aunt Eulalia, but the pink was all wrong for her. And she agreed once she saw the gold bonnet on." Then, without thinking, she blurted out, "She likes my taste."

"She what?" Her aunt advanced on her, menace in her face, hand raised to slap the girl.

Backing away quickly, Fiona cried, "It's true; she does! She asked me to come and work for her as her wardrobe girl."

Aunt Eulalia's eyes widened with shock. "She——you're making this up, you naughty girl. I'll teach you to tell lies to me."

"Please," Fiona begged, "she said so. That's why I stood out in the rain for so long. She asked me if I would go to her home." She could see that business look come over her aunt's face. It was as if she was doing sums that came out in her favor.

"And what did you tell her with that too-quick tongue?"

"I just said I didn't know if you'd permit it."

"You didn't turn her down out of hand?"

"That's all I said. I told her you were my aunt."

"And?"

Fiona hesitated, then thought she'd better tell her aunt the whole truth. "The duke said that something could be arranged, and the duchess said something about money."

"Well, it's only right," Aunt Eulalia said. "They'd be depriving me of my help. I should be reimbursed for your loss of service." She smiled a tight little smile, then added, "But that wasn't the duke; that's her latest lover."

CHAPTER 2

"And watch out for the duke, Fiona. He'll have his hand down the front of your dress or up your skirt every chance he has," Bets warned. "A right old goat, that one. There's even talk that he belongs to the Hell-Fire Club." She stopped and eyed Fiona carefully to see her reaction to this scandalous revelation. Bets was a year younger than Fiona, but she'd been in service since she was twelve, starting as a scullery maid. Now she was upstairs maid at the duke of Lawton's luxurious town house on Millbank. She was much more experienced in the worldly gossip of the *ton* than Fiona.

Fiona, who had just finished carrying the last of her meager wardrobe up to the tiny third-floor attic room she was to share with Bets, hated to admit to her lack of sophistication. On the other hand, obviously Bets was a mine of useful information about the ducal household where she was to work. It would be foolish not to ask questions. Anyway, Fiona was dying of curiosity. "What in the world is a Hell-Fire Club, Bets?"

The squinty-eyed girl, with stringy hair that hung in lank locks from under the ruffle of her mobcap, lowered her voice conspiratorially: "Oh, it's that wicked! It's all lords, and they steal girls from the farms and rape them. And they worship the devil, doing all kinds of awful things. So don't let the duke catch you in a dark corner."

"I haven't even seen the duke," Fiona told Bets as she hung her blue gown on a peg in one corner. "Is he handsome? Young?" She kept remembering the man

18

who had rescued her from death, the man her aunt had said was the lover of the Duchess of Lawton.

Bets giggled. "Oh, Fiona, he's a proper horror, he is—short and fat with bulgy eyes and thick, wet lips." She made a little moue of distaste. "Occasionally he catches me and kisses me. Ugh! And he's years older than the duchess. He must be at least fifty. No wonder she prefers Viscount Huxley." Bets sighed and rolled her eyes. "Now, if *he* pinched me . . ."

"Is he, this viscount, tall and handsome?" Fiona asked. It had to be the same one, unless the duchess had a whole stable of lovers.

"Have you seen him?" Bets asked slyly.

"I . . . he may be the man who was with the duchess when she came to my aunt's millinery shop," Fiona said.

"All of the maids here swoon when he comes to the house," Bets told her, "but he spends all of his time with the duchess."

"And where is the duke while all this goes on?" Fiona's Calvinist upbringing made her uncomfortable at such goings-on. And yet, if the dashing viscount were to pay attention to her, she was sure that all of her training would go right out the window.

"Oh, you know how it is with the lords and ladies. They all have lovers. Marriage is just for convenience, or to keep a lot of money from getting into other hands. They don't marry for love. But then," she added cynically, "who does?"

I shall, Fiona promised herself. *I'll wed only for love.*

Aunt Eulalia had given her advice when she left the tiny living quarters over the shop: "Be a good girl. Don't let men take liberties with you, Fiona. You're much too attractive for your own good. These lords, they think serving girls are made to warm their beds. It's a bad business, that. They get you with child, then kick you out into the streets. Men of that class don't want bastards they've fathered on poor, simple servants. No, keep your skirts down. Someday you may be lucky enough to marry some solid tradesman who'll make you a good husband."

Fiona thought of the ones she knew: Mr. Beeson, the ribboner, a dried-up little prune of a man; Hartwell, the butcher, florid and stout, his greasy gray hair clubbed at his neck; Mr. Holcomb, the draper, who always watched her out of sly eyes and tried to look down the front of her dress. Not for her, one of these, nor any of the young men apprenticed to them, either. They had no prospects—at least not the kind Fiona dreamed of. She knew she had a rare beauty, and she intended to exploit her main asset, her good looks. She'd seen the gleam of interest in Viscount Huxley's eyes when he caught her up to save her from being run over by the coach. The Duchess of Lawton was a beauty, true, but she must be nearing thirty. She would soon be old, while Fiona was in the first blush of youth and beauty. Fiona knew that she would do everything in her power to win the interest of the Viscount Huxley.

The town house on Millbank was very elegant. Bets told her that the duke had a country place in the area beyond Uxbridge: "Oh, a huge mansion. They took me along, once, when one of the maids there was ill. The house is so big you get lost."

"Maybe I'll get to see it sometime."

"No doubt, as you do her ladyship's wardrobe." There was rank envy in Bets's voice. "And how will you get along with Hortense, the French abigail the duchess has?"

"I don't know. I've not met her, either; only the duchess."—and, of course, the Viscount Huxley, but Fiona didn't want to tell Bets about him. It would be her own secret, one she could hug to herself, her secret dream, of loving and being loved by the desirable viscount.

Fiona found out that very day how she'd get along with the French Hortense. The abigail was a scrawny little woman of middle years, her French accent heavy, her dark eyes sullen.

"So, you think you'll win my place away from me," she hissed, her sallow face twisted in anger. "I have been ladies' maid to Her Grace for ten years, now. What do you know of such things?"

Not wanting to quarrel with Hortense, sensing that the abigail might well be important in the servants' hierarchy, Fiona said quietly, "I have no wish to steal your position, Mam'selle Hortense. The duchess engaged me only to see to her wardrobe."

"That is what *I* do!"

Fiona sighed. She could see that things might be difficult here if the abigail remained so antagonistic; but there was little she could do at the moment. In a few weeks, when Hortense saw that she didn't intend to usurp her place, she might become friendlier.

Now Fiona took time to familiarize herself with the apparel that was to be her responsibility. In the suite of rooms the duchess occupied on the first floor, there was one large dressing room the walls of which were lined with deep carved wardrobes enameled white and trimmed with gilt. There were full-length mirrors on all four walls, so that the duchess could see herself from any angle, and, in addition, two gilt-framed free-standing mirrors, which could be moved about, positioned anywhere, to give additional images.

The gowns were so rich and beautiful that Fiona wanted to spend hours there just looking at them, feeling the lush velvets, the smooth satins, the crisp taffetas. There was one complete wardrobe full of hoops of various shapes and sizes, from hip panniers to full bell hoops.

While she was inspecting the gowns, the duchess came into the dressing room. "Oh, here you are,

Fiona. Well," she asked playfully, "do you approve of my taste in clothing?"

"Oh, Your Grace, everything is so beautiful."

"Fiona, there's a ball in two weeks at court, and I must have a new gown made for it. The seamstress will be here in about an hour with the latest fashion plates from Paris, as well as with swatches of fabric. You shall decide what will be most becoming to me."

It was an awesome responsibility. What if she chose something that didn't suit the duchess when it was made up? Would she lose her position?

Just then there was a sound that made Fiona look toward the door. There, ogling her, was a man who had to be the duke, for he fit Bets's description exactly. He was even worse than the upstairs maid's sketch. His paunch was not disguised by the skillful cut of his lavender waistcoat, or by the full skirt of the purple coat he wore. His wig was a mass of tiny sausage curls over each ear and tied in the back with a purple velvet ribbon that matched his coat. His eyes were hot and moist, his expression frankly lecherous. Fiona resolved right then never to let him catch her alone even for a moment.

"Well, well, well! What have we here?" he said, undressing Fiona with his eyes.

With some asperity, the duchess answered, "This is Fiona, my new wardrobe maid. I don't want her leaving the way the last one did, Jonathan." Her inference was unmistakable to Fiona, who recalled the warnings of her aunt and Bets.

He flushed with anger, not shame. "Fie on you, wife! What are maids for?"

"This one is far too clever about clothes to have to let her go in a few months. Have Dashwood provide you with amusement. Surely the supply of virgins in the vicinity of Medmenham hasn't been completely exhausted."

He advanced one menacing step. Fiona cringed

back into the protection of one of the wardrobes; but the duchess just ignored her husband.

"One of these days, Sarah . . ." he threatened.

She only shrugged, showing bare, creamy shoulders above the neckline of her pale-green Lyons silk morning robe.

With a glare at the duchess and another at Fiona, the duke stomped out, leaving the two women alone.

"Don't let him back you into a corner," the duchess said, echoing Bets's words.

Fiona, blue eyes wide, murmured, "No, milady." She certainly wasn't going to allow that old toad to paw her. Innocent Fiona might be, but not ignorant. Her dear mother, when she'd seen Fiona blossoming early, had explained the facts of life, not mincing her words.

So far, Fiona had managed to fend off the eager men who sought to pleasure themselves with her lush body. The duke was an old lecher, and living in the same house with him could make problems; but Fiona knew that she had the duchess on her side, so she was not unduly worried. Now, if that handsome Viscount Huxley wanted to take liberties . . . Fiona wasn't sure that her virtue would withstand the onslaught of such as he.

As if her thoughts had conjured up the young lord, Bets appeared at the door to the dressing room, dropped a curtsy, and said, "Milady, the Viscount Huxley is calling."

"Show him into my boudoir."

"And the dressmaker and her assistant have arrived."

"Good! Bring them up, too. Will can help Fiona select my gown for the court ball."

Fiona's heart raced at the sight of her hero. Today he had not worn a powdered wig but had his own black locks pulled back and tied with a ribbon. His coat was pale-blue satin, his embroidered waistcoat of midnight blue. He made a leg and then dropped a chaste kiss on the duchess's forehead. Then, as he straightened up to his great masculine height, he smiled at Fiona, a heart-stopping smile, and nodded almost imperceptibly, as if he didn't want the duchess to see him greet her wardrobe maid.

Unfortunately, with so many strategically placed mirrors in milady's boudoir—almost as many as graced her dressing room—the duchess could not help but see his interest in the girl. Her brows creased in a frown, which was almost instantly erased, for beautiful Sarah Billings, the duchess of Lawton, knew too well that frowning brought on wrinkles. A bit sharply she said to Fiona, "Well, have Mrs. Kirk lay out the designs." Turning to the viscount, she laid a proprietary hand on his arm. "You must help me decide what to wear to the court ball, Will."

"My pleasure, dear Sarah." And once again he flashed a glance toward Fiona.

She felt her cheeks flush, and went to join the pouter-pigeon-shaped dressmaker and her scrawny little helper, who were laying out the fashion plates on a long gilt-trimmed table decorated with inlays of mother-of-pearl. Fiona knew that these were the very latest fashions from the Continent, brought over by fast packet from France. Mrs. Kirk had an arrangement with a Parisian dressmaker who sent her the designs regularly. They were exquisite, and Fiona's mouth almost watered with envy, wishing that she could have such lovely gowns. Then her skilled eye took over and she busied herself with her job, picking out what would be best suited to Her Grace. Matching swatches of rich fabric to the plates, she soon had the choice narrowed down to three.

"I think one of these, Your Grace," she suggested diffidently. "The style would suit your queenly bearing, and the colors would be most becoming."

Lady Sarah studied the three choices. "Let me see the others," she told Mrs. Kirk. When the dressmaker handed her the sheaf of drawings, the duchess looked

at them carefully, lips pursed until she noticed herself
in one of the mirrors and seemed to remember that
pursed lips also made wrinkles. "And now the fabrics,
Mrs. Kirk."

Fiona felt her spirits plummet. The styles she had
chosen were much better for the duchess than the ones
Her Grace had laid out; and the colors the duchess
chose were not going to do a thing for her, paint or no
paint on her face. Her employer looked up at her, eyes
narrowed a trifle, as if to dare Fiona to object to her
choices. With an effort, Fiona held her tongue. She
wondered, though, why the duchess should pay her the
munificent sum of two pounds a year plus room and
board to advise her on her wardrobe if she intended
not to listen to that paid-for advice.

Turning to Huxley, the duchess asked, "Which would
you choose, Will?"

Fiona held her breath, wondering what his lordship
would do. First he took the three gowns the duchess
had chosen, holding the bits of fabric under her chin;
then he took up the other three plates and the small
samples of satin, velvet, and lace that Fiona had picked
out. Again he went through the same routine, holding
the colors under the duchess's chin (which was beginning to grow a twin).

"I think that Fiona has chosen the most becoming
one," he said, pointing to a lovely gown to be made up
in a deep russet velvet. Then, with a sly wink at Fiona,
he added, "And the second choice would be this one
you selected." It was the best of the three the duchess
had picked. She was not that poor a judge of what was
becoming to her, although she did tend toward gowns
that were a bit too ornate, with too many ruffles and
flounces, too much lace, too many silk rosebuds.

"You really like the russet, Will?" The duchess
turned to Mrs. Kirk. "Do you have the bolt of velvet
with you? Perhaps if I saw it draped over me . . ."

"Of course, Your Grace." Mrs. Kirk snapped her

fingers at the scrawny helper, who scurried out of the boudoir and came staggering back in carrying a huge bolt of fabric. Between them, Mrs. Kirk and Fiona draped the rich fabric about the duchess, pulling it in at the waist, allowing it to fall in deep folds from her magnificent bosom.

"Well?" Lady Sarah said. She had eyes only for Huxley.

"You'll be the most magnificent creature at the ball."

She smiled smugly. "It was very clever of me to recognize Fiona's talent, wasn't it, Will?"

Even as the duchess said the words, Fiona could see a hard look in those hazel eyes. They glittered like opaque stones, cold and calculating. Not being a fool, she realized the duchess was annoyed that Huxley had paid some attention to her, and although Fiona was transported to seventh heaven by his glances, she also knew that if the duchess became jealous of her, she would be out on the street without a reference and probably without her pay. She must be very careful to avoid any compromising situation with Lord Huxley.

The duchess dismissed her, and she spent the next hour conferring with Mrs. Kirk about the gown. Meanwhile, Hortense was in and out of the boudoir as she did the duchess's hair while Huxley lounged on a Chippendale chair sipping chocolate Bets had brought in a steaming silver pot of Georgian design. Each time the abigail saw Fiona she scowled. Fiona wished there was some way she could win the friendship of the French maid, for the woman could work her harm if she chose to. The ladies' maid was a power in any mansion.

When she had finished with the dressmaker, Fiona decided to go down to the kitchen for a cup of tea. As she passed one of the bedchambers, the door opened and the Duke of Lawton said, "Oh, there, Fiona; I've dropped my gold snuffbox. Be a good girl and find it for me. It has rolled somewhere out of sight."

What could she do but go into the room? The duke was her employer. Even though technically she was the duchess's wardrobe girl, Fiona wasn't stupid enough to think that she could refuse such a request by the duke.

Once she entered the room, though, the duke grabbed her in astonishingly strong arms and begin raining hot, wet kisses on her mouth, her throat, and that part of her bosom that was exposed by her low-cut gown.

Struggling mightily, Fiona gasped, "Milord, let me go at once!"

He only laughed, a coarse sound that frightened her. She remembered the duchess's implication that the duke had gotten her last wardrobe girl pregnant. Well, that wasn't going to happen to Fiona!

When the duke caught both of her hands behind her in one of his own iron-strong hands and ripped at the front of her dress with the other, Fiona, more angry than frightened, threatened, "Milord, unhand me at once or I shall scream."

"I like a girl with fire," he muttered, stopping her screams by covering her mouth with his own. Then he took a firm grip on the neckline of her gown and ripped downward, tearing the fabric and baring her to the waist. Catching one firm breast in his hand, he freed Fiona's lips and bent his head to it. By now she realized that she was in true peril of being raped. She tried kicking the duke's shins, but her skirts padded the toe of her shoe and he only grunted at the blow. Now he wrestled her down to the Turkish carpet that covered the parquetry floor of the bedchamber.

"Help!" she screamed, knowing that forcible violation was only moments away. With the duke's full weight upon her, Fiona couldn't possibly escape her fate. "Please help me!" she screamed in terror as Lawton tore at her clothes. Once again he fastened his mouth on hers, forcing his tongue between her teeth,

groaning in his desire. She felt the shreds of her gown
and petticoats being pulled away and then Lawton's
free hand tearing at her chemise.

Struggle though she tried, Fiona was not able to get
away from the man. He was working to hold her down
and pull off his breeches when the door to the bedchamber burst open and Huxley rushed in with the
duchess just behind him.

The viscount reached down and grabbed the duke
roughly, pulling him away from Fiona, while in the
background the young woman could hear the duchess
exclaim, "Really, Jonathan! Not again!"

Frantically Fiona tried to pull the shreds of her gown
about her nudity, with little success. Shocked, infuriated with the duke for his behavior, yet afraid that because she had resisted him she might be dismissed from
this excellent position, Fiona scarcely knew which way
to turn, what to do.

"For heavens sake, girl, go put on some clothes," the
duchess said with asperity.

Fiona picked herself up from the rug and fled, her
face flaming. She couldn't help but notice that the handsome Viscount Huxley seemed hugely amused at her
predicament, and that he had feasted his own eyes on
her bare bosom before she managed to drape a portion
of her torn skirt over her nakedness.

Behind her she could hear Hortense saying, in a self-
righteous voice, "She enticed him, milady; I saw it."

And the hateful duke, quick to accept the abigail's
lie to defend himself, flustered, "That's right, m'dear.
Flaunted her bosom in my face, invited me to touch.
Well, I don't just touch; you know that."

"Indeed I do," the duchess said drily.

Infuriated, Fiona stopped short and whirled about,
ready to defend herself against such lies; but Huxley
was looking directly at her, and he gave the tiniest
shake of his head, warning her away.

CHAPTER 3

"That was quite a performance, Fiona."

Wearing a green cotton stuff dress with a high neckline Fiona stood trembling before the Duchess of Lawton. Was she going to get the sack? "I . . . I'm sorry, milady, but he tried to force me."

"Oh, you don't have to explain the duke to me, my dear. He tries that with every new maid we hire here. Usually, though, they don't put up such a noisy fight." Her eyes narrowed and her face hardened. "Are you a virgin, Fiona?"

Shocked, Fiona said, "Of course, milady."

Arched eyebrows rose over those hazel eyes. " 'Of course' is scarcely the sentiment expressed by most young women in your position, Fiona. Good heavens, your aunt must have been a veritable dragon to have protected your virtue so assiduously."

"Aunt Eulalia had little to do with it," Fiona said with more spunk than she'd thought she possessed.

The duchess shrugged, then said in an offhanded way, "Jonathan knew you'd been a milliner's assistant."

Puzzled at this seeming *non sequitur,* Fiona said, "Yes, of course I was."

"But, my dear, milliners' assistants—shopgirls in general, flower girls—to be your age and still be virgins? It's almost unnatural."

Fiona drew herself up to her full height. "I hadn't been a milliner's assistant for long, milady. My parents died in the smallpox epidemic in Edinburgh."

"Of course! That's where you got that Highland lilt to your speech. Very attractive to the men." She said

29

it as if she didn't like it. "Well, do watch your step with my husband. I did warn you," the duchess added, an edge to her voice. Then, out of curiosity: "How did you get in such a position with him after being cautioned, Fiona?"

Fiona sighed. "He said he'd dropped his snuffbox and asked me to look for it, Your Grace."

The eyebrows flew up again. "That old wheeze! Really, Fiona, you are an absolute ninny when it comes to lusty men."

"I've had no experience with men, milady." Fiona resented the duchess's patronizing tone.

"With your looks and your figure, you'll soon have more experience than you can handle, I daresay. Just be careful how you entice men."

Her voice had gone cold, and Fiona shivered from fear. "En-entice men, milady?"

"Hortense told me that you deliberately enticed the duke."

"That's not so," Fiona cried hotly. "She doesn't like me, milady, and she's obviously determined to have me sacked."

"She's jealous of you, my dear, but she needn't be."

Fiona wasn't quite sure how to take this remark.

"She is an excellent abigail," the duchess continued. "You see to my wardrobe; she sees to me."

"If Your Grace could assure her of that . . ."

The duchess shrugged. "I daresay she'd still resent you—young, beautiful, attractive to men. You'd better learn now that you will go through life being resented by women less attractive than you."

Did she mean herself? Fiona wondered. The duchess was getting on in years. Did she see Fiona as competition? If so, why had she hired her?

"The duke is very annoyed with you. You did rather humiliate him," the duchess said, almost as if she, rather than her husband, sat in judgment on Fiona. "I should avoid another such episode if I were you. The duke can be quite vindictive."

"Oh, I shall avoid him at all cost," Fiona said drily.

Abruptly Her Grace changed the subject. "And what do you think of dear Will?"

"Of whom?"

"Will. . . . Come now, you aren't stupid: Will Huxley, the man who seems to spend his days rescuing you from death—and fates worse than death, as the novelists so quaintly put it."

Fiona knew she must be on guard. Hortense wasn't the only jealous older woman in the house here on Millbank. "He has been very kind, Your Grace." She kept her voice even. "I am eternally grateful to him."

Those hazel eyes seemed to burn holes in Fiona's face. "Don't be too grateful, my girl. He's a man, remember, a lusty man, with healthy appetites. I wouldn't want to have him using you for dessert after he'd dined off my charms."

Fiona's blue eyes flew open with shock. "Milady! I don't do such things!"

"Come, now, are you Papist, slated for a nunnery? All women do such things, sometimes for love, sometimes for excitement, often for more material considerations."

"If you thought I was likely to lure the viscount from your bed, why did you offer my aunt money so that I could come here to work for you?"

"Don't be impertinent, Fiona!" There was a whiplash of authority in the duchess's voice, and her eyes glittered with anger.

"I'm sorry, milady."

"I hired you for your talent with clothes. I should, perhaps, have looked a bit more closely at your talent with men." She smiled then, a cold, smug smile that did little to alleviate Fiona's fear of dismissal. "But then I needn't worry. Will isn't interested in unskilled virgins. He has mature tastes."

Fiona stood there quaking. She didn't try to answer Her Grace's comments. She was going to have to be very careful here or she'd be back in Aunt Eulalia's millinery shop, trimming bonnets.

The smile remained on the duchess's face as she said, "I think that perhaps what you need is a young man of your own, a man who'll keep you occupied. I'll have to see what we can do about it."

Fiona had a cold chill, and it took much willpower not to shiver in front of the duchess. Was she being forced into prostitution by this older woman?

"Well, girl, what kind of man would you like?" Her expression was calculating, and she looked Fiona over as if she were a prize racehorse bound for Newmarket. "Speak up, girl; don't stand there dumb. I assume that with your looks you won't settle for something ordinary —one of the footmen, perhaps or a younger coachman?" She pursed her full red lips and shook her head. "Of course not," she said, answering her own question, not waiting for Fiona's opinion. "Nor should you. With your attributes, we must find something better—perhaps a wealthy older tradesman." Her smile faded somewhat. "I can see that's not to your liking. Well, you're young—sixteen, is it?—much too young to be sensible about your men. No, for you it will have to be a dashing young lord, nothing less."

The duchess leaned forward, cradling her chin in her hand, elbow on her knee. "Ah, I have it, the perfect choice—young Werington! Malleable is dear Thorton. You'll be able to mold him the way cook molds a pudding, if you're clever, Fiona. He might well marry you if you play your cards right. Say no to him and keep saying no. Say yes with your eyes and with your rather nice bosom, but say no to him when he tries to bed you. I daresay his lady mother will have a heart seizure when he presents you as his intended bride, but she's a terrible old snob." A gleam of excitement lit those hazel eyes. "I declare, Fiona, this may turn out to be the most interesting thing I do this season: getting you married off to Werington. It's a hereditary knighthood. You'll be Lady Werington."

"I don't know that I want to plan marriage with a man I've never even seen."

The duchess sat up abruptly, frowning until she remembered the wrinkles. "Fiona McQuade, you are an ungrateful girl! Most young women in your station would leap at the chance to marry so well. Most," she added caustically, "would leap at the opportunity to marry into the nobility, even if the man was three times their age and a fat old lecher to boot. Here I offer you a handsome young man with money, too—his mother is independently wealthy—and you turn up that snippy little Scottish nose? Fie! You're stupid!"

Realizing her error, Fiona tried to make amends. "I didn't say I wouldn't like to meet Sir Werington, Your Grace; but as to marriage, he may not be as eager for it as you."

"Oh, come now! You can get any man you want if you try."

"Thank you, milady." Fiona wondered if that included that most desirable of men, Lord Huxley.

"I'll plan a little musicale. It will be a suitable time for you to meet Werington. Now, you'll need a gown. I'll send for Mrs. Kirk. We must have you looking like a lady, my dear. I'll introduce you as the daughter of a Scottish laird, an old friend."

"But, milady——"

"Surely you aren't going to say that's dishonest? I shouldn't like that, Fiona. I find this whole project very amusing."

"Yes, milady," Fiona said with a deep sigh. She could see that the duchess intended to go ahead with this insanity no matter what she thought. It was degrading, in a way; yet Fiona secretly had to admit that it was also exciting. It would be very enjoyable to mingle with the *ton,* have lords asking for her as a dancing partner. Luckily her parents had not been too strict. She'd even been sent to dancing class. "I hope that I live up to your expectations, milady."

"I'm sure you shall." The duchess's lips drew up into a secret smile.

Fiona could scarcely wait to tell Bets her stunning news. The upstairs maid turned very chilly, though, when she heard of Fiona's good fortune. "I'm sure you'll not be staying up here in our pokey little garret room for long, Fiona."

Impulsively Fiona put her arms around her friend. "Why would I be moving? I'm still just the wardrobe maid. Her ladyship is playing a little game, with me as a kind of doll. She'll tire of it soon enough, and then I'll be back in my old job, sewing ribbons on her bonnets and picking out colors for her gowns. This is all a fantasy, Bets. No young lord is going to marry a nobody like me."

"True," Bets said, cheering up. "But Ned, the youngest footman, has an eye on you. I've noticed it at meals."

Fiona had noticed, too, but she'd not encouraged the young man. No matter how she dissembled to Bets, she had high ambitions. She wasn't interested in this Sir Thorton Werington. She had her sights set on none other than the Viscount Huxley. She could see through the duchess's maneuvers, also, better than the duchess imagined. If Her Grace thought to get Fiona involved with a young man to keep her away from Huxley, then her plan was doomed to failure. Ned wasn't the only man who noticed her; so did the dashing viscount. If he was so completely captivated by the overblown charms of Sarah Billings, Duchess of Lawton, then he'd not be eyeing Fiona every time he came to see his beloved.

"The duchess is having a gown made for me," she told the envious Bets, "but I daresay I'll be allowed to wear it only when she wants me to play her little game with this young man she's picked out for me."

It was a game that Fiona found most enjoyable in the days that followed. Mrs. Kirk made her a delectable gown of deep blue trimmed with Scottish plaid— Her Grace's idea.

"Remember, I'm palming you off as the daughter of a laird. The tartan will be most appropriate."

Invitations went out to the musicale. The duchess engaged a group of harpists for the affair. "They'll play some Scottish airs. You don't sing, do you, Fiona?"

"A little. I am scarcely a performer."

"Let me hear you do some simple Scottish melody."

Fiona sang a folk song she'd known since childhood, and the duchess was ecstatic: "Charming! You'll be the darling of my musicale, Fiona."

Horrified, Fiona cried, "You don't expect me to sing in public, milady?"

"It won't be public; only a few dear friends. I'll speak to the harpists. I'm sure they can include this song in their repertoire." Then, seeing that Fiona was truly terrified, she added lightly, "Don't worry, my dear, whether or not you can sing. The men will all be so entranced with your snowy bosom that they'll pay no attention whatsoever to your voice."

"But the ladies?" Fiona's voice was dry.

"Oh, they'll be so jealous that they'll not hear you either."

"Then what's the point of my singing, Your Grace?"

Instantly the duchess lost her good humor. "Because I wish for you to sing, Fiona. That should be sufficient reason for you. I find you most impertinent at times. You must learn to curb your tongue. Just because I choose to amuse myself by passing you off as a laird's daughter doesn't give you leave to think of yourself as a member of the peerage."

"I'm sorry, Your Grace. Of course I am a nobody."

Fiona was not sure that she'd bettered her lot in life

by leaving Aunt Eulalia and coming here. The duchess blew hot and cold, and it was almost impossible to predict her moods. The slightest wrong word could turn her from pleasant to vinegary in a trice.

To Fiona's surprise, the duke treated her quite nicely after that fiasco on the Turkish rug. "My dear, I must apologize," he said to her the next day, catching her in the hall and blocking her way to the staircase.

Fiona, wary of him, looked around frantically, hoping that she could escape if he tried once again to force himself on her.

The duke smiled quite nicely, though. "No need to fear me. I had assumed that as you were a milliner's assistant, you were quite willing for a bit of a tumble. Most of those girls are well experienced by the time they turn thirteen. I had no idea you were a virgin."

Fiona felt herself flush. Her virginity was too much discussed in this household. Apparently in service you had no privacy at all. "I . . . I'm sorry I raised such an alarm," Fiona said. If the duke wanted to apologize, the least she could do was accept his overtures.

"The duchess tells me she's launching you in society," he said, eyeing Fiona with some of his old lechery.

"It's just a joke she's playing on some of her friends, milord," Fiona hastened to tell him.

"Has young Werington picked out for you. Keep you busy so you can't roll those lovely blue eyes at her latest pretty man, eh?"

"I . . . I don't know what you mean, Your Grace." But Fiona knew exactly what the duke was talking about.

"Have a score to settle with Huxley," he muttered, "but that needn't concern you, need it?"

He seemed to expect no answer, for he smiled and turned away; but there was something about the quality of that smile that bothered Fiona. She had a feeling that the duke really disliked Huxley and meant to do him harm if he could. In all honesty, she couldn't blame the duke for being displeased with the handsome viscount. No man wants to be cuckolded, even one who chases after women. The marriage vows meant little to members of the *ton*, she was discovering. Still, it couldn't be pleasing for your wife to bed a younger, handsomer man, no matter how many serving wenches you had.

The day of the musicale dawned bright and fair. Fiona's gown was a dream, and the duchess had even bought new slippers for her, with cunning high heels of red, all the rage.

Bets was green with envy. "You'll get to dance with the handsome men while I see to the ladies' cloaks and make sure that the combs are kept free of hair in their retiring room."

"Oh, Bets, it's only for this one night, and I could scarcely have refused the duchess, now, could I?"

"Of course not, but I only wish I was beautiful; then I might have such an evening too."

What could Fiona say? Poor Bets was such a homely creature. No duchess was going to be a fairy godmother to her.

Bets helped her dress, pulling on the laces of her stays to make her waist even tinier than it normally was.

"Keep pulling," Fiona gasped, determined that her waist would be the talk of the evening, the tiniest of anyone there. "I can still breathe."

"You'll faint if I lace you any tighter," Bets said cattily.

"As long as a handsome man catches me, then swoon I may."

The duchess sent Hortense to get Fiona.

"What folly," the French abigail said, tone haughty. "Her Grace is only toying with you. She'll laugh at you behind your back. Watch and see, Miss High and Mighty."

Fiona didn't deign to answer. She knew that the duchess was amusing herself; but who knew what might happen tonight? If Will Huxley paid attention to her, the duchess had better look to her laurels. She had a husband, while Fiona was free.

The drawing room was handsomely furnished in the new furniture of Chippendale, so that it didn't seem overcrowded. The older Kent styles went well in the stately homes in the country, where the rooms were enormous and looked bare unless massive furniture graced them; here, though, in this elegant town house, the more delicate lines of the modern furniture designers were admirably suitable. A temporary dais was in one corner, and the musicians were tuning their harps. Before the guests arrived, the duchess wanted to make sure that Fiona was properly gowned and painted. Her Grace had wanted to send Hortense to apply the paint to Fiona's face; but, sure that the French abigail would paint her like a clown to detract from her good looks, Fiona said that she would apply her own paint. She had done it with a very light hand, as her own fair complexion needed only the slightest enhancing. Bets had powdered her hair.

"Charming," the duchess said, smiling as she inspected Fiona. "I assume you aren't laced so tightly you'll faint? I shouldn't want anything *that* spectacular tonight."

"I'm quite comfortable, Your Grace." Fiona dropped a very low curtsy.

"Quite delectable. I understand it's young Werington you're going to charm tonight." It was the duke, done up in scarlet satin, which only emphasized his obesity.

Reluctantly Fiona greeted him, too, noticing that when she curtsied, the duke leaned forward to look down the front of her gown, which was cut sinfully low.

"I do believe that this occasion calls for a bauble," he said. He beckoned to a footman standing nearby and murmured to him, and the liveried servant hurried out of the drawing room.

Before he returned, the butler announced, "The Viscount Huxley."

Fiona's heart raced and she took a deep breath, then wondered if she was going to fall out of her gown with its deep décolletage. Huxley was resplendent in bottle-green velvet, and tonight his hair was carefully powdered and curled. He raised his quizzing glass and peered carefully at Fiona.

"Miss McQuade, daughter of a minor Scottish laird," the duchess said, tongue in cheek. "I can't wait to see the young men make fools out of themselves over our little Fiona."

"And older men, too, I'll warrant," Huxley said drily. He made a leg to the duchess, kissing her hand gallantly. Then he turned to Fiona and paid her the same courtesy.

When his lips touched her hand, Fiona felt she might swoon. Perhaps she had let Bets lace her more tightly than was wise.

With his back turned to the duchess, so that she could not see his face, Huxley let his eyes drink in Fiona's charms, sweeping over the fresh young beauty of her face and lingering on the lush swell of her superb bosom as it rose in snowy mounds from the blue of the gown. Silently he mouthed, "Later." Then, lest the duchess become suspicious, he turned back to her, devoting himself to the older woman.

The footman returned carrying a small inlaid case, which he handed to the Duke of Lawton.

"Come here, my dear," the duke said to Fiona. He opened the hinged lid of the box with his pudgy fingers and took a magnificent sapphire pendant from the case. Handing the empty box to the footman, he beckoned imperiously to Fiona, who had no choice but to move close to him. Then he fastened the gold chain about her neck, carefully positioning the glowing jewel just above the deep cleavage of her bosom, allowing his fingers to trail across her soft skin.

Controlling a shudder of disgust, Fiona forced herself to say, "Milord! You are too kind!"

"I thought the young bloods needed a focal point for their eyes," the duke said slyly, feasting his own lecherous orbs on the sapphire, which shone richly against her white skin.

"Really, Jonathan, you may have gone too far," the duchess said, annoyance in her voice. "They may not be able to keep their hands off her now."

And while she said the words, Fiona's eyes strayed to Huxley. He worked his fingers as if they, of themselves, were determined to caress that luscious skin where the pendant rested.

"I shall make sure that they do not touch," Fiona promised her mentor; but she made a promise to herself that if Huxley wished to caress her, she'd not say no to him.

CHAPTER 4

Sir Thorton Werington was tall, slender, and fair, with one of those overbred faces, all length and bone. His coat was pale-lavender silk and his waistcoat a mass of embroidery of multicolored thread interwoven with gold and silver. The buttons on his coat were amethysts faceted to catch the light of the hundreds of white French tapers lighting the room. His wig was small and tied with gold cord at his neck. A lace kerchief dangled from one cuff, and a quizzing glass hung on a gold chain about his neck. His eyes widened with delight when he was presented to Fiona in her guise as the daughter of a Scottish laird.

"My extreme pleasure, Miss McQuade." His eyes strayed quickly from her face to her bosom. "May I offer you a cup of punch?"

Knowing that this was the young man the Duchess of Lawton had picked for her, Fiona smiled assent, but inwardly she seethed. This young popinjay couldn't hold a candle to Lord Huxley. Werington offered his hand and escorted her to the long table hung with snowy linen and groaning with a sumptuous repast. There he instructed the footman to ladle out cut-glass cups of the potent punch well laced with gin.

Fiona sipped sparingly. She was not accustomed to taking much spirits, and she had no intention of getting tipsy and allowing this young blade with the bold gray eyes to take liberties. Since her virginity seemed to be much discussed, she'd retain it if for no other reason than as a conversation piece.

Soon the drawing room was a mass of beautifully

41

gowned women, well-turned-out men, and a veritable
army of footmen to serve them. The duchess had engaged extra men for the night and extra maids as well.
Fiona found herself the center of attraction, particularly among the men, all eager to ogle her abundant
charms. As she was not used to such attention, it quite
went to her head, and for a brief time she was able to
forget that she was only the lowly wardrobe maid at
this elegant Millbank town house. She felt like a young
lady and was treated as such. When it came time for
the musicale, all of the guests were seated around the
room, and the harpists struck up their airs. There was
polite applause at the end of the first set. Then the
duchess, resplendent in olive-green taffeta, made her
little announcement:

"My young guest, Lady Fiona McQuade, has gra-
ciously consented to honor us with some traditional
Scottish melodies."

With some trepidation Fiona went to the dais, escorted by Werington, who did not resume his seat but
stood nearby, as if to show that she was his property.
The harpists struck a chord, and Fiona sang "The
Waefu' Heart" followed by "My Heart's in the Highlands." She was surprised at the loud clapping that followed her simple songs, for Fiona knew that she had
no great voice. Then she noticed that it was the men
who were applauding so vigorously, not the women.
Curtsying to her appreciative audience, she made to
leave the low stage, but the men cried, "More! More!"
She saw the duchess nod imperiously, so Fiona had no
choice but to consult with the harpists and then sing
"Within a Mile of Edinburgh Town."

"Charming, Miss Fiona," Werington breathed in her
ear. "You are utterly charming. May I call upon you
tomorrow?"

Fiona didn't know what to do. Did the duchess intend for this farce to continue after tonight? Flirting
with the lacy fan she carried, she murmured, "I must

consult my hostess to see what plans she has made for tomorrow, Sir Thorton."

She was glad she'd said it, for now she had a chance to be near Huxley, who was being quite attentive to the duchess, as the duke was busy ogling a well-endowed lady so tall, he had to stretch on tiptoe to look down the front of her bosom, a most ludicrous sight.

Huxley noticed Fiona's amusement at the duke's antics and gave her one of his quick knowing smiles, as if he and she shared delicious secrets they must keep from everyone else. It turned Fiona's bones to jelly whenever he looked at her.

Before Werington had a chance to ask the duchess if he might call on Fiona the following day, the harpists struck up a waltz. At that moment the duchess was in conversation with the Baron of Audley and his good Baroness. While she was thus engaged, and while Thorton Werington was trying to get her attention, Huxley bowed to Fiona, held out his hand, and led her onto the dance floor, which was not crowded. The waltz was still considered by many of the *ton* to be daring, if not downright vulgar, so some of the guests did not dance. Although little experienced in the steps of this newest dance, Fiona found that she could follow Huxley perfectly. He clasped her closely about the waist, so that she was almost overcome by desire to have him so close to her. Round and round the drawing room they swept, dipping and sliding on the polished parquet floor, until Fiona knew her cheeks were pink with exertion, even though she had painted lightly before the affair.

"You are light as thistledown, Miss Fiona from the Highlands," he said softly, so that only she could hear.

"It is your skill in dancing, sir. I am most unskilled."

"I find you an admirable partner," he murmured. "Do you find young Werington to your liking?"

Fiona looked up into his flashing black eyes and

smiled. "He's so young, milord. I prefer my men more mature."

There was no mistaking the invitation in her tone and manner, and Huxley swung her about in an ever more giddy whirl, till she felt almost tipsy from the dance, his proximity, and the excitement of the evening. He waltzed her out of the drawing room, through the wide entrance hall, and into the small salon opposite the main party room. No one was in the room at that moment, and before Fiona realized what was happening, he had pulled her even closer and stopped dancing, and his lips found hers in a passionate kiss that left her breathless. Fiona had been kissed before by many a callow youth, but nothing in her previous experience had prepared her for the rush of emotion that swept over her, leaving her quivering and eager for Huxley's ardent kisses.

His lips slid across her cheek, along the angle of her delicate jaw, and down her throat, sending waves of sensation through her whole body. One hand clasped her to him while the other sought her bosom, cupping one breast as if it had been made to fit his eager hand. Fiona's head fell back as she was caught up in the passion of the moment. No man had ever roused her the way Huxley now did. As his hot lips brushed over the mounds of her bosom, Fiona was rudely brought back to the present by an angry voice:

"And what is the meaning of this public display?"

Fiona's eyes opened and she gasped with fright. The Duchess of Lawton was standing there, face so flushed that the angry red showed through her heavy white paint. She glared at the two culprits.

Fiona, speechless, pulled away from Huxley's embrace.

The viscount, breathing hard, said insolently, "I hadn't known it was to be performed in front of an audience, my dear Sarah. Sometimes you have eyes as keen as a falcon's."

And talons as sharp, Fiona thought, terrified of her mistress.

"As to what the meaning is," Huxley went on, smiling as he regained his composure, "it's all your fault, my dear."

"Don't you 'my dear' me!" raged the duchess, eyes glittering with spite.

Huxley shrugged, the tiniest lifting of his shoulders. He seemed quite unimpressed with the wrath of his lover. "You dressed Fiona up this way and flaunted her in front of all of us, Sarah. And she is very fetching. You must have known that or you wouldn't have initiated this little farce. I'm only human, a man with a man's appetites. Surely you of all people should know that."

The duchess only glared at him.

"Every man dallies with the servants," he went on, his manner so callous that Fiona shriveled up inside.

From the drawing room came the sound of the harps picking out the refrain of a popular minuet. Huxley bowed to the duchess and said, "Would you do the honor of dancing the minuet with me, milady?" He held out his hand to her, knowing she would acquiesce.

"Oh, there you are, Fiona. I'd lost you." Werington, quizzing glass to his eye, stood in the doorway to the salon. He walked across to her, held out one long, slim hand, and said, "I'd like to minuet with you."

Fiona saw it as an escape from an intolerable situation. Not looking at the duchess or at the false, horrid Huxley, she smiled coyly at Werington over her fan and said, "I'd be delighted, Sir Thorton."

As it happened, she had to dance with Huxley in some of the figures of the minuet. When he first took her hand, he leaned toward her and whispered, "I had to do something to save your job, Fiona. That's the only reason I said that dreadful thing about serving girls to Her Grace. Will you forgive me?"

Fiona had been cut to the quick, and she was not sure she wanted to be kind to Huxley, yet when he clasped her hand in his, she found that her breathing quickened so, she was sure the sound of her heart must be audible to him.

"The duchess is a very jealous woman," he went on as they again came together in the dance. "She thinks she owns me; but Will Huxley is his own man. If I could arrange to see you away from the house . . ."

Fortunately the dance separated them just then, so that Fiona did not have to make any answer. What was she to do? There was nothing on earth she wanted more than to see Huxley alone, away from the stifling effect of this house, where she so feared incurring the duchess's wrath.

Again the dance brought them together and Huxley said, "When is your day off, Fiona? We could meet somewhere, go to Ranelagh Gardens—or Vauxhall, if you prefer—take dinner together, go to the theater, perhaps."

In a burst of frankness, Fiona told him, "I'm afraid that my wardrobe doesn't include suitable gowns for such places, milord. I am only a maid here in the house. Don't allow yourself to be carried away by this farce Her Grace arranged for tonight."

"Ah, but you are the most beautiful creature I have seen in London, Fiona. If you wore a milkmaid's linsey-woolsey gown, you would put the beauties of Mayfair to shame."

"Still, I do not have the appropriate clothing for such outings as you propose."

"Then we'll go for a boat ride on the Thames."

Once again they were separated, and now it was Werington who importuned for more times to see her.

"Her Grace has my time so filled . . . ," she lied skillfully. Fiona didn't know, after the contretemps in the small salon, what to expect from the Duchess of Lawton. She might already be sorry she had started this joke. Tomorrow Fiona would be back at work in milady's wardrobe.

Werington would not take no for an answer, though. "I shall petition Her Grace and beg that she allow me to call."

Again the dance changed; again it was Huxley with her. "You haven't answered me, Fiona. Will you meet me? And when?"

"Day after tomorrow I have the afternoon to myself," she said, recklessly accepting his invitation. It was what she'd wanted from the first moment she saw Will Huxley. What harm could there be in a boat ride on the Thames?

"I'll pick you up at the end of Millbank, where it joins Horseferry Road. At two?"

"At two," she whispered.

For the rest of the evening Huxley studiously avoided her, devoting himself to the duchess. It didn't matter. Deliciously happy, Fiona hugged her secret to herself. With something akin to pity, she watched as the duchess flirted openly with Huxley right in front of the duke. That old lecher didn't seem to mind, though; he was too busy pursuing the tall, buxom lady he'd watched so avidly from early in the evening. No doubt he'd bed her tonight while the duchess welcomed Huxley into her own boudoir. It made Fiona burn with envy and jealousy; but she'd soon pay the duchess back.

As the guests left, Huxley made a leg to Fiona but, as the duchess was standing beside her, made no mention of their assignation. Werington was not so shy. He begged to be allowed to call on Fiona, still under the illusion that she truly was the daughter of a Scottish laird.

Fiona could see the look of calculation on her mistress's face, and it chilled her blood. She had made an enemy of the duchess tonight, and she feared she'd pay dearly for her rash little interlude with Viscount Huxley. Still, with the memory of his hot kisses on her throat and bosom, she didn't care what fate the duchess planned for her. She was secure in her knowledge that Huxley found her exciting and desirable. With the viscount as her champion, she needn't be afraid of anything the duchess might do.

Now, however, the duchess seemed determined to keep her options open. Smiling at Werington, she tapped him playfully with her sandalwood fan. "So you find Miss McQuade charming?"

Eyeing Fiona ardently, young Werington declared, "I am completely under her spell, Your Grace."

"Then perhaps if you call tomorrow afternoon, she may find a few free moments for you."

So this charade was to be prolonged, for what purpose Fiona couldn't fathom. It was not, she was sure, for her own pleasure. The duchess didn't do things to please a mere wardrobe maid. No, Lady Sarah had some scheme in mind, a plan that would somehow put Fiona in jeopardy.

When the last guest had gone, Fiona curtsied to the duke and duchess and begged leave to retire.

"Not yet, Fiona." The duchess's hazel eyes were hard as quartz, and she exchanged a look with the duke that conveyed a message without words. "Let us retire briefly to the small salon, since you seem to like that room so well."

The duke and duchess sat side by side on an elegant confidante covered in a delicate brocade. Fiona was not invited to sit, so she stood before them, a prisoner before two judges.

As if Fiona were not there, the duchess asked her husband, "What shall I do about her disgraceful performance, Jonathan?" Then she turned and gave Fiona such a venomous look, the girl's spirit shriveled. "Is Charlotte Hayes still in the market? Virgins are her specialty, I understand."

Now Fiona was truly terrified. Who hadn't heard of

the notorious brothel keeper? Was this to be her fate, to be sold into prostitution by her employers?

The duke, though, laid a pudgy hand on his wife's arm and suggested quietly, "I don't think you should be so harsh with Fiona, my dear. That punch was uncommonly strong tonight. Perhaps she isn't so used to spirits. And it must turn any girl's head to be the belle of the evening, eh, Fiona?"

Fiona was too frightened to answer the duke's question.

Her Grace looked closely at her husband, then nodded. "I take it that you have something special in mind, Jonathan?"

He smiled, and Fiona was more frightened of his good humor than of his anger. He, too, had a score to settle with her. She was sure he'd not forgotten the humiliating incident in his bedchamber.

"You are so perceptive, dear wife. Make sure that Fiona is receiving when Werington calls. And I shall have a very special invitation for him, too. Most young bloods feel honored to get to go to the abbey."

The abbey. Westminster? Fiona wondered if she'd had so much punch that she couldn't think straight, could no longer comprehend the English language. The duchess, though, had no such difficulties. She knew exactly what her husband meant.

"I was very annoyed with Will tonight." This *non sequitur* made the duke smile slyly. "When will Werington's invitation be?"

"You want to go, and take your dear friend?"

"Perhaps he will learn a lesson."

"It could prove amusing, seeing his face when he realizes that the fruit he thought would drop into his eager hand is being tasted by all and sundry."

"Day after tomorrow?"

"I'm sure that Sir Francis can convene the brotherhood by then. He's always eager to worship." He slid a look toward Fiona and licked his thick lips as if in anticipation, his lechery surfacing from behind his new friendliness.

Fiona wondered what plans the Lawtons had for her. It was suddenly imperative that she talk with Viscount Huxley, ask his advice. She was awash with suspicions but had no real grounds for them; only this feeling of evil that now pervaded the small salon.

"You may go to bed, Fiona," the duchess said abruptly. "Tomorrow Mrs. Kirk will be here to sew you another dress more suitable for a picnic." She laughed, an ugly sound.

"A picnic, milady?"

"I choose to let our little game continue for a while longer. Tomorrow we shall allow the eager Sir Thorton to call on you. If he asks you to accompany him on an outing, you have my permission—nay, my command—to say yes."

It was as if she were a puppet, with the duchess controlling her strings. Fiona curtsied and fled to her garret bedchamber, where Bets waited eagerly to help her out of the gown and to hear an account of the evening.

Feigning sleepiness, Fiona promised to tell her all of the gossip next day. She crept into her hard bed with the lumpy mattress; but dawn was lighting the tiny gable window before she drifted into a fitful sleep. The duchess's game was cat and mouse; and Fiona knew that her role was not that of the cat.

CHAPTER 5

Fiona was frantic. How could she possibly get word to Huxley before their assignation? Now that the duchess was making it impossible for her to meet him as planned, she must let him know. But how? Would a letter reach him in time? She didn't even know where he lived. How could she send him a note?

The Duchess of Lawton had dropped her bombshell that morning. Fiona, wearing her new maid's uniform of black and a lacy white mobcap, was called into the boudoir early. Usually the duchess wasn't up before eleven, but by ten Fiona had her summons. She found her mistress still in bed, although Hortense was hovering over her ladyship, combing out the chestnut-colored locks. With some satisfaction, Fiona saw that there were strands of gray running through the russet tresses.

"I've sent for Mrs. Kirk," the duchess said, without any preliminaries, "and she'll bring several assistants so that they can complete your dress by tomorrow."

"Tomorrow?" Tomorrow was her afternoon off, when she was meeting Huxley.

"You needn't repeat everything I say, like a pet parrot."

The duchess's sharp words brought a smug smile to Hortense's face. She was as unfriendly to Fiona as ever.

"You'll be going on an outing with Werington tomorrow—up the Thames by boat, a picnic, and a most interesting afternoon at an old abbey. It isn't every little chit of a maid who gets such a lovely chance on her afternoon off, and you'll make young Werington very happy, Fiona."

51

Her heart sank. There was no use protesting. Unless she was willing to give up her position here, which she didn't want to do, she must obey the duchess. Hopefully in a little while her mistress would tire of this latest game. However was she to let Will Huxley know?

"Fiona does not seem too happy with her good fortune, Your Grace," Hortense said slyly, her spite making her dark eyes glitter.

"I daresay Fiona will change her mind after tomorrow."

There seemed to be a hidden intensity in those words that made Fiona uneasy. Last night's strange conversation between the duke and the duchess weighed heavily on her. Her lack of sleep, the excitement of the musicale, the memory of Huxley's hot kisses—all had Fiona in a turmoil.

"Your Grace is very kind to me," she said belatedly, remembering that her livelihood depended on the whims of this haughty lady in her elegant robes who reclined on the large canopied bed that served now as a kind of throne.

"Until Mrs. Kirk arrives, you may check over my gowns to see if any need mending." Then, as an afterthought, she asked, "Do you have anything to wear today that isn't too tatty?"

Incensed, Fiona said, "I have several very nice gowns, Your Grace."

"Well, we certainly don't have time to make one for today. Mrs. Kirk and her minions will be sorely taxed to get the dress ready for tomorrow. Something simple, I think—maybe in sprigged muslin—and a straw bonnet, if you have one."

"I have a broad-brimmed straw that should keep the sun off my face in the boat," Fiona said, adding a bit nastily, "After all, Aunt Eulalia *was* a milliner."

"Very well. After dinner today, be ready for Werington's call—about three, I'd guess—and when he tenders his invitation, accept."

"Yes, Your Grace."

Bets was dusting the wardrobe room when she went in to go over Her Grace's gowns.

"Tell me everything about last night," hissed the little maid, her squinty eyes aglow with envy. "I saw all of the fine ladies in their silks and satins. You looked as elegant as any of them, Fiona," she added grudgingly.

"Thank you, Bets. It was your help with my hair that did it," Fiona said kindly. She knew how Bets felt. Why should one maid have such a glamorous evening while the other waited on the guests?

"Is the game over?"

"Not yet." Fiona sighed. How she wished she could confide in the upstairs maid; but that wouldn't be wise. Bets might let slip something about the viscount, and it would get back to the duchess via Hortense, who would delight in telling Her Grace something damaging about Fiona.

"Are you going to be at another rout?" Bets asked.

"No, but she has allowed Sir Thorton Werington to call on me this afternoon. And he's to ask me to go on a picnic the next day."

"But that's your afternoon off!" Afternoons off were sacred in the servants' hall.

"I know, but the duchess said that I was lucky to have something so pleasurable to do on my time off. What could I do, Bets? And I'd planned something else, too." She wished she'd not said that, for Bets looked at her avidly.

"What, Fiona. Has Ned asked you to go walking in the park?"

"No." Then she lied blatantly: "I was supposed to go see my Aunt Eulalia."

"Oh, well, you can see her next week," Bets said.

Fiona still had her problem of letting the viscount

know she could not meet him tomorrow. Perhaps he too would call today, and she could see him alone for a moment to explain that the duchess has made other plans for her.

Huxley did call, but by then Fiona was busy with Mrs. Kirk, being fitted for a charming cotton gown of yellow. When she realized that the viscount was calling on her mistress—and his!—she did everything in her power to get away from the fittings to see him momentarily, but to no avail.

"You mustn't keep running away, Fiona," Mrs. Kirk scolded. "It is a monumental task for us to make this gown for you by tomorrow noon. If you disappear, we lose time in the fittings. I've even asked the duchess if we could be served our dinner here in the sewing room so that we can keep on working while we eat."

Fiona next dashed off a very short note to Huxley, putting no salutation or signature lest it fall into unfriendly hands. She'd listen and run down to the door when Huxley left. It would take only a moment to slip the note into his hand. In this she was thwarted also, for when he left the town house, she was standing on a low stool while Mrs. Kirk pinned the skirt of the sprigged muslin to the proper length. She could see, just, from the window of the sewing room; and his tall, unmistakable figure, tricorne placed at a jaunty angle on his head, came from below and got into the carriage that had been waiting in the mews behind the terrace of homes.

Perhaps he'd return later. She was all fidgety, causing one of Mrs. Kirk's drab little assistants to stick a pin in her arm as she tried to pin the frills on the sleeve. Then she had to rush to dress for Werington's call.

It was a strange afternoon. She had scarcely greeted her caller when a footman carried him away for a brief chat with the duke. When he returned, his whole attitude toward her had changed.

"It will be exciting tomorrow at the abbey," Werington whispered, and his teeth nipped her earlobe.

"Sir! You take too many liberties," Fiona scolded. If it had been Huxley . . . Ah, but it wasn't. This young fop in his mauve silk coat and gold-buckled shoes, with his long walking stick and his enameled snuffbox, was a far cry from the robust, manly Huxley.

"The duchess won't mind a bit of familiarity," young Thorton insisted.

"But *I* mind," Fiona told him quite firmly, moving away from his eager hands. "If you intend to behave this way tomorrow, I shall have to stay at home."

Werington laughed heartily, as if this was the funniest joke of the season. "Ah, Miss Fiona, you are so amusing."

The afternoon dragged on interminably. Fiona kept listening for Huxley, but he did not come back to the house on Millbank. The duchess did not spend much time in attendance on the young couple, so Fiona spent her entire afternoon fending off the eager young blood. He hadn't been this way at the musicale. She hoped that she could manage him tomorrow. She could always tip him over into the water if he became too offensive on the ride up the Thames.

"Where is this picnic to be held?"

"You don't know?" Thorton asked in surprise. "At Medmenham Abbey, of course."

"Remember, sir, that I am only visiting in London from my home in Edinburgh," Fiona lied, to keep up the farce the duchess had started last night.

"Then you don't——" He stopped short, then smiled. "How interesting. You'll like the abbey, Miss Fiona. There is to be a special masquerade tomorrow, I understand."

"A masquerade! But I have no costume for such an affair."

"I do believe they are provided," he said. Then, with a rush of confidence, he added, "I've not been there myself. It's very sporting of His Grace to sponsor me for tomorrow."

Fiona didn't know what he was nattering about. "Sponsor?"

"It's very exclusive. Not everyone gets to go there. I understand that the abbey has most . . . *unusual* furnishings, and its gardens are full of exotic statuary. I think you will find it droll."

Fiona came to a decision. As it was impossible for her to keep her tryst tomorrow with Huxley, she must then make the best of a bad situation. The outing should indeed be delightful. A trip up the Thames was always pleasant, she assumed, though she'd been in London so short a time that she'd never actually done this. Very well, she would enjoy herself tomorrow. The next time she had a chance to talk with Huxley, she'd tell him quite truthfully what had happened. He knew that she was in service. Certainly he would understand that she had no say when the Duchess of Lawton planned her time off for her.

"I shall call for you at two in the afternoon," Thorton went on. "We'll take a boat from the old ferry slip at the end of Horseferry Road."

Good heavens! Huxley might well see her as she drove past with young Werington. Fiona made a resolve to be sneezing or turning her head away when they drove past tomorrow. Perhaps she could tie a scarf over her broad-brimmed straw hat so that it would hide her face. At any rate, Huxley wouldn't be watching for her in a carriage. He'd expect her to be walking to their appointment.

The duchess came into the salon then, all smiles. "Is everything arranged for your outing?" she asked.

"I shall call for Miss Fiona at two, Your Grace."

Fiona wasn't quite sure how the duchess managed it, but suddenly Thorton was leaving, though she had expected him to stay for tea. On his way out, he leaned toward her, a daring look on his callow face, and whispered so the duchess couldn't possibly hear, "Get thee to a nunnery," raising his eyebrows as though he'd said something clever.

"Ah, you know Mr. Shakespeare's *Hamlet, Prince of Denmark*," Fiona said.

"As obviously you do too." His words seemed weighted with some hidden significance.

Unbidden, another Shakespearean quotation came to Fiona's mind: "Be thou as chaste as ice, as pure as snow, thou shalt not escape calumny." She shivered as though someone were stepping on her grave.

"Oh, Miss Fiona, do not contract a chill. I should be desolated if you would not be my fair nun to-morrow."

She thought he said "nun," but he must have said "one." Fiona simpered, wishing he'd go away.

Next morning, when Fiona went to have the duchess give approval of the gown, she found her mistress in a rage. She was reading a note when Fiona tapped at the door and entered, bobbing a curtsy. The duchess looked up and crushed the note into a rumpled ball:

"Well! At least *one* of us will enjoy the afternoon."

Fiona, thinking she had done something to anger her mistress but not knowing what it was, stood silent before her. Hortense, ever watchful, glared with Gallic spite at this wardrobe maid in her new finery.

"The gown is finished, all but a bit of stitching, Your Grace," Fiona finally said, voice low, eyes downcast.

"So I see. Well, don't waste more time. Take it off until time to dress for your outing. Now, get to work."

When she had a quick early dinner with Bets in the kitchen, Fiona found out why the duchess was so angry.

"Hortense says that Her Grace is in a rage because

she wanted Viscount Huxley to take her somewhere today, but he had a previous engagement."

"That's what the note was! I saw her read it and crumple it up." Of course; Huxley thought he would be going out with Fiona. What would happen when she did not show up for her appointment?

"She's very possessive of the viscount," Bets babbled on while she shoveled in her meal of beef and boiled turnips. "She's older than he, of course. I'm sure she fears that he may meet some younger woman and marry her. Although," she added cynically, "that doesn't matter to the peerage. They don't have to be faithful."

Fiona had noticed that.

Then she dressed for her picnic. "Don't powder me today," she said to Bets, who was helping her. "I think that natural hair is more appropriate for an outing on the Thames—and for the picnic too."

"I've never been on a picnic," Bets said enviously. "I suppose you'll stop at some lovely spot along the river and eat dainties from a hamper."

"We've been invited to some sort of party at an abbey," Fiona said. "Sir Thorton told me that the gardens are lovely—'unusual,' I think, was the word he used."

In shocked tones Bets said, "An abbey?"

"Ruined, I presume. Probably very picturesque."

"It wasn't Medmenham Abbey, was it, Fiona?"

"As a matter of fact, I think that's what he called it."

"But, Fiona——"

Just then Hortense bustled in. "Not ready yet, you wicked girl? His lordship's carriage just drove up. Hurry!"

"I'm ready," Fiona snapped. She caught up her straw hat and hurried down the stairs to the vestibule, where Sir Thorton stood, resplendent in a suit of fine wool twill.

"Ah, Miss Fiona, how delectable you are," he said,

eyeing her with pleasure, his eyes drawn to the white expanse of bosom the gown exposed. "Shall we be on our way? I have a water taxi engaged to meet us at the old ferry slip."

He whisked her out of the house and into a small open coach. Handing her in, he told the coachman to take them to the river.

As they rounded the corner leading from Millbank onto Horseferry Road, she saw a gig standing there, the gray horse a fine-looking animal. No one was in the carriage; but standing beside it, watching Millbank, was Will Huxley. Quickly she tied the hat down as she'd planned, hoping that he wouldn't notice who she was. Werington ruined her plans.

"I say, there's Huxley. Wonder what he's doing here? I'd have thought he'd be calling on Her Grace."

Eagerly Fiona turned toward her escort, hoping that in doing this, her face wouldn't be seen by Huxley. To her dismay, Werington called out to his driver, "Pull up a moment, fellow. I wish to greet a friend." Then, leaning from the carriage, he called out, "Huxley, old fellow. What are you doing here?"

Huxley turned, smiled, and started over to speak to them. Then he recognized Fiona, and for a moment his expression was blank.

"Fiona and I are off to Medmenham Abbey," Werington said.

"How interesting." His words colder than ice, his dark eyes bleak, Huxley stared at Fiona. "The duchess wanted me to go there today, but I had made other plans. As they did not materialize"—and he gave her a poisonous look—"I think I shall go pay my respects to Her Grace. It may still be early enough for us to enjoy Sir Francis's entertainment."

"I'd invite you to come with us, but I've engaged only a small water taxi. Two more people would swamp it."

"Never mind, Werington. We'll make our own way there, if the duchess still wants to attend."

Throughout all this Fiona sat tongue-tied. There was no possible way for her to tell Huxley what had happened. With Werington sitting beside her, she could scarcely say that the duchess had ordered her to go on this picnic with the young man. If, though, Huxley was coming to the abbey later, she might have a chance then to explain matters to him.

CHAPTER 6

It was a delightful day on the Thames. River traffic was busy, with heavily laden barges of produce being shipped downstream from the farms west of London, while pleasure boats with brightly garbed men and women plied their way in both directions. The smaller water taxis went hither and thither. Since the opening of the New Westminster Bridge in 1750, the horse ferry no longer carried carriages from the north to the south banks of the Thames; there were enough boats on the river, however, that their boatman had to watch where he rowed. Although Fiona was distraught at not being with Huxley, her youthful spirits couldn't long remain low on such a glorious day in May. The sun shone brightly, and she was glad she had worn her wide-brimmed hat; it wouldn't do to let the sun darken her fair skin or redden the end of her nose.

Werington was in a kind of fever of excitement.

"You were not so high-spirited the other night at the musicale," Fiona said. Perhaps the intimacy of the small boat brought out this quality in him, although he had been quite good about not putting his arm about her waist once she scolded him for such impropriety.

"At that time I had not yet received my invitation to the abbey," he said.

Fiona noticed that the boatman glanced at her as her escort was talking, and a sly smile slid over the coarse fellow's face. She turned to Werington to avoid the boatman's eye.

"This abbey—I've never seen it," she confided.

"Old ruins of a Cistercian abbey that Sir Francis has repaired for his frolics."

She didn't much like the look on Werington's face, either. What was happening today? The boatman kept giving her veiled looks and his lips twisted in a leer. Sir Thorton was in a state of suppressed excitement, like the cork in a bottle of French champagne ready to explode at a touch.

"Will there be others there?" Of course there would. She'd heard Huxley say he'd be along later with the duchess. Fiona was determined to find some way to chat with Huxley away from both the duchess and her own escort.

"Always a crowd at one of Sir Francis's parties, I understand." Then, with a little-boy look on his face, Werington added, "I'd not expected to be invited there. It was very kind of the Duke of Lawton to arrange this day for me."

Fiona wished that Lawton hadn't done it. She'd now be with Huxley, perhaps driving through the graveled roads of Vauxhall Gardens or strolling about the rotunda at Ranelagh along the Thames.

It was a long journey to Marlow, and the boatman was sweating mightily when he finally drew up to the small pier and steps where they were to disembark. He steadied the boat while Werington handed her out, then gave Sir Thorton the wicker lunch basket. As he cast off, he called to them, "Have a holy time at the abbey."

"He must be some kind of religious fanatic," Fiona said. "Perhaps he's a Papist?"

Werington just grinned and said nothing. Then they went up the marble steps and walked into the grounds surrounding Medmenham Abbey.

"It's in ruins!" Fiona cried when she got her first glimpse of the gray stone structure. "Is it safe to go inside the walls, Sir Thorton?"

"It has been carefully restored by workmen brought

in from other parts of England," he explained, "to keep the details of building a secret."

"Why should it be a secret?" Fiona asked innocently.

"You'll soon see. But come, let us find a pleasant folly where we can enjoy our picnic before joining the rest of the party. The duke gave me instructions . . . ah, yes, this path to the left leads to one of the Roman temples of love."

The garden was laid out almost like a labyrinth, with twisting paths and exotic plantings. They turned one sharp corner and almost ran into a statue of a nude Venus bending over to take a thorn from her foot. Indeed, Fiona's face was but a few inches from the white marble buttocks, and, flushing scarlet, she hurried past the exotic piece of statuary. Soon they came to a small marble folly of classical design, with upholstered couches set inside it.

"Ah, the Roman temple," said Werington. "We'll lunch here."

Fiona busied herself laying out the sumptuous repast, finding roasted woodcock, sections of guinea hen, and slices of ham, with a variety of pickles, fruit, and nuts. There was a large bottle of claret with appropriate crystal wine glasses. Werington, meanwhile, toured the small folly, looking at murals painted on the walls, chuckling at great rate. Curious to see what he found so amusing, Fiona joined him. To her consternation, she saw that the murals were all highly erotic in content, although they were done in the classical style.

"Copies of murals found in Roman ruins on the Continent," he said.

"They're scandalous!"

"But very clever. Surely the *ton* in Edinburgh are as enlightened as we here in London," he chided.

Fiona wished that she could tell him she had never been a member of the Edinburgh elite; but if she did this, she would incur the wrath of the Duchess of Lawton. "Perhaps we're a bit more provincial in Scotland," she said, scarcely knowing where to look. On every side were the explicitly sexual renditions, which she found to be very embarrassing. Obviously this was the sort of thing the young bloods of London found amusing. No doubt Huxley would think the paintings all the rage. If she was to mingle with high society, she knew she would have to develop a great deal of sophistication, and soon, so she looked at the pictures, trying not to let Werington see how very shocked she was at the lewdness displayed there.

As soon as she could tear him away from the murals, she joined him in the light meal he had brought. They ate quickly, for he told her that when dusk came, the Friars of St. Francis would arrive by boat. "It's quite a sight, I've been told. We don't want to miss it. They come from London in a bright red barge, and they wear white robes with hoods lined with scarlet. They march to the abbey from the quay carrying long lighted black tapers."

"They're Papists?" Now Fiona was shocked, for the Catholics were in very bad repute at this time.

"Papists!" His laughter pealed out in the twilight. "Far from it, Fiona. They all hate the Papists. That's why they mock the mass in their service."

Although from a Calvinist background, Fiona found that such talk of mocking even the Papist mass made her uneasy. She had an innate sense of tolerance that did not allow her to make fun of any religion. She knew, though, from the gossip she'd heard and read since she'd come to London, that the young bloods, the Mohocks and the Blasters, could be very boisterous in their fun, destroying more than was conscionable at times.

Fiona, not entirely ignorant, questioned Werington closely. "This Mass you say they mock—is that what they call a Black Mass?" When he reluctantly admitted that it was, Fiona was properly aghast. "That's witchcraft! It's illegal."

"Oh, come now, Fiona, don't be a cold bath. It's all done in fun, you know. The friars of St. Francis come here to relax, drink some wine, eat, enjoy themselves. They bring their ladies with them. Even the Duchess of Lawton comes—you heard what Huxley said. Do you think your hostess is a witch?"

Fiona would have spelled it differently, but she could scarcely tell Werington what she thought of Sarah Billings.

Just then they heard a bell begin to toll.

"I say, it's the arrival of the friars! Come along, Fiona, we don't want to miss this!" He caught her hand and hurried her along the path toward the landing stage. There were others hurrying toward the Thames, sleek young lords done up like popinjays, macaronis all; and with them were pretty young women in pseudo-rustic gowns, frolicking as milkmaids.

Surprisingly enough, there were several nuns among the group, wearing black habits and black masks. Two of these women approached Fiona and Werington. "Sir Thorton Werington?" one asked of the young man. When he nodded, in assent the nun turned to Fiona. "Fiona McQuade?"

"Yes."

"Please come with us. You have been honored to take a part in tonight's festivities."

"But——" Fiona didn't know what to do. There was something about these nuns that upset her.

"I say, how delightful!" cried Werington. "I had no idea she'd be—— Run along with the sisters, Fiona. I shall see you later."

"Oh, I assure you, Sir Thorton, you'll see a great deal of Miss Fiona," the other nun said, chuckling.

"I won't get to see the friars arrive," Fiona protested.

"Ah, you'll see all of them later," the first nun assured her. "Do come along. We have to dress you for the festivities."

"Dress? Oh, the masquerade."

Deciding that she'd better enter into the spirit of the occasion, and seeing that Werington thought it splendid that she had been chosen for some part in the coming pageant, or whatever it was to be, Fiona let the two nuns whisk her away through the twisting, turning paths of the garden. She got glimpses of statues that seemed to match in marble some of the explicit murals in the Roman folly. Luckily, her escorts did not choose to dwell on them.

The inside of the abbey, Fiona found, had been completely renovated; it was only the façade that was in disrepair. The corridors were filled with the kind of decoration she'd already seen in the Roman folly. She wished she had a bit of time to herself to examine these paintings in detail, for she realized there was a lot to learn about sexual encounters from these explicit works of art, but the two masked nuns hurried her along. "We haven't much time," one muttered. "Someone should have told Werington to bring her up from London earlier." Then they came to a small chamber, and her two mentors ordered, "Disrobe as quickly as you can." With their help, Fiona was soon out of her new gown and the hoops and petticoats that gave it fullness. She stood in her shift and stays, still wearing the fine silk stockings the duchess had so generously provided for her, and her second-best slippers. She'd thought them quite good enough for an outdoor picnic.

"Come, come, Fiona, everything off," cried one of the nuns. "We can't anoint your shift."

"Anoint? I don't understand."

The other nun said, "It's all part of the masquerade. Everyone does it. Come, come, we've seen naked girls before."

A bit embarrassed to strip in front of these unknown women, glad that they were masked so she couldn't see their faces, Fiona took off the last bits of clothing and stood there shivering slightly from the chill of the room and from anticipation. One nun got a silver jar made of some very sheer gauze-like fabric, and Fiona rubbing a rather pungent salve onto her legs. "On the bottoms of your feet, too, Fiona."

Obediently Fiona raised one, then the other, and giggled a little as the nun rubbed the ointment onto the soles of her slim, shapely feet.

"Now, into these for the moment." They gave her plain black velvet slippers, kitten-soft.

"And let me help you with the habit," the other nun said, having a long black garment over her arm. Quickly she slipped it over Fiona's head and tied a sash loosely about her waist. The robe seemed to be made of some very sheer gauze like fabric, and Fiona was slightly scandalized, for she was afraid her body would show through it.

Then the first nun cried, "We almost forgot the potion!" Darting across the room, she poured wine from a tall decanter into a chased silver goblet and gave it to Fiona. "Quickly, drink it down," she admonished. To the other nun she added, in a low voice, "Abbot O'Toole would be most annoyed if we'd forgotten the cantharides for her."

Fiona sipped and almost gagged. "What's in this wine?" she demanded.

"Nothing, nothing; just a bit of something to help you enjoy yourself more, my girl. Everyone has some of it to drink. Come, now, we can't keep the friars of St. Francis waiting. Light the censers, sister."

Fiona took a deep breath and gulped down the doctored wine, hoping that she wouldn't bring it back up. Her feet felt odd, almost as if they had gone to sleep. One of the nuns lighted silver censers, and the pungent incense seemed to penetrate into her brain, numbing it.

Swaying slightly, Fiona said, "I feel . . . feel strange."

"Hurry! We want to get her there before we have to carry her," the nun warned her sister. They got on either side of Fiona, each taking an arm, and walked her out of the room, incense burners swinging on the ends of silver chains. Fiona felt very strange, as if she moved in a dream. At one stage she noticed that both nuns wore crucifixes dangling from their waists; but there was something about the figure—it was a devil, not the Christ. She tried to tell them this, but she couldn't seem to form words. The thoughts were in her head, but they got jumbled on her tongue, which felt thick.

"Leave off the coif and mask until we get to the chapel; she'll get more air. I think you gave her a bit too much of the drugged wine," one nun said.

The words meant little to Fiona. She had difficulty walking. Her feet and legs felt numb, and she was dizzy and disoriented. At the same time, she felt a surge of desire and wished that a man was there, a special man, but she couldn't remember who he was.

They seemed to be floating along vast corridors whose walls alternately expanded and contracted. Somewhere voices whispered: *Hurry! Keep moving! Don't fall! Step down now!* Things looked blurry. Someone was complaining, "Want to lie down, lie . . ."

"Soon you'll get all the lying down you'll ever need."

Then something was put over her head and a mask was tied over her eyes. She tried to pull it off, but strange black-robed figures held her hands.

"Come, Fiona, come into the chapel. Lie down. That's right. Let me open your robe."

Overhead was a blurred picture—a stained-glass window. She tried to see what the figures were doing. Was she in a church? There was more chanting, and a line of white-robed monks filed in, figures swaying, black tapers casting moving shadows. Their faces were hidden by scarlet-lined cowls pulled far forward. What happened next seemed like a dream, disjointed, vague, often threatening. Something cold was set below her bosom, which was bare. The priest held up a black host and chanted Latin words she didn't know. Sometimes he was near; sometimes it was as if she looked at him through the wrong end of a spyglass. Fiona felt desire for this holy man, wanted desperately to give herself to him. When he caressed her bare breasts, she writhed in an agony of lust, opening her thighs, receiving him. Somewhere there was sharp pain, and far away someone screamed; but to Fiona, clutched in the ecstasies of sexual union with this man, nothing mattered but the satisfaction of her primitive feelings.

Then another monk took her, and yet another in an endless orgy of sexual debasement.

Fiona's lust diminished, the strange feelings she'd had were purged, and she began to regain her senses. Something was happening to her. She was lying somewhere in a candlelit domed chamber. Overhead was the most obscene stained-glass window she could imagine. She closed her eyes, disgust swelling up in her throat. "No! No!" she cried in protest.

"Don't say no to me," a man's voice said, harsh with desire. Strong hands were on her body, forcing her thighs apart. As he attempted to enter her, Fiona realized what was happening. With a loud shriek, she fought to get out from under his weight, but he was too strong for her. He took her forcibly as she sobbed and pleaded with him to let her go.

In the background, scarcely heard over her own pleadings, were raucous shouts: "Doesn't seem to like you, Will!" "She didn't fight *me* that way!" "Drug must be wearing off!"

With one final desperate lunge Fiona brought up her hands, her fingers clawing and scratching at his face, pushing back the cowl that hid his features and tearing off his black velvet mask.

With a shriek of despair, she saw the features of Will Huxley, the man she had longed for, but not this

way, not here in this vile place, with a crowd of his
rotten friends watching their performance. The shock
of the day was too much for Fiona. As Huxley, eyes
glazed with lust, had his way with her, Fiona lost
consciousness, falling back onto the obscene altar into
the blessed oblivion of a faint.

CHAPTER 7

It was as if Fiona were up before the magistrates. It was an informal enough setting. The duchess still reclined on her canopied bed, her hair brushed out but not put up. The duke was *en négligé,* his gross body covered with a bottle-green dressing gown, his bald head draped with a matching turban. The pair were breakfasting on chocolate and toast.

"A shocking performance," the duchess was saying, her tone venomous. "When they removed your mask and coif after you pretended to faint, and I saw who had lent herself to such debauchery . . ." She stopped as if it pained her to continue.

"To think that you so abused my goodwill," the duke blustered; but his pig eyes, almost hidden in rolls of fat, were malicious. "I send you along with young Werington so that he'll have a pretty companion for a spring outing and what do you do! You allow yourself to be used by all of the men at the party. Disgusting, Fiona—disgusting."

Fiona, still in a state of shock after yesterday's horrible experience, stood there, tears flowing unchecked, wishing she were dead.

"Well, what do you have to say for yourself, wench?" the duchess cried. "Don't stand there drizzling tears down onto the carpet."

Fiona pulled a kerchief from the pocket under the overskirt of her blue dress. She'd not put on her black uniform this morning. When she'd crept in last night, after Werington brought her home, Fiona was determined to leave this house at the first possible moment.

71

Unfortunately, she found that the butler locked up everything at night, so she could not get out of the house, and before she could escape this morning, she had been summoned into the presence of the Duke and Duchess of Lawton for this mockery of condemnation.

The duchess wanted her to say something. Very well, Fiona thought, she'd tell her! "I was forced into all that degradation yesterday by the two of you," she declared. "You sent me off with Sir Thorton; the duke arranged everything. It was done deliberately to pay me back for refusing to let the duke bed me." Then, as a final insult, she added, "And you resented the fact that Viscount Huxley found me attractive." She didn't tell them that she was to have met Huxley yesterday. If she had, all this would not have happened . . . or would it? Huxley went to Medmenham Abbey with the duchess. He was just as involved with her rape as were the other men there. If she had met him as planned, he might well have taken her to the orgy himself. It was a devastating thought.

"Oh, what impertinence!" The duchess was truly angry now. Her unpainted face was blotched with rage. "You think that Will Huxley finds you charming? Well, he took you yesterday, along with all the other men there"—she shrugged—"but that's what goes on at the abbey. If you weren't interested in such romps, you shouldn't have gone with Werington. Surely you don't think men take well-bred young girls to such places?"

"I noticed that you were there, Your Grace. But then you scarcely qualify as a well-bred young girl, do you?" Fiona regretted the words the minute they were said, but it was too late for recalling them.

With a shriek, the duchess turned to her husband. "What do we do with such an ungrateful, insolent servant, Jonathan?"

"Turn her out without a letter, of course, my dear.

Or arrange for her to be a part of Charlotte Hayes's establishment."

"Of course. Why didn't *I* think of that? An excellent solution to this saucy-mouthed miss." Turning to Fiona, she commanded, "Go to your room and stay until we make arrangements. I can't have you here, corrupting the morals of our other young maids—Bets, for instance."

Without bothering to bob a curtsy, Fiona fled their wrath. She had no intention of allowing them to sell her to the most notorious brothel keeper in London. She might be naïve, but even Fiona had heard of Mother Hayes.

She knew that she was ruined. No decent man would ever be interested in marrying her now that she had been so cruelly used by all of the young bucks at Sir Francis's orgy. Fiona did not intend, though, to let this wicked couple force her into a life of prostitution because of that. No, she'd go back to Aunt Eulalia and work in her shop, try to forget the horrors of that Black Mass in the desecrated chapel of Medmenham Abbey and her ultimate betrayal by Will Huxley. How she had longed for him, and how dreadful had been the fulfillment of that desire. She didn't know what liberties Huxley had taken after she swooned. The next thing she knew, she was in a small room with one of the "nuns" in attendance. When she was able, she had insisted that she be returned to London. Werington obliged, although he had insisted that he be allowed to use her also. "I hadn't had my turn yet," he complained loudly when Fiona rebuffed him.

"You're rotten," she sobbed. "They gave me something to drink, some drug, and I didn't know what I was doing until . . . until . . ." Until she had realized that Huxley was having his way with her there in front of those jeering, cheering scoundrels. She didn't know who among them had used her and who hadn't.

Werington seemed somewhat abashed by her words. "I thought . . . the duke told me——"

"He's rotten too," Fiona said, tight-lipped. "He tried to force me one day, and when I screamed and brought everyone running, he became infuriated. This is his revenge."

And what a revenge it was! Damaged goods now, Fiona could hope for nothing more in life except drudgery and despair.

Werington did try to apologize when he delivered her back to the house on Millbank, but Fiona turned and left him in mid-sentence.

Now, threatened with Charlotte Hayes, Fiona made her own plans. She packed her few belongings in the ancient valise she'd used when she moved here from Aunt Eulalia's. With reluctance she left the lovely tartan-trimmed gown the duchess had had made for the musicale, as well as the pretty yellow sprigged muslin she'd worn yesterday. If she took them with her, no doubt Her Grace would have the constables after her for stealing. She could easily wind up hanging on Tyburn for such a crime.

Bets walked in on her unexpectedly as she was packing. "Fiona! What are you doing?"

"I'm leaving."

"But why? The duchess has been so good to you."

Fiona turned on her roommate, ready to slap her silly face. Bets, seeing the look in her eyes, cringed back into the corner of their pokey little room in the attic.

"If you only knew what they did to me yesterday . . ."

"I tried to stay awake to hear all about the picnic, but you came in so late."

"I don't ever want to think about that horrible day again. I'm going back to Aunt Eulalia, Bets. But if they ask you, just say you don't know where I am." Seeing the doubtful look on Bet's face, Fiona begged, "You don't have to lie Bets; just say I left. Someday maybe

I'll tell you why, but right now I can't talk about it; it's too dreadful."

Fiona was surprised at the look of compassion on Bets's face, combined with understanding and something else—a greedy, avid look deep in the girl's squinty eyes.

"I tried to warn you, Fiona, about Medmenham Abbey. That's where the Hell-Fire Club meets, they do say." Then, curiosity getting the better of her, she wanted to know, "What happened there? Is it true what they say? Do they truly kidnap virgins and do terrible things to them there?"

"Don't worry, Bets, you won't ever be invited to be a part of the terrible goings-on," Fiona said unkindly.

Miffed, Bets said, "Well, that's all the thanks I get for trying to protect you. I guess I was wrong about you, Fiona. You probably enjoyed every minute of your 'picnic.' My mum would skin me alive if she thought I was a dolly-mop." With that final slur, she picked up her black skirts and swished out of their room.

Fiona was too upset to bother with Bets. She had to get out of this house before someone—probably Hortense—saw her and reported her to the duke or the duchess. Carrying the valise, her cloak draped over her arm, Fiona crept down the back stairs to the kitchen, making sure that cook was busy at her pots in the deep fireplace before she scurried across the flagged floor and eased open the back door. Luck was with her. No one noticed that she was leaving. Once outside, she hurried through the narrow passageway that led to Millbank Street.

Just as she reached the main street, a gig drove by, the gray horse familiar. In the seat, handling the reins with expertise, was Viscount Huxley. In a fit of revulsion, Fiona shrank back into the shadow of the town house lest he see her. Her love for Huxley had turned to hate yesterday when the drug had worn off and she remembered that he had used her sexually without any regard for her whatsoever. By now he must know that it was she he had raped so casually; but even if he hadn't known who she was, for she'd been masked just as had he, his actions had been horrifying. How could the man who had rushed to rescue her from the duke's unwanted attention turn and do such a thing to some unknown young woman? If he was a member of the Hell-Fire Club, then he knew what went on there. Even poor, unattractive Bets had heard of the kidnapings of virgins and their deflowering by the members at their drunken orgies.

And she had thought she loved him! Well, all she felt for Viscount William Huxley now was loathing. Someday she'd get her revenge, and not just upon him but upon the Duke and Duchess of Lawton as well, for they had used her shamefully, and she was determined that they would pay dearly for it.

Now her main concern was to get to Bond Street and her Aunt Eulalia. It was a long walk, over three miles, but she had no money to pay for a chair or a coach. An hour later, staggering from the weight of her valise, Fiona opened the door to the milliner's shop, setting the bell to tinkling.

Aunt Eulalia hurried in from the back room, expecting a customer. "Fiona!" With horrified eyes she took in the exhausted young woman, the valise, the cloak over one arm, and making very nearly a proper guess, she blurted, "They've sacked you. What did you do, you wicked girl, to lose such a fine position in such a short time?"

Normally such an attack when she was so tired would have set Fiona to sobbing; but her times for tears were past. She had been shamefully used, and she knew that from now on whatever she made of herself she'd do on her own, with no help from anyone. Straightening her spine, looking up defiantly into Aunt

Eulalia's accusing eyes, Fiona said, "I wasn't sacked; I quit."

"You *what?*"

"I left that evil house on Millbank this morning, and I have walked all the way here, carrying my things." Then, in a fit of audacity, she added, "I should like a cup of tea, if you please, Aunt Eulalia."

"A cup of—— The lass has lost her mind. You'll wind up in Bedlam, my girl, if you carry on this way. Quit your job, ordering up tea as if I were a servant. Fie! Now, tell me the truth. Why did they sack you?"

"Let me tell you about the noble Duke and Duchess of Lawton, Aunt Eulalia, before you pass judgment. I'd scarcely been in the house before the duke tried to rape me. He did manage to tear half my clothes off before a guest in his house, hearing my screams, rescued me. Then, because the duchess's lover—you saw him with her here in the shop—smiled at me, she became insanely jealous. Between them, the pair plotted to have me taken to an infamous Black Mass at Medmenham Abbey near Marlow."

"Black Mass! A Papist gathering? For shame, Fiona."

Fiona laughed bitterly. "It isn't Papist. It isn't anything good, Aunt Eulalia. They worship Satan. There they drugged me with something in my wine, and a group of fine lords proceeded to rape me. Then, their revenge still not complete, the duke and the duchess planned to sell me to Charlotte Hayes. Surely even *you* have heard of her."

"Charlotte—— But she's a notorious brothel keeper!"

"Exactly, so I ran away. I would prefer to work here, sewing ribbons on bonnets, than to be forced into a life of sin by the nobility."

Her aunt was shaken by this recital; it all was beyond her ken. She knew vaguely of the immoralities of the peers, but she shut her mind to such things. She was a God-fearing milliner. What others did was no concern of hers. Now, though, this niece of hers, this orphan she had accepted into her life, was a fallen woman, despoiled by a group of wicked men. What was she to do? "I guess I must take you back," she said grudgingly, "but whatever will become of you, I don't know. I had hoped to marry you to some solid tradesman in time. Now what decent man will have you for his wife?"

"He needn't know."

"Fiona! You shock me. If these are your attitudes, you cannot have acquired them in the brief time you worked for the duchess. You must have believed such wicked things before you came to me. My sister would turn in her grave if she heard you suggest lying to a man who would make you his wife."

"There's no need to lie, Aunt Eulalia; but, on the other hand, I needn't volunteer information, need I?" Fiona was learning quickly that she would have to fight her own battles, protect herself, and if she must use means slightly less than open, then she would. "I was the victim of these people, dear aunt. The duchess ordered me to go to this so-called picnic. She passed me off as a Scottish laird's daughter to play a prank on her friends. What could I do? I worked for her; I had to obey her."

Miss Goodbody sighed. "The ways of the aristocracy are different from ours. Well, get your things put away. Your room is still there, empty. I had considered letting it to some worthy shopgirl, but that will have to wait, I suppose."

With this tepid welcome, Fiona returned to the shop. She had been there only a few days when the Duchess of Lawton came for a new hat. Hearing the familiar voice, Fiona shuddered. She didn't know what would happen if the duchess found out that she was back with Aunt Eulalia. Creeping close to the curtain that separated the shop from the workroom, she eavesdropped.

"Your Grace, how good to see you again," Aunt Eulalia said, using the smarmy voice she reserved for customers.

"Have you heard from that wicked niece of yours who worked for me? I certainly didn't get my money's worth from her. Gone already."

Fiona held her breath. Was the duchess going to demand that Aunt Eulalia return the money she had been paid to release Fiona?

"I am sorry to hear that, Your Grace."

"Did she come crawling back here?" the duchess went on, her voice relentless.

"Yes, Your Grace, some days back." To give her credit, Aunt Eulalia did try to defend Fiona somewhat. "She said that the duke tried to take liberties with her, milady. My dear dead sister, rest her soul, raised Fiona to be a good girl. She is not used to such carryings on."

"Not used—— My dear Miss Goodbody, you foisted off on me a licentious little minx, and a liar to boot, from what you are saying. My dear husband tried to take liberties? I suppose you think that she is a virgin."

"Scarcely that, Your Grace, after the disgraceful goings on at that awful place near Marlow. Oh, she told me everything."

"Did she? That girl has hoodwinked you, Miss Goodbody, just as she hoodwinked me and my husband. Generous to a fault he was with her, and I treated her as if she were a dear daughter of the house, not a lowly wardrobe maid. And how does she repay me? She sneaks away from my house and comes back here, telling you a pack of lies. Wicked!"

It was all Fiona could do not to rush into the shop and confront the duchess, call her a liar to her face. The only thing that held her back was concern for Aunt Eulalia.

"And what has happened to the lying little minx?"

"She is back working with me, Your Grace. She is

quite clever with a needle, and you yourself said she had good taste in hats."

"How I rue that day! She threw herself at poor Viscount Huxley, causing him grievous embarrassment. I must make my position very clear, Miss Goodbody. If you continue to keep a girl like Fiona here in your shop, I will no longer be able to give you my custom. And I shall advise my friends to go elsewhere for their bonnets, even though you do make the most exquisite hats in London."

Fiona knew that her aunt would not be able to stand up to that kind of threat. There was a long, tense silence. Then Aunt Eulalia said wearily, "Yes, Your Grace. I shall pack her off as soon as I can find another girl to replace her."

"Just don't let it be too long," the duchess threatened.

After Her Grace had gone, Aunt Eulalia came into the workroom, her face already set in defensive lines. To spare her aunt, Fiona said, "I heard the ultimatum."

"What can I do?" cried her aunt. "I hate to turn out my only sister's child, but if I keep you on now, we'll both starve." Then, trying to justify herself, she added, "And her story isn't the same as yours, Fiona."

"Of course not! Do you think the Duchess of Lawton would tell you that she sent me off to be raped by her friends?"

"I don't like to hear you use such language, Fiona. Maybe the duchess was right. Perhaps I don't know my niece as well as I thought I did."

"Never mind, Aunt Eulalia," Fiona said, despair washing over her, "I'll leave. I don't know where I'll go or what I'll do, but I won't cause you to lose your business."

"I'll ask around, and why don't you look in *The Gazette*? I'm sure you'll find another milliner willing to hire an experienced girl."

"Of course. I'll manage."

"You don't have to leave immediately. I told the duchess I had to keep you until I find a replacement."

It didn't make much difference to Fiona. A day, a week—soon she'd be on her own completely, forced to earn her own living, forced to find lodgings. She knew that her aunt would ask her to give up her room. The new assistant would need it, and if she didn't, Aunt Eulalia would rent it out.

"I just hope you aren't pregnant," her aunt muttered.

The thought was terrifying, one that hadn't occurred to Fiona. If that happened, what would she do? It would be the workhouse for her—that or a brothel. It was the worst day of her life, barring the day at Medmenham Abbey. Silently she cursed the Hell-Fire Club, consigning them all, Huxley included, to that hell-fire they seemed so proud to profess.

CHAPTER 8

The very next day Fiona found a new position. She had bought *The Gazette,* turning its pages quickly, looking for advertisements of help wanted.

"A Mrs. Jones on Oxford Street is needing a helper in her millinery shop, Aunt Eulalia. Should I apply?"

As nothing would please Miss Goodbody more than to get rid of this niece, she replied, "Do go at once, Fiona."

"She'll want a letter."

"A letter." Aunt Eulalia frowned. "I suppose I can write something." She sighed as if put upon, but she went upstairs to her little desk and wrote a note saying that Fiona had worked briefly for her and was a skillful hat trimmer. "If she asks why you're leaving me——"

"I'll tell her that I fancy the Oxford Street location."

"Yes, perhaps that will do. And see if she has a room to let or knows of one, Fiona. It would be better for you to live near your work."

Just as Fiona had thought, her aunt planned to turn her out. Well, it was expected; nevertheless, it made her bitter—her own mother's sister, and she wouldn't help her out in this time of trouble.

She walked along Bond Street to Conduit and thence to Regent Street, where, unexpectedly, she met up with Sir Thorton Werington. He was just leaving a tobacconist's, and when he spotted Fiona, his face lit up and he swept off his braid-trimmed black tricorne, bowing to her:

"Miss Fiona! I called at the house on Millbank, but

82

Her Grace said that you had returned to Edinburgh, as there was illness in your family."

"Wicked old woman! She lies. And I have no wish to speak with you, either."

Picking up the skirts of her rose cotton gown, she swept past him as if he didn't exist. Werington was not to be put off so easily. He hurried after her, even going so far as to take her arm to get her attention.

"Take your filthy hands off me," she snapped. "Haven't you done me enough damage? Do you want to grind me into the dirt with your elegant red-heeled shoes?"

"Fiona," he bleated, "What has gotten into you?"

She was almost running now to escape him, but Werington showed his stubborn streak, this time catching her by the arm and forcing her to stop.

"You owe me an explanation, Miss Fiona."

"I owe you nothing. You have ruined my life, you and your filthy Hell-Fire Club. What more do you want?"

He was shocked at her vehemence. "But you went willingly, and when the nuns took you away, you made no objection. I assumed that you had no qualms about participating."

"I didn't know anything about where I was going. The duchess ordered me to—— Oh, I don't want to talk about it. I have to see someone on Oxford Street. Please let me go."

Reluctantly Werington loosed his hold on her arm, and she fled, hoping that he was not following her. She didn't even look around but busied herself trying to find the Jones shop. It was tucked in between a draper's and a coffeehouse, where the bloods were gathering to while away their time with coffee, conversation, and gambling.

Mrs. Jones was as short and stout as Aunt Eulalia was tall and thin, her face roly-poly, her triple chins quivering. She wheezed asthmatically as she talked. "Yes, I need a girl. Experience?"

"I've been working off Bond Street for Miss Eulalia Goodbody."

The currant eyes in the doughy face gave her a sharp look. "I've heard of Miss Goodbody. She caters to the finest custom. Has she given you the sack, me girl?"

"No, no. I have a letter from her. I . . . I just wanted a change."

"Don't know if I care for a gadfly who works a week and then flits off," she said, but she took the letter and read it carefully. "Come, let me see some of your work first." She led Fiona into a workroom very much like Aunt Eulalia's and pointed to a partly finished purple velvet bonnet. "Sew the ribbons on it," she ordered, pointing to matching satin.

Fiona's eye was caught by a soft rose velvet ribbon on a reel, narrow ribbon, very lush. "It would look lovely with the rose," she said, picking up the velvet ribbon and holding it next to the bonnet.

For a moment Mrs. Jones said nothing, then wheezed, "By my soul, so it does. Very well, Miss McQuade, finish the hat; then I'll decide."

For the first time in recent days, Fiona felt at peace. The feel of rich fabric between her fingers was soothing, and creating a lovely bonnet was satisfying. When she had the hat to her liking, she took it into the shop, where Mrs. Jones was waiting on a customer—one of the *ton*, by her looks.

"Oh, Mrs. Jones, I like *that* bonnet," the woman cried, voice shrill. "Do let me try it."

Fiona set it on the woman's wig carefully, then handed her the tortoise-backed hand mirror so that she could see how it looked from the back.

When the woman left, she carried the purple bonnet in a box.

"Well, miss, I guess you are hired," Mrs. Jones said to Fiona.

"Do you know of lodgings nearby?"

"As a matter of fact, I do. My greengrocer has a garret room he lets. His wife told me just today that it was vacant."

They arranged wages, and Fiona went off to see about the lodgings, which turned out to be satisfactory. Now all she had to do was walk back to Aunt Eulalia's and pack her few belongings. But she hadn't reckoned on Sir Thorton. When she left the greengrocer's, she found him lying in wait.

"I came into the shop," he said crossly, "thinking that you were buying some fruit, but you weren't in there."

Fiona said coldly, "I was upstairs, looking at their empty attic room."

"At a greengrocer's? Whatever for? Look, there's a tea shop on the corner. Let's have a pot of tea."

Fiona was so tired from the long walk to Oxford Street that she agreed, just to be able to sit down briefly and rest.

After Werington had ordered tea and cakes, he asked, "What is going on, Fiona? I find your actions strange. The duchess assured me that you had rushed home——"

"Home! And where do you think home is? Not Edinburgh, not for months—ever since my parents died of smallpox."

"But what were you doing on Millbank? I thought——"

"The duchess hired me to be her wardrobe maid." Maybe now that she had told this young fop in his exquisitely laced robin's-egg-blue coat, with a darker, teal velvet waistcoat, he'd leave her alone.

"You're joking, Miss Fiona."

"I am not. My aunt is a milliner with a shop just off Bond Street. Her Grace found me there, liked my way with hats, and hired me to work for her." She had to laugh at the stunned look on Werington's face.

"Then . . . but she introduced you as . . . I thought you . . ."

Maliciously she let him flounder on until he stopped, face flushed with embarrassment. "You thought I was a laird's daughter? All a lie. My father was a school-master—nothing more, nothing less. My parents were decent people and raised me to be a decent girl. If they knew what had happened at Medmenham Abbey, they'd——" She broke down then, sobbing.

"I thought you were just a society dolly-mop," he said, covering her hand hesitantly. "The duke told me that you would enjoy a romp. I had no idea . . . I wouldn't have . . ."

She mopped her eyes angrily, wishing she'd not let him see her cry. "It's too late to be sorry," she said coldly, happy to see him squirm with chagrin. "I'm ruined now. No decent man will have anything to do with me. The duke and the duchess saw to that." She gave a bitter little laugh. "I'd been there a day when the duke tried to rape me. One of their guests rescued me." She couldn't bear to say Huxley's name, as he had been the final betrayer. It was he she hated even more than the Lawtons. "And in revenge he arranged everything—the picnic, your invitation to meet me, and the final horror at the abbey. They must have virgins for their rotten Black Mass. They gave me something in wine. I didn't know what was going on until it was much too late. Aren't you proud of yourself?" She was pleased to see how mortified he was at her recital.

"Fiona, I didn't know, I *swear* I didn't. I'd never been to Medmenham Abbey before. I'd heard some of my friends talk about it, but none of my group has ever been invited. Most of the men are older. I thought it a great honor to be able to go, to be sponsored by the Duke of Lawton."

Fiona shrugged. "Now you're one of the elite. I hope it made you happy"—she gave him a thin, cold smile —"even though you said you'd not had your turn with me before I recovered from whatever those wretched women gave me to drink, and I take your word for that."

"If only I could make it up to you."

"My life is ruined and you want to make it up to me?" She started to laugh then and quickly became hysterical. The serving girl came running over to see what was wrong, but Fiona managed to wave her away. Finally she quieted. "I suppose you were a victim of the Lawton's wickedness too," she conceded. "It wasn't really your fault, Sir Thorton."

"Please call me Thor; all my friends do," he begged. Then his clear gray eyes lit up. "I could call the Duke of Lawton out, fight a duel with him."

He was so serious about it that Fiona had trouble keeping a straight face. It would never do to giggle, but she was sorely tempted. "Duels are illegal," she said. "You wouldn't like Newgate Prison at all."

"I wish I could do something. . . ."

Very well, Fiona thought, *I'll let him help me. He owes me that much, after the abbey.* "I don't suppose you have a coach handy, do you? I'm tired, and I have to walk back to my aunt's shop, collect my things, and come clear back here to the greengrocer's."

"Wait right here," he ordered, eyes bright. "I'll get a coach for us."

Aunt Eulalia was properly shocked when Fiona came into the millinery shop with Werington on her heels. As he supervised the stowing of her things in the coach basket, she said, "Well, you certainly aren't the innocent young miss you've pretended to be, coming here with a man, going off to live with him, no doubt, without a thought as to the sin of it all."

"As a matter of fact, this young man has kindly offered to help me move into my new lodgings over a greengrocer's near Mrs. Jones's shop, dear aunt. If you saw the little garret room, you'd know very well that he wouldn't be caught dead in such a dreary, pokey little place. He's very wealthy, with a hereditary knight-hood." Then she swept out of the shop without even saying good-by. Aunt Eulalia had proved to be a very feeble reed on which to lean in time of trouble.

The greengrocer, Mr. Carder, did not like having Sir Thorton in his garret. "You stay downstairs, sir," he ordered, looking down his thin, hooked nose at the young lord. "I don't allow any goings on in my house. I has my reputation to think about, I has."

After the coachey had carried her boxes up to her room, Fiona came back down the narrow stairs into the shop to thank Sir Thorton for his help.

"I do hope to see you again soon, Fiona."

"That won't be possible," she said firmly. "I haven't suitable clothes for——.""

"You looked fetching at the musicale, and the gown you wore for our boat ride up the Thames was charm-ing."

"And both are still hanging in the wardrobe on Mill-bank Street. The duchess had them made for me for her own nasty little farce. They aren't mine."

"Did you wish to purchase something, sir?" Mr. Carder asked pointedly.

"Uh . . . I'll have . . . an orange. No, two oranges." Sir Thorton flushed under the righteous eye of the grocer, paying from a tooled-leather money pouch. "Come outside with me, Fiona. We'll stroll and eat our oranges."

Not wanting to prolong her acquaintance with Wer-ington, yet feeling in his debt for helping her move to her new room, Fiona reluctantly walked with him to a tiny green park nearby, where they sat on a bench and ate the juicy oranges he had been forced to purchase.

"I should be very happy to pay for gowns for you," he said boldly.

"I couldn't think of accepting such gifts."

"Fiona, you don't belong in such drab surroundings

as that greengrocer's garret room. You are a beauty and could be a leader in society here in London."

"Your joke is not funny, sir."

"I mean it."

"Surely"—and her voice was dry—"you aren't suggesting that I marry you. Your mother would have apoplexy."

He flushed with embarrassment and muttered, "Well, she does expect me to marry well."

"I daresay."

"But we could have a liaison," he said tentatively, not sure how she'd take such a suggestion. "I could find a nice little establishment in some discreet location——"

"You are asking me to be your mistress?" A cold rage filled Fiona. "How dare you! First you help to ruin me, then you have the audacity to make such an improper suggestion! No matter what you think of me, I'm a decent young woman who has been sorely misused, thanks to you and your kind." She set down the last bite of orange on the bench between them, got up, and flounced off, wishing she'd thrown the bit of fruit in his hateful face.

"Fiona," he cried, hurrying after her; but she ignored him and hurried back to Oxford Street and her grubby little room.

Next day she was up early in order to be at Mrs. Jones's shop on time. She had agreed to pay extra for meals with the Carders, and found herself facing watery gruel and weak tea. Aunt Eulalia had not given her favors, but at least she had set a good table while Fiona lived with her; and at the duchess's house, she'd had rich chocolate and crisp toast and delicious marmalade. Ah well, beggars couldn't be choosers.

For a few days things went quite well at her new job. Mrs. Jones, recognizing her talent, let her begin designing bonnets, calling her out from the workroom when a favored customer came shopping. Fiona began to feel more secure. She knew she did her work well, and she hoped that all of her troubles were in the past.

One day, as she sat stitching the high crown of a new hat for Lady Teasdale, Fiona herd the bell tinkle as someone came into the shop. In a few minutes Mrs. Jones called for her to come in.

"Her Grace needs a new hat, and I told her that I had a new designer," Mrs. Jones said, all smiles.

Designer! Perhaps she should ask for more pay from Mrs. Jones. And then the elegant lady sitting in front of the mirror turned, and Fiona found herself face to face with her nemesis, the Duchess of Lawton.

Her Grace narrowed her hazel eyes and glared malevolently at Fiona. "Mrs. Jones, don't tell me that this wicked young woman is in your employ!"

Fiona felt that she was shriveling, for she knew too well the power of the duchess's wrath.

"Do you mean Fiona, Your Grace?" Poor Mrs. Jones was a study in consternation. Her pig eyes squinched further shut, and her triple chins quivered with emotion.

"How did you happen to take on such a slut as this? What lies did she tell you, Mrs. Jones? I daresay you thought her to be a proper young woman—industrious, talented—just as I did when I made the mistake of paying her aunt to release her to be my wardrobe maid."

Turning to Fiona, anger making her fat face chalky, the milliner demanded, "Is what she says true, Fiona? Did you work for Her Grace? There was no word of this when you came to me. You told me only of working for Miss Goodbody."

"Her aunt," the duchess put in angrily. "I see that even she can no longer abide such a trollop in her shop."

Fiona could have screamed out the truth—that she was a victim of the duchess's wickedness, not the reverse—but she had learned the futility of trying to get

justice against a member of the *ton*. What point was
there in telling Mrs. Jones how she'd been used by the
Duke and Duchess of Lawton? The duchess would call
her a liar, and the milliner would believe her, not
Fiona.

"Fiona," Mrs. Jones said, advancing on her like a
moving dish of jelly, "you brought me a letter from
Miss Goodbody. She didn't say you were her niece."

"I am. That's true."

"Miss Goodbody dismissed Fiona after I told her she
would lose my custom if she kept on such a terrible
dolly-mop. This young woman consorts with the Friars
of St. Francis—the Hell-fire Club. Have you heard of
its degenerate practices?"

Mrs. Jones clapped a pudgy hand over her enormous
bosom and rolled her eyes. "La, Your Grace, who
would have guessed? Butter wouldn't melt in Fiona's
mouth, and she is skillful with bonnets."

"True. She took me in, too, Mrs. Jones. Do what
you like about the wanton, but know that as long as
you employ her, I won't be returning to your shop; nor
will my friends."

It took Mrs. Jones even less time than it had Aunt
Eulalia to get rid of Fiona. She turned on her, furious
and ordered, "Out!"

"You owe me for——"

"I owe you nothing. You came to me under false
pretenses."

Fiona knew she'd lost. As she went past the duchess,
that worthy lady gave her such a look of triumph that
Fiona could scarcely contain herself. She longed to
yank off the high, intricately curled wig and pull out
the graying hair by the roots. She didn't dare, though;
she would be thrown into prison if she attacked so
noble a person as the Duchess of Lawton.

As she went out the door, Mrs. Jones called spitefully, "And I shall tell Mr. Carder to throw you out

of your lodgings. He runs a decent place. He'll want no whore living with him."

It was the final straw. Tears flowed unchecked down her cheeks as she hurried away from the shop toward her miserable room. If she could get there before Mrs. Jones sent word, at least she'd be able to pack up her belongings and take them with her. She was crying so much that she could scarcely see where she was going. She blundered into a man, almost knocking herself off her feet.

"Fiona! What's wrong?"

Just her luck: it was young Werington. In a fit of self-pity, she poured out her sorry story to him.

"Don't worry, I'll take care of you. My offer still holds good. I shall go with you, help you get your things, and install you at an inn until I find a suitable house for us."

At her wits' end, Fiona knew she had little choice. It was either this or a brothel, so she agreed to accept Werington's offer.

CHAPTER 9

Werington found a lovely little house on Hanover Street not too far from the two millinery shops where Fiona had worked. She didn't care; that part of her life was behind her. From now on she was mistress of Sir Thorton Werington. It was far better than being in one of the infamous brothels of London.

He found a couple, Sal and Rolf Evans, who did for them quite cozily. Of course, Werington still lived with his mother in the mansion on Russell Square.

"What will your mother do if she finds out about us?" Fiona asked, fearful that her good fortune would disappear like fairy gold.

"I'm of age," he said curtly. "All young bloods take mistresses. Mother knows this."

"Isn't she trying to marry you off to some highborn lady?"

"Doesn't every mother want her son to marry well?"

It hurt, hearing him say it. She wondered what would happen to her if Lady Werington arranged a marriage for her son soon. For the first time in her life, Fiona was living the life of a lady. Her only task was to please Thorton in bed and out of it. The first time he had taken her to bed had been traumatic for her. He had got them a room at the famous Golden Cross Inn located at Charing Cross. She didn't know what he had told the landlord, but she felt very self-conscious entering the place with him. Surely everyone there must know she was not married to Werington.

The room had a large canopied bed in it, and a painted three-panel screen hid the pitcher and basin and the chamber pot in one corner. Scarcely knowing what was expected of her, Fiona stood silent after the coachey had carried her boxes to the room and been paid by Werington.

It transpired that Werington, for all his seeming to be a member of the bloods, was as shy as she about their new relationship. That first night at the inn, knowing very well what she must pay for having a protector, Fiona disrobed behind the screen and donned a long ruffled nightdress of fine India muslin, which was the prettiest one she owned. She found that while she had been getting herself ready behind the screen, Werington had undressed and put on a nightshirt of soft flannel. Reluctantly she went to him, scarcely knowing what to expect. All she knew of sex was that one horrifying experience at the abbey.

"At last!" he said, catching her to him roughly and showering hot kisses on her face, her lips, her throat.

She endured it, feeling no love for him or any desire.

"Take off that infernal nightdress," he ordered, stripping off his own nightshirt and revealing his tall, lightly muscled male body, ready for love. Remembering only vague bits about the Black Mass in the abbey, Fiona was stunned at his nudity. She stood there shivering, wanting to cover herself with her hands but knowing that it would only anger Werington. This was the price she must pay for a life of comfort.

He caught her up in his arms and put her on the bed, then mounted her immediately, giving her no caresses that might well have roused her own healthy animal instincts. It was a painful, humiliating experience, as bad as it had been during the orgy.

Afterward, Werington had cried angrily, "You were like a china doll. I watched you during the Black Mass. You didn't act this way at all. Of course, when Huxley had you, you fought him, but no one knew why. You'd certainly been as enthusiastic as any dolly-mop earlier in the rites."

Dismally she murmured, "They drugged me; I told you that. Those two so-called nuns gave me funny-tasting wine and rubbed some kind of ointment on my feet and legs that made them feel numb. Then they lighted censers of some sort of exotic incense, which made me feel very strange."

"They use various drugs in the censers," he said. "I don't know just what they used that day—belladonna, maybe, or hemlock or even mandrake—but it's all part of the game, Fiona. Most people feel a bit embarrassed the first time they participate in a Black Mass—I did— but when you sniff their special incense, it makes you feel more at ease." He frowned, then put his arms about her. "I guess they gave you an aphrodisiac."

"What's that?" she asked suspiciously.

"Something to make you want to make love," he explained. "They often use cantharides. Lots of the older men put it in their wine before those parties, I've heard." He laughed smugly. "They can't perform so well, not like us young men." Then he pulled her to him, and she realized that he was ready to perform again. "Just relax," he commanded her. "I know you can enjoy this, too. I saw you begging Father O'Toole for it. You caught hold of him—here, give me your hand—like this."

Fiona did as he instructed, but still she had no enjoyment from the encounter, though apparently Werington did, even though he complained again of her lack of cooperation in the act. What had she done in the abbey that had made him think that his pleasure with her in bed would be greater?

Humiliated and humbled, she said, "You'll have to teach me how to please you, Thor."

"Oh, I shall; never fear. And I think perhaps I should get some of that drug and give you a bit in wine before we go to bed. Maybe it will help."

"Please don't do that." Her memories of that drug-induced lust were shameful, painful, and terrible. "I promise to try harder to please you; just don't give me that horrid stuff."

"Maybe some wine would help."

Reluctantly he left her and got the wine carafe, pouring large glasses of claret. She wasn't used to so much wine, and he insisted that she drink it so swiftly that Fiona was quite giddy when she'd finished. Perhaps it did help a little; but Werington was not a kind or particularly skillful lover, so Fiona still got no satisfaction from the episode.

"Don't just lie there like a stick," he panted. "Move your bottom about."

"Like this?"

His answering groan told her that she was learning her lesson. Well, if he enjoyed this, she would have to acquiesce. After all, she knew that this was the only reason the young man was setting her up as his mistress. Oh, he would probably take her out, for she was personable, reasonably educated, and if he provided gowns, could look as fashionable as any other young woman in London. But what they were doing now was really all that Werington wanted. If only it could have been Will Huxley—— But she must forget him. He had betrayed her. He was no better than his friends, the Duke and Duchess of Lawton. Yet Fiona knew that if it had been he here with her on this bed she might be enjoying herself far more than she was with Werington.

"I just hope you don't get with child," he said after he had finished and rolled off her to his own side of the bed. "If you do, I'll have to get the name of some granny woman from some of my friends. I've heard them discuss the merits of various ones, but since I hadn't a regular dolly-mop of my own then, I paid little attention."

In horror, she said, "Do you mean what I think you mean?"

"She'd give you something so you'd lose the babe,"

he said. "I wouldn't want you increasing; that would be dull."

Dull! What a horrid young blade Werington was turning out to be. It wasn't that Fiona hadn't heard of abortions. She could even see that at times it might be better to lose a baby than to carry it to term and have it called a bastard. She had, though, heard enough stories so that she knew the concoctions those granny women used were not always safe for the mother. She didn't want to die.

"Now I want to go to sleep," Werington said. "Blow out the candle, Fiona."

She'd wanted it snuffed before their session on the huge bed started, but Werington had insisted on having light so that he could watch her reactions to his lust. Fiona couldn't sleep. She felt degraded. Perhaps she should have tried harder to get some sort of position elsewhere in the city. There were other milliners. Surely the Duchess of Lawton couldn't patronize them all. If she could have gotten out of that district, she might have been able to support herself adequately without having to submit to this arrogant young man who thought only of himself, never of her pleasure. Well, it was too late now. She'd set her foot on a path from which there was no turning back. Quietly, trying not to sob aloud lest she disturb Werington in his deep sleep, Fiona cried for what seemed like hours. She was just drifting off to sleep when her partner woke and demanded that she serve him once more. She pleaded that she was tired, but he cuffed her so hard, she thought he might have broken her jaw.

"Stop sniveling. Stop making excuses. When I want you, spread your legs," he said coarsely.

With his usual technique, he ignored all of her feelings and satisfied himself, although he never stopped complaining at her lack of enthusiasm.

"If I'd known what a dud you were going to be, I'd have thought twice about offering you a lovely home.

Well, I've had to give enough gold guineas as earnest money to the landlord on Hanover Street that I'll try you for a bit longer; but you have to improve, Fiona. I could get a better ride from the flower girl who stands at the corner of Regent Street and Oxford, selling her posies—and herself, from all I hear."

It took enormous restraint on Fiona's part to keep from answering him. She was tired, and sore, and miserable. She had made a terrible bargain, and she didn't know how to get out of it. If she tried to run away from Werington, he might well report her to the constables. As he'd said, he had made an investment in her, and he expected a good return on his money.

Next morning they breakfasted in bed, and then Werington wanted more of her. She hoped that later they could go out, perhaps for a carriage ride, but she discovered that Werington had other plans.

"I'm going to the coffeehouse on Regent Street to see my friends. You stay inside. I don't want the men to get the wrong idea about you. If you go wandering about the London streets alone, they'll think you are for hire."

"I wish I had a book to read," she said rebelliously.

"Perhaps I'll find one for you. I'll see you for dinner."

He dressed in the suit he'd worn the day before, but he expected her to tie his neckcloth for him. When she raised her arms to reach it, he pinched her breasts painfully.

"That hurts!"

"Women like for me to hurt them," he said, pinching even harder, laughing when she gasped with pain.

She hated him then. He'd been the cause of all her troubles. If he'd not been interested in her, she might not have been taken to Medmenham Abbey. In the back of her mind Fiona knew that the real culprits were the Duke and Duchess of Lawton; but Werington was here, hurting her, bruising her already tender breasts. If she'd had a pistol handy, she'd have shot him without a qualm, even if she swung on Tyburn Hill for the crime.

She was glad when he'd finally gone to his wicked friends. Perhaps he would become so engrossed in drinking coffee and gambling that he'd forget to come home for dinner. She poured water into the washbowl from the china pitcher and bathed her breasts, frowning at the bruises already darkening on them. Tonight she'd pinch him and see how he liked it!

Unfortunately, Werington surprised her by returning about two in the afternoon, just as Fiona was beginning to get very hungry.

"I'm starving," she told him candidly.

"Later we'll eat; but first, I've brought you a present." He held out a wrapped package to her.

Fiona, not liking the look on his face, a kind of malicious avidity, was reluctant to take it.

His face darkened with anger. "You wanted a book, and I went to considerable trouble to buy you one. Open it!"

Fearing more violence on his part, wondering how he could have changed from a timid, pleasant young man to this brute in such a short time, Fiona pulled off the paper, opened the book, and discovered, to her horror, that it was a work of pornography, a series of very detailed plates depicting sex in all aspects, as specific as those murals she'd seen at Marlow.

"We're going to work right through that book," he warned. Taking it from her, he leafed quickly through it. "This! I've never done it this way."

From the look on his face, from his quickened breathing. Fiona realized that the pictures were exciting him, although they only disgusted her. "I won't do that," she said, turning away from the explicit picture in distaste.

"You'll do whatever I want you to do, and I want to do it this way." He thrust the book under her nose, then caught at the front of her gown. "Get out of those clothes," he said thickly. "Now!"

"I will not."

Eyes narrowed with rage and lust, he flung down the book, caught her so that he had her hands immobilized behind her, then, with his free hand, ripped open the bodice of her dress, just as the Duke of Lawton had done that day, and flung her to the floor. "Get undressed!"

Aching all over, she obeyed. There was nothing else she could do. Then he forced her onto her knees and parted her buttocks roughly. She screamed with pain, but he only reached forward and clamped a hard hand over her mouth.

Afterward she lay sobbing helplessly.

"Quit crying and get dressed. I'm hungry," he said. "If you don't go out with me to eat, you'll go hungry."

"You've torn my gown beyond pinning," she said.

"Then put on something else. We'll shop for some gowns for you today. I want my woman to be well-dressed. I might even get tickets for the Drury Lane Theater tonight."

It was as if the painful episode hadn't happened. Slowly she dressed, wondering if she could walk to whatever place he chose to eat, she was hurting so badly.

They had dinner at a tavern on Leicester Square. Then Werington suggested a walk in St. James's Park. When Fiona protested that she didn't feel like walking, he glared, waved down a cab, handed her in, and gave the park as their destination. The first person they saw as they strolled was Viscount Huxley.

"Will!" called Werington, as Fiona cringed inwardly. "Haven't seen you since the day at the abbey."

Huxley, exquisitely turned out as usual, whipped off his tricorne and bowed. "Miss Fiona," he said dryly, "I hadn't expected to find you here."

"No; if your friends had their way, I'd now be residing with Charlotte Hayes," she said tartly, to Werington's surprise.

"I was at Miss Goodbody's just yesterday. I didn't see you."

"Did you expect to? Your dear friend saw to it that I lost my job there, as well as the next one I found."

"And how are you managing now, or need I ask?" He eyed Werington almost belligerently. A week ago, Fiona would have been ecstatic at such a look from him; today she was too depressed to care what he thought.

"I've taken Fiona under my protection," Werington said.

"Then she no longer needs me to rescue her from attempted rape, does she?" He bowed and walked quickly away.

CHAPTER 10

"What was all that about with Huxley, Fiona?" Werington demanded as the viscount strode away from them.

"He kept the Duke of Lawton from raping me when I first went to work for the duchess."

"It was he? But I saw him use you at the abbey——"

"I know, I know. I don't want to talk about it, Thor." She moved toward a bench and sat down, not feeling like walking further.

Werington sat beside her and nodded to acquaintances who bowed on passing the couple. "Huxley's a strange fellow. I've heard rumors that he's mixed up with some very peculiar politicians," Werington told her. "He's into some nonsense about bettering the life for the common man in London."

"What's so terrible about that?"

"Good God, Fiona, you wouldn't want the rabble ruling, would you? I understand that the king is very annoyed by such ideas, as well he might be. *He's* the monarch, not the mob. Do you remember the riots of forty-five?"

"I was just a little girl then, living in Edinburgh. What would I know of London riots?"

"Well, there was a lot of destruction, people killed. The mobs in the poor sections of the city rioted, attacked lords in their coaches or chairs, tipped them over, broke carriage wheels. It was a dangerous time, Fiona. Why any peer would be on the side of the rabble is beyond me. I think that Huxley may get himself into a lot of trouble if he keeps on with this course of action. Most of the Friars of St. Francis are also members of the King's Friends. They are dedicated to preserving our way of life. These rabble-rousers have all sorts of dreadful schemes; they even suggest breaking up the large country estates and giving—*giving*—the land to the lower classes."

"They do lead terrible lives, Thor." Fiona herself had been raised in a genteel home. Her parents, although not wealthy, were not poor, either. Her father, a schoolmaster, was educated and respected in his community. Yet she had seen instances of abject poverty in Edinburgh, and she knew that London must be even worse. "Have you ever seen how the poor live in a city? In the country it's bad enough, but at least they have cottages and they can get fresh air. In the cities the poor are jammed into horrid houses with no light, no air. It's a dreadful way to live. No wonder they riot."

"But, Fiona," Werington said reasonably, "what can we do about it? The poor are always with us. Even the Good Book says so. If we divided all of the wealth in the country, most of them still would be poor, but so would we. Do you want to live that way? I notice that you are anxious to have pretty new gowns. Leave politics to the M.P.'s—and Huxley."

It gave Fiona something to think about. "Would what Huxley's doing be called treason?" she asked, hoping she wasn't being too transparent. If Huxley was embarked on a treasonous course and she could expose him—ah, revenge would be so sweet. It would, in a left-handed way, also be revenge on the Duke and Duchess of Lawton, as Huxley was that lady's lover, and any dishonor to him would surely reflect on her and on her cuckolded husband.

"Treason? That's a pretty powerful word, Fiona. He certainly will earn the king's displeasure, though, if he keeps up what he's doing. He seems to be backing a man named Samuel Rogers who is standing for Parliament. This Rogers is quite a champion of the 'little man,' as he calls the poor of the city. He goes about the worst slums of London, haranguing the people, keeping them in a state of tumoil."

"I'd like to hear him speak sometime," she said.

Werington turned and looked at her as if she'd suddenly grown two heads. "Whatever for, Fiona?"

Realizing she was showing too much interest in Huxley, remembering that if she was to survive, she must keep her new protector happy and unaware of her interest in the viscount, she shrugged prettily. "Plenty of people go to Bedlam on Sunday afternoon to watch the mad inmates. It could be just as exciting to be on the fringes of a crowd when this Rogers orates. I've never seen anything like that. It might be amusing."

"It might at that. I'll see if I can find out when this man Rogers is speaking. Maybe we could get up a party of people and make an occasion of it."

Fiona began laying her plans that very day. Huxley had betrayed her, so she would, in turn, do her best to betray him. Every time she could get Werington talking about politics, she subtly quizzed him. One of the important things she learned was that the men who frequented Medmenham Abbey were all prominent in the affairs of the day, politically astute, and much policy was determined by them. They were close advisors to the king. If she expected to learn anything damaging about Huxley, she might find out as much at the abbey as she would on a street corner of the London slums listening to this do-gooder, Samuel Rogers, rave and rant.

So when Werington rather cautiously suggested that they might go again to one of the frolics at the abbey near Marlow, she surprised him by agreeing.

"I realize now, Fiona, that the first time was particularly unpleasant for you. I honestly didn't know you were a virgin when I invited you. The duke suggested that you were just one more dolly-mop, eager as I for a romp. When the nuns took you away, I had no idea what for. I just thought you were to be dressed as a nun and . . . well, I didn't know what. I'd not been there before. I'd heard rumors, but I thought that most of what men told was exaggerated."

"Do they actually kidnap young girls from the farms and force them to participate as I did?"

He had the grace to look embarrassed. "I . . . I honestly don't know, Fiona. I've heard that story, too."

"The upstairs maid at the duke's place on Millbank told me she'd heard it. I didn't pay any attention— that is, until I was the victim of the group."

"I think that virgins are required for the Black Mass."

"That's rather wicked, Thor."

He laughed. "Oh, nobody takes it seriously, Fiona. I understood that Dashwood, when he was quite young, had a horrendous experience during his Grand Tour, and he became converted to the Papists. He believed he saw howling demons with glowing eyes. When his tutor, who was Catholic, realized how frightened the young man was, he told him that the only recourse was to convert. Later, in his cups, the tutor let the real story out—that the 'evil spirits' were just a couple of yowling alley cats—and it got back to Sir Francis. From that day on, he's done everything he could to discredit the Roman religion. And as the Black Mass is a desecration of that, he practices it on occasion. To tell the truth, though, the others go for the drinks and the food and the women. Religion is just a joke with most." He smiled at her engagingly. "So, now that you've been initiated, it won't be terrible for you at all. You'll be with me."

"Would I have to . . . would all of the men there——"

"No!" He was quite vehement in his answer. "You belong to me now, Fiona. If I catch you with another man, I'll take a strap to you."

So that's the way it was to be. Well, she had no

desire to lie with all of those other men the way she had that first awful time during the Black Mass. "Will you be able to get another invitation?" she asked. "I doubt if the Duke of Lawton will sponsor you now."

"He won't know I'm taking you, and you'll be masked when you get there, so he'll never know who you are. In fact, I didn't realize, until you fought poor Huxley like a wildcat, that it was you they were using. I did wonder where you'd got to, but I thought they were going to have some kind of theatrical entertainment later and that you were being chosen for it."

"Oh, it was theatrical, all right!"

She shut her mind to what had happened to her that day and concentrated on being a good mistress to Werington. He took her to the shops and engaged a dressmaker once they moved into their little jewel of a house on Hanover Street. For the first time in her life, Fiona experienced true luxury. Of course, she had to pay a price, but she was learning not to mind that quite so much. She got no pleasure from sex—she didn't know that she could—but she learned to turn her mind off and to please him. It was no more difficult than working as a milliner's assistant, and the rewards were greater. She had a lovely house to live in and two servants. She had gowns and velvet cloaks, French slippers with high heels, even some jewelry, although it was not fine quality. And she had the burning desire for revenge. Huxley would pay, and through him the Lawtons would be humiliated.

Fiona also began to take an interest in politics, a subject that had never crossed her mind. She read *The Gazette* avidly, but now for more than gossip of the *ton*. Occasionally she saw mention of the Viscount Huxley in the paper, and the Duke and Duchess of Lawton; but she also scanned the paper for articles about Samuel Rogers. More and more he was attracting the attention of the people with his inflammatory speeches urging the poor of London to rise and make themselves heard in the City.

"That man Rogers is speaking in Hyde Park tomorrow night," Fiona told Werington as they lay in the huge bed. Her first view of that bedroom had shocked her, for Werington had installed mirrors on all walls—full-length mirrors that reflected them as they worked their way through the book he had bought her at the beginning of their relationship. There was also a large round mirror fastened to the ceiling just above their bed. Fiona kept her eyes closed when Werington made love to her. She didn't want to watch their performance in myriad mirrors. Now, knowing that Werington was satisfied, she decided to ask a favor. "Do you think that we could go and listen to him?"

Half asleep, Werington mumbled, "Listen to whom?"

She raised up on one elbow and looked down at her lover. "To Samuel Rogers. You told me about him."

"Who wants to listen to that old windbag rave and rant? Besides, my mother is having a rout tomorrow night and expects me to be there."

No word of taking her. Well, what did she expect? He would scarcely take his mistress to one of his mother's social events. She wondered if his mother knew about her, but she didn't have the courage to ask him.

Next day, after Werington had left their love nest, Fiona began thinking again about Rogers. If Huxley was involved with this politician, she should get to know the man. Maybe she could use her womanly wiles to find out something that would be detrimental to Huxley. If only she could go to the speech tonight . . . Then she decided, why not? Werington wasn't going to be around. She had only a little money—Thor wasn't too generous that way—but it was enough to hire a sedan chair to take her to Hyde Park and back. He'd never know.

Not sure what kind of crowd she would encounter, Fiona had Sal Evans, her woman servant, help her dress in a very plain gown she had left over from her days with Aunt Eulalia.

"Why you puttin' on such a dress as this, Miss Fiona?" the stocky, middle-aged servant asked curiously.

"I want some air. I'll call a sedan chair. Have Rolf get one for me, Sal. With Sir Thorton out for the evening, I feel caged."

"A pretty cage, though," Sal said drily, just short of being impertinent.

Fiona, not used to having servants, was often at a loss to know how to handle Sal when she spoke out of turn. Usually she ignored the woman, thinking this the best plan.

"I'll not need a linkboy, as it's still light out."

It was much too warm to wear a cloak, which would have helped conceal her face, so Fiona chose a deep bonnet that shaded her features, obscuring them. She also draped a fine silk shawl about her shoulders to help cover her bare bosom. Fiona was learning what inflamed men.

When the chair came, she let Rolf help her into it and close the door. She even pulled the curtains across the windows so that no one could see her. "Go along Hanover Street toward Bond," she ordered. Once she was away from the house, she called out to the bearers to take her to the corner of Park Lane and Oxford Street, where Rogers was to speak.

"That be a busy corner tonight, miss," the lead bearer objected. "Might not be safe for a lady alone in a chair. The Rogers fellow is speakin' to the mob, and ofttimes they get unruly."

"But I want to hear him; that's why I'm going," she told the man. "I'm sure that with two such stalwart men as you, I shall be in no danger. If it looks as if the mob might get ugly, then we'll leave at once."

Finally they agreed to take her and stay there with her, but only if she paid them extra. Fiona realized that it was going to take almost the entire amount of pin money Thor had given her. She'd just have to wheedle more from him tomorrow.

"We'll stay on Brook Street, miss, until we come to Park Lane. There'll be less traffic than on Oxford. This man Rogers has a large following. If he gets into Parliament, he claims he'll make life better for us."

The back bearer sniggered. "But worse for the nobs."

Even on this less-traveled street, there were crowds all moving toward Hyde Park. A few already had linkboys with lit torches moving ahead of their chairs or coaches. Her men had to dodge in and out of the crowd, and she had a bumpy ride. Curious about who was going to hear Rogers, she pulled the curtains aside a tiny crack so that she could look out. There were well-dressed people in chairs and coaches, but the majority of the crowd were on foot and were working people, wearing plain clothes. There were a few women, but most of them were men. One bold fellow reached for the door of her chair, whereupon her back bearer set down his end of the chair so fast that it jolted Fiona, and went after the man with his fists.

Safe at last, they went on toward Hyde Park, although the man in front of the chair again tried to get Fiona to change her mind. "You see what they're like, miss. Many of 'em drunk on beer or cheap gin."

"You both are protecting me admirably. Please go on."

There was a small wooden platform set up in the corner of the park, and Rogers was already exhorting a gathering crowd when they got there.

"Move in to one side but close to the platform if you can," she ordered. "I want to hear what he says."

"Oh, I know it all, miss," the younger bearer said cynically. "Meat once a week for us and plenty of beer.

Every man with a bit of land of his own, taken from the nobs."

"Shh! I want to hear him say it, not you," she scolded.

In the deepening dusk, someone had thrust a number of torches into the ground in front of the platform on which Rogers stood. He was a small man, of slight build, about forty years old. His dress was neat but plain: a stuff coat of light tan, an unembroidered waistcoat of buff with bone buttons, and no wig, only his own unpowdered brown hair pulled back and tied at his neck with a brown ribbon.

Rogers might be plain, but his words were fancy. He was a skilled orator, using his ability to sway the minds of the mob. "You deserve more than a drab existence from cradle to grave," he told them in ringing tones. "You are poor, and the king and his cohorts want to keep you that way. Taxes are impossible. And now they want to put a new tax on every tankard of ale you drink, every glass of gin."

"No! No! Down with the taxing bastards!" someone yelled, and in a moment the whole growing crowd took up the cry. "No more taxes! Let the rich pay for a change!"

For fifteen minutes he talked to them, further enraging the crowd.

"Get the lords!" one ruffian yelled, looking about with wild eyes.

Some unwary peer, his ornate gilt chair embossed with his coat of arms, had chosen to be carried through the park tonight. When the mob spotted the carriers in their fine purple livery, they howled with delight.

"Upset the rascal!" the burly ruffian shouted. "Get him! Beat him up! Break up his chair and pound on him with the pieces."

On the platform, Rogers, his face lit from under by the smoking torches, so that he seemed some kind of demon from hell, tried to restore order. "No violence, brothers!" he shouted, his voice carrying to the fringes of the mob even over the shouts of the crowd. "Let's have no violence."

It was too late. The unruly mob, eager for a brawl, had started after the gilt chair, whose bearers were trotting as fast as they could for the exit to the park, realizing that they were due for trouble. It was the lead ruffian, who came to grief. Just as he drew alongside the sedan chair and reached up to tip it over, the curtain on the window was pulled back and a large silver-handled dueling pistol thrust out. The hand holding it was dripping expensive lace; even so, the pistol was held without a tremor. Too late the ruffian saw his peril and tried to fall back, but the mob behind him pushed forward, yelling for blood.

The chair was now opposite the one in which Fiona sat, cowering back in fright. Her bearer had just caught up the carrying poles to make a strategic retreat from the mob scene when the beleaguered peer yelled, "Stay back or I'll fire!" The mob from behind kept pushing, so that the front ranks were shoved up against the chair willy-nilly.

The next thing Fiona knew, there was a loud report, a flash, and a horrible scream. The nobleman had fired the pistol into the mob, and the instigator of his torment lay bleeding on the ground.

Her bearers started off at a trot, knowing that bloodshed would breed more violence, but it only served to draw attention to the sedan chair in which Fiona rode, clinging to the window frames to keep from being thrown out.

"There's another chair!" someone yelled, and in moments the mob had diverted itself from the gilt chair of the nobleman, who was willing to defend himself with powder and ball, to the plain chair with its unknown rider.

"Hurry, hurry!" Fiona cried.

Her bearers tried valiantly, but another group of

men, coming toward the speaker's platform, cut them off from escape. Caught between two tides of irate citizens, Fiona feared for her life. Whatever had possessed her to come out here tonight alone? She might be torn to pieces by this angry mob, who were further infuriated by the fact that one of their own had been wounded by the lord they had attacked.

A stone thudded against the side of the chair, then another. There was a howl of pain from the younger bearer, and the chair gave an awful lurch, the door springing open and Fiona almost falling out.

"A woman!" one man yelled. "A dolly-mop! Probably belongs to some young Mohock!"

"Now she belongs to us!" another shouted. "Me first!"

Fiona was determined to fight to the death, if necessary, to keep from being the victim of another group rape. Snatching off her high-heeled slippers, she gripped them by the toes, like clubs, ready to hit the first man who laid a hand on her. Then, from the back of the mob, someone cried out, "Enough, men! You don't attack innocent women, do you?"

It was a familiar voice, the ringing tones of the very man who had incited them to riot in the first place. There was grumbling and muttering in the crowd, but the ruffians began to give way as Samuel Rogers worked his way through to where Fiona's chair rested on the ground. Meanwhile, with the mob distracted from him, the lord in the gilt sedan chair had his bearers pick it up and hurry him away to safety. Fiona wished he'd come with that great dueling pistol and helped her; but it was for the politician, Rogers, to rescue her that evening.

Making a low bow, Rogers said, "My humblest apologies, miss, for any inconvenience to you. I trust you've not been injured?"

Fiona took a deep breath to calm herself, then answered, "Fortunately I am all right." Then she saw

Rogers grinning at her. "What's so funny, sir?" she demanded, annoyed at his levity. To her there was nothing amusing about the situation.

"I see you've armed yourself," he said, pointing to her slippers, which she was gripping aggressively.

"With your inciting speech, I had little choice," was her dry reply.

"Well. she ain't hurt, but I got hit on the head by a rock. Raised a big lump, it did," complained her bearer.

Rogers reached deep into his coat pocket, pulled out a plain leather purse, and gave the fellow a penny. "Here, that should make you feel better." Then he turned back to Fiona. "But how do you happen to be here at this hour in this mob, miss? It isn't safe."

"Told her so," the lead bearer chimed in, "but she would come here. Wanted to hear what you were saying, she told me."

Rogers smiled, a charming smile that took away the grim lines from his face. "Indeed, how pleasant. I should like to chat with you about this, miss, if I may accompany you home as a protector?"

Afraid that Werington might be back from his mother's party by now, Fiona said, "I'm sorry, sir. I do not know you, and I think it unsuitable to accept you as an escort."

"Then let me introduce myself: Samuel Rogers, miss, at your service, hopefully soon to be a Member of Parliament, with power to help these poor, downtrodden men."

There were shouts from the crowd of "Rogers!" The mob had quieted somewhat; tempers had cooled. A few even looked shamefaced now that Rogers had chastised them for bothering a woman.

"I'm not sure that inciting to riot is a proper way to campaign for a seat in Parliament, Mr. Rogers," Fiona told him tartly. "Causing a man to be shot . . . If you aren't more cautious, your followers will get completely out of hand and destroy the entire city. Then where will you sit even if you win? Have a care, sir, how you inflame your constituency in the future."

He bowed his head. "You are as wise as you are beautiful, miss. I wish I could have a longer conversation with you about your strong political beliefs."

Not wishing to make any appointment with the man while all of London was looking on, Fiona only said, "Perhaps I shall hear you speak again, sir."

He whipped a pamphlet from his coat pocket. "Then may I give you my schedule, miss? I am speaking in a hall on Oxford Street next week. Perhaps you could come."

"Perhaps. Good night, Mr. Rogers."

He bowed low again and watched as she pulled the curtains of her chair and ordered the bearers to take her out of the park. Not until they were some distance away did she tell them to take her back to Hanover Street. Although she did want to see Rogers again, it was only for the purpose of finding out something detrimental about Huxley. She had no wish for the man to know where she was living. It could be horribly embarrassing if he should ring her doorbell when Werington was at the Hanover Street house. She had no desire for her protector to learn of this little escapade. She didn't throw away the pamphlet, though. She'd look at the schedule later. Maybe there would be a place where she could safely go to make further acquaintance with the politician; otherwise how would she learn Huxley's connection with Rogers?

After a sample of the mob tonight, Fiona was inclined to agree with Werington. It would destroy the whole fabric of England if such men as those came into power. They were guided by emotion, not reason. She knew she had been lucky. If Rogers had not come to her aid, she might now be lying there on the dew-soaked grass of Hyde Park, her clothes torn and her body abused. She shuddered. The scene had gotten ugly so fast that she still scarcely knew how it had happened. It was as if someone had touched a lighted spill to a keg of gunpowder.

If Huxley was behind this man, morally or financially, then he was indeed a traitor to his kind and to everyone.

Fiona smiled as her bearers jogged quickly home. She might yet have her revenge on the handsome, rotten viscount.

CHAPTER 11

"Was your mother's party enjoyable?" Fiona asked Werington when he finally arrived at Hanover Street next afternoon.

He gave her a quick, almost guilty look, then shrugged. "The usual. Such parties are a bore after the excitement of Medmenham Abbey. Incidentally, I saw a friend last night who attends Dashwood's affairs frequently. He's willing to sponsor us. There's to be something there Sunday night, so we'll go with him and his fiancée, the Honorable Maggie Starrett."

"Was she at the party last night?"

"Oh, yes, they are inseparable." Werington guffawed at his own lewd joke. "In fact, if her father, old Starrett, knew how well-connected his daughter and her intended were, he'd have poor Dan horsewhipped, or he might even call him out."

"That would never do. If he killed him, who'd marry his ruined daughter?" Fiona could be catty when she chose. It irked her that Werington hadn't taken her along to the party. She made as good an appearance as any of the other young belles. She'd now seen enough of the elite to realize that many of them were as homely as old witches. Only their aristocratic birth made them acceptable, while she was slighted.

"I'll go along with you Sunday if you'll go to Deacon's Hall with me Friday evening," Fiona bargained.

"Where's Deacon's Hall, and what entertainment is to be held there?" he asked, fondling her bosom.

Fiona pulled away from his embrace. Trying to keep her voice playful so that he wouldn't get angry, she said, "First you promise, then we play, Thor."

His eyes already glazing with desire, he said hoarsely, "All right, all right, we'll go to whatever it is. Now, get out of that gown immediately or suffer the consequences." His eager fingers fumbled with the hooks that held the bodice together over the full breasts. As he exposed the luscious white flesh, he groaned and buried his lips in the valley between her mounds of delight.

Later, as they lay on the big bed, his head cushioned on her bosom, Werington murmured, "What is this engagement Friday all about? Should I invite Dan Ames and his Maggie to go along with us? Is that a new bearbaiting pit? I hear that some entrepreneur plans to go in competition with Hockley-in-the-Hole."

"No, it's not bear-baiting." She ran her fingers through his silky wheat-colored hair.

"A theatrical company? Maybe a naughty farce just over from France?"

"No, it is strictly English," she assured him.

"Aren't you going to tell me, Fiona?"

"Why not let it be a surprise?" she suggested. "Just come in a carriage, and bring your friends if you like."

Perhaps if she met some of Thor's noble friends, they would like her and soon she'd be included in some of the parties given by the *ton*. Although she had an easy life, Fiona longed for more social contacts. She was sixteen and beautiful. Staying in this house, even though it was a little jewel, was boring. Werington didn't bother to take her out often.

"Very well, I'll see if Dan and Maggie want some excitement on Friday night. And now," he said, pulling her against him roughly, "I'm ready for more excitement myself, love."

As she submitted to his hasty loving, Fiona wondered what it would be like to lie in bed with a man who was more sensitive, more eager to please her instead of gratifying only his own desires. Again she thought of Will Huxley, the perfidious, infamous Will.

Would he be at Deacon's Hall Friday night? Or was Werington's information linking Huxley to Samuel Rogers only a rumor, not fact?

When Werington called for her Friday night, Fiona was in an ugly mood. That very day she'd read a tidbit of gossip in *The Gazette* that had upset her greatly:

> *Lady Arabelle Perry's Titian coloring contrasted nicely with the fair good looks of Sir Thorton Werington at a rout held by his mother. Has our Thor finally succumbed to love?*

"Now what have I done, Fiona?" her lover asked as he helped her into the landaulet. "If you dislike me so much, perhaps we should call off this evening's surprise entertainment."

"No, no. I'm entitled to a little fun, too," she snapped.

"What's gotten into you?" he demanded. "I don't have to put up with such nonsense from you, Fiona."

Realizing that she had perhaps overstepped her privileges, Fiona quickly hastened to put Werington at ease. "Oh, I guess it's the hot summer weather," she told him.

Suspiciously, his gray eyes cold as flint, he queried, "You aren't with child, are you? If so, you must tell me at once. The sooner such matters are taken care of, the better."

"No, you needn't worry about that."

"Then what's come over you this evening?"

Exasperated with his questions, Fiona flung caution to the winds and snapped, "I saw *The Gazette* today."

"Oh? What's in the newspaper that has made you so cross? I haven't had a moment today to read it. Some of the men at White's were perusing the news, but I was into a game of cards and didn't bother with *The Gazette*."

"You should have taken time for it," she said spitefully. "Your name appeared in one of the gossip items."

There was a noticeable pause. Then, with an overly casual air, Werington asked, "And just what lies are they spouting about me today?"

"Oh, they just linked your name with that of the Honorable Arabelle Perry, told how your respective colorings complemented each other." She bit off the words as if they were sewing threads.

To Fiona's dismay, Werington flushed a bright red and muttered, "Oh, they're always doing that if a man is a bachelor. It doesn't mean anything." He leaned over, caught her chin in a painfully harsh grip, and kissed her thoroughly. "There, are you satisfied that you are my own true love?" he demanded.

"Of course, Thor." Fiona was worried for the first time since their arrangement. What would happen to her if he did marry Arabelle or some other young lady of aristocratic blood? Would he cease to be her protector? Would he stop paying the rent on her home in Hanover Street? It was a chilling prospect.

As the landaulet rattled up to Deacon's Hall, they saw large placards on the front of the brick building, each with a likeness of Samuel Rogers.

Peering at them, Werington swore. "What's this nonsense, Fiona? Isn't this that politico who's trying to destroy our way of life?"

"You promised we could hear him," she reminded, a bit tartly. "It won't kill you, Thor. It might even be interesting."

"From what I heard at White's, I should have brought along a pistol."

"What do you mean?" Her voice rose dangerously.

"Oh, there's a story circulating that this man Rogers incited a riot in Hyde Park, and the mob attacked Lord Grimes, who was there in a chair; but Grimes fought back and shot a man."

Fiona cried, "Good heavens! Was the man killed?"

This certainly wasn't the time to let Thor know she'd been there.

"No, not grievously wounded. There was a woman there, too, and the mob started to attack her, but I hear Rogers himself intervened. Silly fool. He should have let her get what was coming to her. A woman insane enough to go to such an affair in Hyde Park deserves whatever she gets."

"It . . . it was very foolhardy of her," Fiona agreed. That was one little escapade she hoped Werington never found out about.

"Oh, there are Dan and his Maggie, just getting out of that coach. Here, we'll greet them on the steps." Werington got down from the coach and handed Fiona out.

"Ah, Werington!" the young man called. "Well-timed."

Baron Ames was elegant in scarlet coat and gold-thread waistcoat over black velvet breeches. His companion, Lady Maggie Starrett, had golden hair artfully arranged in a mass of ringlets under a charming round cap with lappets of white lawn that tied under her gently rounded chin. Her blue velvet gown was an exact match for her eyes.

It was to the other woman, though, that Fiona's eyes were drawn. Tall, buxom, her flaming hair partially covered with a bonnet of cinnamon-colored silk, she could have posed for any of the Titian paintings in the royal collection. Fiona heard Werington make a little sound of dismay. As she turned to face him, she found that his eyes were on the redhead, not on her. His face was the classic picture of embarrassment. She didn't need the muttered introductions to know that she was looking at the Honorable Arabelle Perry.

"We mentioned that we were meeting you here, Thor, and Arabelle thought it would be great sport to come along. Had I known," he said to Werington in a stage whisper, "I'd have brought along another man."

"Whatever are we going to do?" Miss Perry asked in a high, overbred voice. "I thought there was to be some fabulous entertainment."

Apologetically Werington said, "My . . . friend, Miss McQuade, thought it might be jolly to hear this man Rogers speak. He's the one who caused a riot in Hyde Park."

"I do hope nothing uncouth happens this evening," she said, distaste plain on her peaches-and-cream face.

"It might be exciting," Maggie Starrett said. Blonde, blue-eyed, slender and willowy, she had a reckless look in her eyes that made Fiona wonder if she was a dollymop. Had she been to Medmenham Abbey with Baron Ames? Or was Fiona the only one who had been tricked into such debauchery? "Is this the man involved in that shooting?" Maggie went on, her voice quick and light.

"He is the one," Ames said. "Old Grimes fired right into the mob who'd come to hear Rogers. Maggie's right. Who knows what might happen."

"I'm not sure it's safe," Werington demurred. "I'm not armed; are you, Ames?"

"No, but I daresay there'll be constables in the hall. A riot in Hyde Park is one thing; a disturbance in a hall is quite another."

"It sounds boring," Miss Perry said, pouting. "I'd not have come if I'd realized . . ." She gave Fiona such a venomous look that she shrank back against Werington's arm.

"This was Fiona's idea," he quickly said, divorcing himself from the idea.

"You said it could be interesting," Fiona spoke up. She wasn't going to let this Titian-haired lovely get the best of her.

"Oh, come on, Arabelle," the vivacious Maggie said, tucking her arm in Miss Perry's, then catching Baron Ames with her other arm. "I want to see what this man looks like."

Scornfully Arabelle said, "You must be blind, Maggie, if you wonder that. His likeness is everywhere." She pointed to the broadsides plastered all over the front of Deacon's Hall.

Maggie shrugged. "Pictures don't tell me what a man is like. I think Rogers may be quite exciting; he must have tremendous charisma to have fired the imagination of the poor of London."

Werington took Arabelle's free arm, then, belatedly, said, "Come along, Fiona," in a very offhanded way. "I promise, Arabelle, that if it is boring, we shall leave."

They started up the steps when a familiar voice called out, "Werington! What in God's name are you doing here?"

It was the Viscount Will Huxley, approaching them from the side. Tonight he was dressed so drably that he might be a clerk from some dreary office. There wasn't a sign that he was wealthy, a peer. His hair was unpowdered and pulled back with a narrow string. He wore the plainest of coats, and his waistcoat was completely unadorned. Sweeping off his black felt tricorne, he bowed to the group. His eyes widened when he saw Fiona, but he addressed himself to her escort.

"Are you mad—and you too, Ames—bringing ladies to Deacon's Hall? Didn't you read what happened in Hyde Park?" He reached out and flicked the gold lace on the baron's scarlet coat. "You couldn't have dressed more conspicuously if you tried, Dan. Do you want to be torn limb from limb by the mob?"

"I see that you aren't a peacock tonight." Werington gave Huxley a suspicious look. "Is it true that you're hand in glove with this fellow Rogers?"

"Where did you hear that?"

"Oh, there are rumors. I warn you, Huxley, you won't be popular with your friends if you begin championing the common man, who wants to take all our money and our land."

"There are many inequities in our land, Werington."

"Siding with the enemy isn't the way to right them," Werington snapped. "Take care, Huxley. This mob will turn on you, and your own kind will ignore your plight."

Fiona found that it was impossible to keep her eyes off Huxley's handsome face. He wasn't paying any attention to her, which piqued her, even though she told herself that she had no interest in the man other than wanting to see him brought as low as he'd brought her.

"I understand that the king himself does not approve of rousing the rabble, Lord Huxley," she said, drawing attention to herself.

"There's unrest all over Europe. There are rumors of trouble in France. The Bourbons have ignored the little man for so long that his plight is desperate. In our enlightened country, the same thing, unfortunately, is happening. King George must open his eyes and give some thought to the masses. If not, who knows what might happen. They're a powder keg about to blow up."

"And they'll do so if you, and men like this Rogers, strike the spark," Ames said, dead seriously. "Huxley, you play a dangerous game."

"I see that you're incognito tonight," Fiona said, scorn thick in her voice.

"Why flaunt my wealth in their poor faces, Fiona?"

"If you are so concerned for them," Arabelle put in spitefully, "you should give all of your money to them and live as they do."

"Well said, Arabelle," Werington said, with such enthusiasm that Fiona felt like slapping him.

"That's stupid," she said to the charming Miss Perry. "What good would that do? Only a complete change in the way these people live will help them. Although Lord Huxley's fortune is reputed to be considerable, it would be but a drop in the bucket."

Huxley looked at her with surprise, as if he were seeing her for the first time. "Thank you, Fiona."

Annoyed with herself for taking his part when she hated him, doubly annoyed that she'd let the too-pretty Arabelle provoke her into such a stance, Fiona just glowered at Huxley until he turned away, puzzled. Then, to her consternation, she saw Samuel Rogers get out of a plain hire chair, pay off the men, and start walking toward their group. Frantic lest he recognize her and say something whereby Werington would realize she'd been the woman in Hyde Park, she opened her white lace fan and concealed her face behind it.

"Huxley! Have you brought some of your friends to try to convert them to our way of thinking?" Rogers asked eagerly.

"Scarcely," was the viscount's wry reply. He quickly introduced Rogers to his friends. When Rogers made a leg to Fiona, she saw recognition in his eyes. She willed him to silence. If he mentioned that he'd given her a pamphlet . . .

Fortunately Huxley forestalled any disaster by saying, "I'm trying to get them to leave, Sam. Dressed up like the latest fashion plates from Paris, they'd cause trouble inside."

"Much as I wish they'd hear what I have to say, I must admit the truth to your words, Huxley. After the trouble in the park . . ."

Fiona felt his hazel eyes on her and she trembled.

"Is it true that some woman was set upon by the mob the other night?" Werington asked avidly. "Silly strumpet, out in such a place alone and at night."

Will Rogers betray me? Fiona asked herself in an agony of suspense.

He gave her a quick look, then said rather coldly, "Perhaps, Sir Thorton, she too is interested in the poor of London. If enough good women got behind my campaign, we might be able to force the king to see all his subjects, not just the ones with money and power."

"I say, old fellow, that's close to treason!" Ames exclaimed.

"Just because I want every man in England to have a chance? If so, then I am a traitor." Rogers said it proudly.

"Oh, let's forget this lecture," Arabelle said, pouting. "I for one am not interested in living the way my abigail does." She turned to Werington and put a slender hand on his arm. "Thor, dear, you promised that we needn't stay if I was bored."

"Well, perhaps this isn't the best idea in the world," Werington said gallantly. "Shall we all go elsewhere?"

"They're baiting a real Bengal tiger at Hockley," the charming Miss Perry added.

"Good; we'll go there, then," Werington said, all smiles.

"But I wanted to hear Mr. Rogers," Fiona said stubbornly, earning herself a scowl from her lover.

"Oh, Fiona, we'd rather go to Hockley," Maggie Starrett said, "wouldn't we, Dan?"

"Huxley seems to think we're not suitably attired for your lecture," Ames said to Rogers, a bit apologetically.

"We don't need another riot," Huxley added.

"Perhaps some other time, Miss McQuade?" Rogers said politely.

She didn't answer, afraid of what Werington might do. As they piled into their carriages and headed for Hockley-in-the-Hole, Fiona wished they could have stayed. There was something charismatic about Rogers. She felt he might go a long way in Parliament if he won his seat.

"What nonsense that was," Werington was saying, his tone aggrieved. "I'm glad that Arabelle had sense enough to suggest something a bit more lively for our entertainment. Sometimes, Fiona, I wonder at your strange ideas."

CHAPTER 12

This time Fiona and Werington had company on their trip up the Thames to Medmenham Abbey: Lady Maggie Starrett and Baron Daniel Ames. It was a beautiful evening, with the long summer dusk casting an enchanting aura over the river. Fiona was not sure how she'd react to another session at the abbey, knowing now what to expect; but Thor had promised her that she wouldn't have to lie with other men, only with him—and that in private.

"Sir Francis had special little rooms around the main Roman hall, Fiona, each with its own bed covered in green satin. There are curtains we can draw so that no one will see us," Werington said lightly.

"And what poor maid will they use for their Black Mass this time?" She was still bitter about that part of her first visit to Marlow.

"That's up to Dashwood, or whoever plays abbott this evening. It isn't always Father O'Toole."

"Is that vile man really a Papist priest?"

"So they say. Excommunicated, of course. The Pope doesn't hold with Satanism." Werington snickered at the thought. "Dashwood gives the man a stipend, I understand, just so that he'll always have an unfrocked priest on hand for the rites."

"Do you have your mask?" Maggie asked her.

Fiona rather liked this woman. Although an aristocrat, she was friendly to Fiona, not at all condescending—*not like the hateful Arabelle Perry*, Fiona thought. "In my pocket. Do we all have to dress like nuns?"

"No, only a few do that. I thought you'd been to the abbey before, Fiona."

"Once." She didn't enlarge on that single syllable.

Maggie gave her a sharp, knowing look, but refrained from comment.

Leaning close to Maggie so that Werington couldn't hear, Fiona asked, "Does Arabelle come to the frolics?"

"Good heavens no! She's much too prim for that kind of fun," Maggie said. Then, with quiet compassion, she asked, "Are you worried about what will happen when Thor marries her?"

Fiona was stunned at the phrasing of Maggie's question—not "if Thor marries her" but "when."

"I can't imagine he'd enjoy her in bed."

"Well, wives aren't for enjoyment; they're for social status, for raising children, for political reasons. Surely you're aware of that."

"I know. Thor isn't about to marry me."

Maggie laid a kind hand on Fiona's. "You're wondering what will happen to your arrangement when he marries? Well, he may well want to continue with it. Many married men have mistresses."

Thinking of the possessive way Arabelle had with Werington, Fiona imagined she'd be one wife who wouldn't tolerate her husband's straying. That he'd be able to maintain a separate establishment for her after he married the Honorable Arabelle was unthinkable.

"Don't worry, Fiona; you're a very attractive woman. There'll be plenty of men willing to pay the Hanover Street rent when Thor leaves."

Fiona hadn't realized how widely it was known about their little love nest. Did Arabelle know about it? This discussion made her feel reckless. Why should she devote herself entirely to Thor, be at his beck and call, go only where he wanted to take her, when at any moment he might discontinue their affair? It made her rebellious. Why couldn't she marry some lord? She was far more beautiful than many of the ladies of the *ton*. She came from decent stock—not the nobility, to be sure, but her parents hadn't been peasants, either. She would make as good a wife for Werington—or for any other young blood—as the next girl.

Perhaps she'd better begin thinking about her future. She had very little money. Werington paid all of her bills and bought her gowns and even gave her an allowance—pin money, he called it—but it was minuscule, and she had no jewels worth any great amount, nor any means of amassing a fortune.

Changing the subject, Maggie said, "I was impressed with that man Rogers. I'd rather have stayed to hear him talk than gone to the tiger-baiting. I really don't much care for animal-baiting."

"Neither do I," Fiona admitted. "It's awfully cruel. But Arabelle wanted to go, so naturally Thor said yes." She gave him a dirty look. Fortunately for her, he and Dan were deep in conversation with their boatman about something or other.

"I was asking Dan about Mr. Rogers. He says that his wife is in Bedlam. She went into a decline when they had a child born dead and finally had to be committed. I think that Rogers comes to the abbey sometimes."

Fiona was surprised at this. "I would think that the men who frequent Dashwood's orgies wouldn't have anything to do with someone who advocates the over-throw of their way of life."

"Apparently he's very witty, and they like to be amused. I understand that he smuggled a monkey into the chapel once, and it caused a riot when the Black Mass began. Some of the friars were so drunk, they thought they had actually conjured up the devil!"

"They do a good enough job of devilment without the aid of apes," Fiona said bitterly.

"What are you ladies whispering about?" Werington called.

"Women's secrets," Maggie countered, relieving Fiona of the necessity of answering. Then she grinned wickedly. "We're comparing notes on your prowess in bed, men."

Fiona was shocked. She could see that Thor wasn't sure whether or not Maggie was joking. Baron Ames, who knew Maggie better, only laughed.

The light had that almost unreal quality of midsummer dusk when the boatmen rowed them to the landing at the abbey. As soon as they had disembarked, Werington told Fiona, "Put on your mask now; then no one will recognize you." He pulled out a black velvet mask of his own, which he donned, and their companions followed suit.

"If you think that this is much of a disguise, you're mad, Thor," Maggie told him. "If we were dressed as nuns and friars, with concealing coifs or hoods, then it might work. As it is, I daresay almost everyone recognizes everyone else."

Fiona was appalled.

"Who cares?" Werington asked nonchalantly. "It's just an excuse. You can pretend not to recognize or be known."

"I understand that Dashwood's wife was in one of the frolics recently," Maggie offered.

"That's not half so bad as Lord Pemberton's sister," Ames said, laughing. "I understand he had her right along with the others. Claimed he didn't know who it was, which I doubt. It's common knowledge that Pemberton's sister lost her virginity at home at the age of twelve, thanks not only to Pemberton but also to his lusty father, who died riding a whore."

"But that's incest!"

"Yes, Fiona," Maggie said, in a slightly mocking tone. "It happens in the best of families."

"That's scandalous!"

'Really, Fiona," Werington chided, "surely by now

you know how it is in real life. All sorts of things happen. Life isn't like a novel."

"They'd ban a novel that was true to life," Ames declared.

Now they had climbed the steps to the gardens. This time, having been here before, Fiona tried not to be too shocked by the statues that were everywhere. They didn't seem to bother Maggie at all. In fact, when they happened on one large statue of Priapus, she cried, "I feel just like Lady Macbeth! 'Is this a dagger I see before me?' " she declaimed, catching hold of the statue. Both men laughed so hard, they had to take off their masks to wipe the tears from their eyes with lace-bordered kerchiefs.

Fiona, still not at ease with this kind of sexual horseplay, particularly in mixed company, felt her face grow hot. She had come a long way from her Calvinistic upbringing, but she still had a long way to go to achieve the casual attitude about sex the *ton* displayed.

As Fiona was to have no part in the Black Mass, no longer being eligible, the four companions wandered about the grounds until they heard the summons to the quay. The friars were arriving. By now the sun had set, and the scene was eerie. On the Thames, arranged in a semicircle about the abbey landing, were a great number of water craft, including barges full of sightseers, all waiting for a glimpse of the infamous Friars of St. Francis as they left their own barge and went in procession through the park to the ruined abbey.

The special gondola in which the friars rode was painted scarlet. The men, as they came up the steps from the landing, were an impressive sight in their white robes with scarlet-lined hoods. They carried long black tapers, and the flames flickered in the gathering dark. A bell tolled from somewhere in the abbey, and Fiona could hear weird organ music all about them, that seemed to be coming from the very sky.

As they moved to follow the procession, there was some excitement off on one side. Fiona heard shrieks, and a young girl wearing only a shift came racing through the shrubbery. In pursuit behind her were two "nuns" and several men.

"No, no, I won't, I won't!" the girl was screaming.

Seeing the four companions, she veered toward them. She was a young girl, probably no more than twelve, or thirteen, although her bosom was well-developed, bouncing enticingly as she ran from her pursuers. Her brown hair had fallen down about her shoulders in a mass of tangled ringlets, and her cheeks were flushed with exertion.

Catching at Fiona's hands, the girl begged breathlessly, "Please, milady, don't let them do it to me. They said I was to bring apples for the dinner, and when I got here, they caught me and took my clothes."

Fiona didn't know what to do. She was appalled that they were going to use this young girl as they'd used her, yet she was powerless to help her.

Maggie intervened. "Come, now, lass, it's not all that bad. They'll give you something to drink and you'll enjoy every minute of it." She turned to Ames. "Give the girl some money, Dan; it'll make it all right with her."

He obligingly took out his money pouch of soft Spanish leather and handed the girl a shilling. She was so eager to take the coin that she forgot her pursuers, who caught up with her and carried her away. Pacified by the money, she had stopped her screaming.

"She's awfully young," Fiona said unhappily.

"At least she gets paid this time. Otherwise it would be some farmer's lad who took her in the hayloft, and she'd not get any shillings from him," Maggie replied.

"Do we watch the Black Mass?" Fiona asked, not wanting to see the child raped by all the friars as she had been.

"No, only the friars get to go. There are twelve

official friars plus the abbott. Sometimes that is Sir Francis, sometimes the unfrocked Father O'Toole."

"We just go to the Roman Room for the banquet, et cetera," Maggie told her.

"Particularly the et cetera." Dan, leering, caught Maggie in his arms and caressed her in a very intimate way.

Afraid that Werington would do likewise, Fiona suggested, "Then let's go to the Roman Room. I don't remember it."

"You didn't stay for the banquet," he said, aggrieved. "You insisted that I take you home after the mass."

"Then you've a treat in store," Maggie told her. "The banquets are fabulous. Wait until you see the food. The chef molds dishes into the most interesting shapes."

"Last time the puddings were shaped like Lady Ducnall's bosom," Dan said, laughing. "What a thing to bite into!"

"And the murals are exact copies from some of the excavations in Pompeii."

"You saw some in the folly where we ate our picnic," Werington reminded Fiona.

She remembered them, all right! Well, this was one time she was glad she was masked, as she knew she'd be embarrassed at the decor, not to mention the things that went on.

When they got to the Roman Room, she found that although the Black Mass had not been concluded, many of the guests were already well into their cups. The long tables, spread with the finest damask cloths and set with heavy silver and cut glass, groaned with food and drink, and above them were beautiful German crystal chandeliers ablaze with white wax candles.

"I see they're serving Breasts of Venus tonight," Maggie said. She pointed to a platter on which two plump pigeons lay side by side, each topped with a juicy red cherry. "And of course all the bread is Holy Ghost Pie. They use that in the mass too."

The place was a riot of color, with the men in their best and most elegant coats of scarlet, plum, mauve, bottle green, turquoise—all the colors of the rainbow—and the women in gowns just as colorful: a draper's dream of satin, velvet, weighted silk, tissue, lawn, and lace. There were a few women who were completely nude except for nuns' coifs and masks. They were helping to serve the men.

"I do believe that's the Earl of Sandwich over there on that couch with the young nun," Werington whispered to Fiona.

Even though he had a mask on, she could see that he was ugly.

"He's the biggest rake here," Werington confided. "He always wants young girls—the younger the better. I'm surprised that he's not helping celebrate the Black Mass with that maiden we saw outside."

"He's too busy with the nun," Fiona said, wanting to avert her eyes. She had a lover, true; but she was not yet used to the idea of sex in public. It was her feeling that intimacy of that sort belonged in the boudoir.

"It's giving me ideas, watching Sandwich," Werington whispered, sliding his arm around her, cupping a breast with one eager hand.

"Thor, you promised me there were private rooms," Fiona said in an agony of embarrassment, for she doubted that the mask she wore was much of a disguise.

"Everyone does it here," Werington argued, his voice persuasive, his touch bolder.

Fiona pulled away from him angrily. "No! You said we would have a private alcove with curtains. I don't intend to run around nude the way that trollop is doing. And I certainly don't intend to do what that couple is doing over there—not with an audience."

"You didn't let that bother you the other time," he

said petulantly. "Everyone at the party had a turn with you except me. What you need is a ride on the rooster hobbyhorse."

"Did I hear you mention the Idolum Tentiginis?" a masked man asked, his voice sardonic. "What's wrong, fellow? Can't you warm your dolly-mop up without that silly rocking contraption?"

"I don't know what you're talking about," Fiona said, cross with the two of them. "It's not polite to talk in riddles."

"Clucky little hen, isn't she," the masked man said, snickering. "Maybe what she needs isn't the hobby-horse but a change of partners." He reached out, caught Fiona around the waist, and pulled her away from Werington. "Come, my surly little miss with the magnificent bosom, leave your man and find out what it's like with a *real* man."

"That's enough, Fiona!" Werington snapped, angry at the insult. "I'll not have you accommodating other men, even though you seemed to like it well enough last time."

"Ah! Been here before with your lethargic lothario."

There was something familiar about his voice, but Fiona couldn't quite place it. The man was of medium height, actually much shorter than Werington, but the wiry arm he had around her felt like a band of iron.

"Fiona!" Werington's voice was dangerous now.

"Please, sir, don't cause trouble for me," she begged.

"My pardon, Miss Fiona." Then, although he took his arm from around her waist, he leaned close and murmured, "Are you the enchanting Fiona I met only last Friday but saw some days before that at Hyde Park? Huxley's charming friend?"

She gasped with dismay. It was Samuel Rogers. No wonder his voice sounded so familiar. She'd come here hoping to get scandalous information about Huxley, but how could she talk with this man with Werington breathing down her neck? "Sir, perhaps we can chat later, over dinner," she murmured as she slid away from his embrace and took Werington's arm.

"What were you saying to that man?" her escort demanded. "Behave yourself, Fiona. Don't anger me, or you'll be sorry. You're not the only beautiful young woman in London, you know."

"Oh, Thor, I wasn't saying anything of importance," she lied. She mustn't get him too angry or heaven knew what he might do. "Let's have some wine," she suggested.

"And then we'll find one of those alcoves you insist on," he said firmly.

By then Fiona had seen where these love niches were. All around the wall of the Roman Room were curtained alcoves. She saw a man chasing one of the nude nuns around, and when he'd caught her, he dragged her off, laughing, to one of the rooms. As he pulled back the curtains, Fiona saw that there was a huge bed inside and mirrored walls. Not all the couples were so modest, though. One pair was copulating on a couch against a wall that held several pornographic paintings. The man was pointing out one of the pictures, asking the woman to copy that example, and she agreed willingly, contorting herself so, Fiona ached just watching her.

Werington brought them large crystal goblets of claret, and he downed his so quickly, his face flushed with the sudden intake of alcohol. Fiona hoped he'd get so drunk that he'd fall into a stupor and not demand anything of her tonight, nor remember tomorrow whether he'd had her or not. Unfortunately the wine he gulped only inflamed his desire, and he insisted that they go into one of the alcoves.

"Can't we wait until after dinner?" she pleaded. "I'm famished, and the servants are bringing in the food."

"This won't take long," he said. "Come on."

Once inside the little room, he told her to get undressed in a hurry, and he fumbled off his clothes in record time. With no finesse, he flung her onto the huge bed, mounted her, and took his pleasure selfishly, as usual. She closed her eyes and her mind and endured it, assuming, from her limited experience, that women were put on this earth to gratify men, with no hope for pleasure themselves.

CHAPTER 13

Although Werington had promised privacy in their alcove, one drunken man blundered in and another pulled back the curtains, looking for a bed for himself and the woman who was with him. It was difficult for Fiona to remember that she had wanted to come here to Medmenham Abbey to try to get evidence against Huxley. His friend, Rogers, was here, but of Huxley himself she'd seen nothing. The masks were a joke. Fiona had been recognized by Rogers, who scarcely knew her. She was sure she'd know Huxley if she saw him, masked or not. If the Duke and Duchess of Lawton were here tonight, she'd not seen them, either. She wondered, trying to keep her mind off Werington and his lust, if Huxley always came with the duchess or if he sometimes brought other women. Was he still calling at the house on Millbank, or did the duchess have a new lover now?

Finally, finished, Werington urged Fiona to dress quickly: "The banquet must be in full swing now, and I'm starved after all that work. Come along, Fiona."

"Let me straighten my hair," she said, cross with him. It looked better when Sal did it for her. "A lot of the powder has sifted out. I look like an old gray granny woman."

He dropped a possessive kiss on her bosom. "Not with that lovely firm flesh you don't. Look on the chest in the corner; there's probably a powder can there."

She found a silver can shaped like a nude man, with a handy "spout" from which the powder was dispensed. Werington sniggered at the lewd appointment. "That Dashwood—he thinks of everything!"

"No, he thinks of only one thing," she said drily. "Here, powder me. I'll hold the bed sheet around my shoulders to keep powder off my gown."

"I feel like a damned abigail," he fumed.

"Well, if you don't want to bother, you can have me looking like an old frump. Then it will reflect on you, Thor."

"All right, all right." He gave in with poor grace. "Now, can we possibly go eat? There'll be nothing left."

"Somehow I doubt that."

Fiona was right. The table groaned with all kinds of exotic foods, and the guests were making gluttons of themselves.

"I see that Sandwich isn't eating that quick snack he has at the gaming tables," Werington said, watching the gross man stuff himself with woodcock pie. "He won't quit when he's gambling. When he gets hungry, he has one of the footmen put a slice of meat on a slice of bread, and he eats it with his hands, so that he won't have to quit the gaming table for the banquet board. Some of the men are beginning to call the meal a 'sandwich.' "

"It sounds interesting. It might be good on a picnic."

"What might be good on a picnic?" It was Rogers again. "This charming young lady would be an ideal picnic companion."

"Do I know you, sir?" Werington asked, annoyed at the attention Rogers was paying Fiona.

The man put a finger to his lips. "Remember, we are all masked for the sake of discretion. You may call me 'Mr. X.' "

"Well, Mr. X, find your own woman," Werington said belligerently. "Fiona is with me."

Rogers bowed and went off, his eye on a nude nun who was pouring wine down a man's throat from a bottle shaped very much like the powder can Fiona had seen. Even Dashwood's obscene articles had a sameness, Fiona thought.

Werington found two places at the table, and the attending footmen saw that their plates were heaped with food and their goblets full of wine at all times. For the first time since they had become lovers, Fiona saw Werington so drunk that he finally slumped over, his face in his plate. Disgusted, she left the table and moved away from the rabble. By now most of the men, and quite a few of the ladies, were drunk. She saw one man drop cherries down the front of a buxom woman's low-cut gown, then go fishing for them with eager fingers. Maggie Starrett and Baron Ames had disappeared, probably into one of the alcoves. In one corner of the room, she saw what looked like a child's toy, a rocking horse, only the body was a swan, neck bent along its back, beak thrusting straight up.

"Surely, Miss Fiona, you don't have to ride that contraption to rouse your passions."

It was Rogers again; he had come up quietly behind her. Fiona felt her face grow hot as she realized what the rocking horse was for. Quickly she turned away from it; but wherever she looked, there was lust or obscene statues or lewd murals, and the company were engaged in a variety of sexual activities in pairs, trios, and larger groups.

Rogers, quickly perceiving her embarrassment, changed his manner toward her immediately. "I'm sorry, Miss Fiona. I shouldn't have made such a bad joke. I thought——"

"You thought that, as I'm here, I wouldn't mind."

"May I say that you don't seem to belong in this scene."

"Thank you, sir. I . . . it's a long story, which I won't tell you, but thank you for saying that to me."

"Your escort seems asleep."

"Yes. He had too much claret."

"Miss Fiona, could we perhaps stroll out in the gardens? They are lighted with torches. I promise you that

I will not lay a finger on you. I would like to talk with you."

Looking around with disgust at the drunken orgy now in progress, Fiona, eager to escape, agreed. Just as they were leaving the Roman Room, they met Huxley and the Duchess of Lawton, neither masked. Quickly Fiona opened her fan, hiding her face, and pulled her skirt aside to make room for them.

As she fled into the night, she heard Huxley cry, "Sam! I didn't know you were to be here tonight."

"Nor I you, Will. Your Grace, I wish you good evening."

She didn't hear the duchess's reply. She did, however, hear Huxley say jovially, "Your lady seems very shy, Sam. I should like to have met her."

"Some other time," Rogers promised, then followed her into the torchlight garden. "I take it you didn't want to see Huxley, Fiona."

"Nor the Duchess of Lawton."

Drawing her down onto one of the marble benches, he said quietly, "I'm sorry if you have differences with Lord Huxley. He's a true friend to the poor of England —if only they'll recognize it—no matter that he's a viscount. He has their good at heart."

"You'd never know it seeing him here," she said, forgetting that she was speaking to the avowed champion of the poor and that he was very much here.

"Ah, these are his friends—at least some of them— and he's been raised this way, Fiona. I wasn't, yet you see me here also." Then, quietly, he added, "And *you* are here. I would not have expected to find you at such a place."

Bitterly Fiona said, "I have my reasons for coming here, Mr. Rogers."

"I'm sure they are good ones, Miss Fiona."

She felt shamed to hear him say those words, for she knew her motives were strictly vengeful. There was something about Rogers, a sympathetic manner, that invited her to tell him the whole sordid story, but it would never do to tell him that his good friend Huxley had betrayed her, had contributed to her downfall.

"I, in turn, am surprised to find you here," she said.

For a moment Fiona thought that her companion was not going to comment. Then he sighed audibly. "And *I* have reasons. You know my aims, Miss Fiona. I hope to win a seat in Parliament. To do that, I need money, of which I have little. And I certainly need friends in high places."

"Huxley."

"Yes. Will Huxley has been very helpful to me, but I need more than that. The men who come here, the members of the Hell-Fire Club, as they're known in London, although they prefer the name Friars of St. Francis, are nearly all very important men, who have influence with King George. Although it may not sound like it when you hear the poor rant and rave—when they become violent—I do not want to foment a revolution. I fear that one is brewing in France. It may not come soon, perhaps not even in the next decade, but the French peasants are seething. The poor are tired of their lot; they are desperate. There will be bloodshed in France before the century is out."

"And you think it will happen here too?"

"I hope not. That is why I want the king's advisors to listen to reason and to make him see the handwriting on the wall. It could happen here. Our people have many more rights and yet the poor have one set of laws, the rich another. Do you realize that a man can be hanged if he steals a loaf of bread to feed his starving children? He can have his hands cut off. A woman can be burned at the stake if she is accused of being a witch. These things seldom happen to the rich and powerful, Fiona. Unless our government changes, it can bring terrible times to our country. There were riots in the streets of London less than a decade ago—houses burned, nobles attacked. It could happen again."

Feeling slightly resentful that he made her feel ashamed of privileged men like Huxley, Fiona said spitefully, "And you think that your inflammatory speeches will help? Sir, they tried to attack me the other night in Hyde Park when I had done nothing except come in a hired chair to hear what you had to say."

"I am deeply sorry for that, Miss Fiona. Unfortunately, there will always be those who go too far. They know they are entitled to more out of life than existing in pain and want. Can you blame them for being desperate enough to snatch at it? You came in a plain sedan chair, true. But not one of those men in that mob could afford a chair. They must walk everywhere. The price of a chair would feed their whole family for a week." He paused, then asked, "You don't come from such a life as that, do you?"

"No," she admitted. "We weren't poor. We weren't rich, either."

"But you never went hungry. You never saw children die because they needed food or a doctor. You probably never saw how such people live. Are you from a country village?"

"No, sir, I'm from Edinburgh."

"Ah, I thought I heard that delightful Scottish lilt in your voice. Well, I daresay Edinburgh has its poor too."

"I came to London thinking it would be better. My parents died, and I came here to work for my aunt. I found, though, that London is only bigger, dirtier, and poorer in many respects than my own city."

"And yet it is alive, vital, the only city I'd ever want to call home. I feel so deeply about it, Miss Fiona. I want it to be the best city in the world. It can be, but it has to change. It must let all of its citizens realize their potential, not just a few. It must provide education for all of the children so that they can have better lives than their parents have."

"My, sir, you are quite a crusader. And how does a

man like the Viscount Huxley fit into your scheme? It seems strange that he, a member of the peerage, should be willing to sponsor a man who wants to destroy his very way of life."

"No, no, I do not wish to destroy anything, Miss Fiona." Rogers protested, a pained note in his vibrant voice. "That is the last thing I want. That would be revolution, and I feel deeply that revolution only destroys. No, I want change—orderly change—brought on by legal means. In the long run, it can only benefit everyone if such a mass of people as our poor can have the quality of their lives improved. We would all be better for it. Huxley realizes this——"

"Yet he comes to a place like this and participates in the beastly things they do. He takes his turn when they rape the poor virgins they drag in here. I saw one young girl tonight—she was nearly nude—trying to escape from her captors." Indignation made Fiona's voice shake. "She pleaded with me to help her."

"And did you?"

Trapped, Fiona muttered, "What could I do for her?"

"Did you protest to your companions?"

"I did, and they only laughed. Maggie Starrett said to give the girl some money, which the baron did."

"And did she take it? I'll bet she took it and went willingly to her fate."

"That's a very cynical observation, sir."

"But true? Confess, now, Miss Fiona, isn't it true? At least she got paid for losing her virginity; otherwise it would have been some country bumpkin who had her behind the cow shed."

"That's what the baron said." Fiona was angry with him for guessing the truth.

"Then don't worry about her. I've been told that some of the young girls Sandwich rapes—and he does like them young and innocent—are grateful to him, for he then sponsors them, gets them rich protectors. Otherwise they'd wind up on the street in the worst slums of the city and grub their lives away, dying early from disease. If they must be whores, they at least are living well."

"It's nice to know what you think of me, sir," she said, her voice icy with rage.

"What I—— Miss Fiona, I wasn't——"

"Come, now, sir, surely you know that I am a kept woman. Werington has set me up in a lovely little house on Hanover Street. I have two servants. I get to come to such interesting places as Medmenham Abbey to see how the *ton* amuse themselves. But I'm a whore."

Rogers, for once, seemed not to know what to say to her.

"I think I must get back inside. Sir Thorton might wake and wonder where I am. He would take a dim view of my being here alone with you, sir."

"I haven't touched you!"

"True; but he wouldn't know that, would he? I daresay he'd assume the worst."

She turned away and started back toward the doorway, realizing for the first time that it was shaped like the access into a woman's private parts. By now she was becoming inured to the lewd decor of the abbey. She passed through the door without giving it a second thought.

Rogers, caught unaware by her sudden departure, hurried after her, calling, "Miss Fiona, please wait."

He was beside her before she got back to the Roman Room, where the sounds of the orgy were deafening.

"I am sorry if I offended you. Who am I to cast the first stone at anyone? I come here. I indulge in all of the activities. You perhaps do not know that I am a married man, but my wife is not able to live with me. I'm only human."

"And," she said maliciously, "you do meet so many important people."

If she thought to disconcert him, she failed, for he said, "I would be the first to admit this, Miss Fiona.

My work is important, and I will do anything necessary to forward my beliefs."

"Can one man do anything to help them?"

"I can try. I can hope to interest other men of good-will. I have already enlisted the aid of one lord; I hope other will join with us."

Fiona couldn't understand why Huxley supported Rogers, and doubted that others would be as foolish. No, the man was living in a fool's paradise.

Inside, the party had deteriorated to the point that Fiona felt out of place fully clothed. Everywhere people were coupling in positions right out of the book Thor had bought for her at the beginning of their relationship, plus some even *that* explicit text had not described. As she headed toward the table where Werington still sprawled, drunk, she heard a familiar voice in one of the alcoves.

"I don't see why we have to hide away in here, Will. All of the fun is out in the main banqueting room." It was her bête noire, the Duchess of Lawton. Obviously Huxley was with her behind the green damask curtains.

As Fiona moved past the alcove, the drapes were parted violently and the duchess, completely nude except for her mask, came prancing out, calling back over her shoulder, "If you won't join me here, then I'll find a more willing partner."

Almost immediately she was accosted by a gross man with pendulous belly who staggered drunkenly. The duchess seemed quite willing to have him paw her.

How could she? Fiona thought, looking the other way. And how could Will Huxley—— But she mustn't think about him. He had played her false, saving her virginity just so that she could be used in the Black Mass. He was despicable! She would yet find something she could use to discredit him. He deserved nothing less than total revenge.

She found that Samuel Rogers was still at her heels.

"Your escort looks much the worse for drink. Would you like for me to see you back to London?"

"No, I dare not, sir. Thor would be furious with me."

"Then let me help you get him to a water taxi."

"We came with Lady Starrett and the Baron Ames. I daresay they'll help me when they are ready to leave."

"I'll look for them," he said. "Meanwhile, would you prefer the privacy of one of the alcoves?" Seeing the look on her face, he hastened to assure her, "Alone, Miss Fiona. I have no wish to force myself on you, although I must say you are a most desirable young woman. Were I free, I would do my best to take you away from Werington, who does not properly appreciate you." He looked over at the drunken young lord and his mouth twisted with disgust. "Come, wait in here until I locate your other companions."

He escorted her to a curtained nook, got her a glass of claret, and then disappeared briefly. He came back soon with the dreary news that both Maggie and Dan were too much involved in some group activities to want to leave the party.

"I told them that I would take you and Werington home," he said.

"But you'll have to leave the party."

"To be in your company, I would leave an affair at court," he told her gallantly.

Quickly he found two of Dashwood's footmen, who carried Werington down to the quay and got him settled in the boat. Then they began the journey through the night back to London.

CHAPTER 14

"It's scurrilous!"

Fiona had hurried to greet Werington, not sure what his attitude would be toward her today. Rogers had hired a coach when they got back to London from Marlow, and had brought her home to Hanover Street before he'd taken her lover on to his mother's home in Russell Square. By then Werington was beginning to come out of his drunken stupor, but he was not recovered enough to realize what was happening.

Frightened at his words, Fiona asked timidly, "What's wrong, Thor?"

He had a rolled-up newspaper in his hand and waved it under her nose dramatically. "This!"

Not knowing what to expect, she took the paper and unrolled it, noticing that it was rather poorly printed. *The London Man,*" she read from the masthead. "What's in it that has you so upset?" Quickly she glanced through it for the society gossip, fearing that some tidbit about Werington was the cause of his anger; but all the articles appeared to be political.

"It's garbage," he fumed, "and I know who's behind it, too—that monster Samuel Rogers."

"The editor is listed as John Everyman."

"A pen name if I ever saw one. All you have to do is read the nonsense he spouts to know it is Rogers who is writing it. That man is a menace. They should tar and feather him and ride him out of London on a rail."

Incensed, she said, "If it weren't for Samuel Rogers, you'd still be lying with your face in the currant pudding at Medmenham Abbey, too drunk to stand on your own feet."

"What do you mean?"

"You don't think *I* wrestled you down to the quay, in and out of the water taxi, and into a coach and took you to your mother's house last night, do you?"

"I assumed Dan———"

"Dan was just as drunk as you," she snapped. "It was a delightful evening for me, you understand—my escort dead drunk with his powdered wig in the gravy, and me left unprotected in that mob. Samuel Rogers was more of a gentleman last night than you or any of your noble friends!"

"Did he . . . did you———"

"No, we didn't. I could have, had I chosen, but I chose to be faithful to you. I feel you buy my loyalty." There was scorn in her voice. "But don't rant and rave about Rogers. Just be glad that he was there last night."

"What was he doing at the abbey?"

"The same thing everybody else was," she said drily.

"Who sponsored him?"

"Obviously he has friends in high places." Then, with a sly smile she added, "Huxley was there last night— perhaps he and Rogers are friends. In fact, *he* probably wrote these articles." She hadn't any idea who had written them. Werington probably was right in suspecting Rogers—from the headings on the articles, it sounded like the sort of thing he was preaching—but maybe she could get the *ton* to believe that Huxley wrote the paper. That should make him monumentally unpopular with his peers, and perhaps the king would chastise him.

She discovered that malicious innuendo took seed quickly in fertile soil. Werington said, "Do you honestly think that Will Huxley would write such inflammatory stuff as this?"

Fiona shrugged, triumphant. She could see that her protector already half believed her fiction. "Well, you know he's a friend of Rogers. He was there at Deacon's Hall, hiding his true identity behind those plain clothes he wore, too."

"You're right." Finally, anger gone, he caught Fiona to him in an intimate embrace. "Why do you insist on dressing in stays and gowns when you know I'm coming to see you?" he demanded, voice hoarse with desire. "Come upstairs, Fiona. To hell with Rogers and Huxley and their rotten newspaper. I have more interesting things to do than worry about them."

The whole time she was in bed with Werington, Fiona's mind whirled about endlessly, planning how she could get revenge on Huxley for what he'd done to her. By now all of her anger focused on the viscount, with none left over for those other villains, the Duke and Duchess of Lawton. If somehow she could prove that it was Huxley who was putting out the seditious *London Man* . . . She didn't have any idea how she might accomplish this, but she intended to cultivate Rogers, for through him she might be able to get back at Huxley.

"Are you staying the night?" she asked Werington later as they lay in bed, sipping claret.

"No! No, I have an early appointment tomorrow, I think it would be better if I went home. My valet can get my clothes ready; you wouldn't want to get up so early. . . ."

All she could think of was a line from one of Mr. Shakespeare's plays—something about protesting too much. She didn't press Werington, though. Her existence was very precarious. Since meeting the Honorable Arabelle Perry, Fiona realized just how precarious. "Will I see you at all tomorrow?"

"I may be busy all day. I'll give you some money when I leave. Why don't you rent a chair, go to Hockley to the bearbaiting or something?"

He'd never suggested such a thing before. Fiona's heart froze. Something was wrong. He acted embarrassed, and the offer of money for the baiting sounded all too much as though he felt obliged to her for some reason.

She didn't question him but said only, "How kind. Perhaps I'll go to Vauxhall." She really didn't care for bearbaiting.

Before Werington left, he laid a gold guinea on the dressing table. "Have a pleasant time, Fiona. I'll see you day after tomorrow." He kissed her quickly and fled.

It was a chilling experience. The gold he'd left was to pay for his guilt, she was sure—guilt for what, she didn't know, but she suspected that it involved Arabelle.

What would happen to her if he married Miss Perry? Could she find another protector? If only Huxley—— But that was a fool's dream, and Fiona was fast learning that dreaming was a poor substitute for living. If Werington left her, would he see if he could find another man willing to have her as his mistress, pay her bills, provide a house for her? In a fit of revulsion, Fiona rolled over and buried her face in the goose-feather pillow, fighting back tears that scalded her eyes. She had told Rogers that she was a whore; but she had never actually felt like one before tonight. Was this to be her life, being shunted from one man to another until she began to lose her looks? Then she'd be on the streets, soliciting.

Soon, though, realizing that tears would get her no place, Fiona got up and dressed. She had the rest of today and also tomorrow to herself, from what Thorton had said. Very well, she'd do something amusing. Now, where had she hidden that pamphlet from Rogers, the one listing his speaking engagements? Ah, here, under a stack of chemises in the chest. She sat on a dainty Queen Anne chair by the window and perused the booklet. Rogers was to be in the park this afternoon. Dare she go there again? The other time was at night. Surely she'd be safe in broad daylight. She knew that Rogers found her attractive. Perhaps he could suggest some way for her to spend tomorrow, when Thor wasn't going to be with her.

Again she told Sal and Rolf she was merely going for a walk so that neither could report on her to their master. Although she was sure now that Werington was spending time with another woman—probably Arabelle—he would take a dim view of her amusing herself with another man. Very well, she'd stoop to subterfuge. Only by cultivating Rogers could she hope to get revenge on Huxley.

This time when she arrived at the corner where Rogers was to orate, he was just arriving by chair himself.

Hurrying over to her, he bowed, tricorne over his chest, and exclaimed, "My fondest hope was that you might be here."

She fluttered her fan, hiding a self-satisfied smile. "I find your political views very stimulating, Mr. Rogers."

"I am gratified, Miss Fiona. May I show you to a bench where you can see and hear with ease, but not be bothered with the crowd?"

Somewhat alarmed at his words, she asked, "Will there be the same sort of trouble as before? If so, I do not wish to stay. I thought that in broad daylight . . ."

His manner was reassuring: "Don't fret, Miss Fiona. I think there is no danger today. I only want you near so that I can see your lovely face and feel I am directing my words to you alone."

"A pretty speech, sir." In truth, his manners were as gallant as a duke's, she thought.

He escorted her to a marble bench set at an angle to the small platform from which he would speak. A crowd was gathering, but it seemed much more orderly than the one she'd encountered at night. There were young couples, obviously out to take the air, who paused to listen. The members of the working class were missing in most part, as they would be at their jobs now. There were poor people there, some looking like ruffians; but the mood of the group was not ugly today.

Actually, Fiona paid little attention to what Rogers was saying. She relaxed in the shade and looked at the fashions other young women wore, sure that her sprigged muslin gown of palest blue was quite the thing. She noticed that many of the gentlemen smiled at her, surreptitiously if they were with a lady. She coyly looked down, then looked back up, masking her face with her fan in approved coquettish fashion.

Roger's words flowed over her, and then there was applause from the crowd and shouts of "You're right, governor! We needs a livin' wage" and similar sentiments. Some of the mob surged forward to speak personally with the orator.

Then Fiona was conscious of someone behind her. Turning slightly, she glanced up over her shoulder and found herself looking into the dark eyes of none other than Viscount Huxley.

His eyebrows lifted and he made a leg, sweeping off the cocked hat he wore today. His hair was unpowdered, and the black locks shone like a raven's wing in the sun. "My word, Fiona, you seem to have developed political tastes."

Annoyed that the man's presence could set her pulses to racing, she said coolly, "I was strolling in the park and thought this a pleasant place to rest."

He looked at the noisy mob clustered around the speaker's platform, then smiled sardonically. "I see you are no longer tired."

"I am rested, thank you." She turned back toward the crowd, hoping that Huxley would go away and leave her alone.

"I trust you got back safely last night?" Huxley went on.

She looked back at him, surprised. She'd not realized that he recognized her at the abbey. "Obviously, as I am here."

"Werington was somewhat the worse for drink."

"Most of the people were," she said drily.

"I had thought you'd be at Lady Blaisdell's soiree this afternoon," he said. "I looked for you, hoping to have some time with so charming a young lady."

Fiona frowned. "And why would you think that I'd be there, sir?"

As if realizing his faux pas, he tried to cover up by saying, "I expect to see such a beautiful young lady as you at all the parties."

The look she gave him was scathing, and he had the grace to look embarrassed. His slip of the tongue had told her much, though. Obviously Werington was at Lady Blaisdell's party. Fiona wondered if he'd gone alone or had escorted Arabelle. She was not about to ask Huxley.

By this time the crowd around Rogers was thinning, and he made his way through them to where Fiona and Huxley waited. "Will! I thought you had a social engagement."

Huxley laughed. "I find some of Lady Blaisdell's entertainment exceedingly dull. Today she had a Swedish soprano who was shrill, so I came here to hear your more dulcet voice."

"Did you notice that more upper-class people listened today?" Then he asked Fiona, "Did you think my talk went well?"

"Very well," she lied, not having listened to one word in fifty.

"Would both of you join me for tea?" Huxley asked.

"If Miss Fiona would be so gracious . . ." Rogers said.

It was reckless of her, but she accepted. If Werington could enjoy other company, so could she.

The took tea alfresco at a table under a spreading elm tree. Fiona was very conscious of Huxley. Although he said little, he let her know he was very much aware of her, in the way men have of saying things to a woman without using words. She noticed also that his left eyebrow went up whenever Rogers paid particular

attention to her or gave her an extravagant compliment.
Very well, if it amused him, she'd play up to the older
man. Perhaps it would make Huxley jealous. She asked
Rogers how his campaign was coming and exclaimed
prettily when he said, with no false modesty, that he
expected to win the seat easily.

"Without buying votes, either," he added.

"Vote-buying is scandalous," she said, having read
bits in the papers about some of the elections. "Is it
true that they carry corpses to the balloting places and
let them vote?"

"I daresay it's been tried," Huxley said.

"What would you do if you learned that your opponent was purchasing votes?"

"Look for a wealthy benefactor," Rogers joked.

Yet under his humorous manner, Fiona felt a vein of
truth. The man was very ambitious. He might well
stoop to such means to win if he thought it necessary.

"It's too bad that I cannot vote, or you surely would
have my ballot to count for you," she said, smiling at
Rogers. There, let Huxley think what he might about
her!

When Huxley went to pay the bill, Rogers asked,
"Would it be possible to see you tomorrow, Miss
Fiona?"

Remembering that Werington would be gone yet another day, and thinking that he probably was paying
court to the Honorable Miss Perry, Fiona said, "It
might be arranged."

Beaming with pleasure, he suggested, "Perhaps we
could spend the afternoon at Vauxhall Gardens."

"I would enjoy that, sir."

"Shall I call for you at——"

"I think it might be best if I met you elsewhere."

"Of course." He understood her situation and did not
question her decision.

They arranged to meet a block from her house on
Hanover Street. When Huxley returned, he offered them

both a ride in his landau, which was waiting at the park entrance.

"I hope I may see you again, Fiona," Will murmured as he handed her into the landau.

She smiled but gave him no answer. How gratifying to have both men wanting her.

Ever mindful of the servants, she said she wished to do a bit of shopping at a draper's on Oxford Street. When Huxley's coach deposited her there and drove off, she walked back home. If she was going to play this sort of double game with Werington, she must be very discreet.

CHAPTER 15

Fiona hadn't realized how little she got out until she and Rogers strolled through the interests and entertainments of Vauxhall Gardens the next day. They had crossed the Thames in a light wherry, a very pleasant boat ride on a fine day. She had not been to the gardens often, lacking the shilling admission; but today she reveled in all its beauties. For a time they enjoyed the winding paths, the statuary—a far cry from the lewd displays at Medmenham Abbey—and the fountains.

"We'll go down this path and be in time for the Waterworks," Rogers told her, and they got to a good vantage point just as the specially set fountains gushed up in a spectacular display, the sun making rainbows in the mist.

"That's lovely," Fiona breathed. "I'd not seen that before."

"My poor wife always enjoyed the Waterworks," he said.

Fiona scarcely knew what to do or say. Maggie Starrett had told her the sad story about Rogers's wife in Bedlam.

"My wife is ill," Rogers went on quietly. "Perhaps you've heard. Unfortunately I had to have her committed to Bedlam—she became dangerous to herself— as I couldn't afford a private asylum."

"How very sad, Mr. Rogers."

"Yes. I miss her, of course, but she'll never get well, I fear, and while she lives, I cannot remarry."

"No, I understand that." Why was he telling her all this?

Then, abruptly, Rogers suggested, "Let's sit here for a while. Later we may be able to hear the musical bushes."

"What are they?"

He smiled, transforming his rather plain face. "Music seems to be coming from the bushes; actually there are musicians in a hole in the ground nearby." He laughed. "I understand that after a rain, the hole fills with water and the musicians get their feet soaked. It isn't one of Mr. Tyers' cleverer amusements, I fear, although most of the gardens are wondrously entertaining. But I wanted to talk with you about your future."

"About *my* future?" Fiona began to wonder what she'd got herself into by coming here with this man.

"I understand about your arrangement with Werington, and I attach no blame to you, my dear. We do what we must to survive. But what will you do when he marries? I understand that the engagement is being announced at a ball tonight." Then, sudden concern in his face, he cried, "Miss Fiona, are you all right? You are white as a sheet."

She fumbled for her vinaigrette, uncorked it, and sniffed the pungent *sal volatile*.

"I am sorry," he murmured. "You didn't know, did you?"

She took a deep breath, put away the smelling salts, and forced herself to smile even though it felt as if her face might shatter in a million pieces. "No, I hadn't heard. Werington didn't bother to tell me the good news. Miss Perry, I presume."

There was pity in Rogers's look, and Fiona resented it. She'd not be pitied. She'd manage somehow when Thor discarded her, as she was sure he would once he married the red-haired Arabelle.

"I'm truly sorry, Miss Fiona. I thought you knew."

"Not that it was official. I knew about her, of course."

"Will you manage after he marries?"

"Oh, yes—quite nicely, thank you."

"Good. He'll settle an income on you, then."

Settle an income on her—what nonsense! Fiona knew her lover too well to expect that. No, he'd feel no obligation to her whatsoever once he married. Maggie Starrett, who'd known Werington much longer than she, hadn't suggested any such thing; only that Fiona could find another protector.

As if reading her mind, Rogers said, "I wish I were rich, my dear. I'd willingly pay the rent on your little house. Unfortunately——"

"How kind of you to think of it," she said, ready to break into tears.

Coming here today was for Fiona an act of defiance; she never dreamed that this would be the day her future would disappear. And this kind man, wishing she could be his mistress but not having the money to support her, almost broke her heart. Life with him would be a far cry from life with Werington, she thought. Rogers, unlike the selfish lord, might well be tender with her.

"Let's walk about the gardens," she said, no longer wanting to sit and chat.

"Of course. Later there will be a concert at the rotunda, and I think I spied a puppet show down one path we passed."

The puppet show was also Fiona's undoing. They were within sight of the stage, and could hear the delighted laughter of children, when Fiona saw a couple who had paused briefly to watch Punch and Judy battle. It was Werington, done up in bright green, and his new lady love in a gown of soft rust that went well with her high color.

Fiona stopped short and uttered a little sound that made Rogers immediately turn to her with concern.

Then, seeing the direction in which her eyes stared, he, too, looked, just as Werington and Arabelle turned toward them to continue their stroll. Acting quickly and instinctively, Rogers moved so that he stood between Fiona and the advancing couple.

"Down this little path to the Greek temple," he urged, breaking her out of her stunned silence. "If we go now, they'll not see you."

Grateful that he'd recognized the danger and acted, Fiona picked up the skirts of her summery gown and fled toward the marble columns ahead, with Rogers following more sedately behind her. Once in the concealing shadows of the temple, she stopped, breathless. "Did Thor see me?"

"I don't think so. He was all eyes for Miss Perry."

"I suppose I should be glad of that," Fiona said bitterly.

"What would you like to do now?"

The day was ruined for Fiona. "If they are having a ball tonight, why aren't they at home resting? Why did they have to come here?" she complained. "I think I'd better leave. I'm sorry, sir, to spoil your outing, but I would spend the next hours in worry that we might happen onto them again."

"As you seem to think that Werington will abandon you, why worry about him today?"

"He can be ugly when he's angered. He owns me, you know."

"That's utter nonsense, Fiona. You aren't a slave; you are a lovely young woman."

"He keeps me, sir, and that gives him leave to be angry with me whenever he chooses."

Roger's face twisted with disgust. "No man should own another person. If it were I——"

"But it isn't," she reminded him gently.

They walked slowly back to the river, making sure that Werington and his betrothed were not in sight. Rogers was uncharacteristically silent while their boatman poled the small craft across the Thames. On the north shore, Rogers hailed a public coach and took her to her home.

"Don't stop at the house but on the corner," she said. "I sometimes think the servants spy on me and report to Thor."

"Fiona, maybe I can help you solve your problems with Werington."

"How, sir?"

"Could you call me 'Samuel'?" he asked diffidently.

Fiona smiled. If they were to be friends . . . "Of course, Samuel. But how can you help me?" He'd made it plain that he couldn't afford to set her up in an establishment as his mistress.

"I have an idea, but I can't discuss it with you yet. Do something for me—and for yourself, incidentally: don't be panicked into any rash situation. Give me a few days. I shall see if I can't work out something."

Curious now, Fiona tried to get Rogers to tell her what he had in mind.

"I'm sorry, but I must consult with someone else. If I do arrange things—— No, I can't ask any commitment from you until I can offer you something certain." Then, sadly, he said, "I must go to Bedlam Sunday to see my poor wife. Do you believe in God, Fiona?"

"Yes, of course."

"This is an age of unbelief," he told her. "So many of the *ton* scoff. I wonder myself why a supposedly loving God imposes such burdens on us. My wife and I longed for a child, and when it finally came, it was born dead. Her mind snapped. I hoped for a time she would recover, but the doctors finally told me that she would always live in that other world of delusions. I loved her, Fiona; I still do, I suppose"—his voice throbbed with emotion—"yet when I visit her and see her as she is, when I know I am tied to her until death, at times I almost hate her. Is that a dreadful thing to admit?"

Sorry for him, for he was greatly agitated, Fiona said truthfully, "It must be very difficult for you, Samuel."

"I long for a true marriage. The time may never come when I am free." He was quiet briefly as the horse clopped along Regent Street. "If I were free, I would beg you to be my wife."

Not expecting such a declaration, Fiona was speechless.

He gave a wry smile. "I shouldn't have said that, I suppose, but it's true." Then, briskly: "But don't despair. I will see if I can't arrange something for you, my dear. It will require some discretion on your part— there'll be things I won't be able to discuss with you— but if it works out, would you be willing for me to be your protector?" He gave a little shrug. "I'm scarcely the young, handsome lord you've been used to, but I would cherish you."

Tears came to her eyes then. What a good, kind man he was. "As it is all now imagination, I shan't give you a firm answer, Samuel."

Could she be happy with him? He was more a father figure than a lover; yet she knew that soon she might be thrown on his mercy, and she would probably accept his offer.

That night, knowing that Werington was being officially announced as the Honorable Arabelle Perry's betrothed, Fiona shed lonely tears. She'd never loved Werington. In fact, she had to admit that she had used him even as he had used her. She had accepted his protection and given herself to him in return. It was a cold-blooded business arrangement; but perhaps all arrangements between the sexes were such. She had little real knowledge of such things. If her parents had ever loved passionately, she could not have known from their actions at home. It was not at all unusual for them to refer to each other as Mr. McQuade and Mrs. McQuade. She'd never seen any overt physical affection between them. Were all marriages like this? Was romantic love found only in novels? If so, life was even bleaker than she had imagined.

Fiona prowled about the house until she saw Rolf in a charming little drawing room. He was in his butler/general factotum guise, and he smiled slyly at her as he poured her claret. He knew. He was aware that Werington was going to marry someone else. Anger flared in her breast. How dare Werington put her in such a position! Yet even as she fumed, Fiona knew that she had no recourse. Her arrangement with Sir Thorton was only that—an arrangement. She had no legal rounds for holding him. She was satisfactory as a mistress, but no young aristocrat would ever consider marriage to her; it simply wasn't done.

Her only training was as a milliner's assistant, but as the Duchess of Lawton had fixed it so that she couldn't work in any good millinery shop in London, she would have to seek work in some other city or continue in her present way of life. Being scrupulously honest with herself, she admitted that this life was far pleasanter than working long hours trimming bonnets for ladies; so she must find another protector once Werington left her. How soon would that be?

This question was answered unpleasantly the next afternoon. She was doing some embroidery in her sitting room when Rolf came to announce a visitor:

"A lady, miss." His tone made it plain that Fiona was not a lady. Indeed, he was ofttimes impertinent.

"Did she leave a card?"

"No, miss, but she said she was a friend. I put her in the drawing room."

It could only be Maggie Starrett, who had never called on her before. Fiona didn't know any other ladies who might call on her. She was still *en negligee,* and ordinarily would have rung for Sal to dress her before she received a guest; but it was only Maggie, who would not stand on ceremony. Her robe was lovely, a rustling creation of rose taffeta in the Watteau sacque style, falling full from her shoulders. Her hair was caught up in ringlets on top of her head and topped with a white lace pinner.

Hurrying down to the drawing room, she swept in, crying, "How nice to see you!"

But it wasn't Maggie's tall, willowy figure carefully ensconced on a Kent chair; it was the Titian-haired Arabelle, looking like the cat who has just been into the cream crock.

Arabelle was the epitome of formal attire. She was in a proper afternoon dress of blue watered silk with an embroidered stomacher; her hands were covered with lace mitts that extended to the elbow; and she wore a fetching broad-brimmed straw hat decorated with silk flowers. Fiona's milliner's eyes assessed the hat as costing upward of twenty-five guineas.

Caught short, Fiona stopped in her tracks, only to see Arabelle's full lips curl in a smug smile. Not to be outdone by the Honorable Miss Perry, Fiona said, keeping her voice cool with tremendous effort, "May I congratulate you on your betrothal?"

Arabelle nodded grandly, the lady acknowledging the good wishes of a servant. "Thank you, Fiona. It is about that engagement that I wish to chat with you."

Indeed! The effrontery of the woman! Fiona was determined not to let Arabelle know how upset she was over Werington's impending marriage. "May I offer you a glass of wine?" When Miss Perry nodded, Fiona moved to the embroidered bell pull and gave it a sharp tug. Sal came in so fast that she must have been waiting outside the drawing room, eavesdropping.

"Madeira for us, please." As soon as they had glasses of the tawny wine and Sal had left reluctantly, Fiona moved to the attack. "Forgive me for receiving you en déshabillé," she said. "I was expecting Sir Thorton." She knew she'd scored by the way Arabelle's nostrils pinched.

"He may not visit you today. We were up very late. He's probably much too weary for the kind of activity he finds here."

"Ah, did you wear him out, Arabelle, celebrating the betrothal?"

Arabelle flushed, a most unbecoming state with her pale coloring. "I do not grant my favors to any man before marriage."

"How quaint! I thought it was *de rigueur* in the *ton.* Do you mean to tell me that Thor hasn't invited you to Medmenham Abbey yet? How dull he must find you."

"Whore!" She spat out the word in spite. "Let me tell you something, Scottish slut: When I marry Thor, you will not ever seen him again."

"I shouldn't want to. I don't share my men with the likes of you." It did Fiona's heart good to see Arabelle's eyes and mouth open to wide *O*'s. Then she had a deliciously malicious thought. "I have a wedding gift for you, if you'll excuse me for just one moment while I fetch it." She swept to the door, then turned back. "It is of such an intimate nature that I don't want my maid to bring it."

In a few minutes she was back, carrying with her the book of pornographic drawings. "Thor gave me this, but I'm sure he'd now want you to have it," she said, leafing through the book quickly to find the particular position she hated. "See? This is what he likes—this and all of the others in the book. You must study it well so that you can please him, or he may seek me out in frustration after you are wed."

She thrust the picture under Arabelle's eyes, laughing in delight as she saw the young woman pale to chalky white, then flush an ugly red, eyes riveted on the explicit details of the picture.

"Thor will be so pleased that I'm thinking of his pleasure," she said smugly. "Arabelle! How naughty of you, throwing Thor's favorite book on the floor! He'll be disappointed in you, my dear."

"Oh!" Arabelle sprang up and fled the house, not even closing the door behind her.

As Fiona heard her carriage rattle off down Hanover Street, she picked up the book and carried it to her room. There was just one little thing left to do. Ringing for Sal, she demanded paper and cord.

"Do you want me to wrap something for you, miss?"

"No, no; just bring me the things. And I'll want Rolf to deliver a package for me."

She wrapped the book of lewd pictures, addressed it to the Honorable Arabelle Perry, and instructed her manservant, "Deliver this by hand to this address on Lamb's Conduit. Make sure that Miss Perry receives it herself. It is not for anyone else."

She only hoped that Werington would be with Arabelle when she opened her wedding present.

CHAPTER 16

Fiona regretted her rash gift that evening when Werington came storming in, livid with rage, the offending book under his arm.

"How dare you! How dare you show such a vulgar volume as this to Arabelle?"

Frightened of him yet determined to fight back, Fiona said succinctly, "You gave it to me and told me to study it so that I could give you pleasure. I was only trying to be helpful. After all, once you are married to the Honorable Miss Perry, she will be sharing your bed, not I. You'll have to derive your pleasure from her buxom body, not mine. And as she is reputed to be not only a virgin but also a prude, I thought that she needed the instruction more than I, so I passed along the book to her."

He slapped her then, so hard that her head snapped back. It was the last straw. Catching up the first thing she laid hands on, a silver candlestick, she swung wildly at him, grazing his chin with the base of it.

"You little whore!" he snarled.

"And who made me that? You did! I was a decent girl until you tricked me into that dreadful time at Medmenham Abbey. Why don't you take your betrothed with you next time you go?"

"She's a decent young lady of good family."

"Most of the people there are members of the *ton*. She'd be quite at home with her own kind."

Fiona fully expected Werington to strike her again; but perhaps he was frightened by her fierceness, for instead he told her that they must talk.

"About what? Your wedding? My position here?"

"All of those things."

"What is there to talk about? Arabelle has been here already, making it plain to me that she won't allow you to see me once the two of you are wed."

"She doesn't have to know everything I do."

Fiona smiled to herself. So Werington was already chaffing at the constraints his bride would put on him. "She isn't stupid, Thor. If you keep me on here, she'll know."

"Perhaps I can find another place," he said casually. Then, as if they'd not quarreled, as if he'd not struck her nor she him, he caught her to him and kissed her with passion. "Let's not fight," he breathed, letting his lips slide down her throat to her white bosom. "Let's go to bed."

"And what if I don't choose to?"

"Then I'll toss you out into the street penniless and naked. I've paid for all of your clothing, don't forget."

There was an ugly undertone to his voice that stopped Fiona from answering him back. He could be very cruel when he was crossed. Now was not the time to anger him further.

He had said he wanted to talk to her; but, with his passion aroused, Werington now had nothing in his mind but bedding her. Even while she submitted and feigned pleasure, Fiona was planning. She knew that her interlude with Werington was almost at an end. He might pretend to her that he would keep her as his mistress after he married Arabelle; but Fiona knew that the jealous Miss Perry would never countenance such actions. She might tolerate his having a mistress; what she would never allow was for that mistress to be Fiona McQuade. So Fiona knew that she must plan for her own future somehow. Rogers had told her he might be able to arrange something; but she put little faith in that. The man desired her, just as Werington did, and that was coloring all of his thinking about her.

When he was done with her, Werington fell into a heavy sleep. Fiona lay awake beside him, not daring to move for fear she would wake him and he would want her again. All kinds of thoughts ran through her mind. She even considered going back to Edinburgh. Maybe she could persuade Werington to give her enough money so that she could set herself up in a small millinery shop of her own and earn an honest living. Perhaps in time she would even meet some decent tradesman who would not know of her lurid past and who would marry her.

Even as she thought it, Fiona knew that it would never happen, for several reasons. First, Werington was inclined to be close with his gold unless it was spent for his own gratification. Second, although she hated to admit it even to herself, Fiona had come to like the good life. She didn't enjoy what she had to do to pay for her easy situation, but she preferred going to bed with Werington to slaving in a shop, catering to the whims of the *ton,* always having to be polite to them the way Aunt Eulalia was, fawning on them, ignoring their insults. Fiona was much too spirited to put up with this.

A good marriage was the ideal solution to her problems; but where was she to find a man willing to take her as a wife, knowing that she was damaged goods? No, her only solution lay in finding another patron when Werington abandoned her. She would talk with Lady Starrett the first chance she had. Maggie, although an aristocrat, was very democratic in her manner. She had suggested to Fiona that she might find another protector. Perhaps she could suggest some man who would be willing to pay Fiona's support if she would accommodate him.

Next morning Werington didn't even mention the talk he had planned to have with Fiona. He even joked a bit about the book she'd passed along to Arabelle. "Did you show her the book or did you just . . ."

Picking up the offensive volume, Fiona leafed quickly

to the vulgar picture she'd shown the prim and prissy Miss Perry. "I told her you liked to do it this way."

"Gad, Fiona! It's a wonder she didn't flee screaming when I called on her yesterday," he sniggered, "although I trow I *would* enjoy having my luscious Arabelle in that position."

"Perhaps she'll refuse," Fiona said spitefully.

His face flushed dark with anger. "She'll be my wife; she'll have to submit."

"I've seen little submissive about Arabella. I daresay she'll have a list of excuses to refuse you long enough to fill a book this size."

"Then I'll come see you," he replied. When Fiona said nothing, he added, "I've been invited to the abbey again. We'll go together."

"And what of your darling Arabelle?"

"I'll make some excuse to her, plead business, tell her I must travel to Bath to look after some property I own there. I've been invited to fill in for one of the regular friars, so finally I'll get to participate in the Black Mass."

Remembering that horrible experience, Fiona felt sick. "And must I serve all of the men as I did that first time?"

"Good heavens no, Fiona; you are no longer eligible. But they want you to be one of the nuns who helps prepare the virgin. If they like you, they'll invite you again. You might even find another patron there once I'm wed."

There, he'd said it, just as she'd thought he would. He had no intention of keeping her on as his mistress once he made the buxom Arabelle his blushing bride. Fiona had no wish to be one of the nuns at Medmenham Abbey, but she knew she had little choice if she went with Werington. If she refused, he might well terminate their arrangement on the spot. Very well, maybe if she kept her ears open, she could get some gossip about Huxley. It was strange that Rogers seemed not to talk about the viscount. Perhaps the stories making the rounds were false. Maybe he just happened to be at Deacon's Hall that night when they'd gone slumming. Fiona recalled that time vividly. It was Huxley who'd cautioned them and told them it was stupid of them to be there flaunting their elegant clothes in the faces of the poor devils who'd come to hear Rogers talk. Yet she was sure he and Rogers knew each other.

Since that one copy of *The London Man,* Fiona had not seen the inflammatory paper again. *Could it be Huxley who wrote the articles instead of Rogers?* Maybe she should ask Samuel the next time she saw him— and she knew that there *would* be a next time. He was interested in her as a woman, not as a political ally. He'd seek her out again. She wondered if he'd be at the abbey this time, too. It still seemed strange to her that the peers tolerated him, for he advocated all the things that would lead to the breakdown of their kind of government, their easy lives.

Finally she slept, an uneasy, dream-filled sleep in which she was once again the sacrifice on the abbey altar.

Maggie Starrett was also playing "nun" that night at Marlow, so Fiona felt a bit better about her role. The two of them drew the job of dressing the virgin for the rites. Tonight's candidate was a buxom farm girl not at all reluctant to take part.

"See, Fiona," Maggie whispered, "you needn't have a bad conscience about this one!"

"When I 'eard about 'ow me friend Moll got two whole shillin's for bein' in this party, I told 'er to get me invited," the girl said, giggling. "Me dad's helper wanted me to do it with 'im in the 'ayloft, but I refused 'im. 'E didn't 'ave no shillin's, 'e didn't!"

This one needed a bath and made no objection to stepping into a tin hip bath and being scrubbed. She downed the drugged wine without a murmur, smacking her beestung lips over it. Even when the drugs began to take effect, she only giggled and let Fiona and Maggie lead her, staggering, down the hall to the chapel.

Masks or not, it didn't take Fiona long to spot both Huxley and Rogers in the Roman Room. Once she and Maggie delivered the virgin to the friars, their work was over. Fiona rather wanted to change out of her "habit," as it was so revealing, but Maggie told her that they had to stay nuns for the entire evening.

She decided that it might be a good time to talk with Rogers, as he seemed not to have a woman at that moment, and approached him. His eyes lighted up when he saw that one of the nuns was interested in him.

Before she realized what he intended, Roger's hand slid through the slits in the draperies that formed her habit, and cupped a breast, his thumb caressing one nipple. To her surprise, it sent shivers of sensations through her body. This had never happened to her when she was with Werington. Her performance with him was completely mechanical, geared to give him maximum pleasure while she got nothing from it. Involuntarily she swayed toward Rogers, then realized what she was doing when he put his other arm around her and pulled her to him in an ardent embrace.

"There's an empty couch over there, dear sister," he breathed into her ear, pulling her along with him eagerly.

The last thing Fiona wanted was to couple with Rogers in front of all these people. It was a paradoxical situation, for she felt a surge of desire for the man even as she was pulling away from his questing fingers. "Please, Samuel, it's Fiona," she begged in an agony of embarrassment.

"Fiona! Oh, I've wanted you from the first moment I laid eyes on you," he groaned, not loosing his hold on her for a moment. "Come, we'll find a more private place than this."

"No, no," she insisted. "Werington will be furious."

"Oh, bother Werington. Where is he, anyway?"

"He's participating in the Black Mass."

"Then he'll be occupied for quite a while. And so shall we, my dear, so shall we."

Just then, though, the door leading into the chapel was flung open and the monks came hurrying into the Roman Room, Werington among them. The ex-virgin was still nude, her hair streaming down to her waist, so that her breasts peeped coyly out of the tresses; but there was nothing coy about the rest of her well-used body. She clung to the arm of one of the friars, perfectly happy in her role.

Fiona pulled away from Rogers. "Werington's here," she hissed.

"They all look alike in those monks' habits."

"I know him," she said drily.

Werington looked about the hall, obviously trying to find her; so she slid out of Rogers's embrace before her lover saw them together.

"I want to talk to you, Fiona," Rogers pleaded.

"Talk wasn't what you had in mind just now."

"Well, I'm a man, and you are an enticing woman. What do you expect when you come to Medmenham Abbey—chastity?"

"Scarcely that" was her bitter reply. "Now I must go." She hurried through the riotous crowd to Werington's side.

"Ah, here you are, Fiona. Come on in this next room, the library. There's going to be a delicious new game the Earl of Bute thought up, called 'pig in a sack.' "

"How do we play it?"

"First get out of all your clothes," he ordered.

"But there are other people in here," she hissed angrily.

"Oh, for heaven's sake, Fiona, act your age. Get

behind that high-backed chair if you must, but get undressed."

Reluctantly she did as he commanded, sliding out of the fall-away nun's habit in moments. "Do I leave on my mask?"

"No, everything off."

As she laid the coif and mask on top of the habit, her lover moved behind her. In a trice, he'd clapped a burlap bag over her head and let it fall down over her shoulders.

Caught off guard, Fiona had a horrid sensation of suffocating. With frantic hands she tried to claw the bag up over her head, but Werington caught the bottom of it and held it in place.

"Fiona, behave! You have to wear this for the game."

"But all the rest of me is naked."

"So I can see, my dear." His free hand caressed her bare bosom, but it didn't send shivers through her as it had when Rogers's hand had found her breast.

"Stop it," she said, trying to hold his hand. "Someone will see."

Then there was a loud call—"Number one!"—and Werington shouted, "That's my number!"

He caught Fiona's forearm in a tight grip and urged her forward. She tried to pull away but couldn't; then she stumbled along, protesting, "Thor, I can't see where I'm going." If she looked straight down, she could see her own feet and a bit of Turkish carpet.

"Come along; I'm guiding you," he said. "We're first!"

"Where are we go——" A door opened and sound burst in on them. "Thor! Not the Roman Room! Not naked!"

He laughed lewdly. "They can't see your head at all, Fiona. It's a marvelous disguise. That's the whole idea."

Then someone caught her other arm, and Fiona was lifted up so that she was standing on something, possibly a table. A loud cheer went up. Horrified, she tried to cover her nakedness with her hands; but she needed as many hands as a Hindu goddess to succeed.

"Don't cover it up, lovie!" someone shouted drunkenly. "Wanna see what I'm bidding on!"

And then Werington's voice, raucous with excitement, called, "Well, gentlemen, what am I bid for this lovely piece of flesh? Do I hear one guinea?"

"One golden guinea!" the drunk called out.

"Two!" another voice echoed.

"Turn her around," someone else ordered. "I can see a luscious bosom, but I want to see her bottom, too."

Someone jumped up beside her and made her turn around. There were whistles and shouts, and the bidding went higher and higher. If she'd had any kind of weapon to hand, Fiona would have killed Werington willingly. She didn't know just what was to happen, but she knew she was being auctioned off to the highest bidder. It was, in a way, even more humiliating than the first night she'd been brought here as an innocent virgin. To her revulsion, she even heard some women bidding on her!

Then two voices were all that were left in the bidding, and both of them were all too familiar to Fiona. She prayed that Samuel Rogers would outbid Huxley, for it had to be his voice that kept raising the bid each time Rogers called out a new figure.

Finally Rogers dropped out of the bidding, grumbling, "I'd sell my soul for that creature, but souls aren't selling well this week—mine least of all."

There were shouts of laughter at his speech. Huxley bid one more time, and Werington shouted, "Sold to the gentleman who bid five hundred guineas. Come and claim your prize, sir!"

Fiona wanted to tear the bag from her head and flee from her fate, but she had no chance to escape. There was the clink of coins, and then she was swept off the table, held in arms like bands of iron, and carried away as the crowd cheered.

"Here's an empty couch!" someone cried.

"I'll use one of the alcoves, thanks," Huxley answered.

There was the brush of drapes as Huxley pushed through them, and she was rather unceremoniously dumped on a large bed. Out in the main banqueting hall, the bidding started again. This time it was Baron Ames's voice as auctioneer, so no doubt he was selling Maggie to the highest bidder. In fact, Fiona heard Maggie's voice, a bit slurred with wine, shouting, "Come, now, milords, surely I'm worth more than a paltry fifty guineas!" Apparently Maggie enjoyed this kind of thing.

"Well, take the bag off your head and let me see if your face is as enticing as your bosom," Huxley said, throwing himself down on the bed beside her and caressing that bosom with skillful hands. "Who are you, my lovely one?" he insisted. "Let's see if I can get out of my clothes before you get your head out of that burlap bag."

This couldn't be happening to her. Not Huxley! Not here! Not again! Fiona rolled into a fetal ball, turning her back to him, only to have him smack her bare bottom affectionately. She heard a thud as his fashionable red high-heeled shoes hit the floor, then rustling sounds as he rapidly divested himself of his clothing. Last time he'd been wearing that revolting monk's habit and hadn't bothered to take it off. It had been hauled up around his waist when she came out of her drugged sleep to find him taking her in that obscene chapel.

"Come, come, you've been coy long enough." With a none-too-gentle hand, he rolled Fiona back toward him and pulled the bag off her head. With a shock of recognition, he gasped, "Fiona!"

"Surely you must have guessed who Werington was peddling." Her voice was bitter. "Well, what are you waiting for? Surely not my consent. You didn't ask it the last time I was here."

Abruptly he pulled away from her, sat on the side of the bed, and reached for the clothing he had so swiftly discarded moments earlier. "I want no woman who doesn't want me."

"A pretty speech, considering that you raped me the other time!"

"Rape! You'd been had by everyone else there, and you'd not only put up no fight, you'd caught each man to you eagerly, begging for it. That's rape? Then when you saw who I was, you started your silly screaming. I've been the butt of all their filthy jokes since then. I don't know what game you are playing, Fiona, but let me warn you, I won't be an unwelcome partner in it. Little trollop, pretending you were a virgin . . . I made a fool of myself at Lawton's."

Furious, she said, "I *was* a virgin. You ought to know that. I was the 'sacrificial victim' at your rotten Black Mass, and you don't use anyone except virgins."

"Well, why did you come here that day if you didn't want to participate?"

"I didn't know what went on here," she spat.

"A likely story. And now I suppose you'll say you didn't know about the auction."

"I didn't. Thor didn't tell me."

"Ah, yes, Sir Thorton Werington, your lover. I know all about him. Don't try that injured-innocence routine on me, Fiona. Everyone in London knows that Werington keeps his own private whore on Hanover Street."

"Oh, you're *rotten*," she hissed. She got up on her knees and swung at him, catching him a resounding slap on his cheek. In a trice he'd caught her hand and twisted it behind her, hurting her cruelly. Her head fell back in pain, and then Huxley was kissing her, deeply, passionately, and Fiona felt herself respond to him as she'd never responded to a man before in her life. He loosed her hand; and instead of pushing him away, she caught him to her with a little moan as his lips went to her thrusting breasts. Desire welled up in her and she fell back onto the bed, pulling him after her so that his weight was on her in a maddening way, and clasping her legs around him in an agony of passion.

"Oh, Will, I want you so much," she murmured.

For answer, he pulled out of her embrace, catching her arms and yanking them from around his neck. "Little slut! I know what you're after. Werington is getting married, and you want another lover to pay your rent. And to think that I fell in love with you the first time I saw you, when I snatched you from under the hooves of those horses! I didn't care who you were, what your background was. You stood there terrified, and I knew I had to rescue you or die in the attempt. I took one look into those blue eyes of yours and drowned in their promise. What a fool I was; how I misjudged you when you cried rape at Lawton's house. I thought I was saving your virginity for myself. What a dunce I was, as easily duped as some naïve country bumpkin.

"Well, you've come to the wrong person, Fiona, if you are looking for another man to set you up in style. You can't dupe me that way. Five hundred guineas I paid for you tonight. I should have let Rogers take you for four ninety-five—although where he thought he'd get that kind of money, I can't imagine. You're an opportunist, Fiona, a calculating little bitch."

This time he did dress and he strode out of the room without a backward glance, leaving her sobbing on the bed, frustration and humiliation feeding her fury.

CHAPTER 17

Fiona suddenly realized that she had no clothes here. Her own were in the dressing room where she and Maggie had changed into their habits. She knew she could go out into the Roman Room naked as the day she was born and not cause even one eyebrow to be lifted, but she didn't want to do that. If Huxley saw her, he'd—— But she wasn't going to allow herself to think about the Viscount William Huxley, churl. How dare he say he loved her and then walk out on her as he'd just done? And why had he waited until it was too late to declare his love for her? She was furious with him and furious with Werington. How she wished now that Rogers had bid just one more time.

She smiled. That's what she'd do. She'd find Rogers and share this bed with him. It would serve both of those rotten men, Will and Thor, right.

Catching the green cover off the bed, Fiona draped it about her as a mock Roman toga, very appropriate for the banqueting hall, and then quickly pulled the burlap bag over her head as a disguise, holding it out at the bottom so that she could see where she was walking. She knew Rogers's distinctive voice. She'd locate him, than take him into one of the alcoves. He wanted her? He could have her. Thor, in putting her up for auction, had forfeited his rights to her, at least tonight.

By now the party had assumed the proportions of an orgy. Fiona saw men and women not only coupling in public but also tripling and quadrupling. Some were dead drunk, lying on the floor, on couches, on the tables. Deciding that she needed to see more than she could by peeping out from under the bag, she pulled it back off her face. Everyone was so drunk by now that it couldn't matter. She saw Thor on one of the green upholstered couches under a lewd mural, and his partner was the buxom farm girl who'd been a virgin when she arrived here tonight. Obviously the ordeal in the Black Mass hadn't bothered her in the least. She was enjoying her session with Thor who seemed almost too drunk to perform.

Her mouth twisted in disgust, Fiona sought further. From one of the curtained alcoves, she heard Huxley's voice. He certainly hadn't wasted any time finding himself another partner. She couldn't find Rogers anywhere. There were plenty of amorous men clutching at her improvised toga. She twitched the draperies away from their overeager hands and went on looking. In one corner she saw a man sketching. He looked up when she came near and asked, "Will you pose for me—in less than that bedcover, hopefully?"

"Not tonight." She recognized him as William Hogarth, an artist popular with the Hell-Fire crowd. His caricatures of life in London were all the rage.

Someone else lurched by, singing hymns at the top of his lungs, hymns to which he'd put off-color lyrics.

Remembering that Rogers liked the gardens, Fiona drifted out of the abbey and wandered about the twisting paths, still not sure what she was going to do or say when she did find the politician. There were other people in the gardens, and several men indicated that they were interested in her; but Fiona told each one that she was meeting someone. She lost track of the time. At least an hour had passed since she'd come outside, and still she couldn't locate Samuel Rogers. Perhaps he'd gone home by boat earlier.

Fiona was ready to give up her quest, go back inside, and have one of the servants direct her to the dressing room where she'd left her clothes. She had a little money in the pocket she'd left with her gown, possibly enough to hire a water taxi to take her back to London. By now she didn't care what Werington said. He'd made it quite clear that her future was her own concern.

She missed the turning of the path that should have taken her back to the main door of the abbey, and discovered she had entered a boxwood maze. Again she made a wrong turning and quickly found herself lost. Fiona wasn't frightened—she knew that eventually she'd get out of the puzzle—only annoyed, as she wanted to get back to London right away. While twisting and turning through the hedges, which were far higher than her head, she heard voices. Good. Others were in the maze; perhaps they'd guide her out of it. She came to a T in the walkway and wondered whether to turn right or left, as the voice sounded directly in front of her, but the path didn't go that way. Arbitrarily she chose the right-hand turning, but discovered quickly that it curved back the way she'd come and led away from the voice. She went back to the place where the path divided, and went left.

Now the voice was louder, and Fiona realized that it was familiar. Luck was with her. She'd happened onto Rogers. She supposed he had some woman with him; however, as much as he was talking, he couldn't be doing too much else! Perhaps he wouldn't resent being interrupted by her. Then she heard a second voice, but it was too quiet to hear well. It was a deep rumble, though, obviously a man's voice, not a woman's:

"I'll see that this article gets in the next issue," Rogers said. "Can you do another one for me, too?"

Just then Fiona brushed against the branches of the hedge, and it made a rustling sound. Immediately all was quiet. In the stillness she could hear the chirp of a cricket, and a katydid sang nearby.

"Who's there?" It was Rogers.

Fiona decided not to answer. Something secret was going on, something that had nothing to do with the usual activities here at Medmenham Abbey. She remembered the speculation about that scurrilous political paper *The London Man*. Werington thought that Rogers was writing it; but Fiona suspected it was Huxley.

She kept very quiet, hoping that they'd start up their conversation again. Easing along the path, careful to keep to the center of it so that she didn't brush against the hedge again, she listened carefully. The moment she heard Rogers's voice, she stopped short and held her breath, straining to hear what he said. Now he spoke much more quietly than before:

"You'd better go," the politico told his unknown companion. "I'm not sure we're entirely alone."

Again the rumble of a man's voice, but no words to tell who he might be.

"I'll need money," Rogers said, "but I think it might work out quite well. I know we have to move it. This would be a clever cover."

The companion said something she couldn't hear. Just then she saw what appeared to be the end of a bench almost concealed by the turn of the path. She caught up the bedcover from around her bare feet and moved toward it as silently as a wraith. Yes, it was a marble bench! If she stood on it, she might be able to peer over the top of the hedge and see who was with Rogers. They were being so secretive about their meeting that she was devoured by curiosity.

With infinite care, she pulled the bedspread up high so that she wouldn't trip over it and climbed up onto the bench. She could just barely see over the top of the hedge. Unfortunately, the place where the two men stood was very dark. Neither had a torch with him, and as the hedge was high and thick at that point, the faint starlight did little to illuminate the scene. If she hadn't recognized Rogers's voice, she would have no idea who he was. As it was, all she could discern were two figures, one tall and the other short. The

short one would be Rogers. Could the other be Will
Huxley? He was about the right height for the Viscount.
It could also be any number of other tall men. If only
he'd come this way, perhaps she could get a look at
his face.

She was leaning forward cautiously, trying desperately to see him, unfortunately she lost her balance
and had to catch at the hedge to keep from falling.
Again the branches rustled, and the men moved in
alarm. The tall man faded into the shadows and was
gone. Rogers came in her direction. She mustn't let him
find her spying.

Scrambling down off the bench, she blundered back
the way she had come. Then, once around the bend,
knowing that Rogers might well find her and suspect
that she'd been prying into his secret business, she
decided on a bold stratagem. Whirling about so that
she was again facing the way she'd been headed before
she fled from the bench, Fiona called, putting a little
quaver in her voice, "Is anyone near me? I'm lost."
Then, to add to the disguise, she added a very con-
vincing hiccup. She also staggered slightly. Let Rogers
think she was tipsy; that was much better than having
him guess that she'd been the one he'd heard in the
hedge. Again she called, this time louder, "Help!
Help a poor defenseless maiden who has lost her way."
Then she giggled loudly. "And lost her clothes, too.
Poor, poor me."

At that moment Rogers came around the slight curve
in the path and confronted her.

"Oh, a man! Sir, kind sir, will you lead me to
safety?" she begged, going toward him with one hand
outstretched, the other clutching strategically at the
bedspread to keep herself covered, but not too well so.
When he came close enough that she could actually
see his face, she cried out in delight, "Samuel! Is it
truly you? I thought you'd run away from me. I've

looked everywhere for you." Then she remembered to hiccup again.

"Fiona!" She heard mixed emotions in his voice: delight, consternation, and a bit of caution. "Have you been here long in the maze?"

"Oh, is that where I am? No wonder I couldn't find you." She moved close to him and reached up to caress his cheek. "It's scary here in the dark. I kept hearing people walking, but I couldn't catch up with them. Will you rescue me, Samuel?"

Dark as it was, Fiona was close enough to him to be able to see the smile that curved his lips, that smile that changed him from a serious middle-aged man to a fun-loving young one. "And where's Sir Thorton?"

"Don't mention his name. He is not a gentleman."

Then, with a shade of hesitancy in his voice, he said, "I thought you were with Huxley. He outbid me in the auction."

"How did you know it was I? Or did you just lust after my lovely young tender flesh?" she teased. "I had a bag over my head."

"Oh, I knew who it was," he said, his voice hoarse.

Her face was tilted up to him, tantalizing him. With a groan, he caught her to him and kissed her so thoroughly she wound up breathless. His lips slid down her throat and he murmured, "I've wanted you for so long, Fiona, since the first time I saw you in Hyde Park. Don't deny me now."

Again his touch aroused her. She had been willing to lie with Huxley, but he had rejected her, a terrible blow to her ego. Thorton had auctioned her off to the highest bidder, an ultimate humiliation. She was ripe to fall into the arms of any man who professed desire for *her*—not for just anyone at the abbey, for that was the usual way of things here, but specifically for her, Fiona McQuade. She let her arms slide up around his neck, forgetting that she was wearing only the green bedspread draped about her without benefit of pins. It slid down off her shoulders with a slither of silk, leaving her nude.

"Oh, Fiona," he groaned, hands caressing her ardently. "I could take you right here and now."

"The dew is on the grass," she murmured, her own voice not obeying her, sounding shivery and breathless.

"Shall we go back inside?" he urged.

"No!" She wouldn't go in there in front of all those drunken, licentious people. Fiona wanted Rogers now, but not in that Roman Room or even in one of those private alcoves where drunks staggered in to stare.

"There's a little folly just outside the maze," he whispered, "a tiny Grecian temple dedicated to Aphrodite. We'll go there." He caught up the green cover and draped it about her shoulders like a cloak—"to keep the evening damp from your delectable skin"—and led her out of the boxwood maze.

The marble temple was softly lighted with candles; it was a temple of love, with a large bed ready for any who wanted it, and wine on a marble-topped table beside it. Rogers quickly disrobed and joined Fiona on the pleasure couch; but the experience wasn't like any she'd ever had with Werington. With great skill and ardor Rogers wooed her, rousing her to a fever pitch she'd not known was possible. When he asked, "Are you ready, Fiona?" she could only cry, "Yes! Oh, yes!" The exquisite sensation built and built until, with a cry, she found the release she'd never before experienced with a man.

Lying there almost swooning, she murmured, "Lovely, lovely." Now she didn't have to ask Maggie Starrett anything. She knew from firsthand experience what love could be like—or at least the physical expression of love. Werington had never once suggested that she, too, might enjoy this ultimate physical contact between man and woman. Rogers, though, had thought of her as well as of himself, and she would be eternally grateful to him for introducing her to the joys of physical love.

They lay there, limbs entwined, and he caressed her, and told her how desirable she was, instead of rolling away and going to sleep, the way Werington usually did. Later they made love again, and it was different this time, less wild, yet sweet and satisfying.

"Fiona," he asked her after a time, "if I can make the arrangement I mentioned, if my sponsor will pay for the house on Hanover Street when Werington marries, will you share it with me? I wish I could offer you marriage, but with my wife ill—mad—there's nothing I can do. I can't divorce her, nor would I even if I could. I owe her at least that loyalty. Before she fell ill, she was a good wife to me and we were happy. I wouldn't put her aside if I could do so legally, even though I desperately want to have you for my wife."

It didn't take Fiona long to make her choice. She knew that her days with Werington were numbered. He'd not told her when the marriage to Arabelle was to take place; but it could be later this summer. She didn't love Rogers and she was sure she never would—not passionately as she might have loved Huxley had he not played her false. She did respect the man, though, admired him for his principles. Tonight she had learned what it was to be a woman, to participate in this intimate act, not just go through the motions to gratify an uncaring man. Poor Arabelle. Suddenly Fiona felt sorry for the Honorable Miss Perry. She was getting no prize when she took Werington for her husband.

"I am willing to be your mistress, Samuel," she said calmly, even though her pulses still raced from his touch. "I cannot lie to you and tell you that I love you."

Humbly he suggested, "Perhaps in time you will learn to love me, Fiona."

"Perhaps." She owed him that word, though she was sure that she'd never love him. Admire him, respect him, look on him as a good friend and an exciting lover—all this she could do; but love him, no.

"I'll make an appointment with Werington and see if this whole matter can't be settled in a genteel fashion. I don't want to cause you any embarrassment."

"Thor may look on you as his deliverer from an untenable position," she said drily. "Now that he is betrothed to the dear Arabelle, I think he finds me an encumbrance."

"Tonight is not the time to discuss your future with him, I think."

"No, he's probably not sober enough to comprehend what you'd say or make sense in his answer." Then she sighed. "I guess I should go back to the abbey now, though. If he does decide to leave, he'll be infuriated if he can't find me. He's spiteful, Samuel. Handle him with care."

They rose from their couch of love, and Rogers dressed quickly as she draped herself in the green bedspread, making sure now that she was modestly covered. She thought about telling her new protector that she'd never before enjoyed lying with a man, but suddenly she felt shy with him. He was a complex man, with virtues and vices. Fiona felt fortunate that he was willing to be her protector. She wondered somewhat about the financial arrangement. From what he said, his unseen mentor would be paying the bills for the house on Hanover Street. It was a peculiar arrangement. For a fleeting moment she wondered if the day would come when this unknown man would exact payment from her in kind.

They entered the abbey together and moved toward the Roman Room, where from the sounds they could hear, the orgy was still in progress. Fiona had just stepped into the bacchanalian party when Maggie Starrett, stark naked, hurried over to her, breasts bouncing.

"Fiona, where have you been? Thor's been looking for you for ages. He's furious with you."

"Did he want to auction me off again to his drunken friends?" Fiona's voice was bitter.

When Maggie saw that Rogers was with her, her eyes widened. Leaning close to Fiona, she whispered, "If Thor sees Rogers, he'll——"

"Trollop!" It was Werington, drunk but not too drunk to see her or Rogers behind her. He stalked toward them, eyes bloodshot from drink, face flushed with anger. "Slut! Whore!" With one hand he grabbed the green bedspread and pulled it off Fiona, leaving her nude before the others. No one else paid much attention, as half the people there were in their bare skins, but it embarrassed Fiona.

"You're drunk!" she snapped at Werington.

"Not too drunk to see what you've been up to."

"As you auctioned me off earlier, I can't imagine why you care now."

"That was different," he said, slurring his words, tongue too thick to get around all the sounds. "I wanted to do it. Made five hundred guineas." He leered at her. "Proves what a clever fellow I am, to have a mistress worth that much. But I didn't get any money from this man." He glared at Rogers.

Rogers, tight-lipped with anger, picked up the bedspread and threw it around Fiona's shoulders to cover her nakedness. "Go get dressed," he said quietly to her. "Then I'll see you back to London."

"Oh no you'll not!" Werington said loudly.

People were beginning to notice that something was going on. Maggie, clever girl that she was, faded into the background. She didn't want to be involved in what looked to be an ugly quarrel. Members of the *ton* didn't like public scenes.

"Fiona is my property, Rogers," he said belligerently, "paid for by me, answerable to me. I didn't give her permission to give you a tumble in the bushes. Ungrateful little trollop! After all I've done for you, and you take up with this . . . this nobody."

"He's worth ten of you!" Fiona cried, cut to the quick. "He's a true gentleman. You're nothing but a boor with money and a knighthood."

She'd gone too far this time. Werington's face darkened and he roared, "Better than *me?* This nothing? This inciter to riot? Very well! He's poor as a church mouse. See how you like living on nothing as his doxy. I wash my hands of you. Your tenancy at the house on Hanover Street just ended. I'd planned to keep you on until the end of the month, but I don't want to see you there again." He turned and raised his voice even more. "Listen, all of you good friends, I make public this announcement: Miss Fiona McQuade, trollop, is no longer under my protection. Any and all who want to use her now have my permission."

She gasped with rage. How dare he!

"Come, Fiona, I'll take you home." It was Rogers, angry but controlled. "Ignore the drunken sot."

"But what will I do?"

"Do? Just what we planned—live with me. I promise you that you'll be back in the house on Hanover Street soon. Until then you will share my humble quarters." He looked with disdain at the frolicking aristocrats. "Nobody, am I? He may learn to his sorrow that I'm a man to be reckoned with."

With all the dignity she could muster, Fiona swept out of the banqueting hall in search of the room where her clothes were. As she left, her eyes fell on a familiar face. One of the curtained alcoves was directly in her path, and peering out of the drapes was the devilish, handsome face of Will Huxley. She glared at him, but he only raised one black eyebrow and smiled sardonically. Beast! How she hated him, even more than she hated Werington.

CHAPTER 18

The rented rooms off Clerkenwell Road where Rogers lived were a far cry from the elegance of Hanover Street. To make things worse, Fiona had only the clothes she had worn to the abbey. Rogers doled her out a few pounds, and her blowsy landlady recommended a cheap seamstress who ran her up a few very plain gowns for the money. Fiona hated them—she'd become accustomed to the rich silks and satins that Werington had provided for her—but she kept her complaints to herself. She knew that she was lucky to have Rogers looking after her. She wasn't hungry or naked, and he treated her with courtly concern. In bed she was stunned at the sensuality of the man and at the responses he elicited from her in his effort to have her enjoy their lovemaking as much as he did. After living with Thor, she found life with Rogers to be a pleasure.

It was nearing election day, and Rogers made speech after speech in many parts of the city. He took Fiona with him whenever she wished to go, and she began to see that what he preached was in large measure true. The poor of London lived in deplorable hovels. Their rooms in Clerkenwell might be shabby, but they were clean, and their window looked out on a tiny park with green trees. There were places in the London slums where the conditions were so appalling that Fiona felt physically ill just seeing them.

After one torchlight parade through one of these meanest of streets, the men following Rogers turned ugly, fanning out to better sections of the city, attacking lords in their gilt sedan chairs, even clubbing one man outside his own door when he tried to escape from them into his elegant town house.

Next morning, as they breakfasted in their rooms, Fiona asked, "Won't such rioting work against you at the ballot box?"

"Perhaps; perhaps not. It gives me much-needed publicity. A lot more Londoners have heard of me than ever knew the name Rogers six months ago."

"I deplore the violence, Samuel. Lord Berklin could have been killed if his footmen hadn't heard the disturbance and come out with pistols to drive off the angry mob."

"Berklin owns some of the rottenest housing in London, and he charges so much that the men who pay his rents to keep a roof over their families have to let those sheltered families starve for lack of bread, Fiona. Don't feel too sorry for him."

There were times when Rogers went to secret meetings to which Fiona was not invited. From one of them he came back all smiles, and pulling a heavy purse from the deep pocket of his blue stuff coat, he said, "Tomorrow we sign the lease for the house on Hanover Street, my dear. You are too lovely a jewel to have to be seen in such a setting as this."

"Samuel, where did you get all that money?"

"I told you that I was making arrangements."

Not being stupid, she asked rather sharply, "And what do we—I—have to do in return?"

"My 'friend' needs a private room for some of his work. We'll provide that for him and ask no questions."

It was the first time in their relationship that Fiona heard a steely edge to his voice, and it stopped her from asking more questions. If this was the price she had to pay to live again in the luxury of Hanover Street, it was small enough.

"There's money for gowns, too. The wife of an M.P. must dress suitably."

She gave him a startled look at the word "wife." "I'm not your wife, Samuel," she reminded him gently.

He flushed with chagrin. "Oh, Fiona, I think of you so much as my true wife that sometimes I forget you aren't." He caught her to him in a passionate embrace. "I love you so desperately," he murmured, caressing her. "I'd do anything for you—anything."

"Poor Samuel," she whispered, roused by his touch. "You do everything for me as it is. Marriage is only a formality."

Yet even as they lay on their bed, even as he aroused her to a fever pitch of desire, even as she welcomed his body and abandoned herself to her own passion and his, Fiona could not bring herself to lie to him and say that she loved him. She felt that she owed him honesty. Sometimes she wished that she could love Rogers, for he was so good to her; yet more and more often she found herself fantasizing as she lay in bed with him, and the man she longed for was always the detestable Viscount Will Huxley.

The move to Hanover Street was accomplished with ease, as she had little to move and Rogers traveled very light. With a wonderful irony, Samuel had leased the same rooms she'd shared with Werington. The look on Sal's face when Fiona was escorted into the house again was comical.

"Miss Fiona! Or is it 'missus' now?" The old sly look was back on Sal's coarse face. Fiona wished she could have new servants here, but apparently the two went with the house. Perhaps now if they were too insolent, Rogers would manage to get rid of them.

"I'm still Miss McQuade," she said coldly to the maid, "but things will be different now. Mr. Rogers will be in residence at all times."

Fiona knew from the narrowed eyes that Sal had gotten her message and hadn't liked it. Good! She'd always been slightly intimidated by the couple. She was sure that they had spied on her and reported to Werington.

"I understand that Sir Thorton is marrying in Westminster Abbey next week," Sal said, eyeing Fiona.

"How nice for him," Fiona replied, staring down the servant. "Now, I'd like for you to get a bath ready for me." Fiona wasn't particularly anxious to bathe, but it gave her pleasure to know that Sal had to carry the cans of hot water for the hip bath from the basement to the second floor.

She felt a little embarrassed by the mirrored bedroom, but Rogers laughed about it with her, removing all the uglier connotations of such appointments.

They'd been in residence only a few days when he told her to dismiss the servants for the day. "And I want you to go shopping, Fiona. I have money for new clothes for you. Take your time, see all the best drapers on Oxford Street."

"I assume that something will happen here that is not to be seen."

"What you don't know, you can't inadvertently mention," he said. Then, seeing the expression on her face, he hastened to add, "My dear, I am not suggesting for one moment that you would say anything deliberately; but sometimes when we know secrets, they slip out. This must remain as silent as the grave."

"Of course." She knew that this was why they were ensconced in the house. Fiona was dying of curiosity, but now was not the time to try to wheedle the secret from Rogers.

When she returned from her shopping, arriving home at the same time Sal and Rolf returned from their unexpected outing, Rolf asked, "Why have the keys to the wine cellar been taken away from me, Miss Fiona?" He put on an injured air, trying to gain her sympathy. "I haven't been at the claret."

"No one ever suggested that you had." So it was the wine cellar that was being used for some purpose! "Mr.

Rogers will see to the wine cellar in the future," she added, doing her best to put Rolf in his place. She hoped that soon they could get rid of the couple and find more suitable servants. Every time Sal looked at her, Fiona felt like a proper whore; it was there in the woman's knowing eyes. And Rolf was always just short of insolent with her.

She found Rogers waiting for her, claret ready on a tray. He asked about her shopping but made no reference to what had happened while she'd been out.

That night there was a big rally at Deacon's Hall, and Fiona went with him. To her surprise, Huxley was there, escorting a lovely young woman who looked scarcely more than fourteen. Had he and the Duchess of Lawton severed their liaison? She whispered this question to Rogers.

"There are rumors afloat that he no longer goes to the house on Millbank," he said. "Frankly, I never could see what Will saw in that woman. She's a fading rose, can't compete with your fresh beauty."

"He seemed interested enough when I worked for her," she said drily. "But he does seem to have someone younger now."

The young woman with Huxley was as dark as he, from the color of her eyes, although her hair was so well powdered that its natural color was completely covered. She was wearing a rather plain gown; but Fiona's knowing eye saw that it was made of the finest weighted silk in a rich rose that set off the girl's high color well. She carried an ornate walking stick of ebony, with rose ribbons exactly matching the dress flowing from a rosette at the top of the staff. Although she was young, her figure was full, with firm breasts creamy white above the décolletage of her gown. She wore a pompon of rose ribbons pinned to her crown, with streamers down her back and over her round, luscious shoulders. Fiona hated her on sight. She had been able to tolerate the idea of Huxley with the Duchess of Lawton, for the duchess was beginning to show her age, but this young woman was of an even more tender age than Fiona. It was annoying to discover that Will Huxley could still fire her emotions.

She turned away from the couple, but Rogers called out, "Will! How nice that you and your friend could come tonight."

To her dismay, Huxley and his woman joined them; so Fiona had to pretend to be friendly.

"This is my sister, Nell," Huxley said, introducing the girl to Fiona and Rogers.

His sister! Fiona was all smiles and greeted the young Lady Huxley cordially.

"Will tells me that you are going to be M.P. from this district," Nell said, smiling at Rogers.

"I hope so. Next week is the balloting."

"If I could vote, I'd cast my ballot for you, sir."

"I told Samuel just the same thing," Fiona said.

"Then I wish that you ladies had the right of franchise," Rogers said, including both Nell and Fiona in his smile.

After Rogers's speech, which went very well, Huxley invited them to have a late supper with him. He had engaged a private parlor at the Oxford Arms Inn, and they all drove there in his town landau, with driver and footmen to protect them from footpads.

They were sipping claret after a delightful repast of roast goose with currants when Fiona saw the Duke and Duchess of Lawton pass the door, which was open just at that moment so that their serving girl could bring in a molded pudding.

"Will Huxley!" trilled the duchess, sweeping into the room unbidden, her hazel eyes as hard as agate. She took in Nell and Fiona and her lip curled in a knowing smile. "No wonder you've neglected me of late, dear Will," she cooed.

Her odious husband, practically treading on the hem of her mauve velvet gown, had his popped eyes fastened on Nell's delectable young bosom. He muttered, "Can't blame the man."

Huxley, standing, made a leg to the duchess and introduced his sister. It disturbed Fiona to see the look of relief on the duchess's face when she learned that Nell was not his current flame, for she'd felt the same way only minutes before.

"Must have you two over to the house," the duke was muttering, completely ignoring Fiona and Rogers.

The duchess, however, was all too aware of Fiona. Once she learned that Nell was Huxley's sister, all of her barbed looks were for her former wardrobe maid. With a sneer she said to Fiona, "I understand that Werington is marrying the Honorable Miss Perry soon."

"She has my sympathy," Fiona countered sweetly.

Fiona stole a look at Rogers, expecting him to be put out at the slight from the Lawtons; but he just stood there with a faintly superior smile on his face, as if he found them vastly amusing.

When they'd gone, and Huxley and Rogers were once more seated with them, Nell, in her girlish innocence, said, "Will, you were very rude just now. You neglected to present Miss McQuade and Mr. Rogers to their graces."

"We've met," Fiona said curtly.

Rogers, more diplomatically, explained, "The duke is not an admirer of my politics, Miss Nell. He feels threatened, as well he might. Sorry, Huxley, I know they're your friends; but they're typical of what's wrong with England today."

"No need to apologize to me, Samuel," Huxley said easily. "I don't see much of them these days."

Fiona couldn't resist the gibe. "I thought you and the duchess were very *good* friends," she said, and gave him a sugary smile.

His dark eyes narrowed, and he glanced at Nell as if to caution Fiona to hold her tongue in front of his sister. His voice, though, was still casual when he told her, "You know how these things are—friends today, not such good friends tomorrow." He gave an elegant shrug that showed off his broad shoulders in his exquisitely tailored coat.

Against all common sense, Fiona's heart sang at the words. So the gossip Samuel had heard was correct. The duchess and Huxley were no longer lovers.

"I've heard in *The Gazette* about the Duke and Duchess of Lawton," Nell was saying. "They're leading members of the *ton,* aren't they? Her salons are famous."

"Even in the depths of wildest Surrey, gossip flies," Huxley said drily; but the look he gave his sister was indulgent.

No doubt, Fiona thought, he spoiled Nell rotten. What must it be like to have such a handsome, exciting—wicked—older brother? For a girl who'd been an only child, it was impossible for Fiona to imagine. Anyway, her feelings toward the dashing Huxley were far from sisterly, she realized to her dismay. She must get him out of her mind. She turned to Rogers and slipped her arm through his. As she was seldom given to such gestures in public, he looked startled, then smiled hugely, covering her hand with his.

"I feel very important sitting beside the next M.P. from this district," she said, smiling up at him.

"What if you don't win?" Nell asked naïvely. "Isn't your opponent a formidable candidate?"

"Pendleton? He is—very rich, and backed by most of the aristocrats. They have him in their pocket, you see, Miss Nell. He's the incumbent, and they know that he'll vote however they tell him to. This is one reason I decided to try for the seat. I'm not in the pay of the likes of the Duke of Lawton."

But he was in *someone's* pay, Fiona knew. With his own meager resources, they'd not be living on Hanover Street but back in the dreary rooms in Clerkenwell. Could it be Huxley's gold that was keeping her in luxury once more? Yet how could it be? Huxley made no attempt to hide his association with Rogers, whereas whoever was paying their bills was keeping very much to himself.

After dinner, when Huxley and Nell departed, Fiona thought some more about the situation. She wished she could be a little mouse so that she could hide in the wine cellar at Hanover Street. The times when Rogers told the servants they could have the day off and gave Fiona money to go shopping or took her to Ranelagh or Vauxhall to spend the day. Someday she'd find out just who was paying their rent, though what good it would do, she couldn't imagine. She'd wanted to get some scurrilous information about Will Huxley, to ruin him, but apparently it was not he who was their secret benefactor. Well, she'd just have to try to get gossip about him the next time she and Rogers went to the abbey, for she was sure they'd go again. Rogers had made it quite plain to her that he went for political reasons, to further his career.

"With your rich friend, why do you need to keep going to that awful abbey?" Fiona had pleaded. "I hate it there."

"True I have a powerful friend who is free with his purse; but he doesn't have the ear of the king, while most of the Friars of St. Francis do. It never hurts to know these men in power, Fiona, for I intend to be one of them myself one day. Who knows? If I achieve some manner of fame as a Member of Parliament, the king might someday make me a knight or even a peer of the realm. Wouldn't you like to be a lady?"

Lady Fiona. She didn't remind him that even if he were made a lord, she still was only his mistress, entitled to none of the courtesy due his wife.

Every Sunday he left her for several hours while he made the sad, painful journey to Bedlam to see his sick wife. Once Fiona offered to go with him, but he refused. "I don't know what Kathleen might say if she saw me with a beautiful young woman, Fiona."

"If she's mad, she'd not notice, would she?"

He sighed, his face drawn. It made him look years older. "Occasionally she recognizes me. I couldn't take a chance that she would be aware the day you visited. It would hurt her terribly to know that I had taken up with a woman."

It was a sad situation, but there was nothing Rogers could do about it, nor she. In a way it relieved Fiona of the necessity of deciding whether or not she wanted to be the wife of Rogers. As long as his wife lived, even though confined to Bedlam, he was not free to marry. Perhaps it was best that way.

CHAPTER 19

The victory parade was through the streets of London by torchlight, with Rogers carried in an open sedan chair high up on his supporters' shoulders. He made sure that they went along Hanover Street so that Fiona, standing out on the scrubbed marble stoop, could see him in his triumph. Pride swelled in her. Samuel was now an important person, a Member of Parliament. She wasn't his wife, had no official claim to the man; but he loved her, he supported her, and he wanted her to be part of his triumph.

There had been wild rumors throughout London all during the day. Rogers had kept a number of runners near him and sent hourly bulletins to Fiona about what was happening at the polling places. Pendleton, suddenly realizing that his supposedly safe seat was in danger of toppling, had resorted to every dirty trick in the books. He'd voted dead men, getting their names from tombstones. He'd sent in the blind and the sick, and there was even a story circulating that he'd had friends bring a newly dead man and they'd held up the corpse to "vote" for Pendleton. It didn't matter. The poor of London were solidly behind Rogers, who had appealed to them with his indignation at their sordid lot. He'd deplored the taxes placed on them, when they hadn't even enough money to feed their families properly or put them in decent housing. He'd fired them with the desire to better themselves. He'd promised that the government would be more responsive to their needs. They had believed him and voted for him.

Fiona waited up for him, although he didn't get home

until four o'clock in the morning, flushed with victory and gin. She saw a familiar coat of arms on the landaulet that dropped him off at the door of their Hanover Street abode. Huxley had been with him in his hour of triumph.

Rogers came in and swept her into his arms, almost crushing her in his joyous embrace. "I won!" he cried. "I wasn't sure I would, but I won!"

"No one ever deserved victory more than you," she said, kissing him ardently.

"All I could think of, when I knew I had bested Pendleton, was getting home to you," he said, looking deep into her eyes. "It's all for you, my dearest Fiona— all for you."

Yet even as he said it, she knew that she never could fully share in his life as an M.P. She could never hope to go with him to official functions or to social occasions where a wife would be welcome but a mistress frowned upon. Still, she was happy for him and tried to hide from him her own feelings of sadness and inadequacy.

He caught her up in his arms and carried her to their bedroom, where she had only one candle burning. Knowing that he liked for her to do it, she helped him disrobe, still keeping on her pale-green negligee but making sure that it was fastened only at the neck, hanging open from there to the floor, giving him tantalizing glimpses of her nude body as she played valet for him. Then they lay together on the bed, their moving images reflected in all of the mirrors on the walls and ceiling. Flushed with his victory, he was even more ardent than usual, rousing her to a fever of desire before he mounted her and entered her willing flesh. She was wanton, the epitome of an abandoned woman, as her eager body moved under his until their mounting passions exploded in an exquisitely sensual climax that led her to cry out in ecstasy. There was no sleep for either of them, for soon he wanted her again—

and then again—until at last they lay sated and exhausted in each other's arms and the candle guttered out.

Sleep came then, only to be rudely interrupted by an insistent knocking on the door to their bedchamber. Fiona, rousing first, called sleepily, "Yes, what is it?"

Rolf's voice answered, "An urgent message for Mr. Rogers."

By now Rogers was awake. "What is it?" he muttered, still fuzzy with sex and sleep.

"Rolf says there is an urgent message for you."

"What time is it?"

"You'll have to light the candle; the drapes are drawn." But Fiona guessed it was morning, for there were streaks of light at the edges of the velvet curtains covering the window.

"Probably someone wanting to congratulate me," Rogers said, sighing with fatigue. "Couldn't they have waited until later?" He got out of bed, pulled on a robe of maroon wool, and went to the door, smoothing his graying hair with his hands as he did. He opened the door, took a letter from Rolf, and then closed the door in the man's avid face.

Meanwhile, Fiona had opened the drapes to let in the early-morning sun. She stood there nude, silhouetted in the light, and turned toward Samuel; but for once he was not feasting his eyes on her lush charms. Instead he was looking at the note, his face contorted with anguish.

"Samuel, what is it?"

In a voice choked with emotion, he said, "It's . . . Kathleen. She died during the night."

Kathleen—his wife—dead at the moment of his triumph. Fiona stood there frozen, not knowing what to do. Should she go to him and comfort him? Or should she leave him alone in his grief? She knew how ambivalent his feelings had been about the mad woman who was legally tied to him. He wanted to marry her,

Fiona, but Kathleen had stood in their way. Now—oh, God!—now that way was clear.

Hesitantly she moved toward him, one hand out-stretched in sympathy. At first he didn't seem aware of her presence. He read and reread the notice. Then a sob burst from his throat, and Fiona hesitated no longer. On flying feet she was across the red Turkish carpet, and her arms went around him, drawing his head to her bosom, letting him cry his grief until his tears were all gone.

Then, surprisingly, his arms went around her, his lips found, captured, devoured hers, and she felt his male-ness hard against her bare flesh. Without a word he caught her up in his arms, carried her to the bed, and took her—quickly, almost desperately, as if he couldn't get enough of her. Finally, passion spent, he lay relaxed on her, saying hoarsely, "You must think me some kind of beast to do this at such a time."

Fiona understood, though. His emotions, so long held in check, had finally escaped their bonds. "You needed me," she murmured, running her hand through his hair, caressing his wiry body, knowing how much she meant to him. "Don't ever feel guilty, Samuel. You loved your wife, but she's been dead to you for so long now. And you have such a capacity for life. It was not being disloyal to her memory to lie with me at such a time; it was an affirmation of your life. She wouldn't have denied you my comfort, my dear, not if she loved you."

"And now I can have the thing I've wanted so des-perately since the first moment I saw you in that tumbled sedan chair," he said, cupping her chin with his hand, looking deep into her blue eyes. "Now I can marry you, have you legally for my wife, take you with me, have you accepted everywhere I go."

Fiona wanted to cry "No, no! I don't love you! I don't want to marry you!" but there was no way that she could say such harsh words to Samuel, not now when he was overcome with grief and feeling guilty that he could enjoy her with such passion when his wife lay newly dead. He had been so very good to her. She *must* marry him.

Inwardly, however, she rebelled. Marriage was until death did them part. Once they were married, she must forget Will Huxley, forget that he'd said he fell in love with her at first sight, school herself to blot out the lovely fantasies of him that filled her mind when Rogers made love to her. Once she was Mrs. Samuel Rogers, she must be faithful to him in mind and spirit, as well as in body.

"Let's not worry about marriage now," she whispered to him. "We're truly married in everything except law, my dear."

He kissed her passionately but did not make love to her again, even though she knew that he wanted to very much.

"I must get up, dress, go to Bedlam," he told her. "There are arrangements to be made—the funeral, a procession. I am now a public figure and I must bury my poor, dear Kathleen in a fitting manner."

Fiona felt hurt. She knew that she could have no part in this funeral for his dead wife; yet she surprised herself by the depth of her dismay. This was the last time, though. From now on, once Kathleen Rogers lay in her grave, she would no longer be excluded from any part of Samuel's life.

Somehow it became known that Rogers was now a widower, and friends called at the house on Hanover Street, some looking with curiosity at Fiona, who had to play hostess for Rogers while he was out making funeral arrangements. There were cards left, and some pathetic grubby bouquets of fading flowers brought by some of the poor, who looked on Rogers as their only champion. Fiona thanked these people, carefully writing their names in a book so that Samuel would know who had come to offer sympathy. There were eyes round at the sight of this lovely home. Fiona wondered if these poverty-stricken people would have been so anxious to vote for him if they'd known that he was living in luxury.

It was hours before Rogers returned home. As Fiona helped him off with his coat, he sighed. "I'm exhausted. Yesterday the election, today planning for a funeral. Poor Kathleen. What a pity that she never was able to share my triumph. Now all I can do for her is to provide as fine a funeral as possible."

Fiona knew how expensive this could be. "Will you have enough money for——"

"I'll get it if I have to go to the moneylenders." He was curt to the point of discourtesy, almost unheard of for him. He'd never snapped at her before. Immediately he begged her to forgive him. "I'm so tired I don't know what I'm saying."

"Will the procession be from here, Samuel? And will the mourners come back here for the funeral meal?"

He looked so embarrassed that she wished she'd not asked. "Under the circumstances, I thought it better to rent a small hall."

"Because of me."

He caught her hand, pleading, "Surely you understand, Fiona. I just won my seat yesterday. Kathleen was my wife. It wouldn't be seemly to have her funeral from here, where I live with you."

"Of course not." It hurt terribly. "I won't be in the group of mourners, then?"

"It would be . . . better . . . if you weren't," he said in an agony of embarrassment. "You understand."

"Yes—all too well."

"Fiona, I'm going to marry you! It's possible now. But, for the funeral, it wouldn't be proper——"

"For your mistress to wear a weeper on her bonnet."

Glad to change the subject, he said, "The draper will deliver the silk weepers tomorrow for the mourners to wear. The procession will be tomorrow night. I've managed to find room for her to be buried in St. Stephen's churchyard in the City. Graves are at a premium. Some places they now are burying the coffins on end to save space, and I saw some churchyards today where the ends of the coffins weren't even covered." He shuddered. "I couldn't bear it if the resurrection men stole Kathleen's body and sold it to some fledgling doctor."

It was a ghoulish picture he called to mind.

"You won't be draping this house with black cloth, then?"

"No. Fiona, everyone knows that Kathleen died in Bedlam, and all of my friends know I live here with you. There'll be nothing said—I hope."

"As long as I stay out of sight."

"Fiona, as soon as it is decently possible, I will marry you."

"Let's not talk about weddings and funerals at the same time," she said drily. Then she changed the subject by showing him the sad little bouquet his friends from the London slums had brought him. "I put them in this crystal vase while they were here," she said. "I felt so sorry for them."

He kissed her cheek gently. "You are a lovely woman, Fiona. I don't know what I've done to deserve you."

Later that evening, Rolf announced that Lord Huxley and his sister were in the drawing room.

"Join me in greeting them," Samuel said. "After all, Will Huxley knows all about us."

"I wonder what he's told his sister."

Both Huxley and his sister were in proper mourning. Although neither wore all black, Huxley's coat was black and his waistcoat a pale silvery gray with only braid for trim, no embroidery. His black tricorne, which he had tucked under one arm, was tied with a black crepe weeper. Nell wore mourning white, with a black scarf draped over her bonnet.

After they murmured the appropriate words of sympathy, Huxley indicated that he'd like to speak briefly in private with Rogers, who took him into the back sitting room while Fiona chatted with Huxley's sister.

"Are you enjoying your stay in London, Nell?"

"Oh, yes. Will has taken me everyplace! Today we saw the rotunda at Ranelagh Gardens, and he's promised to take me to see a bearbaiting at Hockley-in-the-Hole tomorrow—in the afternoon, of course, so we can be in the procession for poor, dear Mr. Rogers tomorrow night." She paused, realizing that perhaps it wasn't quite the thing to say to Fiona. Quickly, to get over the awkward spot, she added, "And we've been invited to a rout at the home of the Duke and Duchess of Lawton the next night. Will didn't want to go, but I begged. I've read in *The Gazette* that all the *ton* go to the parties at Millbank." Then, again realizing she might be making a social faux pas, she said hurriedly, "I suppose you and Mr. Rogers won't be . . . I mean, he's in mourning——"

"No, we won't be there," Fiona assured her, voice dry. She could just imagine how the lecherous duke would play up to the lovely young Nell. No wonder Huxley had not wanted to take his sister there. And if he and the duchess were no longer lovers, she was amazed that even his sister had persuaded him to go to the party. She wondered who he was seeing now. Fiona doubted that Huxley was content for long without a woman. He was too virile, too lusty to live the life of a monk—unless it was the kind of monk who went to Medmenham Abbey.

In a fit of spite, Fiona asked, "Has Lord Huxley taken you to Marlow yet, Nell? There's a fascinating ruined abbey there. You must have him show it to you."

"No, he's not mentioned it to me. I'll remember that. Would we go by boat? I'd love a trip on the Thames."

"Oh, yes, it's lovely by boat."

Just then the two men returned, and after having a glass of wine, the Huxleys left.

"Will didn't want to mention it in front of you ladies —and he wondered at the propriety of bringing it up today—but he is to be abbot at Medmenham Abbey next month and has invited me to be a friar. And you're to come along and be one of the nuns for the evening, help get the girl ready for the Black Mass."

Remembering how eager the last virgin had been to participate Fiona agreed.

"I know you don't like it too well there, Fiona, but if I am to make any progress at all with my programs of social reform, then I must get the ear of the men who are friends to King George. That's the only way I can accomplish anything. And his friends are all devotees of Dashwood's frolics."

"I know." Actually Fiona wanted to go this time; she might still find something against Huxley. If he was to be abbot . . . She closed her mind to the images that brought up. The abbot was the first one to have the virgin at the Black Mass. Well, she'd be in the Roman Room. Perhaps she could help Samuel by being friendly to the many important men who'd be there for the orgy.

"Samuel, do you expect me to lie with all those men to further your career?"

"Good God, no! Surely you didn't think——"

"I hoped not. But I remember how Werington was when he took me to the abbey. At first he gave me orders not to go to bed with anyone, and the next thing I knew, he was auctioning me off to the highest bidder."

"You'll find I'm a very jealous lover, Fiona," he warned. "No, if my success depended on your—— Never! I'd rather be an obscure, unsung M.P. than to have my wife-to-be prostituting herself for my ambition. I thought you knew me better than that, my dear."

It was a relief to hear him say it.

"I think there's trouble brewing for the king not only in London but also in the American colonies," Rogers said. "All we do is bleed them dry of their wealth. They aren't going to put up with that for too long. Before the turn of the century, I expect trouble there, just as there will be trouble in France. Too many downtrodden, it makes for an explosive situation."

"Surely not war, Samuel. How could we wage war across the ocean?"

"That's the problem. I can't imagine that if the colonies decide they want independence, England can hold them. It's not like some countries that are backward, with native populations not as far advanced as we are. Most of the people in the colonies are Englishmen, who expect their rights and will fight to get them. Mark my words, Fiona. The king should pay less attention to his advisors, who are ignoring our lands across the sea. He'd do better to read *The London Man* than to consult with the likes of Sandwich and Bute."

Emboldened by his desire to talk to her about politics, Fiona asked, "Do you write that paper, Samuel? Werington told me that you did."

The look he gave her was piercing. "No. I wish I were that skillful with words. I envy the man who does those articles."

There was something about the way he said it that stopped her further questions. It was almost as if he'd slammed shutters closed. She was sure he knew all about the editor of the subversive paper, and was almost positive that the printing press on which it was printed was in their wine cellar. If ever she had a chance to pry, if she was alone here without the spying eyes of the Evanses, she might try to get into the wine cellar to see if she was right. She had no intention of betraying her Samuel. What he did was his business.

It was only that she was eager to learn the identity of the editor of *The London Man,* for she believed it was he who paid their rent and furnished her with clothes and baubles. If it was Huxley, she could get him into all sorts of trouble with his highborn friends; yet if she betrayed him, he would of necessity pull Rogers down with him. Perhaps she should just turn a blind eye on the wine cellar. What she didn't know for sure, she didn't have to think about or act on. She should be grateful to Rogers for a good life and forget thoughts of revenge against Huxley, since Huxley and Rogers were friends.

CHAPTER 20

Rogers caught her up and swung her around. Considering that he'd buried his wife only two days ago, Fiona was surprised at his exuberance.

"Heavens, Samuel, what has happened?"

He kissed her with ardor. "I've just learned, my dearest love, that it pays to have friends in high places."

"But you've already won your seat in Parliament."

"That's important, but not nearly as important as my private life now. With my wife dead, we can marry. And one of the frequenters of Medmenham Abbey, Lord Laughlin, has the ear of the king. He's arranged for me to get a special license. We can be married in less than a week."

Fiona was stunned at his news. She'd realized that once poor Kathleen was gone, he'd want her to be his wife. What she hadn't expected was that it would happen immediately. With a flash of self-truth, Fiona knew that she didn't want to marry Samuel Rogers, no matter how good he'd been to her. She didn't love him and knew she never could. He had her gratitude and respect; but that did not seem enough to her to marry a man. Fiona was no innocent. She knew that more marriages were arranged for convenience than for romantic love; but she had dreamed of more. She could not, though, deny him. He was her protector. Without Samuel Rogers, she might well be on the streets of London or working in one of its notorious brothels.

"I had thought you'd be in mourning for a while."

"I did my mourning for poor Kathleen when she was

committed to Bedlam, Fiona. There are no tears left to shed."

"But won't people talk? Bury your wife one week, take a new one the next?"

"It will be a very quiet ceremony. I think, under the circumstances, that would be best. I discussed it with the vicar of St. Stephen's when I went to give him a gift for conducting Kathleen's funeral service. He understands. When I explained that you were my mistress, he was all in favor of regularizing our relationship as soon as possible."

Her final excuse was the one every woman has used since the beginning of time: "I haven't anything to wear for a wedding gown."

"I stopped in to see your seamstress before I came home. She'll be here this afternoon. I told her that the gown must be ready by next week, and she assured me that it was possible. So"—he set her on her feet and tilted her face up to him with one finger under her chin—"no more excuses, or I'll think that you don't find me good enough to be your husband."

"Oh, Samuel, never that!" she cried, putting more feeling into her words than she actually meant, because of her guilt about not wanting to marry this man who had been so good to her.

"Is it all right with you if I ask Will Huxley to be one of our witnesses? He's been a good friend to me, one of the few lords who are concerned about the poor of London."

Fiona died a little when he asked her, but how could she say no? What excuse could she possibly give to her betrothed? She could scarcely say that she loved (or hated?) Huxley, or that the viscount had told her he'd once been in love with her, so she was forced to say, "If you want Will by all means ask him."

"And you? Who will you ask to stand up with you?"

Who indeed? She had few friends. There was Lady Maggie Starrett, but Fiona hesitated to suggest her.

And her only living relative, her aunt, had cast her out for living a loose life.

As if sensing her problem, Rogers suggested, "I suppose we could ask Huxley's sister, Nell."

"Yes, of course." Why not?

"I'll arrange everything, my dear." He smiled happily and caught her to him in a passionate embrace. "Let's go up to bed," he whispered, kissing her ear, sliding his lips down to the hollow of her throat. "I want you so much."

How can his touch rouse me so, when I don't love him? she wondered. *Am I wanton? wicked?* Nothing like this had happened with Werington; but, from the very first time, Rogers was able to turn her blood to fire, make her bones melt, with his lovemaking. What would it have been like with Huxley? Now she regretted that they had not lain together at the abbey when he bought her favors from Werington. At least she'd have had that one time to remember forever. Alas, it was not to be. How could she possibly go through with a marriage to Samuel with Will Huxley looking on? Yet she must. Somehow, she would survive it.

Mrs. Tamblyn, the seamstress, made her a simple gown of lavender watered silk, with deep cuffs at the elbow and a frill of expensive Belgian lace that covered her arms halfway to the wrist. The skirt was looped up from an open center front hem, with a petticoat of silver tissue underneath. She wore a lace pinner to match the lace on her gown, and the bodice was trimmed with a stomacher of the silver tissue, laced tightly with plum-covered velvet ribbon. It was a beautiful gown but not gaudy, in deference to the death of Samuel's wife.

He was dressed quietly, in a black coat with a gray waistcoat; but it was richly embroidered with silver thread, and the silver buckles on his knee breeches and on his black calf shoes matched the silver buttons on his coat and waistcoat. It was a handsome outfit. He'd powdered his hair for the occasion, which he rarely did, and it was tied back with a black velvet bow.

The Huxleys were resplendent. They might have been the bridal couple in all their finery, for Will wore a coat of teal-blue satin, and his sister's gown was of aqua velvet, the same hue as his coat but paler.

The service was short, as if the vicar was faintly embarrassed by the whole affair. Then Huxley insisted on buying them a wedding supper at the Oxford Arms, where he had arranged for a private parlor banked with flowers.

"You must have bought out all the flower girls in Covent Garden," Fiona gasped. "It's like a fairy bower."

"It's not every day that I participate in a wedding."

Was his answer ironic? She couldn't tell. Her heart ached, but the deed was now done. She was Mrs. Samuel Rogers, for better or for worse, till death did them part —so she had promised, and Fiona was determined to keep her vows.

The supper was beautifully planned, with more delicacies than was usual, in deference to the two women. There was roast of English beef for the men; but there was also a platter of thinly sliced ham garnished with a variety of pickles, and roast squab stuffed with orange. There was even a wedding cake, the layers iced with pink sugar. It was so pretty that Fiona hated to cut into it. All was washed down with excellent wine.

Later, when she and Nell excused themselves to go to the ladies' retiring room, Nell was full of excitement. Fiona quickly learned that it wasn't the wedding, though.

"I've been invited to a masquerade by the duchess of Lawton," she said. "She tells me that all the *ton* will be there and that I'll have ever so good a time."

Fiona was a little surprised that Huxley was still going to the house on Millbank, for everyone now said that he and the duchess were no longer lovers. Yet she guessed he was happy that his young sister could move in the best set.

"It's to be Friday next," Nell confided. "I can scarcely wait. The duchess is having a special costume made for me. Even I won't see it until the night of the masquerade. She had me measured by her dressmaker."

Friday next, Fiona thought. But that was the night Huxley was going to the abbey. Of course! He didn't want Nell to be alone that evening, so he'd arranged an invitation for her. Perhaps he and the duchess had parted good friends. In the *ton,* many affairs ended that way, with no one hurt and no bad feelings. Yet Fiona remembered how the duchess had hated her because Will showed interest in her. She needn't have worried. He certainly lost interest in her in a hurry, for all his protestations of love at first sight.

That night Samuel was even more loving than usual. He kept murmuring "My wife, my own dearest wife; how much I love you" while he caressed her willing flesh. As her passion mounted, she wished that she could truthfully say the same to him. She cried out in her moment of rapture, but even then she didn't say "I love you" to this man who had been so good to her and who had made her his wife despite all he knew had happened to her.

Later, as they lay in each other's arms, he said, "Now I have the two things I've wanted most. I have been elected to Parliament and I have married you. There's only one thing more that will make my life complete. I long for a child."

A child! The words stunned her senses. It had never occurred to her that Samuel would want children. They'd never discussed having a family. In truth, they'd never discussed getting married. It had just seemed to happen.

Perhaps she was barren. All those months with Werington and nothing happened. And now all this time with Samuel. . . . She said nothing, only caressed him.

Fiona didn't know how she felt about having a child. Of course, now that she was legally married, there was nothing to stand in the way of motherhood. For some reason, though, she shied away from the suggestion. If they had a child, then she would be truly tied to Samuel Rogers for life.

But I am now, she reminded herself. It was her wedding night, she and her new husband had just enjoyed each other's bodies—and she had enjoyed the lovemaking—yet a part of her wanted to hold back from this final commitment, having a child. Well, it might happen anyway. If it did, there was nothing that Fiona could do about it; nor would she want to. She had no desire to murder a babe before it could live.

Then Rogers shuddered. "But I'd be so frightened for you, my love. Having a child is what drove my poor Kathleen mad."

A wave of pity swept over her for this man. "That babe was stillborn; it happens. But I am young and healthy, Samuel. I cannot think that anything untoward would happen if I were to be with child. There are far too many healthy children in the world for childbearing to be that dangerous to the mother." If Samuel wanted a child so desperately, then she hoped she could give one to him.

"I should worry for the whole time, but I'd be so happy if I could see a child of mine held in your arms. I love you so much, Fiona. It would be the final expression of our love to produce from that love a child, flesh of our flesh."

"You keep saying 'child,'" she whispered. "Most men want a son."

"Oh, I want a son . . . and I want a daughter. What man would not want a daughter as beautiful as her mother? And you are so beautiful, my dearest wife . . . so beautiful."

He drew her close, passion rising, and made love to her again, slow, rapturous love that left her feeling so wonderful, she wondered how she could possibly not love him. Then they slept in each other's arms for the first time as man and wife.

Fiona dreamed of a child, when finally she drifted off to sleep; a handsome child, a little boy, who looked just like his father: coal-black hair, flashing black eyes, even that quirky black eyebrow that rose sardonically—— But how could this be her son? It was impossible. The child did not look like Rogers at all, with his graying brown hair, his gentle hazel eyes, which could flash fire when he was exhorting the crowds in Hyde Park. No, her son looked exactly like Will Huxley.

CHAPTER 21

It was one of the days that Fiona and the serving couple were supposed to be away from the house. Samuel went off to Parliament after giving Fiona money to go shopping "for ribbons or a new bonnet," so she knew that their unseen benefactor would be using their home today. She wondered if Rolf Evans and his sly wife, Sal, were curious about what went on in the wine cellar when they were out for the day. She hoped soon to be able to suggest to Samuel that they let the Evans couple go, and get more congenial servants; but, as they were very correct when Samuel was here, Fiona knew it would be difficult for her to make her husband understand just how insolent they were to her when he wasn't around.

Feeling a bit under the weather, Fiona decided to stay in bed for a while after Samuel had gone. When Sal came to help her dress, she said only that she thought she'd lie in for a bit. "Don't worry about me. I know that Mr. Rogers has given the two of you the day off. I'll be fine without you. I'll get up and go out shopping a little later," Fiona told the insolent-eyed woman.

"Very well, ma'am, if you're sure. We was goin' to the bearbaitin' today. Wouldn't want to get there so late we have to stand in back and can't see."

"No, I wouldn't want you to miss such sport," Fiona said, knowing her sarcasm was wasted on Sal.

"Won't you be wantin' breakfast before I go?"

"I think not today. Just pour me a glass of claret."

From the knowing look that Sal gave her, Fiona was sure that the woman assumed she was with child.

Soon the house was quiet, the Evans couple having left as soon as Sal had brought the glass of wine to her on a silver tray. Fiona decided not to make the effort to get up and leave. Their mysterious caller would have no idea that she was up here in bed. The arrangement was that she and the servants were always to be out of the house when he came. She'd be very quiet.

Should she try to see who it was? Fiona wasn't sure if that would be wise. If he glimpsed her, he might well call off his financial arrangement with Rogers and they would no longer be able to afford this nice house. While Samuel now had his pay as a Member of Parliament, Fiona was not sure that they could afford to live on Hanover Street even with that money assured. This was a very elegant section of London.

As their bedroom did not face the street, she could not peek from the window when the man arrived; so she just lay there, listening carefully. It was nearly an hour before she heard the faint sound of the door. He was here! Terror seized her. Maybe he always looked through the house to make sure that it was truly empty before he went to the wine cellar. She now wished she'd not left the bedroom door open so that she could hear his arrival. Should she try to hide? But where? Under the bed? In the wardrobe? Would he hear her if she got out of bed and moved about in the room?

Almost paralyzed with fear, Fiona lay there under the quilt, shivering as if she had ague. Was that a step on the narrow staircase leading up here? Was her benefactor even now creeping up to surprise her? If he found her here, he'd turn from benefactor to enemy at once. She thought she heard the stairs creak, and quickly pulled the bedcovers over her head, cowering in the darkness. Finally, nearly smothered, she cautiously poked her face out into the air. No menacing figure stood in the doorway of the bedchamber. No further sounds came from the staircase.

Then she did hear something, a thumping sound,

muffled, hard to identify. Gathering her courage around her like a cloak, she pushed back the covers and slid out of the high bed, not putting on her velvet slippers but tiptoeing barefoot to the doorway, holding her breath to listen.

There could be only one explanation to the noise, the one she had guessed. There had to be a small printing press in the wine cellar. Copies of *The London Man* were being printed downstairs by—— No, it was truly idiotic to assume that such antigovernment sentiments were written by a viscount. It had to be someone wealthy but not a peer, who, for reasons she couldn't fathom, wanted to push the idea of giving the common man more say in the government. It was revolutionary stuff, and Fiona had studied enough history, her father having been a schoolmaster who saw to her education, to know that revolutions were terrible things. It wasn't that she felt that the poor of the land should always stay poor, that they should keep in their designated place, but rather that the change should be accomplished very slowly, so that the foundations of their kingdom would not be fractured. There were many inequities in the land, as was true everywhere; even so, England still was one of the most liberal, humane nations in the world. Fiona had no desire to see things torn apart.

She remembered that there was a small window in another bedchamber that did overlook the street. If she could get into that room without being heard by her unseen visitor, she might be able to see him when he left. She had no idea how long the man might stay. On the days when Rogers told her to vacate the house, she did not return until late afternoon. If the man stayed that long today, Fiona was going to be very hungry before she had a chance to get a meal. Having had no breakfast, she was already beginning to feel hungry. Her discomfort had disappeared, probably thanks to the claret; but if she kept sipping wine all day, she'd be drunk.

First she'd better dress. If she did have an unfortunate encounter with the printer, she'd be at a terrible disadvantage if he caught her *en déshabillé*. Moving as quietly as a mouse, she quickly put on her clothes, choosing a morning dress of sprigged India muslin. Today she put on soft velvet slipers that had no heels to make clicking sounds. Then she stole out of her room, listening with breath held and mouth slightly open before she ventured from the safety of the bedchamber. The thumping of the press was loud enough to muffle any sound she might make. She even thought that perhaps she could steal out of the house without alerting her visitor. This, though, took more nerve than she had. No, she'd just move into the small room directly above the main entrance hall and keep a vigil by the window to see if she could get a glimpse of the man when he left.

When an hour had passed, Fiona left the window, chose a French novel from the bookcase in the room, and settled herself to read. As soon as the press quit its noisy thumping, she could resume her stance at the window.

Engrossed in the story, she amost missed the man's departure. She had come to the end of a particularly exciting chapter, only to realize that the house was ominously quiet. The printing press was no longer in use. Had the man left without her hearing him? She sprang up, and in her haste she dropped the book. It landed on the flowered carpet with a dull thud, and immediately she heard the door to the wine cellar creak open. Fiona froze, terrified. Had he heard the book hit the floor? Then she heard small noises from the hall below her, so she knew the man was moving about. Afraid he would come up the stairs if he suspected her presence, she stood there like a statue, not daring to move to her vantage place at the window.

At last she heard the front door open and the shout of "Whoa!" from the street. A carriage must have come for him. If she waited any longer, she might not see who he was. Taking courage from the fact that he'd not heard the book fall, Fiona eased slowly to the window, letting the soft-soled slippers slide over the carpet. When she peered out, she found that the window was so high she could see little of Hanover Street unless she opened the window and hung out of it, a maneuver she thought unwise. She could see the top of a carriage. The coachman, distinctive in his typical long coat with the triple row of capelets at each shoulder, was heaving a large box up onto the roof of the coach. Standing on tiptoe, Fiona was able to see the top of the carriage door.

The front door of the house banged, and she heard the key turn in the lock. The man had gone. She was in for a big disappointment, though, for all she could see of him was the top of a very ordinary black tricorne hat and a flash of black cape as he stooped to get into the closed carriage. It might have been anyone.

Now that he was gone, Fiona, feeling better, decided that she had best get out of the house. If Rogers should arrive home unexpectedly, she would have difficulty explaining to him why she was here when she was supposed to be out shopping.

Putting on a wide-brimmed straw hat trimmed with silk roses, she tied on an embroidered pocket filled with money and left the house. She had just gotten to the corner of Oxford Street when a gust of wind blew a bit of dust into her eye. Moving back into the shelter of a doorway on Hanover Street so that she could get out her kerchief and remove the speck from her eye, she happened to glance back down the street toward her house. There, scurrying along as if something was after him, was Rolf Evans, with Sal at his heels. Looking furtively both ways, they darted up the steps to the door, and Rolf unlocked it.

Fiona was shocked. If they'd come only a bit sooner, they might well have encountered the man as he left.

Annoyed that they were back when they were supposed to be at Hockley-in-the-Hole, she quickly attended to her eye, then hurried back to the house. She intended to confront the Evans couple. As she swept up the steps to the front door, she saw Sal peering out at her through a crack in the door.

"Mrs. Rogers! I thought you'd gone!"

"Open that door this instant!" Fiona ordered. "What are you doing here? You went to Hockley, or so you said."

"Well, uh, Rolf forgot his purse. We just came back for—— Rolf!" she called, trying to block Fiona's way into the house.

Furious, Fiona pushed the door open and hurried to the door to the wine cellar. Sure enough, there was Rolf, a long nail in his hand, trying to pick the lock. "How dare you! Get out of this house!"

Caught red-handed, the man turned ugly. "Something's going on in this wine cellar, ma'am, and I intend to find out what it is."

"You impertinent, insolent man! Wait until Mr. Rogers hears of this. He told you that you were to stay out of the wine cellar."

"Makes it sound as if he thinks I've been at the wine," Rolf whined. "Doesn't sound good."

"That's right, ma'am," Sal said, coming up behind Fiona. "Makes it sound as if my Rolf is a thief."

"Wait until I tell my husband that your husband is a picklock!" Fiona said angrily. "He'll have *both* of you up in front of the magistrates. *You* were acting as his lookout, Sal, trying to keep me out of my own house."

"Rolf's just curious, ma'am," Sal said. "Aren't you a bit curious yourself about what the secret is in the wine cellar?" There was that old insinuating way Sal had that Fiona hated so much.

Feeling guilty, for she had tried to spy on their secret benefactor, Fiona was even more belligerent than she might have been otherwise. "You are despicable! I shall ask Mr. Rogers to dismiss both of you."

"I wouldn't if I was you, ma'am," Rolf said, his face ugly. "It might be of interest to the authorities to know what is so secret about the wine cellar of this house."

"You *dare* to threaten me?" It was a very real threat, though. Fiona knew very well what was in the wine cellar, and she knew what a scandal there would be if it could be proved that *The London Man* was being printed here. It would ruin Samuel.

"If you forget that we was here in the house, ma'am," Sal said sweetly, "then I'm sure that Rolf will forget that the wine cellar, which used to be his right to manage, is now locked up against him."

"Besides, what if we told the master that you was here in the house when he thought you'd be away?" Sal's husband said, eyeing Fiona boldly. "Mightn't like that."

Fiona was on the horns of a dilemma. She wanted to get rid of the Evans couple; yet they could cause trouble both for her and for Rogers. Against her better judgment, she said, "Very well, I'll forget it this time. But let me warn you: If either of you steps out of line ever again, I shall ask Mr. Rogers to dismiss both of you without a letter. Do I make myself perfectly clear?"

"Yes, ma'am," they muttered, not pleased with her stand.

"Now, get out of the house and stay out until such time as you would normally return tonight," she ordered. "If Mr. Rogers comes back and finds you here, I shall not lie to him."

They left immediately, with no further pretense about forgetting their money for entrance to Hockley.

Fiona, somewhat shaken by the events of the day, gave them time to get away; then she too left the house. It would not be wise for her to be found here, either, if Samuel happened to get out of Commons early. While on her way to Oxford Street, she heard a newsboy shouting *"The London Man!* Get your copy here, only a penny!"* Beckoning to the urchin, Fiona gave him a penny for the paper. She wanted to see what was being said this time.

One lurid headline caught her attention: KING BE-TRAYS THE POOR. The article was just as inflam-matory, with cogent statements about conditions in London's slums. The blame was placed squarely on the shoulders of King George. It was the most treasonous article she'd yet read in the paper. She tried to hear her husband in the articles, but they just did not sound like Samuel's style. There was a polish to the work that made her wonder once again if Huxley might be the author.

Then she thought of the servants. Perhaps it would be a mistake not to tell Samuel exactly what they'd been up to. However, if she told him they were trying to get into the wine cellar, he'd want to know how she happened to catch them at their nefarious task. Of course, she could tell him the exact truth; but Rogers might never trust her fully again, and she prized this trust. Rogers was the first man who had treated her decently, as if she were a person in her own right in-stead of a chattel whose only purpose in life was to give pleasure to a man. She would hate to lose the con-fidence he had in her.

Therefore, she must keep quiet about Rolf and Sal, although she intended to keep a close eye on them from now on. If they gave her any other cause for dissatis-faction, she would not hesitate to ask Rogers to dismiss them. She was not looking forward to the shared con-spiracy she knew they'd assume with her, the unwanted intimacy, and, frankly, the power that this would give them over her. How she wished now that she had in-sisted on a new couple when she and Rogers first moved into the Hanover Street residence.

CHAPTER 22

It was still early afternoon when Fiona and Rogers stepped from their wherry onto the quay at Medmenham Abbey. Rogers wanted to arrive early, as he had some business to discuss with Dashwood and some of the other men.

"We'll go directly to the house. I think you'll enjoy the gardens." His grin told Fiona that the gardens of Dashwood's mansion probably were similar in lewdness to those surrounding the ruined abbey. "I'll see if he will take you up into the tower so that you can see the layout of the gardens as a whole. It is most interesting."

"Samuel, when you get that look in your eye——"

"But we can't tarry too long, as you are to be one of the nuns who prepares the sacrificial virgin."

"I suppose it'll be another little local slut who can't wait to lose her maidenhead to a dozen lords."

Rogers, always perceptive, took her hand. "You're still very bitter about your first time here, aren't you, my dear wife."

"Yes, I am."

"Yet if you'd not come here with Werington that time, where would you be now?"

"I don't know—certainly not with the Duchess of Lawton. That was her nasty way of getting rid of me when she thought that Lord Huxley was too interested in me."

"That fling is over and done with," Rogers said. "For days it was the talk of the London coffeehouses, how Huxley had tired of her overopulent charms. When he first brought his sister around, people thought she was his new young mistress."

"I thought it, too." Fiona frowned. "But if he and the duchess are no longer a couple, why is he letting Nell be entertained by the Lawtons? I'd think he would try to keep her away from such sophisticated company. She's only fourteen."

"There are plenty of prostitutes several years younger than Nell."

"But they're not the sisters of viscounts."

Rogers laughed raucously at that. "Ah, Fiona, surely you've seen them at the abbey—well-born and well-laid."

"I guess you're right. I believed all the lurid tales about how young girls are kidnaped and brought here to lose their virginity on that obscene altar, but the ones I've seen have been willing victims. I . . . well, I was naïve, stupid, and that nasty drug they gave me did the rest."

"Ah well, they could suffer worse fates," Rogers joked. "They could remain virgins all their lives. How would you like that to have been your fate, Fiona?" and he gave her a very intimate caress.

"You know what your touch does to me," she murmured.

"Unfortunately I must conduct some business before the festivities tonight; otherwise I'd take my wife into one of those charming temples of love and make proper use of it and her this very moment."

Although Fiona had been to the abbey several times, she had never met Sir Francis Dashwood. Today that was remedied, for Rogers escorted her to the mansion to present her. As they walked through the gardens enroute to the house, Rogers said, "See those two mounds of flowers there, with the red blossoms on top?"

"Yes. They look a bit out of place. Who did the gardens for him? Not Capability Brown, I'll wager."

She looked about. "And there's an unsightly clump of bushes over there."

Rogers laughed so hard that tears came to his eyes.

"What's so funny, Samuel? I hadn't realized that my every utterance, no matter how prosaic, would move you to such hearty laughter."

"It has to be seen from the proper vantage point to be appreciated," her husband said, mopping his eyes with a lace-edged kerchief. "If Sir Francis has time, I'll ask him to show you his gardens from the tower."

"That's the second time you've suggested viewing the gardens from higher up. Samuel, what's the joke?"

"Later, my sweet, later. It can't be described, it must be seen. Ah, there is our host."

In his youth Sir Francis had been very handsome, with dark curly hair and a fine physique. Now, in middle age, he was putting on unbecoming weight. His hair, unpowdered and unwigged today, had streaks of gray in it, and his eyes had a tendency to pop. He'd developed both a paunch and jowls, neither of which improved his looks.

He was very cordial, though, to Fiona: "Ah, the new Mrs. Rogers! My word, Sam, you have done yourself proud with this one. I do hope she's taking part in our festivities."

Fiona froze, and she could see that the remark didn't sit well with her husband.

"Only to help get the virgin ready, Sir Francis. She's much too new a bride for me to want to share her with others."

"Ah, but variety is the spice of life, and the lady looks very spicy, if I do say so." He smiled too warmly at her.

Trying to be polite and politic at the same time, Fiona murmured "You are too kind, Sir Francis" and retreated into silence.

"I was wondering if you might have time to show her the view of the gardens from above, sir."

Dashwood grinned hugely. "Indeed it will be a pleasure." He held out a hand to Fiona. "Come, my dear, you have a real treat in store for you."

Sir Francis led them into the opulent mansion, through a magnificent great hall, and to a narrow spiral staircase. He climbed nimbly, with his guests hurrying up behind him. They came out onto the open balustraded roof of the tower, and he led them to the side overlooking the gardens.

"See, Mrs. Rogers, isn't she lovely?" Dashwood whispered.

"Oh!" From here, the layout of the gardens was all too explicit. It was a nude woman. The mounds Fiona had commented on earlier were breasts, the red clusters of flowers nipples, and the clump of shrubbery now showed up as a dark triangle.

"Watch this," he commanded. He waved a signal to a gardener down below. In a moment two fountains gushed out of the "breasts," spouting milky water.

Fiona laughed until she was weak.

"At least you saw the funny side and didn't faint," Dashwood told her. "I invited the local parson to have a picnic of parish children on the lawn, and I brought him up here for the view. When the gardener turned on the twin fountains, the poor man fainted dead away."

When they'd left the roof and Samuel had gone off to conduct his business with Dashwood and others, Fiona was escorted by a liveried footman to the room in the abbey where she was to assist the virgin in robing for the Black Mass.

Entering the room, Fiona was stunned to find Nell Huxley there with the Duchess of Lawton. The girl was just putting down the obscene goblet from which she'd drunk the drugged wine.

"Fiona, how nice to see you!" Nell cried, her words already slurred. Obviously the drugged wine was just another glass for the girl. She was quite tipsy.

"You know each other?" the duchess said, her voice cold. There was something ugly in her expression, a kind of unholy triumph, which chilled Fiona to the core.

"Yes, we know each other," was Fiona's curt reply. "Nell, does your brother know you're here?"

"No, it's to be a surprise. He didn't tell me he was invited to this masquerade too," she pouted. "Naughty Will." Then, looking at the silver cup and realizing it was shaped like a nude male, she giggled and added, "And naughty cup! See, Fiona?"

"I've seen it before."

"Well, get yourself dressed, Fiona, and then we'll dress Nell," the duchess ordered.

Horrified, Fiona didn't know what to do. Speaking sharply to Nell, she said, "I don't think Will would want you to be in this . . . this masquerade. Let me take you——"

"You are entirely out of place," the duchess snapped.

"But I want to be at the party," Nell whined, her eyes getting glassier by the moment. "Lots of fun . . . the duchess promised me, din't you. Said it would be . . . lossa fun."

"Of course, dear. Get into your nun's habit, Fiona."

In a terrible quandry, Fiona quickly disrobed behind a screen paneled with scenes from the villas of Pompeii. By this time Nell had sat down on a chair carved in the form of a satyr, the chair arms being his arms to encircle the unwary nymph. Fiona saw that she was rapidly losing consciousness.

"How much of that vile stuff did you give her?" she hissed to the duchess.

"Plenty. I want her eager for the abbot's embrace."

Then Fiona remembered, horrified. Will Huxley was to be the abbot tonight. That meant that he would rape his own sister! Oh, she'd heard the stories. Incest was nothing to the Friars of St. Francis. Indeed, it was said that all of Dashwood's half-sisters participated in the rites, as well as his stepmother. But her mind balked at the thought of Huxley and his young sister together.

Just then Nell moaned and leaned forward, retching. "So sick," she moaned.

"Damnation, girl, don't do that!" the duchess said. Her face turned green. "I can't stand to see someone vomit." She turned and fled the room, leaving Fiona to care for the miserably sick Nell, who retched and retched, bringing up most of the wine she'd swallowed.

While Fiona knew that most of the virgins brought here participated willingly in the lewd rites, she remembered her own shock at finding that she was being raped by Huxley when the drug began to wear off. Surely, even though Nell wanted to remain, the girl could have no idea what went on here at the abbey. With the duchess out of the room, Fiona decided that it was up to her to rescue Nell no matter how angry it made the duchess, no matter if the child herself protested.

Nell moaned in her sickness. Even though she had brought up everything, some of the drug had gotten into her system.

"Come along, Nell," Fiona urged. "I'll get you to a bed so that you can lie down."

"Can't walk," Nell mumbled. "So sick."

With a strength she didn't realize she possessed, Fiona wrestled the girl to her feet and half led, half dragged her across the floor to the door. There, propping Nell against the paneled wall, she eased the door open, half expecting to find the duchess right outside. There was no one in sight; the long passageway was empty. Perhaps the duchess had gone outside for air.

"Come along," she coaxed, pulling one of Nell's arms over her shoulder and supporting the girl round her slender waist. "Hurry, Nell." Fiona was in an agony of suspense. Any moment the duchess could return to find that her bird had flown.

"Wanna lie down," Nell sobbed. "Feel sick."

"I know, I know; I'm helping you to bed."

She pulled the girl along, wondering where would be the best place to hide her. She knew they had to get out of this passageway or the duchess might find the girl in time to get her into the Black Mass. It seemed forever before they finally reached the end of the passage. Fiona turned left and began looking for a vacant room. The first one had a couple in it on the bed, as did the next. The third was vacant. She dragged Nell over the threshold, then slammed the door behind them with her heel. With a final spurt of strength, she managed to get the girl to the huge bed and let her slump down half on, half off the mattress. Then she bent down, picked up Nell's feet, and swung them onto the bed.

"Sick again, so sick."

Fiona hurried to a screen in the corner and found a washstand with basin behind it. She caught up the porcelain basin, ignoring the pornographic picture painted on it, and held it for poor Nell; then she arranged pillows behind the girl and stayed beside her until she dozed.

Now she must somehow get the girl out of here and back to London. She'd see if she could find Samuel and enlist his aid in smuggling Nell out of here and getting her home.

Fortunately there was a large brass key in the ornate lock. Peeking out of the door, she made sure that no one was around; then she tiptoed out of the room, locked the door, and hurried off, hoping she could find her way to the Roman Room. Surely by now Samuel's business would be finished and he'd be there drinking claret.

She got herself thoroughly lost, though, not being too familiar with the twists and turns of the many hallways in the rebuilt abbey. Finally she heard voices and headed in that direction. She turned a corner and came face to face with Huxley, already in his long scarlet-lined monk's habit, the cowl back off his shoulders.

A man she didn't recognize was saying, "Hurry up, Will, the barge has been sighted. You should be down at the landing already to lead the procession."

The man hurried off, not noticing that Huxley wasn't at his heels.

The sight of the viscount was too much for Fiona. She too was unmasked, though she had on her nun's habit. Like a violent summer thunderstorm, she bore down on Huxley. "I knew you were rotten," she spat, "but I didn't realize the depths of your depravity, Will Huxley. For shame! I guess anything goes at these orgies, but to rape your own sister is the most nauseating thing I've ever heard of."

At first it was as if he didn't understand her. He stood there looking at her with that sardonic expression she was learning to hate. Then, as if the words had finally penetrated, his face darkened with rage. He caught her shoulder in a fierce grip that was painful. "What are you blabbering about, Fiona? Have you been at the claret already?"

Her rage matched his own. She sank her fingernails into the hand that gripped her shoulder until he loosed his hold. "I'm talking about Nell. How many other young sisters do you have here at the abbey?"

"Nell? Have you lost your senses completely, Fiona? I wouldn't bring her within sight of this place. She's only a child."

"Fourteen isn't a child. Everyone knows that the Friars of St. Francis rape children; it's part of their entertainment."

She thought for one moment that he might hit her. His fist clenched, and the expression on his face was terrifying. Fiona didn't intend to be intimidated by this rotten lecher, though. Nell was the last straw, the final nail in Huxley's coffin.

"I think you're a raving lunatic," he grated. "Poor Rogers has bad luck with his wives, doesn't he: one dead in Bedlam and the new one ready to be committed."

"So I'm mad, am I, for accusing you of planning incest? Well, better mad than depraved. Get out of my way! Maybe if I can find my husband, he'll help me get Nell away from here. She's sleeping off the drugged wine now. Fortunately she vomited up most of it. *I* wasn't that lucky."

There was suddenly a change in his face. "Nell isn't here . . . is she? She went to a party at the Duchess of Lawton's today."

"The Duchess of Lawton was the other nun, for your information. By the time I got to the dressing room, she had already drugged Nell with the aphrodisiac and whatever other obscene drugs they give to the Black Mass sacrifice."

"The duchess wouldn't do——"

"Oh, wouldn't she? How do you think I wound up on that altar in the chapel? I had no idea what was going on. She arranged for Werington to bring me here. They drugged me, and when I came out from under the influence of whatever they'd put in the wine, you were raping me."

"Rape! You'd——"

"I was drugged, just as Nell was drugged. And you are the abbot tonight. You'd have been first with her. Rotten—that's what you are, all of you!" She tried to push past him. "Let me by. I must try to find Samuel. He'll help me smuggle Nell away from this den of viciousness and vice."

Again he caught her, his fingers clamped around her arm like iron bands around a hogshead of Spanish wine. "Are you making up this story? But if so, why?"

"Why indeed? Listen, you fool, if you truly didn't know that Nell was to be tonight's virgin, then let me go so that I can find someone to help her."

"I still don't believe you. This is some trick. You are angry with me——"

"Do you want me to take you to your sister?" She pulled the large brass key from her pocket. "I locked her into a bedroom for safekeeping. She was asleep; she'd been dreadfully ill. I think the duchess overdosed her."

His eyes narrowed, glittering black. "Yes, I do want to see Nell. I still don't believe you. The duchess wouldn't do such a thing."

"Are you still lovers?" Fiona asked bluntly.

"No, but we parted friends."

"Maybe *you* thought so, but the duchess doesn't take well to being discarded *or* superceded."

"Very well, when I see Nell here, I'll believe you."

To her dismay, Fiona soon realized that she was still lost. She couldn't find the room where she'd hidden Nell away. All of the long passageways looked alike, and all of the doors were the same. She tried doorknob after doorknob. Sometimes she interrupted couples; sometimes the rooms were empty. If the doors were locked, she tried the key.

Huxley was getting more and more angry with each passing moment. "I don't know what your game is, Fiona. I think you just want to embarrass me. I should be down at the quay right now."

"If you can find the way to the room where they dress the virgins, then I think I can find the room where I hid Nell."

He opened the first door he came to and pulled the bell. In a few minutes a lackey came scurrying to answer. Huxley told him what they wanted, and the man guided them along the halls with ease.

"It is just around this next corner, milord," the servant said.

Huxley dismissed him, not wanting an audience when he found his sister—*if* she was indeed here at the abbey. He and Fiona were just about to turn the corner when they heard a familiar voice raised in wrath:

"Where is she? And what happened to that Rogers

slut? Find that girl! Now!" It was the Duchess of Lawton; there was no mistaking her voice.

"It's *Sarah*," Huxley said, astonished. "But she's supposed to be at Millbank, entertaining."

"I told you. Now I hope you finally believe me."

There was the sound of footsteps coming their way.

"Quick, Will, into this room. We'll get Nell away as soon as they pass. I can find the room now, and it is locked."

They locked themselves into the room, holding their breath when a servant rattled the doorknob. Then the footsteps receded. Cautiously Huxley turned the key, trying not to let it grate in the lock. He opened the door a crack, put his eye to it, then motioned to Fiona that the coast was clear. Quickly she led him to the room where she had locked Nell away for safety.

Once inside the room, Huxley strode to the bed, where his young sister still slept. "God! She looks terrible! What did they give her?"

Fiona shrugged. "Cantharides, maybe belladonna . . . I don't know. Sometimes there's a tiny amount of aconite or henbane in the wine."

"It could have killed her."

"Fortunately she didn't keep it down."

Impatiently Huxley cast off the monk's habit he had on over his shirt and breeches. "I wonder if we can rouse her."

"I don't know. She was quite sick."

"Never mind; I'll carry her. But we may need help. Can you find your way to the Roman Room and get Samuel?"

"Yes, I think so. I realize now where I missed a turn in the passageway."

"Get him here. We'll spirit Nell away."

"What about the Black Mass? I thought you were abbot tonight."

He winced at the bite in her words. "I deserved that, Fiona. There'll be no Black Mass tonight, no abbot, no

virgin. Let them find some other more willing victim."
He looked down at his sister sleeping her drugged sleep,
her eyes puffy, her face pale. "God, it could have been
Nell on that altar, and I'd not have known until it
was too late. I thought all of the girls came willingly."

"Oh, Will, it's the talk of London that they kidnap
the local rustic belles to be their victims."

"Most of them are interested in the money they
get."

Fiona knew from experience that this was true, yet
she also knew, from her own horrifying trial here, that
not all of the girls were willing victims. Some were
duped, as she'd been—and as Nell would have been
had she not rescued her.

"Hurry and get your husband," Huxley urged. "And
be careful, Fiona. Don't let Sarah Billings see you."

"I know the duchess all too well, believe me. I'll be
very careful."

Then Fiona went looking for Samuel to help Will
get his sister out of this obscene place and back to the
safety of London.

CHAPTER 23

Fiona hadn't gotten to the Roman Room when she met Rogers.

"What's happened?" he asked. "There seems to be some delay. Everyone's looking for Will Huxley. They say he was here early, but——" Then, noticing her expression, he caught her arm. "What's wrong, Fiona?"

She glanced around to make sure they couldn't be overheard. "Come with me, Samuel; I'll tell you in private."

Just then one of the rowdier lords, well into his second bottle of claret already, caught at Fiona's revealing nun's costume and drawled, "I'm in need of spir . . . spirchul conso—consum—mation!" He and his companions roared raucously at his lewd slip of the tongue.

"Not just now," she snapped, yanking the panel of her robe out of his clutching hand. "Come on, Samuel; it's urgent," she whispered, glancing about anxiously, afraid they might meet the Duchess of Lawton at any moment.

She and Rogers fled down the passageway, away from the drunken revelers. When they were alone, she told him in a few breathless phrases what had happened. "Will needs help in getting Nell out of here and into their boat."

"Good God! Sarah Billings did that to him?"

"Why not? She duped me the same way."

"This is going to take some maneuvering to get the girl away secretly," Rogers said as they hurried toward the room where Nell was hidden. "There are people everywhere."

237

"If we could get her down to the quay as the procession makes its way to the chapel——"

"Without Huxley as abbot, will there be a procession?"

Fiona hadn't even thought of that. "Ah, here we are." She made sure the corridor was empty, then tapped lightly on the door. "Will, it's Fiona," she called.

The door opened quickly and they slipped inside. Will locked it behind them, to keep out any curious drunks. "Did Fiona tell you——"

Rogers nodded. "Yes. I'm shocked, Will. Thank God Fiona was one of the nuns tonight."

Huxley was pale. Fiona sensed a leashed rage in him, a frightening amount of bottled-up anger, which could explode at any moment.

"I thought maybe we could get her out during the procession, Will; but Samuel reminded me that you are supposed to be abbot tonight. Without you, and they're already looking for you——"

"What we need is a stand-in for you," Rogers said. "I'd do it, but I'm not nearly as tall as you."

Huxley's eyes narrowed. "With the cowl pulled over your face, maybe no one would notice. It would just be to distract their attention long enough for me to get Nell to our boat. They can't have the Black Mass without their virgin, but by the time they realize that Nell is gone, we can be well downstream. The minute you can get away, just discard the robe and leave."

"I could put something on top of your head to make the cowl higher and you look taller," Fiona suggested.

"I'm willing to do it," Rogers said. Quickly he donned the friar's habit, and Fiona found a small pillow and stuffed it into the hood to make it stand up from his head. "I'll leave now. Don't start until you hear the bell begin to toll," he warned. "You'll know the procession is coming up from the Thames then."

Huxley let him out, then relocked the door.

"We should try to cover up that nun's habit Nell is wearing," Fiona said, "but her clothes and mine are in the other room. Dare I try to get them?"

Huxley shook his head. "The dear duchess will be waiting there, I daresay, but if you could get to the Roman Room and filch some cloaks . . ."

"I'll do my best. Let me mask first so I won't be recognized."

She hurried to the banqueting hall, paying little attention to the men who tried to embrace her as she passed them. She knew where the cloakroom was located, and she got rid of the liveried footman in charge of it by telling him that Sir Francis needed him at the outer door to help carry a guest who was too drunk to walk. When he had gone, Fiona caught up three cloaks, paying no heed to what they were, and raced back to the room where Nell was hidden.

Inside, she found an appalling sight. Nell had waked and was trying to pull her brother down on top of her in her drug-induced desire.

"God! Help me, Fiona!" he said. "Nell, Nell, wake up! It's Will, your brother!"

"Love me," she kept begging, clutching at him. "Love me."

Fiona got the pitcher of water from behind the screen, wet a towel, and began bathing Neil's flushed face, hoping to help her recover more quickly from the effects of the drugs. Huxley put on the largest of the three capes and fastened his mask over his eyes. Fiona helped him wrap Nell in a scarlet cloak, pulling it taut about her so that she couldn't wind her eager arms about his neck, then draped herself in the third cloak, a blue velvet so long that it swept the floor, and also masked her face. Nell's face they covered by pulling the hood of the red cape over it.

Then Huxley picked up his sister, Fiona unlocked the door, and they made their cautious way along the passage toward the exit to the gardens. As they moved into the torchlit night, the first sonorous notes of the bell began sounding through the air. There were shouts of "Here come the Friars of St. Francis!" and the thud of running feet as the guests hurried to see the spectacular sight as the robed monks, carrying their flaming tapers, marched in slow procession to the chapel for their Black Mass.

Then, off to the right but all too close to the escaping trio, came a call: "Nell! Nell Huxley! Where are you?"

Huxley checked so abruptly that Fiona, racing along at his heels, almost collided with him. "That's the duchess," he hissed. "She's still looking for my sister."

"We'll have to move around to the left so that she won't see us," Fiona said.

Again, this time closer, they heard the Duchess of Lawton: "Nell! It's time for the masquerade. Where are you, you sly, naughty girl?"

To Fiona's horror, Nell, who had been a limp deadweight in her brother's arms once they'd wrapped her securely in the scarlet cloak, now roused herself. "I'm here!" she cried in a light, clear voice that carried over the distant shouts of the watchers.

"Oh, hush, Nell!" Huxley said fiercely. "You little fool!"

"I hear you, Nell," the duchess instantly called back. "Where are you? It's time for the party."

Huxley shifted his hold on his sister so that he could get one hand over her mouth to silence her. "Be quiet, Nell. You'll be sorry if you don't."

The Duchess of Lawton called for the girl yet again, and this time her voice was even closer.

Huxley turned and said quietly, "We've got to move away from here, even if we go back toward the abbey for a bit. Stay in the shadow as much as possible, Fiona."

Fiona only hoped they wouldn't get lost in the maze,

for she realized now that the shadows into which Huxley urged her were the beginning of the boxwood horror. "We're in the maze."

"It's all right. I know the way through it."

But on their heels came the duchess. "I see you," she cried. "You can't get away from me by going into the maze, Nell. I know its twists and turns, and you'll get hopelessly lost."

Fiona knew they had to do something. "You go ahead with Nell," she said. I'll go another direction and try to lure the duchess away from you."

"All right," he said "When you get to the statue of Ariadne and Theseus in the heart of the maze, take the passage behind it and keep bearing right. It will bring you out of the labyrinth near the path to the boat landing."

Then he was gone, carrying a now struggling Nell to safety. Fiona watched carefully until she saw movement behind her; then she moved noisily through the pathways.

"Nell, wait!" the duchess cried, her voice angry.

"Catch me!" Fiona called, trying to make her voice higher and lighter to sound like Nell's.

She played her cat-and-mouse game with the duchess until she finally penetrated to the heart of the maze. There, in one last attempt to fool the duchess, she whipped off her concealing cloak and hung it from Ariadne's arm so that it gave the illusion of a standing hooded figure. Then she fled into the path behind the statue, being as quiet as she could and keeping to the center of it so as not to brush the boxwood walls and give away her position.

Behind her she heard the duchess cry out in triumph, "Aha! I see you, Nell, you naughty child." Then, moments later, there was a roar of rage from the frustrated woman when she found that the girl she thought she'd captured was nothing but an empty cloak of dark-blue velvet.

Fiona rushed on, taking each right turn as she came to it, remembering Huxley's instructions. With great relief she emerged from the maze just as he'd predicted, with the quay in sight just down over the green lawn. Unfortunately, the duchess knew the maze far better than Fiona did, and was waiting for her as she came out of the boxwood path.

"Aha! Caught you, Nell!" she cried in triumph, snatching at Fiona's revealing nun's habit.

Now masked, Fiona realized that the duchess didn't know who she was. Being younger and fleeter of foot, she counted on being able to outrun the Lawton woman easily, and twisting out of her grasp, she fled toward the quay. Even in the darkness she could see a boat moored there, a lantern lighted in the bow and another in the stern. It had to be Huxley, waiting for her.

The dew had already formed on the grass, making it slippery underfoot, and as Fiona raced along at breakneck speed, her foot slid on a slick patch and she fell headlong.

The duchess, long in the tooth though she might be, was on her in a moment, pouncing down and catching her in a firm grasp. "Now, now, enough games, Nell. Get up and come back to the abbey like a good girl. We're all waiting for you. The masquerade can't start without you."

Momentarily winded, Fiona lay there, regaining her breath. She didn't say a word to the duchess. It was to her advantage to be anonymous right now. The older woman urged her to get up, putting an arm around her and half lifting her to her feet. Then, as Fiona tensed herself to break away and make a final dash to the waiting boat, the duchess seemed to realize that she didn't have Nell captive at all.

"Who are you?" she demanded. "You aren't Nell Huxley." Before Fiona realized what she was going to do, the duchess snatched off her velvet mask. "Fiona!

I might have known! What have you done with the Huxley girl?"

"She's escaped you, my dear duchess," Fiona said gleefully. "Will rescued her. She won't be sacrificed on that rotten altar tonight." Then, emboldened by the stunned look on the woman's face, she gave her a hard shove that toppled her over on her generous backside. Free now, Fiona fled down to the pier, raced along it, and accepted Will Huxley's helping hand into the wherry.

"London!" he barked at their boatman.

They were well out into the river when the duchess reached the quay. Her angry voice echoed out over the water: "You'll be sorry, both of you—just wait!"

"What about Samuel?" Fiona asked, suddenly realizing that her husband wasn't with them.

"He'll understand. It was vital that I get Nell away immediately." He held her cradled in his arms. She seemed to have dozed off again, her eyes closed, her head on his chest.

It was cool on the water, and Fiona shivered, for her nun's habit was more illusion than substance. Noticing, Huxley pulled off the concealing cape he'd worn and handed it to her. She wrapped herself in it gratefully.

They said scarcely a word to each other for the long miles from Marlow to London. Huxley had the boatman put in at the slip at Horseferry Road, where his coachman was waiting patiently for him, dozing on the box of the landaulet. He came to with a start and stared as his master carried the sleeping girl to the coach.

Huxley got Nell in on one seat, then handed Fiona in so that she sat beside him on the other. "Home," he commanded the coachman.

"I hope you don't mind going to my house first, Fiona; I want to get Nell to bed. Do you think I should send for a doctor to look at her?"

"I don't think so. She brought up a great deal of the drugged wine, and she seems to be sleeping off the rest of it. The less said about tonight, the better, Will. The doctor might well gossip. Although"—she shrugged—"it will be the talk of the *ton,* no doubt. The duchess will not pass up such a juicy morsel, I fear."

"I should call the duke out," Huxley said with suppressed violence. "He was in on this too, the lecherous old goat."

"You don't have to tell *me* about him, Will," she reminded Huxley. "You're the one who kept him from raping me, only to have a hand in raping me yourself." She couldn't keep the bitter note out of her voice.

"God, Fiona, I should be horsewhipped for that! I thought . . . frankly, I thought that you'd been playing me for a fool, that you were the typical milliner's assistant. Most of them are blatant tarts. When I discovered that it was you there on the altar, and you fought me off after having invited the caresses of all the other men——"

"It was the drug. You saw how Nell acted."

He shuddered visibly. "How can I ever thank you enough, Fiona? I'd not have known it was Nell. Their faces are always covered with the nun's coif and wimple. I should kill Lawton . . . *and* his bitch wife."

"And hang on Tyburn? Don't be ridiculous, Will. They aren't worth risking your own life. Nell is all right. She probably won't even remember much that happened tonight. Just keep her away from the house on Millbank after this."

"I'm sending her back home. I can't take care of a young lady!"

Then the coach drew up in front of a lovely house dating from the time of Queen Anne, and Huxley was lifting Nell out.

"Come in, Fiona. As soon as I get Nell's abigail to put her to bed, I'll see you back to Hanover Street."

"I wish I had something else to wear home. My maid is too curious by far about what I do. She'll make much of this revealing costume I'm wearing."

"I'll have the abigail find you something of Nell's to wear," he promised as he carried the sleeping girl up the white marble steps to the door. "I should have thought of that without being reminded. Sorry, Fiona; my brain isn't working too well tonight."

"It's all right, Will; you're forgiven."

And as she said the words, Fiona realized they were true. At some point in the hectic events of the night, she had quit hating Will Huxley; in fact, she admitted to herself that all of the old attraction was back. But Fiona was no longer free to love this handsome, exciting viscount. She was now a married woman.

CHAPTER 24

When Huxley came back downstairs, he said to Fiona, "I've had the abigail give me a sacque of Nell's. Do you think it could go over that just to cover you until you get home?"

"Of course. It's so kind of you, Will."

Then somehow he was standing in front of her, and the longing in his eyes matched her own. There was nothing Fiona could do, or would do, to resist the devastatingly attractive viscount. She swayed toward him, and his arms opened to hold her. It was as if she had always belonged there. As their lips met in a passionate kiss, Fiona realized that she loved Huxley, had always loved him—from the first moment she'd seen him at Aunt Eulalia's shop—and that she would love him until the day she died. He was not the only one who'd fallen in love at first sight! She melted against him as though she were French candle wax and he the flame. His hands, accustomed to the revealing nun's costume worn at the abbey, slid through the slits and found her willing flesh. As he caressed her breasts, she moaned with desire.

"Oh, Will, I've wanted you for so long," she sighed.

Erased from her mind was the horror of that Black Mass when she woke from her stupor to find him enjoying her body. Gone was the resentment, the hate, the bitterness of that dreadful encounter. Introduced to the delights of physical love by her husband, Fiona now longed for that ultimate embrace with Huxley.

His lips were on her eyelids, on her throat, on her

bosom. His hands tore at the flimsy drapery she wore, even as Fiona's fingers undid his waistcoat and tugged at his linen neckband. As they cast aside their clothing, passions rioting, Fiona could think of nothing except the culmination of her love for Huxley. Together they sank onto the Turkish carpet, their bodies joining in the ever-quickening rhythms of love. Fiona was the ultimate of sensuality as she gave herself in abandon to this man she loved so desperately. Passion built until she thought she must die from the intensity of her feelings. Finally, in a rapturous, blazing moment, their lovemaking climaxed in a burst of sensation that left her fainting.

When she recovered, Huxley was murmuring, "Fiona, beloved Fiona, I love you so much."

"And I love you," she breathed.

Still clasping each other, legs entwined in the most intimate of all embraces, they kissed tenderly, passion spent for the moment.

Later he lifted her from the floor, laid her on a velvet-upholstered sofa, and made long, slow, wonderful love to her. She responded with all the ardor of her youth, wondering how she could have thought that Samuel's lovemaking was fulfilling. Nothing in her life had prepared her for the depth of feeling, the complete giving and receiving, she had experienced just now with Will Huxley. She was shaken to the bottom of her soul.

Then, as they lay together kissing, caressing, loving, she realized what she had done. "What will Samuel say?" she cried. "He has been so good to me, and I have repaid him this way."

"Fiona, Fiona," Huxley said, voice hoarse with desire, "you love me. Why did you marry Rogers?"

"Why?" She laughed bitterly. "What else was I to do?"

He was silent too long. "I should have asked you to wed me," he finally said, quietly, sadly.

"You thought I was the worst kind of trollop," she reminded him. Even as she said it, she regretted the words. How could she say such harsh things to him as they lay together, bodies one in flesh, emotions one in spirit? Yet they came to her tongue unbidden.

"Damn Dashwood, damn his friars, damn Medmenham Abbey!"

"Damning them doesn't get us out of our disastrous fix," Fiona told him. "I'm married now."

He stopped her words with a passionate kiss, his lips moving on hers, his tongue seeking her own, his hands moving on her flesh, rousing her again to a fever pitch, so that she opened her thighs and welcomed his body into her own. This time there was almost a desperation in their passion. It was as if they felt they might never be together again, so they had to plumb the depths of passion, explore every sensation, give and take wildly to satisfy their love. Finally sated and exhausted, they lay there dozing for a long time.

It was Fiona who said, "This is madness. I must get home, Will. By now surely Samuel has left the abbey. He'll be worried when he gets back to Hanover Street and doesn't find me there."

Huxley sighed but got up from his bed of love. "What are we going to do, Fiona?"

"Do? Nothing."

He caught her chin in his hand and forced her to look at him. His eyes blazed with both passion and anger. "What does that mean? Surely after tonight you can't go back to Rogers. Your marriage with him would be a mockery."

Tears came to her eyes and spilled down over her cheeks unheeded. "I can't leave him, Will. He has been too good to me. It would hurt him terribly if I told him that . . . that I loved someone else and wanted to be free."

Huxley caught her shoulders in a harsh grasp, his fingers biting painfully into her bare flesh. "You don't love him, Fiona! You love me! You told me so to-night."

She closed her eyes, shutting out the sight of his face, darkened with anger. She loved him so utterly, so completely. How could she bear to go back to Samuel, to share his bed, to give herself to him as she had been doing? He'd know; he'd sense a difference in her. But he had been her salvation.

"No, I don't love my husband; I never did. I never told him that I loved him. But he loves me, Will. He took me in when I was desperate. I would have been on the streets if it weren't for Samuel Rogers. I don't love him, but I am beholden to him. I owe him, and I must pay my debts."

"But what about us?" he cried out in anguish. "What of me? I love you too. I *need* you." He caught her to him and kissed her with a wild passion that left her limp. His lips were on her breasts, on her thighs; he demanded response, and her body responded with the abandon she felt. But even this final act of love could not change Fiona's decision.

Sobbing wildly, she begged, "Oh, Will, don't ask me to betray Samuel's trust in me. I love you. I have always loved you and I always will—forever—but I owe him too much. I cannot leave him for you."

"Then you don't love me." He thrust her away from him, caught up his clothes, and dressed hurriedly. "If you loved me as much as I love you, Fiona, no other man could come between us. It's just as I believed. You are wanton. Any man can have you—*anyone*. All he has to do is undress you and you give yourself to him."

She shrank from him, dying a little at the dreadful words. "Oh, Will, how can you say that?"

Then he was on his knees, clasping her in a grip of iron. "Fiona, forgive me. I was mad to say that to you. It's just that I love you so much; I want you so much—all of the time, not just now and then when we can hide from your husband. I want you to ask Rogers for a divorce."

"Divorce! Will, I can't; I just told you that. He's been too good to me to treat that way. It would destroy him."

"But it will destroy *me* if I don't have you."

She put a hand on his head, caressing him, loving him. "You are strong, Will, and you must be stronger still, strong enough for both of us. I want you so much that my bones melt at the thought of you; but it would not be honorable for me to leave Samuel after he took me in the way he did. I must stay with him. A divorce would ruin him, destroy the career in Parliament he has worked so hard to achieve."

He rose and caught her fiercely to him. "Then what are we to do?"

"We must not see each other again." If she lived to be a hundred, never again would Fiona have to say such a difficult sentence.

"Not see each other! After tonight? Fiona, my flesh burns for you. You will be in my thoughts night and day. I cannot live without you! We must meet; we must love."

Fiona was sure that her heart would break. She wanted Will so much. She didn't want to stay married to Rogers now that she and Huxley had declared their love for each other. It was, though, the only honorable road she could take.

"It's better not to see each other again alone, Will." Fiona would rather have died than have said those words. She knew, though, what would happen if she and Will Huxley were alone together: they would not be able to keep from making love. It was too much to ask of them. Therefore, they must never be in this position again.

"It would be easy, Fiona," Huxley said. "I'm frequently at the house on Hanover Street. Did you know that? You're never there, of course. Samuel makes sure that the house is empty."

She had to smile then, remembering. "I was there the last time you came to print up your inflammatory articles."

His eyes opened wide with shock. "But I thought——"

She told him the story. She also told him how the Evans couple had tried to break into the wine cellar.

Now his face grew grave. "Did you tell Samuel?"

Fiona admitted that she had not, as she was afraid that Rolf would betray the secret of the printing press to the authorities.

"He knows the press is there?"

"I don't think so, but he knows something secret is going on. He's shrewd and a born snoop. When he threatened to go to the authorities, I know I should have bluffed him, told him to report us and be damned; but I didn't want to get Samuel into trouble. I didn't know who the mysterious printer was. I had wondered if it might be you. You're the only lord I know who is on Samuel's side in his drive to force the king to see to the needs of the poor."

"It would have been better to have told your husband immediately, Fiona."

She sighed. "I know that now, but at the time——"

"Well, I'm afraid we have to let Samuel in on the secret now. Your servants are dangerous to our work. They'll have to go."

She shivered a little. "They'll know I reported them."

Huxley's voice was hard when he answered her. "That can't be helped, Fiona. The work is too important to jeopardize." He smiled then and caught her to him in a warm embrace. "Don't fret, my lovely one. I'll protect you from the Evanses."

"Now I must go. Let me get into Nell's gown." Her reluctant fingers did up the hooks. How she wanted to stay here with her love—how she hated having to go back to Hanover Street—but she had to go, and the sooner the better.

Their carriage drew up in front of the house just as a hackney cab, coming from the other direction, rounded the corner. It was Rogers, finally home from Medmenham Abbey.

"Sorry to leave without you," Huxley apologized to Rogers, "but the Duchess of Lawton discovered that Fiona and I had rescued Nell, and we were not able to wait for you."

Rogers insisted that the viscount come in for wine.

"You missed all the excitement," he said with a laugh, eyes sparkling. "When the friars found they had no virgin, they just went into the Roman Room and got even drunker than usual. I saw the Duchess of Lawton with fire in her eyes, so I chose to make a hasty exit myself." Then, sobering, he inquired, "Is Nell all right?"

"Thanks to Fiona, yes. She was sleeping off the effect of the drugs, with her abigail in attendance. I insisted that Fiona come in and put on one of Nell's gowns. What she wore as one of the abbey nuns would have caused your servants to have apoplexy." He hesitated, glanced at Fiona, and then added, "I'm afraid we have a problem here, Samuel, with your servants."

"Problem?" Rogers's eyebrows raised and he looked at Fiona, a question on his face. "Fiona hasn't mentioned any problem with the servants."

"I . . . I didn't want to have to tell you, Samuel," she murmured, and felt her face flush with embarrassment.

To spare her, Huxley quickly told an abbreviated version of the story, not telling Rogers that Fiona had been in the house the whole time he'd been at the printing press in the cellar. He made it sound as though Fiona just happened to come home early and catch Rolf trying to get into the locked room.

"That's terrible! Fiona, you should have told me!"

"Rolf threatened to report us to the authorities if I did," she said, taking the easy way out Huxley had provided for her.

"They have to go," Rogers said flatly. "I won't have servants who spy and pry and make trouble."

"Yes, they must be dismissed," Huxley agreed, sipping at the claret Fiona had poured for him. "But we must do it circumspectly, my friend. This Rolf sounds like the kind of man who, if you dismiss him, just might go to the magistrates to spite you. If so, they might well come with a search warrant and find the press."

"There's no law against having a printing press in your wine cellar," Rogers said stubbornly.

"True; but we're vulnerable, you and I, with so much sentiment for and against our little paper. I think we must move the press temporarily. Then we find a logical excuse to let the servants go. Perhaps Fiona could claim that she has poor Scottish relatives she must hire."

Just then Fiona, who was facing the closed door of the parlor in which they sat, saw the doorknob turn cautiously. Holding up a quick hand to silence the two men, she pointed to the door and mouthed, "Rolf."

With a speed that surprised Fiona, Rogers was across the room even ahead of Huxley. He flung the door open, catching the luckless servant a blow on the nose that sent him reeling backward, hand covering his face as he howled with pain. "What's the meaning of this?" Rogers demanded, ignoring the blood that was seeping between the manservant's fingers. "Spying on us? How dare you!"

Frightened, Rolf blustered, "Thought I heard someone . . . might be footpads who broke in to steal . . . was creeping up on them——"

"A likely story," his master said, voice cold. "We were talking in normal tones. Surely you must have recognized my voice. No, you wanted to eavesdrop, so you were trying to open the door a crack to make it easier for you."

"Them's harsh words, Mr. Rogers," the man shouted.

"Truth is often harsh. Go pack your things. I want you and your wife out of here within the hour."

Rolf, clad only in a long flannel nightshirt and a matching nightcap, fought like a cornered badger. "Fire me, will you? I can make trouble, and I will, I promise you. Wait until I tell about the locked wine cellar."

"And wait until Mr. Rogers explains that he had to lock it and keep the key himself because you'd been drinking up all his claret," Huxley put in, voice calm but firm.

"That's a lie!"

"Prove it," Huxley said.

Fiona shivered at the look on her lover's face. She'd not want him for an enemy.

Just then her husband said sharply, "I see that Sal is up, too." He could see through the doorway into the hall. "My wife was going to put herself to bed to spare waking you, but since you're up and about, you shall help her."

Wondering what the men would do about the printing press, wanting to stay there to see the end of this drama, Fiona knew she had no choice but to go up to their bedroom with Sal.

The abigail, clad in a nightgown and shabby robe, her gray hair in two long plaits covered with a plain nightcap tied under her chin, was disgruntled and let Fiona know it. "It's hard to be the only woman servant in the house," she whined. "Must cook and clean and tend to you at all hours."

"Then you'll be glad to leave my employ," Fiona said, triumphant to get rid of the insolent woman.

"Here, now, only a dress on? I dressed you complete earlier and in another gown. Fine goings on from the *ton*."

"What I wear is no concern of yours." Earlier, Fiona

would have been so intimidated by Sal that she'd have made up some ridiculous story about falling into the Thames. Now, knowing the servants were finally to be dismissed, she felt she owed no explanation at all to the woman.

In a few minutes Rogers came in, saying, "Hurry, woman. You have to help your husband pack. You both are to be out of here before dawn."

"Throwing us out on the street! For nothing!"

"Spying on your employers is nothing? Be glad I don't search your belongings to make sure you aren't walking off with some of the plate."

When Sal finally left the room, Fiona whispered, "What happened to Will? What are you going to do about the press? I wouldn't put it past Rolf to set the law on us."

"We know that. Will has gone home for crates. His coachman is completely trustworthy. They'll come back the minute the Evans couple leave and transfer the press to his home until we see what happens. If he does make trouble, they can search our whole house and they'll find nothing."

Fiona was filled with foreboding. The Evanses were sly and vindictive. She feared that they still would make trouble for the three of them.

CHAPTER 25

"They asked a question in the House today about an article in *The London Man*," cried Rogers in glee when he got home next day. "It's beginning to have some effect, Fiona, when a little paper like that can manage to embarrass the government."

"Then the men who publish it are in trouble," she said drily.

"But no one knows who it is."

"Many blame you, Samuel; you know that. And there's been gossip about Huxley, too, because he's so often seen with you."

"Anyone who knows me knows the articles aren't my style. I couldn't write that skillfully. I'm good at the spoken word, but I'm a dud as an author."

"But those who hear you speak know that you're saying the same things they've read in that paper, Samuel. You'll get in trouble, and so may Will. The government doesn't want to be embarrassed. King George will get very ugly if the criticism keeps up. Kings don't like to be told publicly that they are doing a poor job of ruling."

"Parliament rules, Fiona, and I'm part of Parliament."

"Don't let King George hear you say that or you may find out how much power the monarch has, my dear husband." Fiona had never had any interest in politics; but being married to a politician, and being loved by another, was rapidly changing this attitude. She found that she was getting engrossed in the issues of the day.

"I was surprised when Huxley told you that he was the author of *The London Man,* Fiona."

"After last night it could scarcely be kept a secret. I just hope that Rolf and Sal don't suspect the truth about what was kept in the wine cellar."

"Probably they don't, but any gossip they start could cause problems. Why else do you think Huxley moved the press temporarily? It will keep us from publishing next week, I fear, but we don't know what Evans may tell, and others more clever than he might make the connection and guess that we have been printing the paper downstairs."

"Do you actually think that they'll come here to search?"

"I hope they do."

Fiona was shocked at his answer. "Good heavens, Samuel, why would you want that?"

He grinned. "Because the press is not here. They'd look, find nothing except the wine, and listen to my hints that I had to lock the cellar to keep Rolf from drinking up all the best vintage. Then we'd be in the clear and Will could bring back the crates containing the press."

She admitted that it did make a kind of sense; still, she wanted no part of the legal process. Having bailiffs in your home was not tantamount to proof of guilt; but there'd always be neighbors who'd whisper about having fire where there was smoke.

Several days passed, though, with no unwanted visitors. Fiona had no chance to see Huxley. Although she had told him that they must not meet again, she found that every time she went out for a stroll, and whenever she and Rogers took the air at Vauxhall or Ranelagh, she kept watching for the tall figure she loved so well. He did not appear anywhere. Finally, trying to make the query casual, Fiona asked Rogers what had happened to the viscount and his sister. "I thought perhaps they might call."

"Just heard today in White's that he's packed her off back home. It's just as well; there's a lot of ugly gossip going the rounds in the *ton,* too many rumors flying. I think that Lawton and his wife are working their tongues overtime, spreading the word that Huxley had planned to use his own sister in the Black Mass ritual."

"That's not true!"

Fiona herself was amazed at how much she'd changed in these last few days. She'd tried so hard to find out something scandalous about the viscount, and now, when there was a truly delectable tidbit, she was defending him, not spreading the vicious tale. How she longed to see him; her flesh burned for his touch. When she lay in bed with Rogers, she fantasized about Huxley even more than she had before. Now she knew what it was to love him.

"We know the story about Huxley isn't true," Rogers agreed, "but the duchess is a very influential woman in the *ton,* Fiona. All of society wishes for invitations to her parties. The duke is one of the most powerful men in London, a member of the group known as the King's Friends. When people like the Lawtons lie, people fall over themselves to believe them."

"Samuel, we could tell the truth."

"Ah, Fiona, we could, but who would believe us?"

"Surely they'd believe Will Huxley if *he* told the truth."

Rogers shrugged. "Well, there are lots of people who would discount his denials. After all, he was going to be abbot in the Black Mass, and they do use a virgin each time. He is scarcely blameless."

Oh, how true!

"There are those who would say he intended his sister to be part of the ritual, but when he was found out by you, he pretended he'd known nothing about it, that Nell had been brought there secretly, unbeknownst to him."

"She was, Samuel. Nell thought she was going to a

masquerade—she knew no more than that—and Will thought she was going to the house on Millbank, where she'd be entertained royally, have a marvelous time, while he was cavorting at Dashwood's chapel." Her mouth twisted in disgust. "It's really an ugly place, Samuel. I wish we didn't have to go there ever again. Oh, I know, I know, you do it for career reasons. Even with Huxley's backing, I know you need to convert a lot more men who have influence with King George." Then she smiled slyly. "You never enjoyed lying with the women, of course—playing games with the nuns!"

He grinned. "Oh, my motives were of the purest. But I think Huxley would prefer to let the story about Nell die. If we tell the true version, it will just blow the whole thing into a real scandal. Let's stay out of it, Fiona."

"Whatever you say, Samuel."

It bothered Fiona to have such dreadful accusations leveled against the man she loved. She wasn't convinced that silence was best. It annoyed her inordinately that the Duke and Duchess of Lawton should once again be able, with their lying tongues, to spread malicious stories. Fiona felt that someone should stand up to them, make them retract their vicious lies. Poor little Nell might have her blameless reputation besmirched because of their gossip. However, if Huxley didn't deny the stories, then she and Samuel could scarcely do anything to help.

"I'm surprised that Huxley doesn't call the duke out," Fiona said. "I know, dueling is illegal, but many of the bloods still fight."

"I'm sure he would like to, but he has to be practical, Fiona. Huxley is a sensible man. A duel would just fuel the fires of gossip. No, another scandal will replace this one soon. They'll forget all about Nell and Medmenham Abbey." Then he asked her about the couple they'd hired to replace the Evanses.

"Isaac was going over the household accounts with

me today. He told me that the Evanses had cheated us blind. You should have heard him. It's two shillings for five pounds of potatoes, but Rolf would list four and pocket the difference. He went over the figures with me until I think I could start my own stall in the market." She smiled as she mimicked the low-class dialect. "Boilin' beef, two pounds at two and a ha'pence the pound. Loaf sugar, shillin' and a half the pound." Suddenly angry at having allowed the servants to cheat her, she said, "I should have paid more attention to what was going on in the house. I'm afraid I'm not a very good wife for you, Samuel."

To her consternation, he caught her to him, gave her a long, slow, passionate kiss, and murmured, "You belong in the bedroom, Fiona, not in the kitchen. Who cares if you can manage a house? You are wonderful in bed, and that's where we are going to go now."

The thing that shocked Fiona was that she still enjoyed Samuel's lovemaking, even after her glorious experience with Huxley. Perhaps he'd been right about her. Maybe she *was* horrid and wanton. She certainly felt more tolerant of the women who went to the orgies at the abbey. Perhaps they enjoyed physical love with all of the men. Maybe that was as normal a way of life as being faithful to one man and one only. Certainly the members of the *ton* seemed to put little store in monogamy, for they all took lovers and traded them as often as they traded partners in a minuet.

"But Lettie probably has dinner ready."

"Let her wait."

It was the next day that the bailiffs came with their search warrant, duly executed and signed by a magistrate. Rogers was attending to his duties at Parliament when Isaac, solemn in his gray coat and black knee breeches, announced that there were men at the door demanding entry.

"They have a paper, madam, and insist that I let

them search the house." His angular face showed incredulity that such effrontery would be used.

So, it had happened. Although Fiona knew that there was now nothing at all incriminating in the house, that the press was somewhere that Huxley had hidden it, she found that her heart was thudding madly and her palms were damp with a cold sweat.

"I'll come at once. If these men are from the authorities, we must let them in, Isaac. As we are innocent of any wrongdoing, we have nothing to fear."

"Perhaps that couple who left were criminals," he muttered. "Cheating on the accounts . . . why, they may have been stealing and hiding the loot here."

Fiona wouldn't have put it past Rolf and Sal, but she knew that in this instance the authorities were here because of the printing press, although Rolf surely never knew exactly what secret lay behind the locked door.

The men were suitably burly, in truth caricatures of their offices. They presented the search warrant with some belligerence, and seemed put out when Fiona granted them the run of the house.

"I shall be in the drawing room after you have finished your search," she said calmly, though inwardly she still shook. "If you wish to speak with me, I will be available."

She noticed that Isaac dogged their steps, as if he wanted to be sure that they did no damage, planted no false evidence. Without her asking for it, Lettie brought tea on the best silver tray, tea with conspicuously one cup.

"The bailiffs won't be taking tea with madam," she said, not asking.

Fiona had to smile at such loyalty in a new servant. "No, Lettie, they won't be taking tea here. Thank you for bringing it to me."

The woman, gray hair done up in tight little sausage curls, mobcap snowy as her apron, went to the door of the drawing room, then turned hesitantly. "They won't find anything, will they, madam?"

With assurance, Fiona said, "There's nothing to find."

Still the maid hesitated. Then she came back into the room. "Madam, I . . . I heard some gossip yesterday when we went to market. The cook two houses down was there buying cabbages." She stopped, as if waiting for permission to go on.

Fiona didn't like servants' gossip; but Lettie did not seem at all like Sal, avid for any juicy morsel that cast a bad light on someone. Realizing that the woman was truly distressed about what she'd heard, Fiona said, "What did you hear, Lettie?"

"I understand that the couple you let go—Rolf and Sal Evans—were taken on immediately by the Duke of Lawton."

Fiona started. That was bad news indeed.

"You know His Grace?"

"I know him." No need to go into details.

"Madam, I've been in service for the *ton* here in London since I was thirteen. Started as the scullery maid and worked my way up. I've seen and heard things that would turn your head, I have. I never worked at that house on Millbank, but I've heard stories."

It was no secret, and Fiona sensed that she would gain Lettie's friendship if she told her. "I worked there as a wardrobe maid myself, Lettie. When I was forced to leave, the duchess made it impossible for me to get another job and keep it."

A tight little smile crossed Lettie's plain face, then was gone almost before Fiona realized she'd seen it. "I'd heard, Madam. And I can understand why a man would find you more attractive than Her Grace. I've seen her."

"Thank you, Lettie." Fiona wanted to tell the maid to bring another cup and have tea with her, but just in time she realized that Lettie would think this unseemly. She was mistress of the house, and Lettie the maid; they had no social meeting ground. It didn't matter that such a short time ago Fiona had been in service. Now she was in charge of a fine home, and Lettie would not have it otherwise.

"The duchess is saying that you are wanton, that you came back to London nude. And the woman who was your abigail," she added, lips pinched indignantly, "tells similar stories."

Fiona said quietly, "As a matter of fact, there is some truth in the story. What they don't tell is that I helped to rescue a young girl from rape. The duchess herself had arranged it as a revenge on a former lover."

"I thought it could be nothing bad about you, madam. I am a good judge of people," the maid said matter-of-factly. "It distresses me to hear you said bad of, madam."

"We know the stories aren't true. We shall ignore them, shan't we, Lettie."

"If you say so, madam. Now I must get back to the kitchen. I hope the bailiffs didn't upset too much there."

So, the duchess was still trying to do damage to Huxley through her. Fiona was frightened. She knew that the Lawtons were very powerful. Will Huxley was in a very precarious position. If anyone found out and could prove that he wrote *The London Man,* the king might well have him arrested for treason. Samuel might be elated that questions were asked in the House about the paper; but she was uneasy. Suspicion had been planted, and obviously the duke had enough power to get this search warrant. She knew it had to be the Lawtons behind the search, with information garnered from Rolf Evans. Vindictive servants, vicious peers—it spelled trouble.

Finally the bailiffs finished their search by poking

about in the drawing room while Fiona sat there, outwardly calm, inwardly queasy.

"If you'd tell me what you are looking for, I might be of some help," she said, willing her voice not to shake.

"A printing press, madam." The man looked at her with little pig eyes set deep in a lardy face.

"A printing press! Surely you joke, sir."

"No, madam."

"Then I could have saved you this search, for there is no printing press here."

"So we found, madam. Good day, madam."

With the sketchiest of bows the two men left her to her tea, which had grown cold. Fiona found that she was shaking. There was a discreet cough, and she saw that Isaac was standing just inside the drawing room.

"Yes, Isaac?"

"You seem agitated, madam. Perhaps a glass of claret?" He went to a small but solid walnut table done by Kent, poured wine from a cut-glass decanter into a delicate goblet, and brought it to her.

"Thank you, Isaac. It was . . . distressing to have the house searched."

"Yes, madam. I understand that the former butler told anyone who would listen that the master kept the wine cellar locked."

"That is correct."

Isaac smiled the same kind of fleeting smile his wife had smiled earlier. "No doubt to keep him from the claret."

She didn't say yes or no.

"Madam, I have also heard other rumors . . . about a certain paper that is much read by those of us who feel life could be better. Not," he hastened to add, "that I do not find my position here to my liking. I am well paid and treated like a human being by you, madam, and by the master."

"I hope we treat you decently, Isaac."

"The story is circulating that perhaps the locked wine cellar held more than claret. The bailiffs were looking for a printing press. I assured them there was no press here."

"As did I." What did this strange conversation mean?

"Madam, I wish to tell you that my wife and I would be proud to have even a small part in the production of that certain paper that is dedicated to the common man. And if the wine cellar should be locked at some future date, I would not make any attempt to enter it."

He knew! For one shattering moment Fiona wondered if once again she and Samuel were to be subjected to blackmail from servants. Then she absorbed the full meaning of Isaac's words and realized that he was telling her that she had nothing to fear from him, and that the printing press could be brought back and put to work again.

"It would seem a pity if that fine paper could not be published as usual, madam. My wife and I read it with almost as much fervor as the Holy Bible. The man who writes it has my heartfelt thanks." He paused, then said diffidently, "If you'd mention it to the master . . ."

She smiled. "Of course. He'll be very happy to hear this, Isaac." And so would Huxley. This meant that the press could be brought back immediately.

As if reading her mind, the manservant gave a deprecating little cough and said, "Now that the bailiffs have searched and found nothing, they won't be coming back, will they? If you'll excuse me, madam, I must polish the silver."

Fiona couldn't wait for Rogers to get home. Obviously the Newburys were going to prove to be as loyal as Huxley's coachman, who always helped him with the bundles of papers that were printed here.

She knew that the Lawtons were back of today's search. All of the servants of the big houses in London were tuned into the grapevine, knew what was going on. Rolf had known exactly where to go with his scurrilous tales of secrets in wine cellars; and the duke and his wife hadn't waited a moment to strike at both Huxley and Fiona. She only hoped that they could not damage Samuel's career too much with their vindictiveness.

CHAPTER 26

"Huxley will be around this evening," Rogers told Fiona when he returned from his duties at Parliament. "I told him that the bailiffs had searched yesterday and found nothing." He grinned. "See, my sweet, I was right. Now they won't be back again."

"Unless Rolf thinks up some other mischief."

"You're sure it was he?"

"Who else could it be, Samuel? He was so very curious about the wine cellar, and he knew exactly where to go with his suspicions. The Duchess of Lawton doesn't take Huxley's defection lightly—or my intervention for his sister. She can be terribly vindictive, as I learned from sad experience."

"I'm surprised that the duke goes along with this. Surely he knew he was being cuckolded by Huxley. It's not possible that he was the only man in the London *ton* who was unaware of who his wife's lover was."

"He's always so busy trying to force the maids that he has little time to worry about what the duchess does." She added, after a moment, "He tried to rape me when I worked there. I think he hasn't forgiven me for that fiasco. He is the one who arranged for me to be taken to the abbey—with his wife's eager connivance, of course. Oh, Samuel, I'm frightened. They are formidable adversaries. They can ruin you easily, after you've worked so diligently to get where you are."

He put his arm around her, drawing her close. "Don't worry your pretty head about the Lawtons, my dear. I have all of the common men of London behind me. With someone to direct them, they will be a force for reform, mark my words."

But Fiona did worry. And she dreaded seeing Huxley that night though she longed for him. Would she be able to behave with propriety when he came calling? Samuel must never guess that there had been anything between her and Huxley. What had happened at the abbey that first time was one thing—Rogers hadn't even met Fiona then—but if he learned that she had been unfaithful with the dashing viscount, she didn't know what he might do. He seemed to be the mildest of men, yet she thought there were hidden depths in her husband that she had never seen.

That night, when Isaac announced the viscount, Fiona's heart throbbed so hard, she feared Samuel would hear it. Huxley was the soul of propriety when he came into the elegant drawing room. He bowed over Fiona's hand formally, but as he raised his head, he gave her one piercing look from those flashing black eyes that nearly undid her. She snatched her hand away from his as if his touch burned her, as it did.

Huxley was so handsome in his silk coat of deep maroon trimmed with matching braid that she couldn't keep her eyes away from him. Luckily Samuel didn't notice the crackling tension between his wife and his guest.

The viscount chose a massive Kent chair across from Fiona so that he could keep looking at her without being obvious about it. He sipped wine and seemed relaxed, but it was the relaxation of a prize Bengal tiger, with leashed power ready to be released at a moment's notice. "We must make a decision about the printing press," he said, coming directly to the point.

Rogers smiled. "No problem. It seems that the new couple we've hired are staunch supporters of the sentiments they read in *The London Man*."

Huxley's black wings of eyebrows raised at this.

"Isaac must have guessed what was being done here when the bailiffs told him they were looking for a hidden printing press, because he told me he would be proud to help in any way possible in the publication of

The London Man. So the press can be brought back," Fiona said.

"The bailiffs will scarcely come looking again," Samuel added.

"Excellent." Then Huxley paused, thinking. "For their own protection, though, your new couple should probably be out of the house on the days when I come here, just as before. It relieves them of any responsibility. They can truthfully say, if asked on oath—I hope it never comes to that, but it might—that they have no knowledge of any activities in the wine cellar, that the master keeps it locked as a matter of principle, getting up the wine himself."

"Fine," Samuel agreed, "although poor Isaac may feel cheated that he's not allowed to run the press."

"Tell him that by keeping our secret he does enormous good for the project."

"And what about me?" Fiona said, then wished she'd bitten off her tongue before the words were formed.

Samuel answered before Will had a chance to reply: "I think it wisest for you also to leave as usual, Fiona. The same holds good for you as for the servants. You know, of course, but still you could swear in a court of law that nothing treasonous had ever transpired while you were here."

"Good thinking, Samuel," Huxley said.

His words were a crushing blow to Fiona. He had begged to see her alone again and yet, when they might have had a legitimate excuse to be alone in the house together, he agreed with her husband that she should continue to go shopping on those days he printed *The London Man.*

How she longed for Huxley's embrace. Just remembering how it had been made her blood run hot. If only—— But there was no solution to her problem. She had married Rogers out of gratitude, and the terms of her marriage had not changed; she still was grateful to him for what he had done for her. If Huxley had not—— No, she mustn't blame him. She was as much a part of what had happened at his house as he was. The loving had been inevitable. They were drawn together the way iron filings were drawn to a magnet.

Fiona knew that she would love Will Huxley until she died; she also knew there was nothing they could do now about the situation without hurting Samuel terribly, and this she was not prepared to do. Much better, then, that Huxley had agreed she should be absent from the house on the days when he printed the paper. She wondered where he had learned the printer's trade. She wouldn't have expected a lord to do such menial labor. "Where did you learn the art of printing?" she asked suddenly.

Huxley grinned. "At Oxford," he replied. "Several of us wrote this absolutely scurrilous sheet—it was pretty bad—and we got access to a printing press and learned to use it in order to keep our activities secret. If they'd ever have found out who we were, we'd have been packed off home in ignominy. So I learned two good things at university: printing, and keeping it a secret."

"You have hidden depths, Will," Rogers said.

Ah, yes, how little her husband knew, Fiona thought unhappily. He'd be crushed, humiliated, if he ever found out she had been unfaithful with his good friend and mentor the Viscount William Huxley.

As Huxley was about to leave he asked Rogers if he had any notes about pending legislation that might make a good article for their paper, and the moment Rogers left the drawing room, he was beside Fiona whispering, "Be here the days when I come to print the paper. Leave as usual when the servants go, but come back. Please, Fiona . . . I cannot live without you. After the time with you, the bliss, I must have you again. Don't say no."

"You know I mustn't," she said, but her heart sang at his words. What he'd said before was just for Samuel's benefit, to keep him from guessing that they were lovers.

"Don't do this to me," Huxley pleaded. "I must have you again. My flesh burns for yours, my beloved. Promise me that you'll be here. I'll be moving the press back tomorrow, and then I shall come the following day to run off an issue of *Man*. Be here, I beg you. Samuel will never know."

"I can't promise anything. It's wicked of me even to listen to such—— Do you think that the paper really has an effect on the king?" she asked brightly, for she'd seen Rogers in the hallway on his way back to the drawing room.

Huxley, understanding her ploy, said, "Such pressure must eventually bring about reform, Fiona. If not, God help England. Just as the injustices in France under the Bourbons are festering, so will it happen here. You cannot keep the masses under your heel forever. Englishmen have a tradition of freedom. The man in Cheapside wants it just as much as the Duke of Mayfair. If the rulers of a country do not change with the times, then they are changed by the times."

"Bravo! Spoken like a true London man," Rogers said, and applauded.

They made final arrangements about returning the printing press to the wine cellar, and Huxley took his leave. When he was gone, Fiona wished he'd kissed her while Samuel was out of the room. Perhaps it was best that he hadn't, though. One of his kisses was so inflaming that she would not have been able to sleep for hours, wishing for a true fulfillment of her desire for him.

Later that night, when Samuel made love to her, it was almost more than she could bear; yet he still was able to rouse her. She felt that she was betraying Huxley when she lay with her husband, and betraying Samuel when she let Will make love to her. Was ever a woman so torn, so tortured, as she was?

It was arranged that she and the servants would be out of the house when the printing press arrived. Before Rogers went off to Parliament in the morning, he called Lettie and Isaac into his study and explained the situation to them.

"I am deeply touched that the two of you are so much in accord with the work being done by *The London Man*. For your own protection, though, we wish you not to be here when the press is going. That way you could swear in court, if it ever came to that, your lack of true knowledge of what goes on in the locked wine cellar."

The Newburys were disappointed, for they had seen themselves as folk heroes in the struggle for equality in London, but they accepted Rogers's edict, acknowledging that what he wanted was sensible. "But remember, sir, that if you ever need us in the fight against oppression, Lettie and I will do anything to help."

"Even if it means winding up in Newgate," she added.

"After the bad servants I was cursed with, it is indeed wonderful to have the two of you to keep my home for us here."

On schedule next day, Fiona, wearing a weighted silk gown of deep green, with a cunning little matching bonnet she had made for herself, strolled out along Oxford Street, ostensibly shopping. Tomorrow . . . What would she do when the time came? Would she dare go back to the house to see Will alone? It was what she wanted more than anything in the world. The time with him when her love had been consummated seemed a dream She wanted more than dreams to sustain her. She wanted the reality of his arms about her, his lips on hers; she wanted to feel his body against hers; she wanted the culmination of their lovemaking once again.

She was startled out of her reverie when she heard someone cry, "Fiona! How have you been?"

It was Maggie Starrett, spectacular in a rich red gown with the overskirt looped up to show a gold tissue petticoat. She carried a parasol of the same gold fabric to protect her delicate pink-and-white complexion from the rays of the late summer sun.

"My, marriage certainly agrees with you," she said, eyeing Fiona candidly. "I must say we all were surprised to hear of your wedding, but happy for you, too."

"Thank you, Maggie." How ironic, Fiona thought, that Maggie should congratulate her on her marriage just as she and Will had finally discovered that they loved each other.

"Let's go into the park and have tea," Maggie suggested.

Once they were ensconced at a table under a shady elm, with a pot of tea between them, Maggie began telling Fiona all of the latest gossip.

"I've heard the most delicious scandalous story about Will Huxley," she said, leaning over the table, lowering her voice confidentially. "You do know the viscount, Fiona?"

"Yes, I know him."

"Of course! We met him with your husband—not your husband then, I know—that night when we all went to hear Rogers speak. Well, I've heard that he did the most wicked thing. He planned to use his own little sister—scarcely more than a child—on the altar at Medmenham Abbey when he was abbot, but the Duchess of Lawton managed to rescue the girl with her virginity still intact—though why anyone would worry about such a trifle as that is beyond me. Of course, it is a mite much to use your own sister, but there have been stories about Dashwood——"

"That's a rotten lie, Maggie," Fiona said, anger making her eyes flash fire. "I know what happened there that night because I was there, and nothing Her Grace says can be believed on oath."

Maggie sparkled with interest. "My word, Fiona, you look like you could scratch out dear Sarah's eyes."

"I could." Fiona told her the whole truth about Nell Huxley. "I am the one who discovered the plot, and Will and I—with Samuel's help—spirited Nell away safely. She'd been heavily drugged; but nothing else happened."

"Ah, I wondered. I know that Will is a real rake, but his own sister? It did seem out of character for him."

"Well, it was. The duchess is furious with him because he tired of her; this was her revenge. I just happened to be at the right place at the right time to help Nell escape. And the stories the duchess is spreading are outright falsehoods. I guess she knows that it would put her in a bad light if the truth were known."

Maggie grinned happily. "My, my, wait until I have a chance to tell this delicious little story to everyone. Frankly, I wondered if dear Sarah wasn't spreading the story about her ex-lover a bit freely. So *that* is what happened. I daresay Will Huxley is furious. I'm surprised he hasn't called Lawton out."

"I think he feels the story will die down sooner if he ignores it. I really shouldn't have told you the truth, Maggie. If you start this counter-rumor, it will keep the story alive. Could you just forget it?" Fiona was worried now, remembering that Samuel had wanted her to stay out of the controversy.

Maggie said, "Well, it's a juicy tidbit, and I hate not to offer it with tea to my friends; but if you insist . . ."

Fiona wasn't at all sure that the temptation to tell such a marvelous story wouldn't be too much for Maggie to resist. Why hadn't she held her tongue? She'd wanted to defend Will, naturally; but, by doing so, she might well have prolonged the gossip he'd hoped would quickly die.

Then suddenly, as if it had arrived in the nick of time to get Maggie's mind off the story about the abbey, Fiona felt faint.

"Fiona, are you all right? You're white as a sheet."

She could hear Maggie's voice, but it sounded as if it was coming through a barrel. In a moment there was the sharp smell of *sal volatile* as Maggie held her smelling-salts vinaigrette under Fiona's nose. The pungent odor made her cough until her eyes watered.

Pushing at Maggie's hand, Fiona gasped, "I'm all right now, thanks."

"Your color is better," Maggie acknowledged. "Did you feel faint?"

"Just for a moment. I hope I'm not coming down with the summer fever." She sat there breathing deeply, still a bit shaky but no longer faint.

"You gave me a scare," Maggie said. "Are you sure you're all right, Fiona? Let me call a chair to take you home. I'll come along to make sure you're all right."

"No, no, I'm fine!" Then, seeing the surprise on Maggie's face, Fiona tempered her tone and added, "I'd rather just sit here for a bit. Maybe we could get wine instead of tea."

"I think it would be better to——"

"Don't fuss, Maggie. I felt faint for only a moment. I'll be fine if I can sit still for a bit."

Fiona had remembered just in time that she couldn't possibly go back home now, certainly not with Maggie Starrett in attendance. Huxley and his coachey might still be moving the printing press back into the wine cellar. Maggie had a curiosity bump as big as the dome of St. Paul's. She'd be sure to ferret out Huxley's secret. And Maggie was a terrible gossip, not that she was particularly malicious; she just couldn't resist repeating a "juicy tidbit." In a day the story would be all over London. No, Fiona had to sit here until she was sure it was safe to go back home.

Seeing a buxom serving girl carrying tankards of ale to a party at the next table, Fiona motioned to her and ordered Madeira for them. When it came, she sipped gratefully at the amber liquid, letting it relax her.

"How is Samuel doing in Parliament?" Maggie asked.

"He enjoys it, and hopes to be able to sponsor legislation to help the poor."

"Personally I think it is like trying to stop a flood with one building brick."

"But someone has to make the start, Maggie. I've

seen some of the places in the slums; they're so appalling."

"I know, I know; but what can one man do, or even a handful of men?"

"If they can get the ear of the king, they can accomplish miracles," Fiona insisted staunchly. Then, quoting Huxley, she added, "The mob are like a keg of gunpowder, Maggie. One spark and they can explode. I don't remember the riots of a decade ago, but I understand that they were frightening in their intensity. It's little things like putting another penny tax on a mug of cider that infuriate the poor."

"What's a penny more or less?" Maggie asked reasonably.

"To us, nothing," Fiona conceded; "but to a poor man with a family, a man who earns only a few shillings a week, it can be the difference between hunger or food at times."

"But the money to finance the government projects has to come from somewhere. The landowners protest constantly that they're taxed poor. The amount my poor father has to pay is sinful."

Fiona didn't answer. Maggie's father's taxes would support a poor family for months and he would still live in luxury.

"Besides," Maggie went on, "they shouldn't keep having more brats if they can't feed them. It's a disgrace."

"How can they help it?"

A look of amazement made Maggie's lovely face almost comical. "Fiona, Fiona, I keep forgetting how naïve you are. I'd thought by now, with Werington and the abbey and marriage, you'd know how simple it is to take care of these things. Why do you think Sir Francis keeps a doctor just for his lady friends at the abbey if not to perform abortions when needed? Now, don't look so shocked!"

But Fiona was shocked. No matter how much she

had participated in the orgies at Medmenham Abbey, she still was not able to be so blasé about such things.

Then Maggie's eyes widened until the white showed all around the clear blue of the iris. "Fiona, you aren't expecting, are you? This faint spell——"

"No, no, nothing of the sort. I just remembered that the pheasant we had yesterday was very high. It's probably just that. I must tell Lettie not to let the birds hang for so long next time."

"Because if you were, there'd be no problem," Maggie forged ahead as if Fiona hadn't answered. "If you didn't want it, Sir Francis could easily arrange——"

"Samuel would kill me. He wants a child very much."

Maggie shrugged. "Oh, well, in that case . . ."

Fiona dawdled over her wine until she was sure the house on Hanover Street was vacant. Then she told Maggie that she felt quite well and would prefer to walk home rather than take a chair.

"You're sure, Fiona? Then I think I'll go along to Oxford Street. I saw the daintiest little sandalwood fan in a shop there—imported from China, the shopkeeper claims. I do think it might be just the thing to go with the brown merino suit I'm having made for fall."

The house was quite empty when Fiona got back. Huxley was long gone, but he'd be here again tomorrow. What would she do? Come back as he requested, or be a good, faithful wife and go shopping all afternoon? Even as she asked herself, she was planning to wear her new raw-silk dressing gown. It was a becoming buttercup yellow, and the silk was so soft, the lines so simple and flowing, that if she wore it with nothing under it, her figure would be tantalizing—not to mention the fact that there were no hooks down the front, only a sash to keep it closed. It wouldn't take Will more than a moment to undo the sash and bare her willing flesh to his loving touch.

CHAPTER 27

While they breakfasted lightly on toast, marmalade, and cocoa, eating from a tray in their bedroom, Fiona admitted, "I'm frightened, Samuel. What if someone saw the press being brought in? They moved it in broad daylight."

Rogers sipped the steaming chocolate and said indulgently, "You worry too much, my dear. Surely you don't think that Will Huxley is stupid? The crates didn't look like parts of a printing press. Some of it was disguised in a nice walnut chest. If the neighbors wonder, it will be what kind of new furniture we're acquiring, nothing else."

"What if Rolf is still spying on us?"

"Come, now, Fiona, if he goes to the magistrates again claiming that we're running a press in the wine cellar, he'll be laughed out of court. They sent their men to search and found nothing. I'd say that Rolf Evans—and, hopefully, the Duke of Lawton—aren't considered the most reliable of informants about now. All that trouble to get a search warrant, and then nothing in the wine cellar except bottles of good vintage."

"It was different before, when I didn't know who was putting out *The London Man*. He was just a faceless benefactor then, the man who made it possible for us to live here in comfort. Now that I know it is the viscount . . ." She kept having trouble saying Huxley's name to Samuel. Fiona feared that her tongue would betray her. Samuel must never know that she loved Huxley.

Rogers patted her hand. "Keep remembering that it

is the same man it's always been, Fiona. He has kept out of trouble all these months, and he'll be nimble enough to elude his enemies now." He reached for the bell pull and tugged the embroidered tape. When Isaac came, he motioned to the breakfast things. "But first, Isaac, I want to give you some money. We think that it might be best if you and Lettie went across the river and spent the day at Vauxhall. You'll need money for a boat and for the various amusements there. Enjoy yourselves."

"Sir, I thank you. Lettie does like the concerts they have in the gardens." He took the coins from Rogers with a respectful bow, then removed the tray and went off to give the good news of their outing to his wife.

"And you'll be out of the house, too, by ten?"

"Yes, dear. It seems a bit silly, now that I know who is coming, but if you and Will think it best——"

"We are trying to prevent later trouble, my dear. Buy yourself a new bonnet, or perhaps you'd like to see the latest play at the Drury Lane Theater."

"I'll decide later," Fiona lied. "I daresay I'll just shop." If, when he got home, she told him she'd gone to the theater, he might ask questions about the play that she couldn't answer.

As Fiona started to get up from the table where they'd breakfasted, she suddenly felt faint, just as she had yesterday in the park. Not wanting the arrangements to be jeopardized, she settled back in the chair, hoping that the spell would go away quickly so that Samuel wouldn't notice that anything was amiss. He was putting on his coat, a fine new one of brown velvet with brass buttons and brown braid down the front and around the bottom of the full skirt, so he didn't realize that she was feeling ill.

"I must hurry, my dear," he said, tilting up her chin with one possessive hand and kissing her warmly. "How I hate to leave you," he murmured, his hand dropping to caress her bosom. "I count the minutes until I can be with you again."

It gave Fiona the most awful sense of guilt; but she knew that no matter how guilty she felt, she still was going to come back to the house so that she could be alone with Will Huxley. Poor Samuel—he deserved better than this. She must never, never let him know that she was deceiving him.

She and the Newburys left the house at the same time, Fiona turning toward Oxford Street while the servants hurried off to find a boat to take them across the Thames. She decided that she would spend at least two hours shopping. She must have purchases she could show Samuel tonight when she lied to him and told him how she'd spent her day.

As a sop to her conscience, she bought an elegant neckcloth for Samuel, one made of the finest Irish linen, edged with delicate handmade lace. For herself she got a charming ruffled parasol, and then thought about buying a bonnet. Perhaps she should go around to Aunt Eulalia's shop to see her. Now that she was a respectable married woman, her aunt might look more kindly on her. What deterred her from this visit was the fear that the Duchess of Lawton might still take her trade elsewhere if she learned that Fiona had as much as set foot inside the shop. It wasn't fair to her aunt.

By lingering in the shops, taking her time deciding on her purchases, Fiona managed to spend two hours. Then she had a light repast in a pretty little tea shop. Surely by this time Huxley would have his printing finished.

Suddenly she could wait no longer to see him. Instead of walking back to Hanover Street, she took a sedan chair, crowding into it with her bundles. When she had paid off the bearers, she stood looking at her house. There was no way of knowing whether or not anyone was inside. Fear clutched her throat. Had

Huxley thought she wasn't coming back? Would he still be here, or would he have left, not knowing whether or not she intended to meet him and deciding not to wait?

She flew up the snowy marble steps to the door, fumbled the key in the lock, and arrived breathless in the reception hall. Was she too late? Had her own perversity denied her the pleasure of loving Will? No, over the thudding of her heart she could hear the reassuring thump of the press as Huxley printed the latest edition of *The London Man*.

She smiled. There was an ornate gilt-framed mirror hanging over a small table, and as she put her bundles down there, Fiona saw her glowing happy face. *I should wear a veil like the ladies in the harems of Araby*, she thought. *Anyone seeing my face would know I'm in love.*

Should she go to the wine cellar to let Will know she was here? No, she'd hurry upstairs and disrobe and be ready for him when he finished his work.

With gay abandon she flung off her gown, petticoats, stays—which nipped her waist in so tightly, Huxley could span it with both hands—chemise of embroidered silk, and French silk hose. Then she put on the yellow silk robe, fastening it loosely, slipped her feet into matching slippers decorated with tiny silk forget-me-nots, and unpinned her hair, letting the black tresses fall like heavy rain onto her shoulders. Artfully she arranged one long curl to hang over her bosom, which was nearly exposed by the deep décolletage of the robe, and leaned forward to her mirror. No need of mercury water to whiten her already lovely skin. No need for carmine on her lips, which were moist and ready, or for her cheeks, which blushed like a spring dawn.

She went into the upper hallway, and realized that the sound of the press no longer echoed through the house. Fiona stood at the head of the stairs listening intently; soon she heard the sound of the footsteps below. From where she stood, she could see the table where she had piled her purchases. Just then Huxley came into view. He had taken off his coat, and his teal waistcoat fitted him like a second skin. He'd worn a plain silk shirt without frills at the wrists, no doubt aware that they might get ink-stained. He stopped short when he saw the packages on the table, then turned and looked up, seeing Fiona for the first time as she waited for him on the upper floor.

He was up the stairs two at a time and caught her in his arms, crushing her to him, his hot lips seeking hers, kissing her as if he might never have the chance to kiss her again. One hand tangled itself in her silky black hair, and he rained kisses on her eyelids, her cheeks, her lips, her throat. She sighed in rapture and flung her head back, and his lips moved to the hollow where her throat and bosom met.

"Oh, Fiona," he breathed, "I was afraid you'd not be here."

"I shouldn't be," she whispered huskily, "but how could I stay away from you?" Her arms stole up around his neck, and she strained her lithe young body toward him, nearly swooning with desire.

"Where's your bed, my darling?" he asked, sweeping her up in his arms so that she nestled against his chest as a child would.

There was nothing childlike about Fiona's feelings, though. She burned for him even as she breathlessly directed him to her bedchamber. It was shameless of her to take him into the bed she shared nightly with her lawful husband, Samuel; but Fiona had no shame where Will Huxley was concerned.

Once inside the room, Will stood her on her feet and loosed the sash that bound her robe, which fell from her shoulders and slipped to the floor in a pool of brilliant yellow. It looked as if she was standing in the center of a giant buttercup. Quickly, with nimble fingers, she helped him disrobe, unbuttoning the gold buttons of his waistcoat and the smaller buttons of his silk shirt, baring his chest to her loving touch. He snatched off boots and trousers, undergarments and hose, then lifted Fiona onto the bed and lay beside her, drawing her so close that they were as one.

Both were too eager for each other to wait for tender lovemaking. They came together, bodies joining in an explosion of sensation, as if nothing else in the world mattered—only their love. They matched their rhythm in an ever-increasing tempo until Fiona thought that she could not survive any more rapture. In a blaze of ecstasy they cried out together as their love culminated in exquisite bliss.

"I love you, Will," she gasped, showering kisses on his face. "I love you desperately."

"Marry me, Fiona," he begged. "I long for you constantly. When I think of you in Samuel's arms, I die a little. I hate him; I even hate you, and how can I hate you when I love you so completely?"

"Poor, dear Will," she murmured. She drew his head down onto her breast, her fingers tracing the lines of his face, outlining the flashing eyes now closed in love, following the line of his strong jaw, touching the black brows that could make his face loving, sardonic, or frightening just by their position. "What can we do? I am tied to Samuel. I'm his wife, and I cannot ever tell him that I want to leave him for another man. It would kill him."

"I know," Huxley groaned. "I know. But when I'm with you like this, all I can think of is how much I want you, how much I need you. I try to put Rogers out of my mind. I fill my whole being with thoughts of you—of your soft, hot lips, of your satin-smooth skin, of the swell of your breast and its delightful weight in my hand. I long to explore every inch of your lovely body. I never want to leave you."

As he said his words of love, his eager hands were caressing her, tracing the lush curve of her hips, the smooth length of her thighs. He kissed her snowy breasts, and she felt the surge of passion again as he roused her to a fever pitch of desire.

This time his lovemaking was slow and sweet, and Fiona responded in kind. As their bodies met again, it was giving and sharing, not taking, as it had been when they were so desperately eager for each other after having been apart for what seemed an eternity. But the rapture was as intense as before, and Fiona clung to him, willing him never to leave her. The weight of his body on hers gave her such pleasure that she almost fainted from the feeling.

Afterward they lay entwined with each other, bodies sated, emotions quiescent for the moment. Fiona wished they could stay here forever; but she knew this could not be. Huxley would have to leave soon, for the servants would be returning from their outing and Samuel could return home at any time. What would he do if he got back early and found his bride in bed with his friend and collaborator? She shuddered at the thought.

"Are you cold, my dearest? Here, let me pull the coverlid up over us," Will said, reaching for the colorful quilt.

"No, no, I'd be so comfortable I might go to sleep," she protested, frightened now lest Samuel find them together in his bed. "We must get dressed; it's late."

As if to punctuate her remarks, the little gilt clock on the chimneypiece chimed three.

"I didn't realize what time it was. When I'm with you, time stands still," Huxley murmured, still caressing her.

This time she pulled away from his importuning hands. "No, Will, please, no. If Samuel should get home early . . ." She left it for his imagination to finish the sentence.

Reluctantly Huxley agreed. Their lovemaking for that

day had to come to an end. "Fiona, if we were married——"

"But we're not!" she wailed.

"If we were, we could spend as much time in bed as we wished—no watching the clock, no worries about whether or not we'd hear an unwelcome key in the lock or a dreaded step on the stairs. We'd be truly one."

Tears filled her blue eyes and brimmed over onto her love-flushed cheeks. "Please, Will, don't even talk about it," she begged. "It can't be. I cherish these hours we steal for ourselves, but I never forget for a moment that they are stolen. I just hope and pray that we never have to pay the criminal's price for this theft."

"Theft! It's Samuel who steals you away from me," he protested bitterly. "It's I you love, not Samuel."

"I'm his wife," she said.

There was something final in her voice that made Huxley realize he'd not be able to win her over to him today. He got up and dressed slowly. Fiona, fearful now that she had been so carried away with her sensual experience with the viscount that she'd lingered too long in bed, flung on her own clothes, putting on the gown she'd worn when she went out ostensibly to shop. If the servants came back soon, she could always pretend she'd gotten in just before them.

"When is your coachman coming for you, Will?"

"Four."

"But Samuel might be home by then."

"Tell him I was still here when you got in, Fiona."

"No, no, I might give something away. No, I have to leave and come back later."

"My dear, that's ridiculous."

"I have to do it," she insisted, now in a fever to get away from the house. "If the servants find us here——"

"They know about the press, Fiona."

"But they don't know about *us*," she said, her voice all sweet reason, "and they must never know. I hate it when the servants look at you that sly way that Sal and Rolf did when I was living here with Werington."

"I understand that his wife is giving him a child," Huxley told her.

Scarcely listening to him, fingers fumbling with the hooks on her bodice, Fiona mumbled, "That's nice."

Huxley, dressed except for his coat, which was still in the wine cellar, caught her to him in a final embrace. "I wish that you were having my child, Fiona."

"Oh, God! Don't say such a thing!"

"Why not? Wouldn't you like to have my child?" Disappointment was obvious in his hurt tone.

"But we can't . . . we mustn't . . . ," she said, almost sobbing.

She didn't tell him that Samuel, too, wanted a child by her, longed for a child. It wasn't the thing to tell your lover. A terrible thought popped into her mind, an unanswerable question, one she'd never thought about before. If she became pregnant, whose child would it be? She was Samuel's wife in every way. He made love to her, just as Huxley did. There'd be no way for her to know which of the men was the father of her child.

Pulling out of his embrace, she said, "Oh, Will, let me go now. I must get out of the house before anyone gets here. I couldn't carry off a lie, not after the way we've been." Then, at the last moment, she remembered, "I must straighten the bed. It would never do for Lettie to find it like this. She might suspect——"

"She's only a servant, Fiona. You don't owe her any explanations."

"I know, I know, but . . ." Frantically she pulled at the bedclothes, smoothing them, fluffing up the pillows. While she'd not made a bed for some time, now, Fiona had been raised without servants, and the old learned skills came back quickly. "There, she'll never suspect a thing."

She flung her arms round Huxley's neck in one final embrace, then wriggled out of his arms as they tightened about her. Down the stairs she flew. Fiona caught up her bundles and parasol and dashed out of the house, terrified now that she might meet either Samuel or the Newburys on her own front stoop. A quick glance up and down the street reassured her. No one was in sight. She raced along to Oxford Street, then relaxed. In a little while, after she'd heard the big clock in the church steeple strike four, she could safely go home to an empty house.

CHAPTER 28

Fiona fainted the night she and Rogers went to the King's Theater in the Haymarket to hear the Italian Opera Company sing an opera by Bononcini. She'd been quite excited about the evening's entertainment, not having heard much opera. One of Rogers's friends from the abbey had given him the tickets when he'd learned he'd be unable to use them, and they were excellent box seats. Lettie had laced Fiona into her finest gown of white satin trimmed with gold lace, the petticoat of gold tissue showing down the front, with a gold flounce about the bottom, and gold lacing the bodice.

"Not so tight, Lettie," Fiona had gasped, grasping the posts of the walnut four-poster as the abigail pulled on the strings of the corselet. "I can scarcely breath."

"The gown won't fasten if I don't pull you up tighter," Lettie said between clenched teeth. "You must have put on a bit of weight, madam."

Finally the maid got Fiona's waist small enough so that she could hook up the gown, although poor Fiona felt that she couldn't possible draw a full breath laced so tightly. The stays nipped in her waist and pushed her bosom up so high, she wondered if the bodice would contain the creamy mounds, which felt tender from the tight binding—and perhaps from Huxley's lovemaking. He'd been able to see her only once a week for the past month, on the days when he came to print his newspaper. She was always waiting for him, longing for his ardent embrace. So far they had been able to carry on their affair in secret. The servants

288

stayed away, as arranged, and Samuel seemed not to suspect that he was being cuckolded by Huxley.

Rogers had been enchanted with Fiona's appearance when she came down the stairs in her white and gold gown. "No one will pay any attention to the singers, my dear," he murmured, taking her in his arms gently so as not to disarrange her hair, which Lettie had dressed high for the formal occasion and powdered liberally. "You are the most beautiful woman in London."

She wished she could be pleased with his compliments; she truly wished she loved her husband. Fiona was a realist, though, and she knew that no words from Rogers could change the fact that it was the Viscount William Huxley she loved.

"I bought you a little trifle today," he said, handing her a prettily wrapped package. "I see I chose cleverly. It will go splendidly with your gown."

Loving surprises, Fiona opened the package and cried out with delight. It was a delicate fan with gilded sticks and gold lace. "Oh, Samuel, you're much too good to me." She felt contrite that he loved her and she didn't return that love. Opening the fan, she flirted with him, hiding her face, peeping at him with her blue eyes over the frilly edge.

"No one could be too good to you, my dear," he said. "Let's leave, or I shall carry you upstairs to bed and we'll never get to the opera at all."

"The tenor would not survive if we weren't in attendance," she joked. "Is the carriage waiting?"

"It just drove up." He draped a lovely silk cloak about her shoulders, flung on his own black cape, and they were off for the Haymarket.

It was during the first interval that Fiona felt very warm and dizzy. Fanning herself frantically as she and Rogers promenaded about with all the glittering company, she murmured, "Samuel, I think Lettie laced me too tightly; I feel faint."

Instantly his arm was about her, supporting her.

They hurried toward their box; but before they reached the curtained doorway, everything went black.

When Fiona recovered, she was lying on a sofa in the gallery, with a uniformed maid holding smelling salts under her nose, and a distinguished-looking gentleman taking her pulse.

"Ah, madam, feeling a bit better?" he asked in a deep baritone voice.

Over his shoulder she could see Samuel's frantic face. "How silly of me to faint," she said, her voice surprisingly weak. "My maid laced me so tightly, and it is warm——"

"Of course, madam. Let us see if you can sit up." He slid a firm arm under her shoulders and raised her to a sitting position. For a moment Fiona felt giddy, but then she seemed to be all right. Someone proffered a glass of wine, which she sipped slowly.

"I think, sir, it might be best to take madam home," the doctor was advising Samuel.

"But we'll miss the rest of the performance!" she protested. "There's the bell now."

The crowd moved away from this little drama, hurrying to take their seats before the next act should begin.

"The doctor's right, my dear. We can come to the opera another night. Right now I want you home and safely in bed."

Although she continued to protest, the doctor and her husband were adamant. When she was swathed in her cloak, Samuel helped her down the curving staircase to the waiting coach, and in a moment they were rattling over the cobblestones, Fiona resting her head on her husband's shoulder.

"I would have been quite all right," she said a bit crossly, disappointed to miss the rest of the opera, for the singers had been in fine voice.

"Another time. I do hope you aren't coming down with a fever. Have you had any other giddy spells recently?"

"No . . . well, I did feel a bit faint one day in the park when I met Maggie and we had tea; but it was a warm day."

They said no more about it that night; but the next morning Fiona was very sick, vomiting into the china washbasin Lettie held by her bed. Then, once her stomach was relieved, she felt quite all right and insisted on eating breakfast.

Samuel, not yet gone to the House of Commons, was very upset. "My dear, I don't think you should try to eat anything."

"But I'm starving," she said crossly, "and I don't feel a bit sick now." She turned to the abigail and ordered breakfast.

"The doctor who helped us last night gave me his card," Rogers told her. "I want to send a message to him at once. I think he should come here and examine you. Maybe you need to be bled."

"Ugh!" She shuddered. "I hate leeches. I absolutely refuse to let him put those horrid things on me, no matter what he says."

"But you will let him see you?"

Fiona sighed as if she'd been asked to perform some impossibly difficult task. "Oh, very well; but I feel quite all right now. It must have been something I ate." Then, realizing that Lettie was standing by, she added, "Not that I think it's your cooking, Lettie. Sometimes things upset us for no reason."

As Samuel went out of the room, Lettie followed him closely, and Fiona could hear the sound of their voices in the hall, though they spoke so quietly she couldn't understand a word they said.

When Dr. Ingham came later, his first question was, "Are you expecting, Mrs. Rogers?"

"I——" Her denial was cut off before it began. Fiona thought back and realized that she hadn't been keeping close watch on her calendar. "I . . . I might be." It was a stunning development.

He smiled. "My congratulations, madam." His examination confirmed his suspicions. "You are a healthy young woman. You should have no problems with your pregnancy."

Pregnant! And she didn't know whether the child belonged to Samuel or to Will Huxley. What was she to do?

Seeing her agitation, the doctor, with the bedside manner of all successful doctors, reassured her again. "I'm sure that Mr. Rogers will be happy to learn he is to be a father."

"Yes. Yes, he wants a child very much."

The doctor patted her hand. "In a few weeks you'll not have problems with morning sickness. In fact, you may well feel better than you ever have in your life. Many ladies tell me this, particularly with a first pregnancy."

She forced herself to smile at him. Poor Dr. Ingham. What would he say if he knew that what was bothering her was not her health but the fact that she didn't know who the father of her unborn child was. What would Will say when he learned that she was pregnant?

Samuel was, as she'd anticipated, ecstatic when she told him the news—she couldn't keep it a secret; he'd have had word from the doctor if she'd tried to hide the coming event—but he was also very frightened. "You must stay in bed most of the time, Fiona," he insisted. "I don't want anything happening to you or to our child."

"I'm not Kathleen," she said irritably, regretting it instantly when a shadow crossed his face. "I'm young and healthy, Samuel. It's not good to spend all of the time in bed. Dr. Ingham insisted that I live a normal life, go walking even more than usual, so that the baby will be healthy."

"Well, if the doctor says so . . ."

"He does, so that settles it."

"I'll move into the other room," he said.

"Whatever for?"

"I wouldn't want to injure the child."

Now she was in a true dilemma. The doctor had assured her that normal conjugal relations would not be harmful. She intended to continue her affair with Huxley—that is, unless he no longer wanted her when he learned of her impending motherhood. There was no need for her husband to sleep away from her, yet if he did, she'd be able to give herself to Huxley completely.

The first day that Huxley printed *The London Man* after Fiona learned that she was expecting a child, she scarcely knew how to approach him. She came back to the house on Hanover Street as usual, went immediately upstairs, and disrobed in preparation for him when he finished printing the paper. She stood in front of the free-standing, walnut-framed, full-length mirror looking critically at her nude figure. Was her waist beginning to thicken? Were her breasts fuller than usual? No wonder she fainted the night of the opera, for Lettie had had to lace her tighter than usual in order to get her dress fastened. Would Will notice any difference in her? Should she tell him today? And what would he say?

What he said as they lay together after their usual glorious lovemaking was, "The child is mine!"

"Will, how can you be sure? Even I don't know," she sobbed. "The child could be Samuel's. He's my husband, and he has been expecting his marital rights." She'd never told Huxley that she enjoyed lovemaking with her husband, too, although the rapture she felt with the viscount was absent when her husband lay with her.

"The child is mine," Huxley repeated, laying his hand on her abdomen. "Mine, I know it. And I want this child for my legal heir. Fiona, you must tell Rogers about us now. You have to get a divorce so that we can be married before the child arrives. When is it due?"

"Probably in May," she whispered. Divorce? She

couldn't divorce Samuel, no matter how much she wanted to be married to Huxley.

"You have to tell Rogers that the child isn't his."

"I can't do that, Will, it may be his child, and he wants a child so desperately since his other child was stillborn. He is so excited about my condition——"

Huxley groaned. "Fiona, Fiona, how can you be so cruel to me? You tell me that you love me, you demonstrate that love in the most glorious way, and yet you won't marry me. I want my child."

She dissolved in tears. "It may not be yours," she sobbed. "How do I know whose child it is? It could just as well be Samuel's. Do you want to cheat him out of his heir?"

Furious, Huxley got up from the bed and paced, nude, like an irate tiger. His muscles rippled with leashed power. Fiona loved every inch of his tall, strong body—it gave her such pleasure that the very thought of him made her weak—yet she had a sense of honor that she could not wall out of her life. She was Rogers's legal wife. This child she carried under her heart might well be his. How could she know? How could anyone know? She could not ask him for a divorce now. He was living on a heavenly cloud, thinking that he was to be a father at long last. It would be unutterably cruel to tell him that the child might well belong to Huxley.

"Will, please don't be angry with me," she begged. "You are a gentleman, a man of honor. Can't you see my position?"

Huxley quit his angry pacing and lay again with her, pulling her tenderly into his embrace. Lips against her coal-black hair, he murmured, "Honor—I've always thought that it was the most important thing in life. But now I've learned that there's something else more precious to me than my honor; it's you, Fiona. I'd willingly become the most dishonorable man in England if only I could claim you for my bride, if only this child you carry could be legally mine."

"Oh, Will, you don't mean that," she cried, tears falling onto his face. "You couldn't live with yourself if you did the dishonorable thing, nor could I. We'd come to hate each other all too soon, for we'd both know that we had wronged Samuel dreadfully. Oh, my dear, I love you so much, but I can't do what you ask. I can't tell Samuel that this child may not be his. I can't ask him for a divorce so that you and I can wed. If I did, I'd never be able to look at myself in a mirror again. My eyes would be eternally accusing. And you'd feel the same way; you know you would."

He clutched her so tightly that she almost cried out from pain. "Oh, Fiona, you're right. You're good, and noble, and I love you so desperately. How can I bear it? Yet, you are right. We must go on living a lie, for we cannot bring dishonor onto our two households."

CHAPTER 29

"Samuel, Will Huxley has gone too far this time," Fiona said as she read the latest issue of *The London Man*. "He's named Sandwich and Bute as two men who advise the king to the detriment of the public. They'll be furious."

"But it's true, Fiona, every word. And reaction is already running high in the poorer sections of London. They're burning boots and petticoats everywhere, and even the lowest sweeper knows the significance. The boots are a play on Bute's name."

"And the petticoats?"

"A reference to the well-known fact that Bute seduced Princess Augusta, gaining much power through her."

Fiona shivered. "I'm worried, Samuel. You and Will are treading on hot coals. What if the king calls this treason?"

"They have to prove who wrote the articles."

"Too many think you did, and I know some suspect Huxley because of his association with you."

"It takes more than suspicions, my dear. This is England. Our laws require proof of wrongdoing, not just suspicions."

"But history has shown that when you step on the toes of the powerful, sometimes proof is found . . . or manufactured."

"Don't worry; it's not good for our son," Samuel chided in loving tones.

Fiona's pregnancy was beginning to show. Lettie had

to hitch her hoops up higher and higher to cover her increasing girth.

"But I do worry," she complained. "Samuel, I think that Rolf Evans is still spying on us."

He looked up quickly, eyes unreadable. "What makes you think that?"

"Last time Will was here, when I came home I met Evans as I turned in Hanover Street from Oxford." She could scarcely say she'd seen someone lurking in a doorway down the street when she slipped out of the house after her rendezvous with Huxley, and on her return she came face to face with the villain, realizing he'd been the vaguely familiar shape she'd seen earlier.

"Huxley doesn't use his own coach when he comes here on business. And I know he always has the collar of his cloak turned up, as if to ward off a chill river breeze, and wears his tricorne down low to shadow his face."

"But what if they search us again?"

Rogers was all concern for his young wife in her delicate condition. "I'll talk with Huxley. Maybe for a time the press should be moved to a new location."

"It might be safer." But then how would she ever see Will? Now he had an excuse to come to their home. With the press gone, what could she tell Samuel if Will was seen coming and going from this house when Samuel was away?

"We'll work out something, Fiona. I won't have you worrying at this time; it might mark our child."

Fiona was even more worried the next day when she read *The Gazette*. Apparently the king's wrath was enormous after he'd seen the latest issue of Huxley's paper. He was muttering words such as "treason" and "the Tower." Samuel came home from Parliament with a worried look that matched Fiona's.

"Huxley certainly precipitated a furor this time. There's been trouble in the streets. Crowds of men are roaming about, upsetting carriages and attacking various lords in chairs. I understand that they beat old Tomkins rather severely."

"But he must be seventy!"

"They don't hurry first to Somerset House to look at the records, Fiona. They're angry men."

"Violence—I don't like it, Samuel. Is it right to provoke such actions? Someone will get murdered; then how will you and Will feel?"

"I deplore violence too, but sometimes people reach a boiling point after years of oppression. It's hard to blame them, even when they overreact."

That night, though, after dark, they had reason to be even more fearful than they'd been. There was a hammering at the door, and in moments Isaac ushered in a man in Huxley's livery. He was gasping as if he'd run a long way.

"Sir, they've arrested his lordship. Before the constables took him away, he managed to whisper to me, told me to come here and tell you to look to the wine cellar."

"Thank you, my good man." Samuel pulled out his purse and gave the man a penny. After the servant had gone back into the night, he rang for Isaac. "We have to dismantle the press at once. We may be searched again."

"Where can you hide it?" Fiona asked frantically.

"First let's get it out of the wine cellar. Can you and Lettie empty any trunks we have that are full of stored clothing?"

"Of course," she replied. But if the bailiffs came again, they'd go all over the house as before. They'd open trunks, peer into wardrobes, get down on their knees to look under beds.

Samuel and Isaac worked all through the night, taking apart the printing press and stowing the parts in three large trunks that Lettie and Fiona had emptied stowing the extra clothing in drawers and cupboards and in already crowded wardrobes. Fiona wanted to stay up with them, but Samuel, fearing that the excitement might bring on a miscarriage, insisted that Lettie put her mistress to bed.

Fiona slept only fitfully, dreaming of prisons and scaffolds when she did sleep, and woke unrefreshed when Lettie brought in her morning tea.

"The men?" she asked, as soon as she'd opened her eyes.

"Finished packing the press, madam. There's no sign that it ever was in the cellar. His lordship has always been very neat in his work there," she added with approval.

Samuel came in then to share a light breakfast with her. "I've tried to find out about Huxley, but all I know is that he's in Newgate Prison. His solicitor is trying to get him released."

Newgate Prison! The words struck ice to Fiona's heart. "Will they come here again, Samuel?"

"I would have said no, as they searched previously. Now, however, with Will in prison . . . Are you sure you saw Rolf Evans hanging about?"

"Positive."

"Will thought it dangerous enough that he sent his man to warn us last night. I must carry through."

"What will we do with those trunks full of press pieces?"

"That's what I've thought of all night. I'm going out right now to rent rooms in a slum section of London. I hate to ask you to help, but——"

"Samuel, I'm your wife. Whatever affects you affects me. I *want* to help."

"I'll say that I'm looking for temporary rooms for my wife and her abigail, that you're having a complicated pregnancy and we've come in from the country to consult a London physician. Then you and Lettie will have to arrive with the trunks. You will spend very little time there. You can tell the landlady you have friends elsewhere—anything—but at least the trunks will be safe."

"Someone may recognize our name."

"I'll rent the rooms under my mother's maiden name of Yeoman. Who'll ever guess?"

"What will Will Huxley say to your plan?"

"Fiona, I can't wait to ask him. I have to get that press out of here immediately. In fact, I'll take the trunks with me now and leave them at an inn briefly. That should throw off any pursuit. When I find suitable rooms, you and Lettie will go to the inn, have the trunks loaded on your hire carriage, and then go to the rooms."

"If it will help, I'll do it, and I'm sure Lettie will, too."

Waiting was agony. She had no idea what had happened to Will. Would they be able to keep him in prison? Was there any firm evidence against him, or was it more of Rolf's malicious rumors? Fiona knew that the rich peers had a better chance to escape imprisonment than the poor, but in this case the king himself had entered into the picture. He was furious with the man who wrote *The London Man*. No matter that England was considered a constitutional monarchy; no matter that in theory Parliament had a large voice in running the affairs of state—in the final analysis, if the king was angry, someone had to pay, and this time it was her beloved Will.

She sketched out the plan of action to Lettie once Samuel left with the trunks in a hired coach. Before he left, Isaac scouted the entire street, making sure that Rolf Evans wasn't hiding in some doorway waiting to spy on them. Fiona was vastly relieved when the trunks were carried out and the carriage pulled away from the house. It was not yet light, but Samuel wanted the press away as soon as possible. She wasn't dressed when Isaac, all concern, came to tell her that the bailiffs had returned with another search warrant.

Wearing her severest robe, Fiona swept down the stairs and confronted the stolid men with their accusing paper. "Gentlemen, this is too much!" she said with a firm voice, though inwardly she was shaking. "You have searched this household once recently and found nothing. What mischief is this? Who accuses us?"

"Madam, we has our orders," the older man said, "and we has the authority." He waved the offending search warrant under her nose.

"Very well, search," she said coldly. "And much joy it will give you. We have nothing to hide, nor did we the previous time."

She made a pretense of breakfasting in the small salon while the men went about their work, but the food stuck in her throat and momentarily she feared she might be sick. What if Samuel hadn't had the foresight to get the press away before dawn? What if they hadn't been warned by Huxley? She and Samuel might be sharing cells with Will in Newgate Prison. Then she had another worry. What if Samuel returned while the bailiffs were conducting their search? Might he say something incriminating if provoked by them? She rang for Isaac to remove her breakfast tray.

"Where are the bailiffs?" she asked in a whisper.

"In the wine cellar again, madam."

"Wait outside at the corner. Try to flag down Mr. Rogers when he returns. Have him wait until they have gone before he comes in."

Isaac, no fool, saw the wisdom of her words immediately. "At once, madam." He snatched up the tray and hurried from the room.

In a few minutes she heard the front door close quietly, and shortly afterward the bailiffs appeared in the salon.

"Well, are you satisfied?" she asked coldly.

"We found nothing, madam."

"I told you there was nothing to find. I am becoming

increasingly annoyed by this nonsense. Don't come back."

"We comes if we is sent, madam," the older man said stubbornly. Then, pig eyes narrowing, giving his fleshy face a mean look, he asked, "Where's the man-servant off to?"

"Market." She made no further explanation, and finally the men took themselves off. Fiona hoped she'd seen the last of them.

It was several hours before her husband returned, and by that time she and Lettie were dressed to go out. Fiona had chosen the plainest gown she had, and a severe bonnet, to look the part of a country wife in for medical care.

"I have news of Will," Samuel said the minute he was in the house. "He's been released, I understand. They had no proof of his complicity. Apparently his home was searched——"

"As was ours again," she cut in.

"Thank God we got the press out in time."

"Now Lettie and I are ready to do our part in this affair."

"I've told the hired coach to wait. Have you packed anything?"

"A few clothes. We thought it would look strange to arrive only with three large trunks. As it is, our land-lady may wonder that we have such large wardrobes."

"The rooms are off Lincoln's Inn Fields, in a very poor neighborhood. I daresay the landlady is interested only in the shillings she'll get for the rooms. They're reasonably clean, but that's about all."

Even as she and Lettie rode along the streets toward their destination, Fiona's mind was working overtime. Now that Will was free, maybe they could meet in these new rooms. There was no way for them to be together on Hanover Street. With the press gone from the wine cellar, there would be no reason for the servants to leave one day a week. She could give them time off, of course, but then Samuel might find out about it and wonder. She could, though, come alone to the rooms in Lincoln's Inn Fields—no need to tell the servants where she was going—and Will could meet her there. Any thought of denying her flesh now was incomprehensible. She was so deeply in love with Huxley, and he with her, that they were in misery when they were apart. If they couldn't see each other often, Fiona didn't think she could go on living.

CHAPTER 30

"Why do you keep glancing back over your shoulder, Fiona?" Will asked. "Surely you don't think we're being followed? No one knows of the lodgings except you, Samuel, and your two loyal servants."

"I know, I know, but . . ." Her voice drifted away. How could she explain to Will this feeling that they were being watched? She'd not seen Rolf Evans since that day on Hanover Street, but she wasn't sure that he hadn't sniffed out her new hideaway.

As if reading her mind, Huxley said, "You don't think that Evans scoundrel is still on our trail, do you? What difference would it make if he were? The press is now out in a deserted cottage on my country estate. I have every good reason to travel there each week. No one could guess that my trunk contains paper and supplies of ink, and that there are copies of *The London Man* in it when I come back to the City. There's nothing for Evans to find even if he does spy on me."

"He'd know about us."

"I'm a friend of the family, Fiona," Huxley said, laughing.

"You know you're much more than that. If Samuel found out——"

"What's he going to find out, my dear? That I have taken you out for tea? What we do in your grubby little room turns it into a palace of delight."

He wasn't even touching her, but his very words thrilled her, bringing with them a surge of desire. How wanton she had become. Nothing mattered to her now except being able to lie with Will on this lumpy mattress in this dingy room. He was right. When they were together, their surroundings didn't matter at all; nothing mattered but their sensual delight in each other, the exquisite pleasure they shared with the coming together of their bodies.

"I'd not want gossip about us to be whispered throughout the *ton*, Will."

"Sometimes I wish that the story did get back to your husband," he said, frustration on his handsome face. "Then you'd have to divorce him and marry me."

It frightened her when he said such things; the intensity of his feeling was like a volcano ready to erupt.

"Will, you promised me you'd not say that again."

"I know, but I want you so desperately, Fiona. I sit at my desk at night, quill in hand, paper before me, and the words that should come, the words to fill *The London Man*, turn into love sonnets for you."

"Will! You never told me you wrote poetry."

"I don't. It's the most awful doggerel—the words don't nearly express my feelings—but you're interfering with my work, my dear."

In dismay she cried, "You mustn't say that, Will! What you are doing is so important; you must forget about me."

"You might as well expect me to forget to breathe."

They had been strolling across the expanse of Lincoln's Inn Fields. The grass was taking on the faintly yellow tones presaging autumn, and the trees were beginning to show color in their leaves. There was a nip in the air that brought color to Fiona's cheeks, and she pulled her cloak closer around her.

Immediately Huxley noticed. "Are you cold? I shouldn't have kept you out so long, let you walk so far."

"Nonsense! Dr. Ingham says that walking in the air is good for me. You and Samuel would wrap me in cotton wool and not let me move a muscle if you had your way."

She saw his mouth tighten at her mention of Rogers; but Fiona knew she had to keep thinking of her husband or she was lost. How easy it would be to yield to Huxley's pleading and allow him to arrange for a quiet divorce—quiet, that is, if Samuel didn't contest it. But her first loyalty was to Rogers, who had saved her from a life of degradation, and she must never forget it.

As they came back to the cobbled street, a carriage that had been standing there suddenly started up, the driver whipping the horses so that the coach raced past them, spattering them with gobbets of mud in its mad dash. There was a crest on the door of the well-varnished body of the landau, but the carriage passed them so rapidly, Fiona couldn't see what the coat of arms was. Huxley swore loudly.

Fiona, glancing at the mud on his breeches, said, "How can people be so thoughtless?"

"That was done deliberately, Fiona. Didn't you recognize the crest? It was our old friend and nemesis the Duchess of Lawton."

She felt a sinking sensation in the pit of her stomach. "Are you sure? Oh, Will, she'll spread it all over London that we were together."

"What matter if she does? We're engaged in an innocent walk——"

"But what excuse would we have for being here in Lincoln's Inn Fields? I think it is time to abandon the lodgings, Will. Now that you've taken the press out of London——"

"But I've not mentioned that fact to your husband."

"He knows you can't run the press in the lodging-house. Sometimes you don't give Samuel credit for having any sense at all," she said crossly. She was caught between Scylla and Charybdis with her emotions. Love and duty warred constantly, making her short-tempered even with the man she loved.

"If you give up the room, will you come to mine instead?"

"Oh, Will, someone would see me. How can I?"

Their dilemma was not resolved when Huxley left Fiona at the lodginghouse. He wanted to take her home in his coach, which he'd left waiting while they strolled through the fields, but Fiona, now supersensitive about gossip, said it would be better if she hired a coach or a chair to take her to Hanover Street. She was adamant. Finally Huxley stormed off, furious with her for being so stubborn.

More tired from the walk than she wanted to admit, Fiona used her room to lie down and rest for a while. She knew that soon Samuel would realize there was no further need for this particular pretense. How she and Huxley would get together then was a problem she refused to think about; it just gave her a headache. As she lay resting, the child she was bearing moved, filling her with a rush of maternal feelings. Was the child Samuel's or Will's? That was another problem she pushed behind her, refused to think about. She might never know unless the babe looked so much like one of the men that there could be no question about paternity. What would she do if the child obviously belonged to Huxley? What would Samuel do? It was terrifying to contemplate.

She had been home only a short time when Samuel arrived, all smiles. "Last time we went to the Italian Opera, you fainted and we missed most of the performance. Tonight we'll see it all. I've managed to purchase two seats."

"If I faint tonight, just leave me lying on the floor while you see the performance, and you can tell me about it later," she joked. Then she began worrying about what to wear. "I may not be able to get into any of my better gowns. Lettie and I may have to rip the seams."

"My dear, you'd look delightful in whatever you wore," Samuel said gallantly. "And think how important it is for our unborn child to be introduced to such things as Italian tenors at such a tender age."

By pulling Fiona's hoops up almost under her chin, Lettie finally got Fiona dressed in a rather elegant gown of deep copper silk. "If you wear this separate blouse under the bodice, madam, it will seem to be part of the gown," she said, slipping the soft white ruffled blouse over Fiona's head. "See, I can use much longer ribbons for lacing, and it will give you plenty of room."

"Lettie, you are a jewel," Fiona murmured. "Shall I wear my hair high?"

"Yes, in an elaborate style, I think, madam, to call attention to it and away from your increasing waist-line."

Samuel's eyes lit up with that old familiar gleam when she came down the stairs. He'd not stayed out of her bed for long once Dr. Ingham told him that it was not necessary to stay apart from his wife this early in her pregnancy, and Fiona knew he'd want to make love tonight after the opera.

Attending the opera was an exciting but strange experience. The tenor was in fine voice, Fiona thought, though she didn't understand a word of Italian. Samuel consoled her with the opinion that scarcely anyone there spoke the language.

"But most of the men who go to Medmenham Abbey know Latin."

"Believe me, that's not Italian," he said, laughing. "Even I had a smattering of Latin in school and a bit of Greek, but if you think I understand that howling on stage . . ."

At the interval they joined the promenade, coming face to face with the Duchess of Lawton, simpering on the arm of a dandy in lavender who was young enough to be her son. Samuel tried to sidestep them, but the duchess, malice on her chalky face, blocked their way.

"How charming," she shrilled, so that all conversation within hearing range automatically stilled. "Mr. and Mrs. Samuel Rogers, legally wed." She smirked at Fiona, who was seething inside but kept a social smile pasted on her face. "And I see that dear, dear Fiona is expecting. How quaint. Whose child is it, my dear?"

There was a gasp from someone nearby, and a titter of laughter ran through the crowd. Fiona's hand was resting on her husband's arm, and she could feel his muscles tense at the insult.

"Fortunately for me, it isn't His Grace's," Fiona said, her voice as carrying as the duchess's. This brought even more laughter, but now it was at the expense of the duchess.

Her Grace flushed, an ugly blotched look under the white paint coating her aging skin. "Little slut! I'm surprised you could get any man to marry you." She turned to Samuel and said, in a travesty of sweet sympathy, "I do hope you don't expect this child to look like you, not when your wife is seen in the company of such lechers as the Viscount Will Huxley." She reached with her fan and tapped Fiona's thickening waist. "Carrying a little bastard, are you?"

Fiona was stunned speechless. She should have known, when Will told her that it was the duchess in that carriage, that her secret would become public property; but for it to come to poor Samuel's attention so publicly . . .

Samuel lost his temper. His voice, instead of rising, dropped an octave and was icy: "Madam, if you were a man, I'd call you out."

"Oh, how darling," she cooed. "He wants to fight a duel with me. You should save your fury for the man who is cuckolding you—the dastardly William."

Fiona pulled at Samuel's arm, trying to drag him away from this vixen with the virulent tongue; but Samuel was not going anyplace yet.

"Madam, apologize to my wife this instant."

"Apologize to my ex-wardrobe maid? Sir, you are

insane, as mad as your first wife. You do have bad luck with your wives, don't you, Mr. Rogers? One in Bedlam, the other in bed with anything in—or out of—trousers."

Fiona feared that Samuel might suffer a stroke of apoplexy, so infuriated was he. "Ignore her," she whispered frantically. "Pay no heed——"

"You are vile, madam," Rogers said to the duchess. "Retract your lies this minute."

"Lies? *Lies?*" she trilled, making sure her audience could hear her every word, projecting her voice above the babble in the background. "Sir, I saw them with my own eyes only yesterday, strolling through Lincoln's Inn Fields."

"And? What of it, madam? I see that you are here in public with this young popinjay who is not your husband."

The young fop flushed and blustered, but the quarrel was not with him, and the duchess silenced him with a scowl. "Sir, if my husband, the duke, were present, you would not dare speak thus to me."

"If your husband were here, I'd say it all over again."

"Oh, Samuel, hush!" Fiona pleaded, knowing how vindictive the duchess could be. "Come, there's the bell."

The crowd, loath to leave such drama, hung back; but the liveried ushers began herding them back to their boxes so the curtain could go up for the final act.

Fiona was shaking from anger and fear. What would Samuel say about her being with Huxley? She soon discovered, nothing. All he could do was fume about the lies the duchess spouted:

"The woman is insufferable, Fiona. She's a menace. If she were a man, I'd strike her, challenge her to a duel."

"Hush, Samuel! No more talk of illegal duels. Ignore her. Everyone in the *ton* knows she is a terrible liar and a troublemaker."

"I won't have my wife slandered thus," he continued, "nor my friend Huxley. Hasn't that bitch caused enough grief for you and for Will? Someone should do something about her to keep her in check."

"Samuel, she's very powerful; you know that. She can cause us untold agony. Please ignore her. Forget what she said. Don't talk about revenge. No one wins in such a situation, particularly when she holds all the high cards."

"Wait until Huxley hears of this."

"Don't tell him!" she wailed. "It can only cause trouble. Please, Samuel, the curtain is rising. Pay attention to the opera; that's why we came here tonight."

Neither of them concentrated on the music, though. Samuel fumed visibly; and Fiona wondered how soon he'd begin to think about the substance of the duchess's accusations instead of the tone. When he did, he might wonder why she and Will had been together where the duchess had seen them.

She could see that they were being surreptitiously watched by the members of the *ton* who were at the opera. More quizzing glasses and lorgnettes were trained on their box than on the stage, where the soprano died noisily in the tenor's arms.

When the performance was over, Fiona held back, not wanting to be caught in the crush. By the time they left the King's Theater, the duchess and her newest gigolo had gone. Fiona breathed a sigh of relief, glad that they could go back to Hanover Street without further turmoil.

Morning brought the continuance of the trouble, though. While she and her husband breakfasted in their bedchamber, Isaac brought up a hand-delivered note for Samuel.

"Whatever can it be this early in the morning?" Fiona said as she sipped the hot chocolate.

She saw Samuel's lips tighten to a harsh thin line

when he looked at the wax seal. Before she could see what imprint it bore, he broke it open angrily, scanned the contents, and then asked, "Is the messenger still here?"

"No, sir, he left immediately on delivery of the letter."

"Very well; that's all, Isaac."

The moment the servant had gone, Fiona demanded, "What is the letter, Samuel? Who sent it?"

"The Duke of Lawton."

Fear paralyzed her voice momentarily. When she could speak, she asked, scarcely recognizing the sound, "What does he want? Does it have anything to do with last night's ugliness?"

"Everything. He has challenged me to a duel. It seems I insulted his dear wife in public last night."

"Samuel, you can't fight a duel with him; it's illegal!"

There was an adamant look on his face that terrified her. "Fiona, duels are fought regularly, illegal or not. I intend to have satisfaction in this matter. As he has challenged me, I shall have choice of weapons. I'll choose pistols. I'm a dud with swords, but I'm quite a good shot."

She thought she would faint. "Samuel, you are mad! Think of me!"

"I *am* thinking of you. I will not allow that wicked woman to bandy your good name about as she's doing. My mind is made up. I shall accept the challenge."

"You can't go without a second," she said, sure he'd not be able to find anyone foolhardy enough to oblige him.

At that moment Isaac knocked and announced, "The Viscount William Huxley, sir and madam."

Will strode in, his face a thundercloud. "What's this nonsense I've heard that the rotten Sarah is spouting?"

"It's all too true, Will," Rogers said. "And her husband has just challenged me to a duel."

"Are you going to accept the challenge?" Fire lit his dark eyes, and Fiona hoped to hear him tell Samuel not to acknowledge the challenge.

"Of course I shall fight him," her husband said, stubborn to the last.

"Good; then I'll be your second," Huxley declared.

CHAPTER 31

Fiona wept, she pleaded, she argued, to no avail. The two men were in accord. She had been insulted, so they would accept the Duke of Lawton's challenge and meet him two mornings hence at dawn in one of the deserted areas of Hyde Park.

"You're insane, both of you. You should be committed to Bedlam. Samuel, you might be killed; then what will I do? Your child left fatherless, me a widow —have you no thought for me at all?"

She saw Huxley open his mouth, then close it quickly. She knew what he'd started to say—that he'd take care of her if anything happened to Samuel—but luckily he'd realized in time that it was not appropriate under the circumstances.

Then Rogers surprised both of them by asking Huxley, "If anything should happen to me, will you take care of Fiona?"

"Nothing will happen to you," Huxley said crossly, wanting Fiona but not wanting to appear to.

"That's ridiculous!" she flared. "Samuel is going to ask for pistols. He could easily be killed."

"The duke is probably a rotten shot," Samuel said, trying for a light touch but not quite achieving it. "I'll wing him; then honor will be served."

"Couldn't you both just fire in the air with no intent to injure?" she asked.

"It's been done, but I'd not trust Lawton to do it," Huxley said, frowning. "No, there's no getting out of this duel, Fiona, with honor intact. It has to be fought."

"Oh, honor be damned!" she cried, incensed at the

stupidity of the two men who meant most to her in life. "Rather than have my husband killed, I'd take dishonor."

Rogers took her in his arms and said, "But don't you see, Fiona, I can't do that? I couldn't live with myself if I allowed the dearest person in the world to be maligned by such as the Duchess of Lawton and her vile husband."

"I don't care what she says!" Fiona said doggedly.

"But I do."

There was an implacable tone to Samuel's voice that left no room for Fiona. He was going to fight this dreadful duel, and nothing she could say would stop him. Bitterly she pulled out of his embrace. "I'm tempted to go to the authorities and tell them what you men plan to do," she threatened. "If you show up in Hyde Park with dueling pistols, they can haul you up in front of a magistrate."

"You'd do that to me?"

She sighed. "No, of course not, Samuel. But you"— and she rounded on Huxley—"I'm disgusted with you. Why not try to dissuade this insane husband of mine instead of encouraging him by agreeing to be his second?"

There was a play of emotions over Huxley's face— love, chagrin, despair. "Honor is important, Fiona; surely you must realize that."

"Nothing is as important as Samuel's life."

"Maybe I'll be lucky and kill the duke."

She thought she might faint when her husband said this. "And go to prison, wind up on Tyburn with your neck fitted with a hemp neckcloth? Samuel, stop now before it is too late. Ignore his challenge. What matter that he gossips in the coffeehouses for a week? We've withstood gossip before."

"This time he's gone too far." Again that adamant tone.

She turned to Huxley, but she got no help from him.

He was as much in favor of the duel as her husband was.

"If Samuel ignores this challenge, then I must call out the duke," he said quietly. "It's my name he's bandying about, too, Fiona. You don't think I could let this pass? In fact, once Samuel finishes with him, I may well call him out on my own account."

"Enough! I don't want to hear another word about it," she said, anger fighting with fear. She swept out of the room and climbed wearily to her bedchamber, where she called for Lettie to get her ready for bed. Both of the men in her life had taken leave of their senses. There was nothing she could do now except pray for them, and she had long since given up prayer.

Next morning she did not even ask Samuel what had been decided. He told her, though, as they drank their morning chocolate together, that he had sent an answer to the duke.

"Tomorrow at dawn."

"Will you let him provide the pistols? He'll probably arrange for you to have one that misfires," she said cynically.

"I'll be using Huxley's dueling pistols. This afternoon he and I will go out to try them." He smiled at his wife over the rim of his china cup. "Don't worry, dear, I don't intend to be killed. I have too much to live for."

She didn't answer. All she could foresee was disaster. If he wasn't wounded—or worse—then the authorities would hear of this duel and he'd be put in prison. Either way, he couldn't win.

All day while he was gone from the house, Fiona fretted. How could she stand the suspense next morning not knowing what had happened, wondering if she was a wife or a widow? Finally she realized that there was only one thing for her to do—see this duel for herself. She wasn't foolish enough to think for one minute that Samuel and Will would let her go with them to Hyde

Park, but she could get there by herself by chair. She'd have to arrange it today. She'd find a public chair and engage the bearers to come for her in the morning just after the men had gone to their rendezvous. If she were there watching, perhaps the whole affair would come to nothing. Surely they wouldn't fight with her as an audience? Even if Samuel and Will were determined to go on with the duel, the duke would not want anyone watching.

Next morning Samuel was surprised that Fiona was already up when he woke. "I'd hoped you'd sleep through this nonsense."

"Sleep through—— You're stark-raving mad." Then, as a final try, she asked, "May I go too?"

"To watch the duel?" When she nodded, he just shook his head. "Fiona, it is out of the question. It would be too traumatic for you and the babe. Please, go back to bed and try to sleep."

"Sleep! With you out there being shot at?"

He caught her to him in a rib-cracking embrace and kissed her as if it might be the last kiss they would ever share. "I'll be back before you know I'm gone," he promised.

Once he was out of the house, Fiona threw on her heavy cloak, pulling the hood high, made sure she had money for the sedan-chair bearers, and slipped out onto the front stoop to wait for them. She didn't want the servants to know that she was going anyplace. Isaac might well have gotten wind of this dreadful duel and would suspect something if he saw her ready to go out. She waited and waited. The sky lightened to a pearl gray and still the chair did not come. Fiona was desperate. If they didn't come soon, she couldn't possibly be at Hyde Park by dawn. She wasn't even sure of the exact location where the duel was to be fought. She'd have to look once the chair discharged her at the edge of the park. She wouldn't dare let them take her closer, for security reasons.

She was in a quandary. Should she wait here for the chair she had engaged, or should she hurry to Oxford Street and hope to find bearers at this hour? Just as she decided to risk Oxford, she saw a sedan chair coming around the corner and up Hanover Street. Not wanting to lose even a moment, she hurried down toward it, waving frantically to the men when she came opposite them. It was the bearers she had engaged yesterday.

"You're late!" she cried. "Oh, hurry, hurry!"

They helped her into the chair, picked up the carrying poles, and went off at a trot, with no chance to explain why they were late. The minutes passed and Fiona fretted. She peered through a gap in the curtains of the window, and saw only an occasional coach clatter by and a few people hurrying along the streets. Would she be in time to stop the duel? She should have insisted on going with Samuel. She shouldn't have let Will influence him. What could she do to stop this insanity?

Then the green trees of Hyde Park showed down the street. She was nearly there. Should she keep the chair and have them carry her deep into the park? No, they might well wonder what a pregnant matron was doing in Hyde Park at dawn.

Dawn! While her bearers had trotted along, the sky had lightened gradually. Now the sun was peeping above the tops of the trees in the park. Was she too late?

They came to the intersection where Oxford Street joined Bayswater Road, and the bearers put down the chair.

"Speaker's Corner, ma'am," the head bearer announced. "Sure this is where you wants to go? No one about at this hour, it seems."

She reckoned quickly. The duel wouldn't be here; it was too public. Where was it that they usually fought? She tried to remember. Near the Serpentine, she thought, off The Ring somewhere. It was much too far to walk.

"I think I want you to take me into the park," she decided, "where The Ring crosses The Serpentine."

"Cost you more, ma'am," the man said, tone surly. "You told us Speaker's Corner yesterday."

"Yes, yes, but my plans have changed," she said. "Please hurry. I'll pay the extra willingly."

She thought she heard the man grumble "Women!" but it didn't matter. She had to find Samuel and stop him before it was too late.

After she promised them each a penny extra if they'd hurry, the men trotted along at such a clip that she had to clutch the window edges on either side to keep from being thrown out of the chair; yet she didn't complain. Speed was all that mattered now.

It was growing lighter by the minute when the bearers told her that she now was on The Ring at The Serpentine. They helped her out of the chair, doubt on their rough faces.

"Are you sure this is the place you wants to be, ma'am?"

"This will do fine." Quickly she paid them.

"Should we wait for you? Not safe for a lady to be alone in the park. Lots of footpads around."

It was a temptation, but Fiona shook her head and gestured for them to leave. Dueling was illegal. It wouldn't do to have two witnesses if she could find the combatants.

Reluctantly the men picked up the chair and trotted off. Now Fiona didn't know what to do, where to go. Hyde Park was so large; the men might be anyplace. How foolish of her not to have asked where specifically the duel was to be fought. Here she was, alone, anxious, and her presence was truly foolhardy. Should she start out across the grass toward those trees, or was it better to cross the bridge?

Just then shots rang out, and there were shouts

over to her right. Picking up her skirts, she ran awkwardly, her pregnancy making it difficult for her to make such speed. Once she was into the trees, all was silence. Had the shots come from here? Sounds could be so deceptive. It was a wild area, and more and more Fiona regretted her decision to come here alone. She should have brought Isaac along with her. He'd have been very supportive, a tower of strength.

Then she heard the pounding of feet ahead and hurried toward the sound. She found a path and ran along it until, turning a slight bend, she came to a clearing where a dramatic tableau opened before her. The Duke of Lawton stood to one side with someone behind him. A man lay on the ground, another bent over him. She stopped dead in her tracks, feeling faint. The man on the ground was Samuel, and beside him was Huxley, a pistol in his hand.

From the other side of the clearing, men came racing forward, men in uniform. "Halt in the king's name!" one of them cried.

Fiona rushed forward, not heeding them. That was her husband lying there, obviously wounded. "Samuel!" she cried, her voice shrill with fear. "Will, oh, God, what has happened?"

At the sound of her voice, Huxley sprang to his feet, still holding the long, wicked-looking dueling pistol. "Fiona, don't come over here," he called, anguish in his tone, in every line of his body.

She paid no more attention to his words than she had to the constables, who now were spreading out to encircle the four men. She rushed to Samuel and fell to her knees, her skirts billowing about her like a flower. He was terribly pale, unmoving, and his eyes were closed. "Samuel?" She looked up at Huxley, beseeching.

Gently he lifted her to her feet and pressed her face against his chest. "Poor Fiona," he whispered, "My poor, dear Fiona."

"Is he——" She pulled away from his embrace and looked back at Samuel, lying there so still. "Will, he isn't——"

Then, interrupting her frantic question, the duke's voice rang out: "Arrest that man, the Viscount William Huxley," he shouted to the soldiers. "He just murdered Samuel Rogers in order to marry Rogers's wife. Look at them together! See how brazen he is?"

Everything seemed to spin around her. Huxley's face was a terrible blur; the duke and his companion did a crazy dance; the constables were part of the whirlwind that swept her away from reality. With horror she managed to concentrate on Huxley's face so close to her own. He was like a stranger to her. The planes of his handsome face were harsh and cruel, his mouth was grim, his eyes unfathomable pools of dark water that threatened to drown her in their depths.

"Will?" Was that her voice, that feeble, anguished cry? "Will, did you . . ." She couldn't say the dreadful words.

Fiona felt him retreat from her, emotionally as well as physically. His arms fell from around her, and she swayed, putting out an imploring hand, resting it on his shoulder to steady herself.

Voice icy, Huxley asked, "How can you believe that of me? I thought you loved me."

She saw that he still held the dueling pistol in his hand. Near Samuel's lifeless right hand lay the twin to it. They were Huxley's own pistols. He'd brought them to the house yesterday so that Samuel could try them, accustom himself to them.

"Why do you have one of the pistols?" she whispered.

This time she was interrupted by the official voice of one of the constables: "Milord, I am placing you under arrest for the murder of this man, Samuel Rogers."

"I didn't kill him!" Huxley shouted, rounding on the constable.

With a flick of his head, the constable summoned his deputies, who caught Huxley's arms and wrenched them behind him. The chief constable took the pistol from his fingers.

"It's a lie!" Huxley yelled, struggling to free himself. "The Duke of Lawton is the murderer. He shot Rogers in the back before the end of the count, then tossed the gun down here. I picked it up. Ask his second. He'll tell you what happened. It was a duel——"

"Dueling is illegal," the constable said, manner stolid. He was a burly man, probably about Huxley's age. His hair was flaxen, his eyes so pale a blue that they were almost colorless.

"The man lies," Lawton said, hurrying over to defend himself. "He wanted the wife." The look he gave Fiona was malevolent, making her shudder. The man hated her and hated Huxley. He'd tell any kind of lie in order to have Will hang on Tyburn Hill.

"Ask his second," she insisted, echoing Huxley's plea.

"Second? I have my manservant with me. We were taking the air when we heard shots and hurried here. We found this ugly scene—Rogers lying dead, Huxley standing over him with a smoking pistol in his hand."

The chief constable then turned to the duke's manservant for confirmation of one story or the other. Fiona saw for the first time who it was, and her heart plummeted. The man the duke had chosen for his second in this tragic duel was none other than Rolf Evans, the spying, wicked servant she and Rogers had dismissed.

"It's like His Grace says," Rolf muttered, glancing at Huxley out of the corner of his eye as if afraid the viscount would get away from his captors and attack him bodily. "His Grace and me, we came on this . . . this murder." He said the word boldly, with that hateful smirk on his face that Fiona had always despised.

"The viscount's a murderer and a traitor, even though they never proved it. Carryin' on with the poor dead fellow's wife. Shockin' behavior."

"Shocking!" the duke echoed, looking triumphantly at Fiona as the constables dragged Huxley away.

CHAPTER 32

If it hadn't been for the Newburys, Fiona would not have survived. She had no experience with planning funerals. When Samuel's first wife, Kathleen, died in Bedlam, he had kept her out of the entire procedure for obvious reasons. Now she needed advice on finding someone to come with the embalming oils to prepare Samuel's body for burial. As he'd been a Member of Parliament, there was a certain amount of ceremony to be followed. Then too, as a champion of the little man, the poor, her husband had a public following that almost overwhelmed Fiona. She ordered black crape weepers but soon ran out, having to send Lettie around to the shops to buy more. It was Isaac who told her to send for William Hunter, the most famous embalmer in London.

Meanwhile she was uncertain of Huxley's fate. There were rumors; there was even an article in *The Gazette,* but all she learned from it was that he was imprisoned in Newgate.

Isaac found her weeping in the small salon, her tears falling onto the paper, blurring the hateful words. "It's very serious, madam, is it not?"

"I don't know what happened," she sobbed. "By the time I found the dueling grounds, my husband was dead and the viscount was kneeling over him, a smoking pistol in his hand."

"He never killed the master. There's treachery afoot."

Fiona raised her tear-stained face to meet his eyes. "I know he didn't. But the Duke of Lawton and Rolf swear that his lordship shot poor Samuel."

"I wouldn't believe that Rolf Evans if his hand was on the Bible, madam. He's a scoundrel."

"But what can I do? I didn't get there in time to see what happened, and now the Lawtons are blackening my name and Huxley's."

"Mrs. Rogers, I swore an oath that I would keep secret the fact that his lordship publishes *The London Man;* but if this were known in the City, there'd be such an outcry from his followers that the king would be forced to intervene and conduct a fair investigation of this sad matter."

She didn't know what to do. She needed desperately to consult with Will, see what he wanted done. "Would I be able to see the viscount if I went to the prison?"

"I should think so, particularly if you dropped some shillings in a few hands there. The guards are very grasping, I daresay." Then, diffidently, he added, "I'd be honored to go with you, ma'am, as protection, if you'd have me."

She burst into tears. "Oh, Isaac, I would so like that. I'm all alone in the world, with my husband dead and my good friend in prison. Does he have a solicitor?"

"I'm sure that his lordship is well served by counsel."

They decided to visit Huxley as soon as the funeral was over. It was impossible for Fiona to get away before that, as she was constantly besieged with mourners who came to pay their respects. Samuel's body lay in state in the main salon, the bier draped with black. Isaac had obtained black cloth from friends who sympathized with Samuel's ardent espousing of the liberal cause, and he hung great swatches from the upstairs windows, anchoring them on the lower window frames, to show that they were a house in mourning.

The funeral was from St. Stephen's, with the vicar who had buried Kathleen and who had married Fiona and Samuel conducting the impressive service. There were many mourners there from Parliament, with the notable exception of the devotees of Medmenham Abbey. Fiona assumed they all were rallying around the Duke and Duchess of Lawton.

After the funeral, Fiona had to endure the feast at the house on Hanover Street, with Lettie calling in some extra maids for the time the mourners gathered to eat the huge collation prepared for them. When finally all of them had gone, Isaac and Lettie helped her upstairs to bed—a lonely, solitary bed—and there at last she wept for Samuel, for what he'd meant to her—and what he'd not. She regretted never having been able to love him, but she knew that despite this, he had been happy; at least she had that consolation. The baby kicked, and she remembered how happy Samuel had been to learn she was pregnant. She still had no idea if this was his child or Huxley's. It was all too terrible to contemplate.

Lettie brought her mulled wine and insisted that she drink it and get some sleep. "Tomorrow Isaac will go with you to Newgate Prison, ma'am. For that you need your rest."

Fiona thought that she wouldn't ever sleep again; but her weary body defied her, and she dropped into a deep slumber almost immediately.

When she woke, it was light outside. Lettie came when she rang, bringing a cup of tea and toast with marmalade. Then she laid out one of the black mourning outfits Fiona had ordered. A seamstress and her assistant worked full time making her several outfits, all of them also suitable as maternity dresses.

"What a tragedy," the seamstress said as she fitted the black bombazine and taffeta to Fiona's heavy figure. "So young to be a widow and with a child coming—sad, sad."

She knew the woman meant well, but Fiona wanted to scream in rage, anguish, despair. What was she going to do? How could she possibly manage alone? Was Isaac's idea workable? She couldn't imagine that the poor of London had any influence on King George.

What could they do? March in protest along Pall Mall? Who could care? They'd be chivied and harassed by soldiers and driven home with broken heads.

Now, waiting for the closed carriage that Isaac had ordered to take them to Newgate, Fiona wondered if she'd be able to maintain her calm when she saw Huxley behind bars, caged like a common criminal. She must be brave. She had to give him hope, not more worries.

Lettie fastened heavy black veiling over her black silk mourning bonnet so that no one could see who she was. When Isaac announced that the coach was waiting, she made sure she had her vinaigrette and sufficient coins to pay for the carriage and bribe the prison guards. Then she let Isaac escort her to the closed hackney and they clattered off for Newgate.

It was raining, the sullen rain of autumn, making the day dreary and frightening. What if they wouldn't allow her to see Huxley at all?

"Should we have tried to contact his lordship's solicitor before we made this visit?" she asked her manservant, who sat facing her.

"No, madam, I think it would be best to approach the guards as a sorrowing woman. Gain their sympathy or line their pockets, but nothing official about it. An official request for a visit might well have been denied, whereas if you appear at the gate, kerchief in one hand, shillings in the other, your chances will be much better to see the viscount."

"I daresay you're right, Isaac. I've never visited anyone in prison before."

"And I hope you never need to again, Mrs. Rogers." Then he reached into the deep pocket of his black stuff coat and pulled out a plain pewter flask. "I took the liberty of bringing a small flask of brandy from the cellar, ma'am. I'll keep the guard distracted with drink to give you a chance to confer with his lordship in private. Try, ma'am, try to get him to see reason. If I can pass the rumor that he's the man who writes *The London Man,* that he's been arrested falsely, then we may get him released. Otherwise it will be a public trial —and circus, mark my words. We must get him out before that happens."

"I'll do my best."

The bleak prison almost broke her resolve. When they approached the gray walls streaming with rain, Fiona wanted to turn and run away; but that would not help her beloved Will. She left the negotiations up to Isaac, who clinked shillings and had her whisked inside so fast that she was stunned. The odor of the prison sickened her, but she opened her vinaigrette and sniffed, keeping it handy as the slovenly guard led them through dank corridors, past barred cells where prisoners pleaded with them for help, and finally into another section of the prison a little less grim than the rest of it. These cells were for those who could pay for comfort.

Fiona wasn't allowed into the cell, but she put her arms through the bars to embrace her love and lifted her face for his kiss.

"You shouldn't be here," he groaned, "but oh, how I've longed to see you! Are you all right?"

"As right as I can be until you are a free man, Will."

"With Lawton and his toady lying the way they are, the only time I'll see the light of day will be en route to Tyburn."

"Don't say that!" She was appalled that he seemed to have lost heart. "Isaac and I have a plan." Quickly she outlined the venture to him and begged him to consent.

"I don't know. If I do escape hanging, my use as the writer of *The London Man* will be at an end. It was my anonymity that made my work valuable."

"You can start up another paper under another title," she begged. "Oh, Will, let us try. Don't give up! I need you so desperately. Your child needs a father." It was the first time she had ever said that the child was his. She still didn't know, but this was no time for such fancy sophistry. If it gave him the will to live, if he gave his consent to the plan, she'd tell him anything he wanted to hear.

"Very well, but with Samuel dead and me in prison, don't expect miracles. The mob need someone to lead them, to whip them into action."

"Isaac will do that. He longs to help the cause."

There was no more time for talk. They heard the clank of keys as the warder came back, smelling of brandy, to tell Fiona that her visit was at an end. One last kiss and she tore herself away from Huxley.

In the carriage en route to Hanover Street, Fiona told Isaac that he could go ahead with his plans. "Although his lordship thinks it won't help. He's very low in spirits."

"Don't you worry, ma'am, we'll have him out of there in days. He'll not hang on Tyburn."

Nothing happened for several days, at least nothing that was obvious to Fiona. Isaac was gone from the house all hours of the day and night, but Fiona and Lettie made do without him. Then the first little notice appeared in *The Gazette:* just a brief mention that there had been a parade to Newgate Prison to protest the incarceration of Sir William Huxley on what the marchers called "trumped-up charges." The movement caught on like wildfire, sweeping through the City. There wasn't an hour of the day or night that didn't see marchers parading somewhere, some carrying hand-lettered signs saying FREE HUXLEY. Powerful lords began to go armed through the streets; but this didn't save them from the angry mobs who attacked their chairs and coaches, setting fire to them, toppling them over, and threatening their very lives. Word spread that a petition was being circulated, a petition to be carried to King George, and so many signed it—or made an X

if they couldn't write—that it took three men to carry
the bundles of signatures.

Each day Fiona made the trip to Newgate Prison to
keep Huxley posted on what was happening. As the
days passed, the newspapers were filled with nothing
else.

"They're asking questions in the House about the
duel," she told him. "Many are saying that the Duke of
Lawton is not noted for his probity. They are hinting
that he is lying."

"My solicitors are working hard, too," he told her.
"At first everything looked so black; but now they have
hope that they may be able to get Evans to change his
story."

"Isaac suggests paying him more than the duke has
paid."

"I suggested that myself. My worthy legal counselors
were shocked until I explained that if they could persuade Evans to take a bribe and sign a paper to that
effect, then they had grounds to have him prosecuted
for perjury."

"Will it work?"

"We don't know. Much depends on which magistrate
would hear the arguments. Lawton is still very powerful. I hear that he has Dashwood and all of the Friars
of St. Francis behind him, and they have the ear of the
king."

"But you were one of Dashwood's friends too!" she
cried.

"Ah, Fiona, fair-weather friends. Now that I'm in
trouble, now that the word is out that I'm the author of
The London Man, they've all turned against me and
are backing Lawton."

"You owe them a lot. I hope you pay them back in
kind."

"I shall. Never fear, dear Fiona, I shall."

The plan to try to bribe Evans in favor of Huxley
never got off the ground. The masses took care of

Evans first. Isaac made sure that the true story of the duel was told everywhere. It was hard for the mob to get at the Duke of Lawton, for he had guards with him everywhere he went, armed men alerted to shoot first and think afterward. He himself carried a pistol at all times. But Evans, when his use as a false witness was over, became once again nothing more than a servant in the house on Millbank, and the Duke of Lawton didn't demean himself by associating with the help. Thus, while the duke went out only under heavy guard, Evans was left to fend for himself.

The men set to watch for him saw him slip away one dark night and trailed him to a local tavern, the Cock and Hen. While some stayed to make sure he didn't leave the tavern, the others raced about the streets, getting recruits for the "court" they intended to have. Soon thousands of angry men converged on the Cock and Hen, clubs in hand, to mete out summary justice.

Isaac, alerted by friends, was there to see what happened and to make sure that the mob, in their fury, didn't kill Evans. "We need him as a witness against the Duke of Lawton," he kept warning. "Don't kill him. Frighten him into telling the truth and then drag him before the magistrates."

While Isaac was out with the mob at the Cock and Hen, Fiona had an unexpected caller.

"A Miss Goodbody to see you, ma'am," Lettie announced.

"Aunt Eulalia! What a pleasant surprise."

Her aunt, upright as ever, looked about the elegant salon, deigned to give her cloak and bonnet to Lettie, and then came forward to embrace her niece. "I understand that your husband died. I should have come sooner, but——"

"I know, I know; don't fret about it. You have to live; we all do." It was a dismal truth that Fiona knew well.

Her aunt sat stiffly on a Kent chair, her straight back

not touching the upholstery. "I hear many things in my shop. The *ton* seem to think I'm deaf. They discuss all manner of privacies in front of me as if I didn't exist. I've not seen the Duchess of Lawton recently, although she ordered a fall bonnet, which is ready and waiting for her. Today I was fitting a new hat for the Countess of Montmorency, and she had that foppish lover of hers along. They talked about 'dear Sarah' in front of me, and it did my heart good. I never felt right about letting you go, Fiona, but the duchess could have ruined me with a word. Then it would have been the workhouse."

"It's all right, Aunt Eulalia. She was hitting at me through you. I've never blamed you. And it all worked out for me."

"I see you're expecting—poor babe without a father —but that's not why I came. I've heard all about the duel and the story that the Viscount Huxley was supposed to have killed your husband. The *ton* snicker about it—none of them likes Huxley now—but of course they've all been afraid of Lawton. Well"—and her voice took on a triumphant ring, and she smiled a tight, cold little smile—"Lawton's gone, and good riddance to him and his duchess."

"Gone? What do you mean, Aunt Eulalia?"

"Got too hot for him here. Oh, I hear from the *ton*, but I also hear from the masses—a milliner is suspended between both worlds. Lawton, on discovering the king himself is most distraught over all this turmoil in the City and holds the duke personally responsible, packed up everything and left for Paris with his wife for a 'protracted stay.' The house on Millbank is closed. Deserted that scoundrel Evans, too. But then, good riddance to them all."

"Oh, Aunt Eulalia, what wonderful news! Will the king free Lord Huxley?"

"Probably. He's seen the handwriting on the wall, just as that ancient king in the Bible saw it. And I'm glad I can be friends with my own flesh and blood again, Fiona."

Fiona rushed to her aunt, dropped to her knees, and hugged that tall, bony body. "Oh, Aunt Eulalia, I'm glad too!"

"I'm already planning the finest baby bonnet a child ever possessed," her aunt said, returning the embrace a bit awkwardly, for the lady had never been much to show affection. "It'll be a bonnet fit for royalty."

Suddenly Fiona's spirits lifted. Everything was going to be all right; she knew it. If Lawton had fled, then there would be no one to bear witness against Will. Rolf Evans, deprived of his wealthy sponsor, would buckle. They'd free her beloved—they'd have to—and they could finally be together.

CHAPTER 33

Fiona was dreaming. Will had come in from somewhere and was getting into her bed. She was so sleepy, but she moved toward his warm, ready body, eager for his love. His lips moved on hers, and her tongue met his invitingly.

"Oh, Will, I do love you so much," she breathed. Then Fiona was awake, and Will *was* there in her bed, his hands demanding on her flesh. "Will! You're free!" The dream was gone; but the reality was even better than the dream had been. "What happened?"

"I'll tell you later," he said, his voice hoarse with desire. "Now all I want to do is to love you. Oh, Fiona, it's been so long, so long. I missed you so much."

She drew him down onto her own eager body, opening her thighs to his maleness, moaning with pleasure as he entered her. Nothing else mattered now but Huxley and the love they had for each other. Both, starved for love, were ablaze with passion. Their ever-quickening rhythm raised them to an intensity of feeling they had never before experienced, even in their most amorous encounters. Sensual delights enraptured them, leading them higher and higher until, with a wild burst of emotion, they found the bliss they had sought so avidly.

Later, his lips against her silken hair, Huxley murmured, "There were times when I despaired of ever holding you in my arms again, Fiona. I knew I could wind up on Tyburn, if the Duke of Lawton had his way."

She shuddered, remembering how dreadful these past

days had been, and burrowed against his body as if she wanted to meld their flesh truly into one flesh.

"Are you cold, my dearest?" He gathered her even closer in his arms to warm her with his body.

"We don't have to worry about anything now," she said, and told him the news her Aunt Eulalia had brought her.

"So Lawton cut and ran, taking his darling bitch of a wife with him!" He roared with laughter, an almost hysterical note in it.

Fiona knew then how frightened Huxley had been that he would be hanged by the neck until dead for the death of her husband. Gently she caressed him, now being the one to comfort him as he had been comforting her. "It's all over, Will. All of the bad life is behind us."

"Nothing but good forevermore. Mrs. Rogers, will you be my wife, to have and to hold, from this day forward, till death do us part?"

"Oh, Will, I want nothing more than that; but what will people say if we marry so soon? There will be those who whisper that it was true . . . that you did kill Samuel so that we could marry."

"Who cares what anyone says?" He kissed her so fiercely that he bruised her lips with his ardor. "We'll leave London and go to my place in Surrey. The village vicar will marry us. I won't wait, Fiona; I've waited too long for you now. By this time next week, if I can get a special license, you'll be the Viscountess Huxley—officially, irrevocably, forever. And the child you carry—my child—will be born in wedlock, with no nonsense about his legitimacy. Remember, someday he'll be the Viscount Huxley. It's an old and honorable name, and you shall bear it."

"There's nothing I want more," she breathed. "If you don't mind the gossip, then neither do I."

Later, as they breakfasted together in bed, with a beaming Lettie to serve them, Huxley gave a great shout of laughter that startled Fiona so, she almost spilled chocolate on her creamy bosom.

"Tell me the joke so that I too can laugh."

"We'll give the *ton* so much to think about, they'll have no breath left to talk about our hasty marriage, my dear. And I'll pay back the Friars of St. Francis, who ignored my plight when I was in prison falsely accused by their friend, the Duke of Lawton. Oh, Fiona, it's a marvelous idea, one that is in keeping with this whole affair." Then, seeing that she was consumed with curiosity, he told her, "I moved the press down to Surrey, you know. It's in an isolated cottage on my estate. I'm going to start up a paper again just as you suggested, only it will have another name—the *Voice of Truth*, perhaps. What I intend to do is document all of the happenings at Medmenham Abbey. The thing the Friars of St. Francis can't stand is publicity. Once people know what goes on there, the crowds will gather. Every curiosity seeker in London and the surrounding counties will want to have a first hand view of the orgies. They'll overrun Dashwood's estate, unless he hires an army of guards to keep them off. It will destroy the abbey more than anything else I can think of."

"Do you really think it will work?"

"I'm positive," he said, nuzzling her throat. "But I don't want to think of revenge now, not with you here in my arms, so warm and willing." His lips moved to her breast, and Fiona forgot everything but the urgency of his desire, which was matched by her own hot blood. This time they loved each other slowly, savoring each moment, rousing each other to a peak of love that exploded like a display of fireworks.

Later, as they dressed, Fiona remembered their faithful servants, Lettie and Isaac Newbury. "What will happen to them when we give up the lease on this house, Will? They have helped us so much."

"I shall take them on to work in my own London town house or at my Surrey estate. Do you want Lettie for your abigail? If so, then they can go back and forth with us, staying at whichever establishment we are using. I can always find something for Isaac to do. He can help me put out the *Voice of Truth*. And I may even resurrect *The London Man* from time to time if I feel the political climate needs it."

"Who will become the champion of the poor now that Samuel is dead?"

"I'll do all I can. I know that I cannot reach them the way he did—my title works against me—but I hope that another leader will rise, to whom I can give my backing and support the way I did for Samuel."

The following week found them traveling to Surrey in a large, comfortable berlin. With fall upon them, the air was brisk and nippy. Lettie had heated bricks so that Fiona could rest her feet on them and keep warm. The Newburys followed in the older landau with all of Fiona's boxes and trunks.

"I keep thinking that I'll unpack my trunks and find a printing press tucked away in them," she joked, clinging to Huxley's hand.

By next week they would be man and wife Will had made all of the arrangements for special license, vicar, everything, and the seamstress had fashioned her a lovely wedding gown of pale-blue weighted silk, a Watteau sacque that flowed from the shoulders with fullness to help conceal her increasing size. Fiona hoped that Samuel would rest peacefully in his grave. Would he have approved of the hasty marriage? He'd done the same when he married her, for Kathleen had scarcely been put in her grave when he obtained the special license.

Huxley's home, Fairfax, in Surrey was a lovely place, an old Tudor manor house that had been modernized. The half-timbered building was surrounded by tall elm and oak trees, now in their autumn reds and golds.

"We'll not be deserting London permanently," Huxley promised. "I think that I'm going to spend more

time in the House of Lords from now on. Perhaps, with
a direct approach in the Lords and an indirect kind of
needling through my new *Voice of Truth,* changes can
be brought about to benefit the common man."

Fiona was very tired from the trip, so Lettie put her
to bed in the master suite. There was no coy nonsense
about separate bedrooms until the wedding day, as both
Lettie and Isaac knew that Fiona and Huxley were
lovers. The viscount and Isaac immediately left for the
isolated cottage so that they could get the printing press
set up and in working order.

That night Huxley sat up late, the candle burning
low, as he worked on the first issue of the *Voice,* the
one exposing the Friars of St. Francis and the orgies at
Medmenham Abbey. Fiona coud hear him chuckle as
he wrote the devastating exposé. Finally, bone weary,
she drifted into sleep, not waking until the sun was high
next morning. She found that she was alone in the bed,
although Will must have slept there, for the pillow beside her was dented. Where had he got to so early? She
rang for Lettie, who soon bustled in carrying a breakfast tray.

"Where's his lordship?" Fiona asked.

"He and Isaac are off to print the paper, ma'am—or
I guess I should start calling you 'your ladyship.' "

Fiona hadn't even thought of that. She'd never been
a lady. It would take some getting used to. "Well, let's
wait until the wedding," she said, smiling at her abigail.

"His lordship left you a letter, ma'am." Lettie pulled
aside her white apron to get at the pocket tied under
her draped skirt.

It was a copy of the lead article for the *Voice:*
ORGIES AT MARLOW! She was shocked to find that
he had named names, accusing men like Bute and Sandwich of all manner of ugly things—all true, of course.
He detailed the deflowering of virgins, the blasphemy
of the Black Mass, with its unfrocked priest in attendance, the lewd statuary in the gardens surrounding the

rebuilt abbey. He even announced that there always was a special mass and orgy on All Hallows' Eve, which was only two weeks off. Fiona was torn between fear and laughter. If any suspected that Will was the author of this article, they might well tar and feather him the next time he showed his face in the House of Lords—or at White's Coffeehouse, for that matter.

At noon he came striding in from his work, his dark eyes glittering with fiendish glee. "Well, my dear"—he gave her a resounding kiss—"what do you think of my latest literary effort?"

"Bute and Sandwich may sue you for libel."

"They have to prove that I wrote it, first. That's going to be hard to do. I saw three other radical papers on the streets of London last week. I started a trend with *The London Man*. Now others are taking up the fight against the corrupt men the king has around him."

"Is this true about a big orgy on All Hallows' Eve?"

"Yes; they try to follow the old witchcraft calendar, or their usual mockery of it. I'll bet that the Thames will have so many boats on it that night, it will be difficult for the boatmen to row. Everyone in London will want to see the spectacular. It will be better than the entertainments at Vauxhall, and it won't cost them a penny."

She giggled. "I wish I could be there. It might be fun to see how the crowds deport themselves. Do you really think they'll actually invade the gardens? I should think they'd be afraid of Dashwood's guards."

"There'll be some bold one who'll start things off. Then his friends will decide they want some of the fun, too. Pretty soon everyone will be there, swarming over the place. I shouldn't be surprised if they carry away some of the smaller statues."

"How are you going to get the papers to London?"

"Isaac has volunteered to see to it."

"It would be interesting to see the faces of the friars when this hits the streets."

"I'm sorely tempted to ride to London with Isaac, but I think it wiser to be away when the first issue circulates. I'll get reactions aplenty from my neighbors, I daresay. Besides, I'm getting married next week. I shouldn't want to miss that."

"I should hope not!" she scolded with mock severity, and then rushed into his waiting arms.

The day of their wedding dawned bright and clear, with a fresh, clean snap to the air. They had invited no guests, both of them agreeing that a private ceremony was in order for many reasons. The ceremony was to take place in the local squat Norman church, with Lettie and Isaac as their witnesses. It seemed too good to be true, Fiona thought as they stood together before the altar of St. Auden's in the Dell. She had loved Will for so long; but everything had conspired to keep them apart. Now at last they were together for all time.

The day of All Hallows' Eve was another bright, crisp autumn day.

"Are you feeling well enough for a rather long coach ride, my dear?" Huxley asked her that morning.

"I feel wonderful," she said with that special voice he loved to hear, an intimate tone he understood.

"I thought it might be interesting to ride to the Thames across from the abbey and see what happens tonight. I hear there's been a lot of furor about what I wrote in the *Voice*. Baron Wilkerson saw me yesterday as he rode by, and stopped to chat. Said he'd been to London the day before and all the *ton* were talking about the impending orgy at Medmenham Abbey. Those who frequent the place lied and said nothing of the sort ever happened there. But there are too many who have talked about it—too many who've been there —and the people believe what I wrote."

"Well, they should; it's the truth." She looked up at this man who was now her legal husband, and saw the mischief in his eyes. "I'd love to see the show," she said.

"We might even be able to get a boatman to take us out nearer the other bank so we could see better what happens."

"It might be wise to wear masks," he suggested. "There are plenty of men who know we both used to go to the abbey. I think this is one night I'd rather not be recognized!"

"They might well dump us into the Thames," she agreed.

Normally they'd have gone in a gig; but because of Fiona's delicate condition, Huxley chose to take a landaulet, with driver and footmen, armed, as guards. At night the highwaymen were a menace on the roads. It paid to have well-armed men with you for protection.

They left Fairfax at noon, with a picnic basket and a bottle of hock along for supper later. The roads were in good condition, as it had not rained for several days, and they made good time heading north to the river. All of the trees were in their fall colors, which added to the pleasure of the drive. They stopped several times at inns so that Fiona could get out of the coach to rest and have a glass of wine.

Dusk was falling when they reached the Thames. Across the river stood the renovated ruins of Medmenham Abbey, the stones rosy in the glow of the setting sun.

"Will! Look at the river!" Fiona exclaimed. "It's clogged with boats of every description, and they're not going anyplace; they're just rowing or poling enough to keep their places."

"I told you this would be the free entertainment of the season. Come, let's see about hiring a boat. We can eat our supper on the river."

One of the footmen carried heavy robes lest the damp chill of the Thames be bad for Fiona, and now he handed them to Will. Although it seemed that every boat for miles around was already hired, Huxley managed to engage a wherry and a boatman for the two of them. They were on the dock, ready to embark, when Fiona cried, "Listen! What's that?"

It was the tolling of the abbey bell, the signal that the barge carrying the Friars of St. Francis and their "nuns" was approaching from downriver.

"Let's wait here until the procession goes up to the abbey," Huxley suggested. "We'll see better from here than from a boat. Once they're inside, we'll row across the river to get a firsthand impression of the mood of the crowd."

"What if they're afraid to invade the gardens, Will?"

"Then they'll have to have a leader, won't they. Be sure to keep your mask on. We may find ourselves at the head of an irate army, Fiona."

Fiona had seen the procession from the abbey side; but from here it was even spookier, more eerie. The torches reflected off the white robes and made the red linings of the monks' hoods glow like flame. The nuns paraded demurely; from this distance, one couldn't see that the habits were made to reveal rather than conceal the naked charms of those chosen women.

As the last of the procession passed out of sight in the shrubbery surrounding the ruined abbey, Huxley said, "Let's go, Fiona." He gave her a hand into the wherry, tucked the robes about her, then settled himself beside her. The boatmen lighted torches at either end of the boat and began to pole them out into the expanse of the Thames.

"No one's following the procession," Fiona said, disappointment in her voice. "I thought you said the gardens would be invaded by all these curious onlookers."

"I guess I overestimated the mood of the mob. Well, there's only one way to precipitate action, Fiona. I'll leave you safe in the boat and I'll lead the crowd myself."

"Oh, no; you're going nowhere without me. I'm your wife, and I have as much at stake as you in destroying the ugliness that exists here at Medmenham

Abbey. I'll be right there beside you, leading them through the gardens to the abbey door." There was a reckless gleam in her blue eyes.

Huxley tried to dissuade her, but she was adamant.

"If we don't start this, nothing is going to happen, Will." She turned to the boatman. "Pole us to the pier, my good man, and wait for us there."

Realizing that his wife was determined to go with him, Huxley reluctantly agreed. Once the decision was made, he began shouting to the others in their boats, "Let's go, men! I want to see what happens at this abbey! Are you with me?"

With someone to lead them, the crowd surged forward, and with Will and Fiona at their head, they scrambled ashore and raced after the chanting friars onto the private grounds of the abbey. As the last of the procession passed out of sight in the shrubbery surrounding the ruined abbey, there was a surge of spectators behind Fiona and Will who left their boats and hurried into the abbey gardens.

Knowing their way, Will and Fiona could lead the mob to the special door of the abbey. Will had snatched up one of the torches planted at the water's edge to light the procession, and now he waved it high, crying, "Follow us, men! I know the way into the secret places of the abbey."

Fiona caught at his sleeve and shouted, "Here come some of Dashwood's men with staves."

They were powerless against the mob, however, and retreated to the safety of the abbey walls.

"Take more'n staves," one man chortled. "Hear all kinds of tales about yon abbey. All kinds of wicked things agoin' on, so they say. Heared tell there was somethin' about it in a London paper, there was. Big doin's tonight, bein' it's All Hallows' Eve. They say they use virgins, beggin' your pardon, ma'am."

"Everything you heard is true," Fiona said, lagging

behind. Racing along when one was pregnant wasn't easy.

"Fiona, stay here," Will commanded. They had come to one of the little temples of love, and Fiona sank gratefully onto one of the upholstered couches. "I'll just see that they find the proper door into the chapel and then I'll be back. I don't want to stay here; the crowd might well turn ugly." He gave her a quick kiss, then hurried on with the raucous mob.

Left alone, Fiona began to feel uncomfortable. What if something happened to Will? What if Dashwood's guards used firearms on the crowd? She was too restless to sit quietly and wait for her husband. She peeked out of the doorway of the small folly and saw that people were now running away from the abbey, streaming past the small building where she hid. What did this mean? Oh, why didn't Will come back?

She was just ready to go looking for him when his familiar form materialized out of the dark. He still carried the torch, but he also had something tucked under his arm.

"Quickly, Fiona; I don't know just what is going to happen. The mob broke into the chapel and rescued the virgin, but she may receive the same treatment from them. One look at all of the erotic fittings and they went mad."

They hurried toward the Thames and luckily found their boatman waiting for them.

"Wasn't goin' to wait much longer, milord," he grumbled. "Lots wanted to use this boat."

Huxley handed him an extra shilling, which quieted him immediately. He poled away toward the opposite shore.

"Just in time," Fiona murmured. "Look at that mob!"

The common people were running back to the river, some pursued by liveried lackeys now carrying pistols or blunderbusses. Many of the rioters carried small statues in their arms, ignoring the shouts of "Stop, thief!" A few shots were fired, but no one seemed to be hit by the bullets.

When they'd gone some distance, Fiona whispered, "What do you have hidden under your cloak, Will?"

He grinned and showed her one of the infamous drinking mugs made in the form of a nude man, with its convenient "spout" for pouring.

After she got done laughing, she asked, "Do you really think that this will be the end of the Friars of St. Francis, Will?"

"Not just this one time. But every man who came tonight will talk about it, and the next time the friars meet, there will be even more here to watch and to harass them."

"How will they know when the next Black Mass will be?"

Huxley threw back his head and roared with laughter. "How, darling Fiona? They'll read it in the *Voice of Truth.* I can guarantee it!"

CHAPTER 34

Yuletide was a joyous season for Fiona. By now she was becoming accustomed to being Lady Fiona, the Viscountess Huxley. She and Will spent most of the time at Fairfax, for her pregnancy was so far advanced that she found coaching most uncomfortable. There was a good midwife in the village nearby, so Fiona knew that when her time came, she would be well cared for.

The house was decorated with boughs of holly and fir, and candles gleamed softly in the windows. On Christmas Eve a group of children from the parish came to sing carols, and Fiona gave them sweetmeats and sugarplums as a treat.

They limited their entertaining, for Huxley was afraid that she might get overtired, owing to her delicate condition. Fiona felt marvelous, better than she'd ever felt in her life, but she obeyed her husband's admonitions; she didn't ride or go out coaching, and limited her exercise to walks through the gardens, now brown and sear with winter.

Aunt Eulalia was invited to spend Christmas with them. She engaged a helper to keep the shop open, as many ladies wanted their new bonnets for the holiday season. Huxley traveled up to London several times a month, and he escorted Miss Goodbody back to Fairfax on one of his trips. He was bringing out weekly editions of the *Voice of Truth,* and those times he did not go to London, he sent Isaac with the papers. So far no one had guessed who the author was.

Aunt Eulalia, stiff and formal as ever, had some choice gossip for her niece. "All of London is talking about that dreadful Medmenham Abbey," she said, scarcely waiting to shed her heavy maroon travel cloak before she told Fiona the latest word from the *ton*. "There was a furor about the place on All Hallows' Eve."

Fiona, scarcely able to keep a straight face, poured tea for her aunt, not daring to look at Huxley for fear she'd burst into laughter.

"And what was that furor?" he asked.

"There's a new paper in London. I've seen it; it's called the *Voice of Truth*. Just before All Hallows' Eve, this paper published an exposé of the abbey. What shocking things went on there!"

Fiona, knowing how knowledgeable her aunt was about the doings of the *ton*, didn't think for a minute that this upright lady had been surprised at what she'd read.

"They say that the king was furious."

Fiona was disturbed by this. She didn't want Huxley doing anything to make King George angry, not again. He'd escaped once; next time he might not.

"What perturbed our monarch?" Huxley asked, cool as winter snow. "He's no saint himself."

"That may be true," Aunt Eulalia said, lips stern, "but so many of his advisors were involved that it created a scandal. No king wants that during his reign."

"What did he do?" Fiona asked.

"From what I hear, he ordered the Friars of St. Francis, as they call themselves, to disband. No more orgies are taking place at the abbey. I understand that Sir Francis Dashwood has put the property up for sale."

"So that's the end of the Hell-Fire Club," Fiona said thankfully.

"I wouldn't be too sure of that, my dear," Huxley said. "Those men are rakes. They'll start up somewhere else, I daresay."

"Have the Duke and Duchess of Lawton come back to London?" Fiona asked her Aunt Eulalia.

"No. The house on Millbank is still closed. The servants were dismissed with only a week's wages. And the duchess never collected the hat she commissioned, nor did I get paid for it."

"Sell it to someone else," Fiona advised.

Her aunt gave that tight little smile and said, "I sold it the week after they left. I can't hold bonnets for ladies who rush off to Paris when scandal brews. I'd be in the poorhouse in short order if I conducted my business that way."

Huxley laughed until tears ran down his cheeks. "Ah, madam, the Duchess of Lawton met her match in you."

Christmas Day was one of feasting, with roast goose as the main dish and plum pudding for a sweet at the end of the meal. Aunt Eulalia stayed until Twelfth Night, when Huxley escorted her back to her shop in London.

"I shall come at the end of March and stay until your babe is born," Miss Goodbody told Fiona. "As your only relative, it is only right that I should be with you then."

"Will will come for you," Fiona told her. "Don't think of taking the stage."

Time passed happily for Fiona. She sewed on a layette for the child, walked about when the weather was not too severe, and saw to Will's comfort. He looked forward to fatherhood eagerly, telling her all of the things he would teach their son.

"And what if this child is a daughter?" she chided gently. "Will you disown her?"

"Fiona! What a thing to say! If she's like her mother, I'll love her with all my heart. You wouldn't mind sharing my love with her, would you? She'll be beautiful, like her mother." He tipped up her face, one warm hand under her chin, and kissed her with love. "And when she's grown, all of the young bloods in the county will be dangling after her."

"Oh, Will, if only she can be as happy as I am."

Fiona still could not believe her good fortune. After all of the bad things that had happened to her, she now was the wife of the man she truly loved and was expecting a child, which, even though it might be Samuel's, Huxley thought of as his own. She was incredibly lucky. She couldn't even hate the Duke and Duchess of Lawton anymore, for they had to flee into exile, while she remained in England as the wife of the Viscount Huxley.

Will still championed the cause of the poor in his paper, but so far no man had risen to lead them the way Samuel Rogers had directed their efforts. At times Fiona wondered if the condition of the poor would ever improve. There had always been people under the grinding yoke of poverty; no doubt there always would be. Still, her husband thought that their lot could be bettered, so she hoped that they, too, could someday live happy lives.

Winter now lay over the land, and the days were dark and short, with bitter winds whistling about Fairfax; but the house was snug, the fires were huge, and Fiona was never uncomfortable. She moved more slowly as her size steadily increased. Sometimes she joked with Lettie, wondering if she was going to give birth to an elephant, so large had she grown.

March came, and with it the promise of spring. Huxley planned to go to London to bring Aunt Eulalia back to stay until after Fiona's baby had been born. Fiona was reluctant to have him leave her; but she knew she couldn't expect Aunt Eulalia to make the trip to Surrey by herself.

"Be careful, my love. Don't let the highwaymen attack you."

Huxley grinned. "They wouldn't dare." Seeing the devilish look on his face, Fiona decided that any highwayman rash enough to approach her husband would deserve his fate!

That night she retired early. "I feel so weary, Lettie," she said, "and my back aches."

"I'll bring a warming pan to make your bed toasty, milady, and some mulled wine to help you sleep." When she had her mistress in bed for the night, Lettie said, "If you need me during the night, milady, just ring."

The pains started sometime during the dark of the night, waking Fiona. *But it's not time yet,* she thought. *It can't happen now, not with Will away in London.* She tried to convince herself that the pains might be indigestion. *I shouldn't have had the game pie,* she temporized. *It may have been spoiled. But it tasted all right.* The pains eased and she turned over heavily, hoping that she'd fall asleep again. Then they hit again —pains like she'd never experienced before. They came and went, but each time when they returned, it was with increasing severity. Finally, no longer able to lie there alone, she rang for her abigail.

Lettie came at once, clad in a dark-blue wool wrapper, her gray hair in two braids down her back. She took one look at her young mistress and went to the bell pull, tugging it several times. "I'm sending for the midwife, milady. Your babe isn't going to wait for the appointed time."

"But his lordship's away," Fiona wailed. "I can't have the baby until he returns."

"Ah, but that's exactly what you *can* do, milady." Lettie smiled and patted Fiona's hand. "He's done his job, and now you must do yours. Whether his lordship is here or not, the child will arrive."

The next hours were a blur of pain and labor, with the faces of Lettie and Mother Miggs, the village midwife, always there, comforting, encouraging, and supporting her.

"Push hard, milady," Mrs. Miggs would order, and Fiona would obey.

Finally the child was there, and Fiona closed her weary eyes when she heard the midwife exclaim, "A fine healthy boy, milady." There was the sound of a smack and then the indignant wail of the newborn son.

"A boy! Will wanted a son. He'll be so pleased."

Moments later the pains started up again, and Fiona cried out in terror, "What's wrong?"

Mother Miggs soothed her. "Nothing to worry about, milady. There's another child wanting to be born. You are having twins."

The second child came quickly, a little girl.

As Fiona lay there with the babes cradled in her arms, an enormous happiness swept over her. The boy was a Huxley; there was no denying the look. His head was covered with black hair, and his eyebrows were so much like Will's that her heart melted at the sight.

"Congratulations, milady," Mother Miggs said. "Two fine healthy babes. The boy's the spit and image of Lord Huxley; and the girl, she has her mother's beautiful face."

"Now, may I take the babes? They'll both share the cradle until we can have another made," Lettie ordered, all thought now for her young mistress, who was exhausted from her labors.

Fiona kissed each baby, marveling at the soft hair and tiny perfect features. Then she fell into a deep, healing sleep. When she woke, the first thing she saw was her husband's face, full of love and wonder as he gazed at his children in the cradle next to her bed.

"Will! Will, are you pleased with your new family?"

He turned at the sound of her voice, came to the bed, and kissed her tenderly. "Oh, Fiona, you've made me the happiest man in all of England. A son and a daughter—not many men can boast of that!"

"We'll name him William, for you. And our daughter, what shall we call her?"

He was thoughtful for a moment; then he said, "The children are mine, just as I knew all the time. Poor Samuel. He never had a child, and he didn't leave one to carry on his name. I think that we should call her Samantha, in his memory."

"That is a lovely thing for you to do, my dearest one," she said, tears filling her eyes.

"Don't cry for the dead, Fiona; smile for the living. We were lovers and then man and wife. And now we are parents. We have a long, glorious life ahead of us."

She slid her hand into his. "Together, love, together."